REPUBLIC SHATTERED

Sins of Before

By Michael J. Brooks

Wars of the New Humanity

Book Three

Paperback ISBN: 9781737929383
Hardback ISBN: 9798218576028
Ebook ISBN: 9781737929390

Library of Congress Control Number: 2024922691

Printed in the United States of America

Michael J. Brooks
Mount Rainier, Maryland 20712
www.authormbrooks.com

Paperback and hardback wholesale and retail orders: Ingram

About this Book

A Message for New Readers

This book includes a recap of the previous two, titled "The Story Thus Far," making it easy for new readers to catch up and dive into the story. Additionally, you can refer to the glossary at the back for explanations of important terms and phrases.

Content Warning

Republic Shattered: Sins of Before is an action-filled science fiction book that contains violence, strong language, and detailed scenes of lovers making love.

Content Meter

If you are a new reader, welcome, and if you are a returning reader, welcome back.

Praise for Republic Shattered

"With succinct prose, Brooks weaves a layered and intriguing plot, treating me to intergalactic politics, futuristic technology, warfare, love affairs, action, adventure, thrills, and a dynamic and fascinating cast. The plot twists and tone of the storyline had me on the edge of my seat. The elaborate depictions that often created a vivid sense of movement and atmosphere made the novel cinematic. Brooks uses refreshing and well-paced dialogue, alongside a depth to the storyline that brings out the emotions and complex traits of the cast. This allowed me to connect with them and understand their conflicts in a morally complex universe. This is an incredible third installment."
—Keith Mbuya for *Readers' Favorite*

"This book, *Republic Shattered: Sins of Before*, has what great books entail: action, adventure, surprises, and love. This is an amazing and interesting science fiction novel, beautifully and intricately crafted, and is indeed worth the read, I must say."
—*LitPick*

"Michael J. Brooks creates a thought-provoking story that hosts a wide range of characters; each with their own special abilities and interests. His insertion of ethical and political reflections will especially appeal to readers seeking more than just military-style battle encounters, while his ability to build just the right amount of tension, then juxtapose it with psychological growth and new directions, keeps the plot vivid and unexpectedly fluid."
—D. Donovan, Sr. Reviewer, *Midwest Book Review*

The Story Thus Far

Eden, the utopian motherworld of humanity's intergalactic republic, the Commonwealth, was a beacon of luxury and prosperity. In stark contrast, Satellite One, its less fortunate counterpart, offered only mediocrity to its inhabitants, despite the Commonwealth Government's assurances of equality. Tensions between the two worlds grew, and colonies One, Four, and Six of Satellite One declared independence. The Commonwealth Defense Force (CDF), equipped with mechanized combat suits known as Shells, was deployed to Satellite One to quell the rebellion.

Republic Falling: Advent of a New Dawn

In *Republic Falling: Advent of a New Dawn*, Randal Scott was Linked (cerebrally connected via a nanoimplant) with his mother, Kathleen Scott, when she was killed in a devastating explosion. Traumatized and seeking vengeance, Randy joined the CDF to bring justice to the man responsible for both her death and his emotional scars. That man was his father, Arson Scott. A decorated former CDF captain, Arson had mysteriously defected to the Coalition of Rebel Factions—the insurgency threatening to collapse humanity's intergalactic republic—and participated in his wife's murder.

Randy, his girlfriend Stacie Spencer, and his best friend Jarius Ford deployed as newly initiated CDF Guardians to Colony Four, where Arson led his insurgent faction. While on deployment, Randy began to see a darker side of the CDF. Colony citizens were being treated cruelly by the very force he served.

Randy encountered Kesley Whittaker, a colony citizen and, unknown to him, a Coalition rebel. She opened his eyes to the harsh realities that drove colonies One, Four, and Six to revolt, leading Randy to question whether the rebellion was, in fact, justified.

Randy was captured by the Coalition during an assault on Arson's hideout. While aboard Arson's escape ship, Randy learned more about the legitimacy of the rebellion and was shown damning evidence of the Commonwealth Government's corruption.

Arson disclosed the Coalition's plan to infiltrate the Parliament Building and use its broadcast center to transmit the evidence across the net. The operation was code-named Hammer Fall. Randy wrestled with the decision but ultimately sided with the Coalition, believing that overthrowing the corrupt government and freeing the oppressed colonies was the right choice. Jarius, who had also been captured, joined him.

Randy eventually began to forgive Arson, accepting that his mother's death had been a tragic accident and that Arson, a former colony citizen himself, had aligned with the Coalition out of a sense of duty.

Randy and Jarius' unit launched a mission to rescue them, attacking Arson's second hideout. Both Randy and Jarius decided against returning to the unit, instead remaining with the Coalition. During the firefight, Randy encountered Stacie and gave her files confirming that her parents—members of a powerful group of entrepreneurs called the Eight Elite—were involved in the government corruption.

After reading the files, Stacie went back to Eden and confronted her parents on Babylon Island, only to be disowned for opposing their criminal ways.

Amid Operation Hammer Fall, Randy and Stacie faced off on

the Parliament Building's lawn, now on opposite sides of the war. Through their Link, Stacie uncovered Randy's brief affair with Kesley Whittaker, a moment of weakness he deeply regretted. Infuriated, Stacie fought Randy at full force. He defeated her but ensured her safety inside the Parliament Building, which the Coalition had successfully seized.

The Coalition leader, Arman Reza, was expected to pursue peace after exposing the corruption. Instead, he killed Chief Executive Cornelius Gould and proclaimed himself the Commonwealth's new leader. While Cornelius was a power-hungry megalomaniac who had secured the Chief Executiveship by assassinating the previous Chief, Jared Kerner, killing him was still wrong.

Outraged by Reza's betrayal, Arson and Randy teamed up to eliminate him. With Reza dead, Parliament Chairwoman Oviereya Amaechi, who had been a maternal figure to Stacie, became the new Chief Executive under the government's rules of succession. As an immigrant—a former colonist permitted Eden citizenship through the lottery—she pledged to fight for equality, end corruption, and reform the CDF.

Scarred by the war, the loss of Stacie's love, and the burden of killing both rebels and Guardians, Randy took a break from military life. As for Stacie, she inherited her parents' fortune and organization, Spencer Enterprises, after they were killed by Arman Reza's justice squads. She planned to assemble a team to bring down the new heads of the Elite—the men and women who had seized control of their own parents' criminal empires following similar assassinations.

Republic Under Siege: Threat from within

In *Republic Under Siege: Threat from Within*, the Commonwealth's civil war was over, but peace remained elusive.

Randy returned to the CDF and transferred to the Expedition Task Forces, specialized teams responsible for hunting down human and alien criminals. Among the Guardians of his assigned team, Vanguard Alpha, he became close to colony immigrant Akane Sugimori. She, along with two other Guardians of Vanguard Alpha, secretly belonged to a clandestine social-justice organization called RISE.

While RISE's mission of advocating for colony and immigrant equality was noble, their methods were far from legal, branding them as vigilantes. Akane admired Randy for his role in emancipating the colonies as a former Coalition fighter and sought to recruit him into RISE. She gradually introduced him to the organization while concealing its illegal activities for the time being.

Through Akane, Randy learned of a growing threat within the Commonwealth. Known as Purists, they were violent ultra-extremists determined to preserve the classist society oppressing colonists and immigrants. At the same time, Stacie, who had formed her own combat team, targeted the criminal empire of Damien Sykes, a member of the Elite now running for Chief Executive. Registered as a bounty-hunting entity, Stacie's team was able to legally obtain weapons for their less-than-legal war against the Elite. The bounty-hunter registration was just a smokescreen for Stacie's true objective.

Oviereya Amaechi, Stacie's friend and the Commonwealth's new Chief, informed her that Defense Force Intelligence (DFI) was investigating Damien Sykes. Stacie asked to go undercover for

DFI, leveraging Damien's lingering attraction to her to infiltrate his network and gather evidence to dismantle his trafficking operation. While undercover, she discovered that Damien was also the leader of the largest Purist organization, the Brotherhood for Humanity's Salvation.

As Randy became more involved with RISE, he realized their actions—though rooted in a desire for equality—crossed legal and moral lines, including election interference. He faced a difficult choice: expose RISE's headquarters to DFI or continue protecting them. Despite his feelings for Akane, Randy decided to report RISE, but he kept Akane's association with the group a secret. When he confessed his actions to her, their budding romantic relationship dissolved.

Before the CDF could act, the Brotherhood attacked RISE headquarters, killing Akane's Eden-family and leaving her emotionally devastated. Akane and one of the last surviving RISE members, Jamie (Jay) Lister, vowed revenge on Damien Sykes.

Randy and Stacie teamed up to stop Akane and Jay from assassinating Damien at one of his campaign rallies. Despite Damien's crimes as a human trafficker and Purist leader, keeping him alive was essential for DFI to destroy his criminal empire and save lives. After defeating Akane and Jay, Randy chose to shield Akane from the consequences of her vigilante actions, opting not to turn her in. He urged her to take a sabbatical and visit her parents on Satellite One.

During the mission to stop Akane and Jay, Randy and Stacie had Linked, allowing Stacie to fully grasp how deeply Randy still loved her. As a result, she decided to give their relationship another chance, finally forgiving him for his past entanglement with Kesley Whittaker. Now, the story continues.

Epigraph

"So the CDF is a bunch of contract mercenaries, is that it? Just fucking guns for hire?"
—**Ahmed Hawsawi** (*Republic Falling: Advent of a New Dawn*)

"We're (Guardians) human beings for goodness' sake. Does the CDF want us to be cold-blooded or something?"
—**Randal Scott** (*Republic Falling: Advent of a New Dawn*)

"Seems like the CDF adopted a culture of brutality."
—**Randal Scott** (*Republic Falling: Advent of a New Dawn*)

"It's not like the CDF has been the universe's do-gooders all the time."
—**Akane Sugimori** (*Republic Under Siege: Threat from Within*)

"I'm pretty sure Lars was gonna blow me away just because I wondered if there was some legitimacy behind the CFP protesters' actions. I was gonna get blown away by my superior. Apparently, being a freethinker is a career killer in the CDF, *literally*."
—**Jarius Ford** (*Republic Falling: Advent of a New Dawn*)

"It could be only a matter of time before Commonwealth antagonists, opposed to our planetary-impact missions, strike Eden soil or the colonies."
—**Arman Reza** (*Republic Falling: Advent of a New Dawn*)

PROLOGUE

THREE YEARS AGO

Planet Mabbeon
Nation of Khanoria

Zataldra's heart wouldn't stop palpitating. Anxiety gripped her as she watched her father, Jud'Zarr Gor'Ronn, don his ornate robe of vibrant hues. Defiant in the face of tyranny, he had paid no heed to the warnings and looming death threats. Zataldra couldn't help but curse his fearlessness and dedication, qualities she had always revered—just like her dearly departed mother had. Yet now, those qualities were endangering his life.

Father, you're too noble for your own good, she thought. *I pray an early grave isn't your future.* Already robbed of her mother, she feared a cruel fate would claim her father as well?

Of all the Grand Elders, Jud'Zarr was the most vocal critic of the High Sorin's oppressive reign. He was driven by righteousness to decry injustice and defend the mistreated. Even now, he only thought of others' welfare as he prepared to uplift the flagging spirits of the locals corralled outside his and Zataldra's earthstone abode. These men and women were relying on him to allay their fears, give them hope, and show them a path forward. He would not let them down, nor all of Khanoria.

Despite the Sorin's warnings, death threats, and intimidation tactics, his resolve remained inextinguishable. Feeble souls caved under pressure; the strong remained sturdy in their conviction and would rather die than renounce their obligations, even in the face of life-threatening repercussions.

The Khanoria he and everyone knew was being ripped from the seams by the Sorin. Seduced by power, the Sorin no longer consulted the Council of Elders for guidance, a practice honored by his predecessors throughout history. Instead, the Sorin chose the path of absolute power, and his offenses to Khanorian society were vast. Long-practiced religions were now prohibited. Hallowed lands were being exploited for profitable resources, uprooting aborigines from their homelands. Those who taught or spoke the Ancient Languages faced hefty fines. And anyone who dared challenge the Sorin's authority faced severe consequences, from imprisonment to execution by firing squad. Jud'Zarr knew the self-proclaimed supremacy of the Sorin had to be brought to an end.

The rise of the Khanorian Revolution was a sign that brighter days were on the horizon. The revolution had ignited a tide of spirited dissidence, clandestine rebellions launched in secrecy behind closed doors. Denizens across provinces were rallying against the authoritarian regime, some taking up arms.

Jud'Zarr placed a pendant around his neck that bore the signet of the Grand Elders, figures the public respected as magnates of wisdom and leadership.

He looked into the mirror in front of him and gazed at Zataldra's reflection. She stood behind him in a dress of flamboyant colors, her chin lowered in concern. He was proud of her. Zataldra had earned admission into the esteemed Khanorian science guild called the Shaho'Gkodii, which was at the forefront of Khanorian society's scientific advancement. Her mother would've been proud too.

Noting the unsettling expression on Zataldra's face, Jud'Zarr turned from the mirror and beckoned her to speak her thoughts. "Daughter, what is it that ails your heart?"

Zataldra's voice quavered. "Your criticism of the Sorin incurs his wrath. He may sic his new allies on you, this . . . Commonwealth Defense Force. I've heard about these humans' indisputable atrocities. These beings are savage." Her eyes flicked toward the window. The storm clouds shrouding the sky felt like an ill omen, a presage of something terrible. "I beg of you, Father, cancel your oration."

"I am a Grand Elder, Zataldra. That means I am duty-bound to the people, obligated to denounce the defilement of our society." Jud'Zarr's tone was stern and unfaltering. "The Sorin has dismantled the fundamental principles that form the bedrock of Khanorian civilization. He even has the gall to enslave beings from other worlds to labor for him. Despicable. No Sorin has ever stooped to such depravity."

Zataldra fidgeted with the embroidered cuff of one of her sheer sleeves. "Yes, but—"

Jud'Zarr silently raised a hand, ending any further remonstration from Zataldra. "Enough, Daughter, I have no time to argue with you."

The panic wrenching Zataldra's heart remained incurable. Exhaling an acquiescent sigh, she looped an arm around her father's to escort him outside. "Allow me to be by your side onstage."

Jud'Zarr okayed her request with a nod.

When they emerged from their home, the boisterous locals who had congregated hushed. Within the crowd, Zataldra spotted her closest friends, Navexira and Geznan. They had also come to listen to Grand Elder Gor'Ronn speak.

Zataldra said, "Father, I will join you shortly. I want to speak to Geznan and Navexira."

"Of course, my child." Jud'Zarr proceeded up the wooden stairs to the stage.

Zataldra strode to her friends and hugged them. They held a special place in her heart. Since the three of them met five years ago, when Zataldra was twenty years old, they had shared memorable times together, supported each other's aspirations, and lifted each other up in difficult times. Besides her sister and father, no one else meant more to Zataldra.

Geznan registered the despair etched across Zataldra's face. "Are you alright?" He rested a hand on her shoulder. "You look stressed."

Zataldra's nerves were fraying by the minute. "It's just that . . . I fear for Father. The Sorin has cautioned him against continuing his objections, and now he does this: holds *another* assembly. I have a bad feeling. This might be the final provocation the Sorin will tolerate from Father."

Navexira knew that since Zataldra had already lost her mother to a terminal illness, losing her father today would butcher her heart. To offer some comfort, she told Zataldra, "I will keep him in my prayers."

"I appreciate that." Hearing her father begin, Zataldra rushed off to the stage.

Jud'Zarr's gift of oration captivated his audience. "The regime in power does not respect our time-honored traditions, the order that has guided us since the dawn of our civilization. They refuse to consult us Elders. They restrict religious diversity. Their affronts to our society have grown numberless—grown intolerable. Intolerable to where . . . conventional means of removal are . . . feckless."

In his prime, Jud'Zarr had been a warman in the National Protection Force, but he had long since adopted a life of nonviolence. Nevertheless, he'd wield arms again to overthrow the Sorin if need arose, allowing the dormant warrior inside him to resurface.

The audience applauded Jud'Zarr with fulsome cheers, but the distant rumble and sputter of approaching vehicles caused their standing ovation to fall silent.

A man broke out in a cold sweat. "It's them, the Sorin's new allies—the humans, the footmen of the Commonwealth Defense Force!"

Fearing the rising revolution, the Sorin sought to enlist the aid of humanity's military forces, which had earned a reputation as hired guns. After negotiating a lucrative compensation package with the Sorin, the Commonwealth Government greenlit the deployment of the CDF. The deployed Guardians bolstered the numbers of the Sorin's undermanned National Protection Force to help him curtail the widespread civil unrest.

BUSs, the CDF's all-terrain soldier carriers, were closing in on the crowd fast.

Zataldra's stomach knotted. On the other hand, Jud'Zarr stood unperturbed in the face of the CDF's arrival. Being the calm within the storm was a skill he had perfected through grueling trials.

The BUSs chuffed to a halt among the earthstone dwellings. Guardians in M-X01 Shells disembarked, deadly weapons rattling. They fanned out, encircling the gathering area—setting up a dragnet for Jud'Zarr.

A Guardian raised his coarse voice above the Khanorians' overlapping murmurs, hollering into his helmet-mic, "I'm Sergeant Cochran! I'm in charge of this force!" His helmet's audio system translated his words into the Khanorian language.

Bodies shuddered at the menacing alien soldiers. Heart rates went way up. Faces paled.

Cochran narrowed an intimidating glare at Jud'Zarr. "You must be the troublemaker we're looking for. You're Grand Elder Gor'Ronn, correct?"

"I am," Jud'Zarr replied bravely.

Acting as a two-way translator, the audio system in Cochran's helmet relayed Jud'Zarr's response to Cochran in English.

Peril looming in the air, Zataldra's legs trembled. "We should leave now," she whispered, clutching Jud'Zarr's sleeve in a viselike grip.

Zataldra understood Jud'Zarr's aversion to fleeing. As a former warman, he wasn't accustomed to showing weakness or backing down—to anyone. But being aware of the CDF's uncompromising nature, Zataldra knew that attempting diplomacy with these Guardians was out of the question. Fleeing was the only sensible option.

Cochran advanced. His armored chassis' servo-mechanisms whirred with each step of his mechboot. "The Sorin has ordered us to take you into custody, Grand Elder, so you're coming with us."

Jud'Zarr frowned. "And what offense have I committed to warrant arrest?" He shrugged off Zataldra's grip. "I do nothing but enlighten my people about our traditions, culture, and moral doctrine. Does that truly warrant reprimand by the Sorin?"

"You're being taken into custody for inciting violence and civil insurrection," Cochran said.

"I have not—"

Cochran cut Jud'Zarr off before another word could leave his mouth. "Shut your trap and come with us! This isn't up for discussion, oldtimer!" With a foreboding edge to his tone, he added, "And any resistance might be fatal to your supporters here, get me?" He gestured, issuing an order. In response, the Guardians lifted their rifles, and articulated instruments of death sprouted from their Shells' built-in weapons system.

Jud'Zarr's countenance twisted into a scowl. "You would turn your weapons on defenseless Khanorians who pose no threat?" His words oozed pure disdain. The warrior within him awakened. He wished there were a battalion of Khanorian warmen at his side to confront these arrogant alien brutes.

Cochran wasn't someone to be trifled with, and he was intolerant of defiance. "Are you fucking hard of hearing or something?" His nostrils flared.

Jud'Zarr let out a resigned sigh. Not complying would put the safety of the gatherers and his daughter at risk. "Alright, I surrender."

Zataldra snatched his arm, holding him back. "Father, please don't." Her voice was brittle, about to crack.

Jud'Zarr drew her into a gentle side hug. "Everything will be fine. I will be okay. Guard your sister well until I return."

Growing impatient, Cochran made a displeased sound in the back of his throat. He was about to blow a gasket. "Don't keep me waiting, Elder!"

Jud'Zarr descended the stage's stairs.

Zataldra's pulse skittered. She wondered what fate awaited Jud'Zarr. A lengthy prison term? Execution?

As the crowd witnessed their beloved Grand Elder hand himself over to the aliens, their anger simmered. They refused to be intimidated. They refused to allow Jud'Zarr to be detained in some holding cell. Emotions rising, they hurled stones, bottles, and other projectiles at the Guardians, while yelling things like "Leave our nation" and "Go away."

Cochran shouted above the clamorous grousing, to his men, "Enough of this bullshit!" A bottle shattered against his Shell, splintering into fragments. "Threat level elevated! Open fire on these malcontents!"

A young male private dared to question Cochran. "But, Sergeant, isn't that level of force . . . overkill?"

Cochran got in the private's face. "Are you disobeying my orders, Private Weissman?"

"Uh, no, Sergeant," Weissman stammered.

"Then be a good little grunt and do what I fucking tell you!" Cochran clapped a palm against Weissman's chest, propelling him back a step.

Weissman swallowed hard. "Yes, Sergeant," he said flatly, hesitantly bringing up his rifle.

A homicidal grin hitched the corners of Cochran's lips at the sound of triggers being pulled.

All Guardians' weapons flashed and crackled.

Khanorians dispersed in multiple directions, shrieking and stumbling. Bullets whizzed through the air, shattering the earthenware and tchotchkes showcased atop market stalls. Mortally wounded bodies crumpled into haphazard heaps.

Zataldra recoiled in horror. "Father!" she screamed from the stage, voice drowned by booming gunshots. Her eyes scanned the chaos for Jud'Zarr.

A scholar of the science field, she was a far cry from anything resembling a warrior. This was her first encounter with live gunfire. The harrowing screams, wild sprays of blood, and ceaseless thundering of killing devices overwhelmed her.

As fight or flight kicked in, her mind went haywire. Should she run away? Seek cover? Where was her father? She raced down the stage's stairs and into the swarm of Khanorians—some fleeing, some banding together in solidarity to stand their ground—and got swept up in the melee.

Bodies crushed against her, jostling her aside.

A man slammed into her by accident. She stumbled but recovered her balance, avoiding a fall onto her face.

An unending stream of bullets pierced flesh indiscriminately—men, women, children.

Zataldra's searching eyes snapped left and right. *Father, where are you?* Her brows rose and jaw hung when she saw Jud'Zarr lying prone, a purplish puddle of blood seeping into the earth underneath him.

A sick feeling swelled inside her, and she forced herself not to retch.

Jud'Zarr inched toward his firstborn daughter in a slow, painful crawl, his fingers raking grooves into the earth. "Z-Zataldra—" he rasped. Blood trailed behind the drag of his body. He was clinging to his last vestige of life.

The world came to a standstill for Zataldra as dread accumulated in her chest.

A bullet narrowly missed her temple, instead hitting a nearby shopfront's window.

Her body shuddered at the crash of glass.

Shedding the paralyzing grip of fear, she darted through the dispersing mass of Khanorians to get to Jud'Zarr, arms swinging with the beat of her feet. Nothing was going to stop her.

Possessed by emotion, she plunged into a state of tunnel vision. She zeroed in on reaching her father at all costs, shoes kicking up dirt. The gunfire now appeared trivial, as though she had become bulletproof. Without apology, she shoved anyone in her way onto the ground. Her arms became battering rams clearing her path. She'd have to reckon with guilt later; right now, all that mattered was her objective.

She made it to Jud'Zarr and came to a full stop, silver whorls of hair settling around her mauve face.

A whirlpool of cherished memories churned in her mind. *No,* she thought. The ache was small at first. Within a blink, it multiplied tenfold. Tears flooded her rheumy eyes and pattered the ground in droplets.

The weight of sorrow dropped her onto her knees. A broken woman, she wept. Her father had transitioned.

Cochran said to his soldiers, "Cease fire!" Weapons hissed, cooling down. The life-scan readings streaming across his HUD confirmed Jud'Zarr's demise. "Dead or alive was our orders. Looks like the mission has been accomplished," he declared smugly. After taking snapshots of Jud'Zarr on his HUD for proof of elimination, he marched over to Zataldra.

Heart lodged in her throat, she cradled her father's lifeless body in her arms. She was one of the most brilliant scientists of the Shaho'Gkodii, but she couldn't help but feel that her genius-level mind was powerless in preventing massacres like this.

Cochran's faceplate slid up, unveiling cold, unrepentant eyes and the ear-to-ear smile of a remorseless soul. "Let everyone know that all who defy your nation's Sorin will be punished by the Commonwealth Defense Force. Got that?"

Receiving nothing but silence from Zataldra, he nudged her rib cage with his mechboot, prompting a response.

Zataldra's gaze flew to him, and she gnashed her teeth. Her goldish eyes seared. The death of her father had smashed her world into pieces. She was on the razor's edge of losing it. *"Leave—me—alone, you butcherer!"* Sobs and sniffles disjointed her words.

If she had the power to, she'd disembowel every one of these foreign bastards and relish in the joy of dancing over their mutilated corpses. And she'd gladly serve Cochran's rifle to him, shoving it down his gullet and pumping the trigger.

Cochran snorted and spat in her face, the glob sliding down her cheek. "Stupid Khanorian bitch."

Zataldra growled, brows twitching.

Cochran signaled his Guardians to load up and head to the next stop. He felt no sympathy, regret, or remorse. He had completed the mission, proving that crossing both the Sorin and the CDF could be fatal. Basic Combat Training ingrained in Guardians the importance of being ruthless, regardless of whom the Commonwealth Government ordered them to point their weapons at. Instructors hammered into Guardians that showing mercy to the enemy was unacceptable and might get them killed, so when deployed, Guardians were to establish dominance right away. Their goal was to instill fear in *whoever* their enemy was, which included civilians like the Khanorians that Cochran and his team had just terrorized and murdered.

The Guardians left in their BUSs.

With the violence over, the area fell into an unsettling stillness. No one could hear even the faintest rustle of a breeze.

Everyone who had ensconced themselves behind locked doors tentatively ventured back outside. Bereft, they dropped to their knees on ground lathered in blood, bawling over dead loved ones.

A forever-wounded soul, Zataldra couldn't stem the flow of tears.

She held her father's corpse, her features set in a mask of revulsion. *Humans are nothing but sowers of death and ruination.* Her eyes promised retribution for their sins. *They will answer for what they've done here, I swear.* Animosity hardened her gentle heart.

A voice called her name. It was Geznan, and Navexira was with him. They had survived, having found a safe place to hide during the massacre.

I am sorry for your loss, Geznan thought, watching Zataldra let out gut-wrenching wails.

Though Zataldra was relieved that her friends were alive, she simply cast a tearful glance their way before tightening her embrace on her father.

Geznan was about to go console her, but Navexira grabbed his arm, restraining him. "She needs space," Navexira said.

Understanding that Navexira was right, Geznan stayed put, giving Zataldra the space she needed to grieve.

Amid the mewls of the Khanorians around her, Zataldra laid her father down and stared at her bloodstained palms. The emotions choking her were a battle cry for vengeance. She hoped her thoughts would reach the ear of the divine. *If it is your will, allow me to be your wrath, your blade, your avenger.*

Thunder crashed, and forks of lightning scarred the murky sky. It was as if the heavens itself was furious.

CHAPTER ONE

PRESENT DAY

Planet Dilaxus

Randal Scott's muscles tensed, and pressure mounted inside his chest as he and his Vanguard Alpha teammates, in their Shells, ventured into a canyon. Ahead of them lay the carcasses of fallen comrades, some decayed beyond recognition. The deceased's Shells bore evidence of a fierce fight—blast punctures and other structural damage. The whole scene reeked of an ambush.

Randy's visor scanned the busted-up Shells. He'd be devastated if his best friend and former battle-buddy, Jarius Ford, were among the dead. *Please, Jarius, be alive,* he silently implored. The drumming in his chest worsened.

Jarius had elected to commission into the Ambassador Corps of the CDF, the branch dedicated to diplomacy and intergalactic relations, with some convincing from Randy. He and two other ambassadors had deployed to negotiate the release of several Guardians detained by the Commonwealth's new mysterious enemy, the Collective. While they were returning to Eden from a

Mission World, a Collective boarding party attacked and infiltrated the Guardians' vessel. Randy suspected the Collective had no intention of negotiating with the ambassador delegation. Consenting to a meeting with them had been a setup from the start.

Randy's worries evaporated in a wave of relief when he confirmed that none of the bodies belonged to Jarius. The other two lieutenant ambassadors weren't among the dead either. It was likely the Collective took the three of them captive, but that didn't guarantee they were still breathing.

Lieutenant Carl Breckenridge contacted the other task forces deployed to locate the ambassador delegation and their team of bodyguards, bodyguards who now lay dead. "This is Lieutenant Breckenridge to all task forces. We found them," he reported over audio comms. "The ambassadors aren't here, though."

Randy contemplated the Collective's intentions. *What in the universe could the Collective possibly be after? What the hell's their objective? It appears their sole mission is to . . . eliminate Guardians and disrupt the Commonwealth's trade network.*

The emergence of the Collective was a sudden and enigmatic development. They had attacked Commonwealth vessels, bombed Commonwealth embassies within protectorates, and targeted Guardians engaged in planetary-impact missions. Their actions seemed driven by a relentless desire to undermine the Commonwealth at every conceivable turn, ruling out any notion that they were mere intergalactic pirates.

"Attention, everyone," Carl said in a commanding voice. "Plug into these Shells and check out their video logs. Let's take a look at what went down here."

"Yes, Sir," the team of five replied in unison—Specialist Randal Scott, Sergeant Jenny Pines, and newcomers Specialist Arturo de

León, Private Brayden Warnock, and Sergeant Royce Thatcher.

Vanguard Alpha fanned out, dry earth crunching beneath their mechboots.

Randy knelt beside one of the fallen Guardians, whose faceplate had been shattered during the battle. The sight of flesh-eating parasites nibbling on the decaying remains tightened his features into a wince. Jerking his head away, he shook off the disgust and regained his bearing. Then he glanced down at the Guardian's name tag: HARLOW.

He inserted an interface cable into the port at the back of Harlow's helmet. His Shell's CPU synced with Harlow's, granting him access to its memory bank. And that memory bank contained footage of the battle, because a Shell's visuals were always being recorded and archived by its CPU.

Through Harlow's perspective, Randy observed:

Brilliant flashes from Harlow's energy gun danced across his Shell's visor.

One of the Collective soldiers, encased in his own mechanized armor, crumbled to the ground after taking too many shots from Guardians' weapons.

Harlow shouted, "Damn it, they've got us outnumbered!" Enemy gunfire pummeled his Shell and tore into its metal rind. The reverberating impacts vibrated Randy's eardrums as he watched on through the feed.

Harlow retaliated, pivoting his gun's muzzle from one direction to another while pumping the trigger. The will to survive and protect his comrades took root, transforming him into the deadliest version of himself.

Enemy gunfire rained from above, battering the earth.

Harlow tilted his visual perspective upward and zoomed in on the cliffs. He sighted more hostiles standing atop ledges. "Shit, there are more of them, up there!" He elevated his aim. The errant plasma blasts discharged from his gun struck the cliffsides, sending debris cascading down.

A Guardian screamed in the distance after the strident boom of an explosion.

Harlow's stress level hit the ceiling. "Fuck, Talbert's down!" Blasts pelted him from all sides: left, right, front, and back. Shell breached by the storm of gunfire, he crashed to the ground with a thud. Within the cracks and lacerations of his Shell's exterior, exposed hardware and circuits disgorged smoke and crackling sparks.

All that filled Randy's visor was the sky as Harlow lay on his back, struggling to oxygenate his lungs.

Life ebbing away slowly but surely, Harlow knew death was coming sooner rather than later, so he paid no mind to the damage reports blinking on his HUD.

The cacophony of roaring weapons faded, giving way to the enemy's voices mingling with Harlow's labored breaths.

One of the Collective soldiers said, "Zataldra, we have secured the envoys." The CPU in Harlow's helmet translated the language being spoken.

"Good. Take them to the ship," Zataldra replied.

Randy pondered, *Could this Zataldra be the Collective's leader, or at least an authority figure within their ranks?*

Vital-sign overlays scrolled across Harlow's HUD. Numerical indicators pulsed, plummeting from three digits to two to one— and then zero. Harlow's body was slowly surrendering to death. Any second now, he'd be gone.

Feeling for his fellow Guardian, Randy chewed the inside of his cheek, and his throat constricted. Then his heart rate ticked up a notch when he heard Jarius demanding, "What do you people want? Why are you doing this?"

Zataldra replied in a frigid tone, "What we seek is retribution, retribution for *all* beings who have suffered because of you humans." The device she wore around her neck translated her words.

Harlow wheezed his final breath, and his vitals flatlined. A morbid electronic beep caused Randy to shiver. Next came the sounds of a scuffle between the three ambassadors and their captors. At that point, Randy closed the video log, his blood running cold.

Randy unplugged the interface cable and rose to his feet. Harlow's last heartbeat and the ambassadors' clamors of resistance stuck with him. He initiated an analysis of the language spoken by the Collective attackers. His CPU identified it as Khanorian. Randy's memory stirred. He recalled something from the Academy's archives about a Khanorian Campaign that took place years ago.

Specialist Arturo de León approached Randy. "Hey, chin up, war hero. I know you're stressed out about your buddy, but the fact that he isn't on the KIA list is a positive sign, right?"

"Well, it's certainly better than the alternative," Randy said dully. "I'll manage."

"Alright, but if you need to talk, you know I'm here."

"Thanks."

It seemed Randy couldn't catch a break. His best friend was missing, possibly enduring torture or worse. Moreover, being sent on missions to combat human and alien criminal forces often kept him galaxies away from Stacie for weeks at a time, while they were in the midst of rebuilding their relationship. And future missions might even wrest him away from Stacie for two or three months at a stretch. He didn't want to be an absentee boyfriend. But he understood that his career as a Task Force Guardian would inevitably test his relationship with Stacie.

The ships of the other task forces assigned to search for the missing delegation descended from the sky and touched down.

Carl lifted a fallen Guardian into his arms. "Let's help get our comrades-in-arms back home."

Vanguard Alpha rallied around Carl, helping to transport the Guardians to the waiting ships.

Randy worked alongside his teammates, thinking about Jarius. *If you're still alive, the CDF will find you, buddy.*

◆ ◆ ◆

Lieutenant Ambassador Jarius Ford was an outgoing man of infectious charisma. Big personality, smooth talker, confident swagger, charming smile. He was a prime candidate for a lieutenancy in the Ambassador Corps of the CDF. His collegemate, battle-buddy, and best friend, Randal Scott, was the culprit who motivated him to apply to Officer Candidate School (OCS) and commission into the Ambassador Corps. The transition was the right move beyond a shadow of a doubt. The Ambassador Corps seemed to fit him more so than his prior service branch, the Land Combatant Corps. Leave it to Randy to steer his career in the right direction.

After graduating from OCS as a second lieutenant, he met up with Randy for a night of celebration, and to his surprise, Stacie Spencer was with him. Jarius was genuinely happy for Randy, glad that he and Stacie had decided to mend their broken relationship, one step at a time, of course. And from an outside observer's perspective, their renewed relationship seemed to be progressing well. Three days later, Jarius crossed paths with the woman of his dreams, Jazzlyn Rochelle de' Medici. Black and Italian. Good-looking. Saucy attitude. Ambitious. Lieutenant in the Reserves of the CDF's Air & Space Corps.

He, Jazzlyn, Randy, and Stacie double-dated and created timeless memories. Jarius and Jazzlyn even established a Link, consummating their relationship through the intimacy of mental communion. And within just two months of meeting her, Jarius proposed. To many people, tying the knot at this stage might seem impulsive, but to Jarius, it felt entirely right. Why play the field when he had scored a remarkable woman like Jazzlyn? With her at his side, he was on the biggest high of his life.

Now he lay on the dingy floor of a grungy, unventilated detainment cell as a prisoner of war. The fetid reek of unbathed flesh filled his nostrils, his uniform was begrimed, and the wounds from recent beatings throbbed. How many days had it been now? Four? Maybe five? In BCT, cadets were told they'd have to embrace the suck when out in the field; this was beyond *suck*.

Why he and the other two ambassadors were being kept alive by the Collective remained a mystery to Jarius. No amount of further interrogation could unsheathe any valuable insights from him or his fellow ambassadors. What they had divulged was already common knowledge to the Collective. The truly sensitive data relative to the Commonwealth's defense capabilities and innovative weaponry in development was in the hands of people way above his pay grade.

Jarius' cell door creaked open. He squinted to blunt the shaft of light stabbing his eyes as it pierced the darkness. In the doorway stood Zataldra. She was clad in a purplish outfit accentuated by an armored corset-like garment hugging her midsection. Completing the ensemble were bicep-length gloves and thigh-high boots. On her face was a decorative nose chain, a hallmark of traditional

Khanorian women's attire.

The outfit exuded an air of boldness, signifying a notable shift in Zataldra's demeanor. The gentleness her eyes once held had been supplanted by a fierceness that was totally uncharacteristic of her former self. The woman who had once felt powerless witnessing her father's demise had undergone a transformation. She had shed the fear she'd previously harbored toward the alien soldiers who took his life, the CDF's Guardians. In its place was an aura of strength, fearlessness, and authority. Never again would she be the victim, but always the victor.

She gave Jarius a nasty look—a look he interpreted as unbridled hatred. His people's military had supported the Sorin's tyrannical regime in squashing the first wave of uprisings that had threatened to unseat him, executing a mass-scale civil enforcement operation known as the Khanorian Campaign. Zataldra and the Collective had deemed that the time of reckoning for the human race was now. If it weren't for the CDF, that first wave of uprisings would've forced the Sorin to abdicate the seat of leadership.

Zataldra tapped the interspecies translator collared around her neck, enabling her words to be conveyed in the human prisoner's language. "What is the purpose of this?" she demanded, holding aloft a nanochip nipped between her thumb and forefinger. She had extracted it from one of the Guardians the delegation had been sent to rescue. "I've been conducting numerous experiments on this micro device, and though knowing its exact function isn't pertinent to the success of my experiments, I'm curious what it is and how it actually benefits your people."

Jarius shifted upright, bracing his back against the stone-block wall. His arm and leg shackles chinked and rattled. Features cringing with scorn, he said, "Maybe you should've asked my colleague, the one you *ripped* that cerebral implant from the brain of, *murdering* him." He had let anger dictate his words, a grave folly for an ambassador. He needed to stay cool and somehow negotiate his release from captivity.

Emotional wounds from the past resurfaced within Zataldra once more. Who was this human to speak with such disdain? Her face contorted into a scowl. "And, just like all of your *foul* species, he deserved nothing more than death."

Fighting back the flush of anger triggered by Zataldra's ruthless assertion, Jarius unwrinkled his brow and schooled his face into an amicable expression. He had to listen with a receptive ear. He had to be understanding of her pain—like an Ambassador Corps liaison should be—and not bow to heated emotions. Allowing reckless, insensitive words to compromise this opportunity to reason with Zataldra would be foolhardy. Though reasoning with her would most likely be a hapless endeavor, he had to give it a shot.

Smoothing out his voice, he said, "I get why you hate us, but we—"

Zataldra steamrolled over the rest of his words. "Silence your mouth, ingrate!" The condemnation in her tone nearly nailed Jarius to the wall. "Tell me, what is the purpose of this . . . cerebral implant?" She took an aggressive step into the dark, confining enclosure. Jarius could feel fury radiating from her. She glared inquisitively at the small invention of alien neuroscience in her hand. "Is this micro contraption some sort of . . . wetware enhancement mechanism?"

"It allows us to establish a mental Link," Jarius replied calmly.

Zataldra's features pinched. Then puzzlement sowed its way across her face. "What?"

Jarius explained, "Linking allows humans to send and receive thought. It's a cerebral bond shared between two consenting individuals. Linking was created to foster empathy, understanding, and compassion among people—to bring them closer together."

Zataldra regarded him for a moment. *Empathy? Understanding? Compassion?* she thought. Was this human being earnest? She laughed, her hand clapping the wall in utter amusement. "A . . . most noble pursuit for such a barbaric species, *if true*. But I don't believe candor is a trait your race possesses."

"I'm aware Khanorians have suffered because of the Commonwealth Defense Force. We were wrong in supporting your people's oppressors. So, yeah, we're guilty as charged. And we've done some terrible shit to citizens of other worlds too. But the Commonwealth Government is 'under new management.' Our current leader would *never* compromise the Commonwealth's integrity just for . . . incentives." Jarius and all the Commonwealth knew Chief Oviereya Amaechi was incorruptible. "We're trying to redeem ourselves and redress our wrongs. We want to—"

"Redress your wrongs?" Zataldra spat angrily, interrupting Jarius mid-sentence. Her lips twitched. For countless nights, she had cried herself to sleep over her father's death. "Can you revive the dead? Can you reverse the annals of history and undo your atrocities? Can you restore what you took from me?"

Jarius redoubled his efforts to make peace with Zataldra and said, convincingly and wholeheartedly, "We're not asking for absolution, but we wanna rectify the damage we've done. Please, you've gotta believe me."

Zataldra answered his passionate entreatment with a harsh laugh. She refused to lend credence to the notion that the human race was anything more than a malevolent species. To her, evil was baked into their DNA. "Like I would actually believe a word you say," she sneered. "You humans destroy lives at no cost to your conscience. That, I have observed firsthand."

The emotive memory of innocent Khanorians—and her father—being slaughtered dragged Zataldra back in time, agonizing screams and the sharp cracks of gunfire mixing. "To support the High Sorin's tyranny, soldiers of your Defense Force deliberately reined terror across this nation, quashing mass protests and resistance with unwarranted violence. Women became . . . trophies to them."

Jarius bit his lower lip, remorse burgeoning and thoughts cursing the bad actors within the Defense Force. They had defaced its reputation for all Guardians. And those bad actors included high-ranking officers right down to the lowest of the enlisted.

Zataldra's narrative continued. "After witnessing so much death, I forsook my scientific endeavors to stand alongside the rebels fighting to overthrow the Sorin. We gave our best effort against your Defense Force, but they eventually beat us into submission. As soon as your Defense Force fulfilled its contract, every single Guardian departed Khanoria.

"The year following their withdrawal, the flame of resistance reignited. The voices of dissent grew louder than before. Without your Defense Force's manpower, the Sorin was overthrown during the second wave of the Khanorian Revolution.

"If it weren't for your Defense Force, the Sorin's defeat would've come much sooner. The lives of decent people wouldn't have been lost. Women wouldn't have been . . . stripped of their dignity. So why should I believe anything you, a human, says? Why should your people not face punishment for their crimes?"

Zataldra pivoted to leave out the open door, the footfalls of her flat-heeled boots clicking.

Jarius wasn't going to be an apologist for the CDF's wrongs, but he wasn't going to demonize the entire CDF either. They were more than the sum of their sins. He said, "Not all Guardians are a buncha amoral dicks. And you can't hold every single human being accountable for—"

"Zer'Katro, Bingrew," Zataldra addressed two men in the corridor, disregarding Jarius, "bring the prisoner, just in case I require another test subject for the demonstration."

"What the hell? What demonstration?" Jarius demanded.

Zataldra's two acolytes rushed into the cell, grabbing Jarius beneath his armpits and hauling him off the floor. They were both robust men, strong and built.

Jarius writhed against their hold in a bout of fierce resistance. "Let me go, man!"

While Zer'Katro kept Jarius restrained, Bingrew discharged a chemical aerosol into Jarius' face from a handheld dispenser of some sort. Then Zer'Katro released Jarius from his grasp.

Jarius eyesight blurred and swayed. *Damn it.* In an act of desperation, he swung a fist at the two men, but with the shackles restricting his reach, air was the only thing he struck.

As his neohuman immune system struggled to overpower the foreign agent invading his bloodstream, his lungs burned and vertigo unbalanced his feet. Losing the battle to remain standing, he sank to one knee.

His brown complexion turned ashen, and his motor functions faltered. Then he succumbed to unconsciousness, slumping to the floor.

◆ ◆ ◆

Jarius awoke, thoughts muddled. His arms were secured above his head, fastened to a wall by manacles. Sweat induced by the aerosol wet the dark scruff on his unshaven jaw.

A pair of blurry figures to his right, manacled to the wall as well, came into focus. They were the two lieutenant ambassadors he'd gone to Dilaxus with, seeking to secure the freedom of the Guardians being held prisoner by the Collective.

"Arlo. Cruz," Jarius murmured, the fog clearing from his mind. He saw they were all in an unfurnished, featureless stark-white room.

"You look like you've been through the wringer, but good to see you're still alive and kickin'," Cruz remarked.

Depending on what Zataldra had planned, Jarius wasn't sure how much longer that would be the case.

The doors leading into the room slid open, and Zataldra, Bingrew, and Zer'Katro walked in.

Apparently, Jarius and his fellow ambassadors were being given a front-row seat to Zataldra's "demonstration"—whatever it entailed.

After Zataldra ordered the room's virtual aide to translate their language into the humans' and vice versa, a computer-generated voice acknowledged her command. Now, the loudspeakers in the room would echo everyone's words in their respective languages.

The wall screen flashed to life at the designated hour, revealing the rugged bluish-gray visage of a man with high-composed features and a sharp underbite. He watched eagerly, awaiting Zataldra's demonstration.

Jarius' brow furrowed with contempt. He recognized the man from the Academy's archives. He was Dafulton, a dictator the CDF had toppled during one of their respectable planetary-impact missions. Jarius wondered if he was the Collective's leader.

Zataldra said, "Dafulton, we will now proceed with the demonstration."

Dafulton nodded silently.

Zataldra tapped her wristlet. A faint blue light on the device blinked. Instantly, an agonizing pressure coalesced in Cruz and

Arlo's skulls.

Cruz's teeth clicked together. "The pain . . . It's too much—"

Hair-raising screams from both Arlo and Cruz echoed throughout the room.

Watching them suffer, Jarius wiggled his wrists, as if his manacles would budge. "What are you doing to them?" His voice was strained with emotion.

Once the two ambassadors stopped screaming, they began grunting and thrashing against their restraints like feral beasts.

"Now, release them," Zataldra instructed Bingrew.

He pressed a button on the remote he held, setting Arlo and Cruz free.

Zataldra inputted a sequence of commands on her wristlet, and the ambassadors locked eyes. Primal rage glazed over their unblinking gazes. They were itching to kill each other.

In an eruption of violence, they collided, fists pounding into flesh.

Horror wrenched Jarius' heart. *What the fuck is going on?* Arlo and Cruz no longer recognized each other. They had been transformed into bloodthirsty savages. "Guys, cut it out!" Jarius yelled. There was no acknowledgment of his plea in their deadpan eyes. They weren't in their right minds.

Cruz rammed his forehead into Arlo's nose, producing a sickening crunch. Arlo staggered backward with blood streaming from his nostrils, before falling onto his back. Cruz then straddled Arlo's torso and rained down punches, reducing Arlo's face to an unrecognizable mess of blood, broken bones, and bruised flesh. Gripping Arlo's head in both hands, Cruz slammed it twice into the floor, killing him with blunt force trauma.

An epiphany dawned on Jarius: Zataldra had devised a way to hack a cerebral implant—the gateway into the human mind.

Subverting human beings' will to turn them against their friends, family, and loved ones—making them obliterate each other—was one of the most horrid weapons Jarius had ever encountered during his time in the CDF.

Cruz rose to his full height, knuckles drenched in red liquid. Arlo's blows had left noticeable injuries on his face.

Searching for another person to clobber, Cruz panned his crazy-eyed gaze across the room.

Zataldra's wristlet lit up after she entered a new command, and Cruz froze in place. Not a single muscle in his body moved, yet sorrow, agony, and remorse flickered in his eyes. He was aware he had ended Arlo's life.

"Now, on to part two of the demonstration," Zataldra said as Dafulton continued observing. "Release the third prisoner," she told Bingrew.

Bingrew pressed a button on his remote control, and the manacles holding Jarius' arms aloft clicked open.

In a split-second reaction, Jarius lunged toward his captors. He figured he'd at least go down fighting.

Zataldra keyed her wristlet, and the signal transmitting from it rooted Jarius' feet to the floor, stopping him in his tracks.

Jarius ground his teeth, an ache pulsating behind his eyes and setting his brain on fire. Questions mobbed his thoughts. Was Zataldra subjecting him to the same manipulation that she had subjected Cruz and Arlo to?

Zataldra removed her energy gun from its holster and extended it to Jarius. "Take the weapon."

Against his will, Jarius' hand accepted the gun. He was conscious of everything happening but unable to fight Zataldra's influence over his mind. He was a prisoner within his own body. All he could do was watch helplessly as his limbs followed commands that weren't his.

"Now aim the weapon at your comrade and pull the trigger," Zataldra said.

Jarius wanted to scream and protest, but his mouth remained sealed shut. He was about to be a spectator of a murder being performed by his own body.

Jarius rested the gun against Cruz's temple. Cruz's swollen, puffy face carried an expression that begged *"please don't."* Jarius fired at point-blank range. Cruz's head disintegrated, showering Jarius in a backwash of blood and brain matter.

"Return the weapon to me," Zataldra ordered. Jarius handed her the gun, and she stowed it back in her holster. Then she turned to Dafulton, who appeared to be pleased, and said, "Part two of the demonstration is complete." Her voice beamed with pride. "As you have witnessed, my progress has been significant. We can even transmit the mind-control signal via unmanned aerial systems."

Dafulton wore a toothy wicked grin. "Excellent."

Tears streamed down Jarius' cheeks although his expression remained blank. He stood there as an unwilling accessory to murder.

Zataldra said to Dafulton, "Geznan and Navexira are already on the humans' primary homeworld, preparing to conduct the weapon's most extensive test yet." There was no one she trusted more than Geznan and Navexira to accomplish this mission. They had fought with her against the CDF during the first wave of the Khanorian Revolution. They had stood beside her even in her darkest moments, like after her father's death. They knew how much the extermination of humanity meant to her, which might hinge on this weapon.

Still paralyzed by the mind-control signal, Jarius flinched internally at what he had heard. The Collective had two operatives on Eden, who were about to execute a large-scale demonstration of the weapon's capabilities.

Dafulton's eyes were alight with malicious glee. "I would like three of your control devices delivered to my ship to conduct some tests of my own," he said to Zataldra.

"Consider it done."

"Good. If you require any more test subjects, there are plenty aboard my ship. Enough to meet your needs." Dafulton was referring to the Guardians the ambassador delegation had been sent to rescue.

He signed off, and the wall screen cleared.

Zataldra released Jarius from her hold, the lights on her wristlet blinking as she punched buttons.

Now back in control of his body, Jarius dropped to his hands and knees, wheezing. He felt like he was about to vomit up his innards, and his muscles were taut with tension.

Zataldra crouched next to him. "How does it feel to watch helplessly as someone you care about dies, as I had to?" she asked, her voice icelike. Jarius held back the unsavory words coming to mind. "Nothing? Not surprising."

The continuous mental replay of him killing Cruz watered Jarius' eyes, tears peppering the floor. Being used as a test subject in someone's scheme to destroy humanity was a horror he wished on no one. Maybe Defense Force Intelligence would intercept the Collective operatives on Eden and thwart their agenda before it could harm any unsuspecting civilians. But he worried that was wishful thinking.

Zataldra drew herself up, her hard-hearted disposition unsoftened by Jarius' distress. "Take him back to his cell," she instructed Bingrew and Zer'Katro, "but make sure he gets cleaned up. I tire of his stench."

A buzzer sounded, signaling that someone was outside the doors. They chirped open, and a teenage Khanorian girl strode in. She wore a hip-length, short-sleeve skirt paired with pants that puffed out slightly where they were tucked into her boots. Her facial features bore an undeniable resemblance to Zataldra's.

"Sister, what's going on here?" the teen asked. Her gut clenched as she took in the grotesque sight on the floor—the bludgeoned face of Arlo and the headless corpse of Cruz. She covered her mouth, forcing down the bile rising in her throat. She wasn't a noob to blood and gore; it was impossible for her to be. She had seen much of it during the Khanorian Revolution—too much. But such sights still made her insides twist.

Zataldra said, "Iya, what are you—" Then she remembered. "Oh, that's right. So caught up in my work, I forgot about your visit today. My apologies."

Confusion blanketed Iya's face as she pointed at the two dead ambassadors. "Yes, but what in the name of the Gods is going on here?"

"Though I owe you no explanation, I will provide one later. For now—"

Iya's eyes shifted to Jarius. One slow, sure step at a time, she started toward him. "You're in pain. Do you require medical attention?"

Jarius wondered why Iya was different. Why wasn't she fuming with rage at the sight of his kind?

Bingrew stepped into Iya's periphery, stone-faced. He extended an arm to block her from further approaching Jarius. "Caution, young one, he is dangerous. Just like the rest of his race."

Iya stood akimbo, staring squarely into his eyes. "I'm sixteen now, Bingrew. I know danger when I see it, and this human appears to have been rendered harmless. Even if he's guilty of some misdeed, the Korahh'Havaell teaches us to respect all sentient beings, whether they are prisoners or—"

"Enough, Iya!" Zataldra said, her voice a whirlwind of fury. "This is neither the time nor the place for religious doctrine." *It seems you're more like mother and I'm more like father,* she thought. More like their father when he was a warman.

Jarius' mind conjured up theories. *Korahh'Havaell? Maybe that's a scriptural text of some sort.* He clearly saw that Iya's belief system contrasted with Zataldra's.

An insistent voice inside Iya urged her to act on her growing sympathy for Jarius. He was doing his damnedest to fight off the nausea and headache working in tandem to keep him on his hands and knees. "That human appears to be quite unwell. I will help him —"

"No, Iya, you will do nothing," Zataldra said firmly. "This is my domain. I decide what happens here. While you may stay, as you are my sister, you must respect my authority."

"Fine. But do remember I'm sixteen now and that it's the Gods who guide my steps. And please, don't let your descent into apostasy overshadow the Korahh'Havaell's teachings, the teachings our mother lived by and used to instill morals, values, and compassion in us—even if we chose not to become devout followers, like you have." Iya left, the doors snapping shut.

Zer'Katro and Bingrew assisted Jarius in getting to his feet.

Zataldra's wristlet chirped, drawing her attention. The message displayed on its small screen softened her irritable expression. It had been a while since she had last spoken to Grand Elder Drosaide Varanz, her father's closest friend. He had always been there for her, Iya, and Jud'Zarr, especially after her mother's premature passing.

Zataldra knew a Khanorian did not disregard an invitation

from a Grand Elder. So, though she was busy, she would meet with Varanz and hear him out.

Bingrew and Zer'Katro marched a resistless Jarius through the doors. He had no fight left in him, body fatigued by the aftereffects of mind control.

He trudged forward, legs shaky and about to buckle, his head hanging low. Though his future looked bleak, he held onto hope, thinking of his fiancée and best friend. *Jazzlyn. Randy.*

CHAPTER TWO

Commonwealth
Planet Eden

On a morning run, Stacie Spencer and Jazzlyn de' Medici raced across a paved jogging trail winding through woods. The lattice of leafy tree branches overhead filtered the sun's rays, casting a patchwork of light and shadow over the two runners.

Both Jazzlyn and Stacie were in the zone, each striving to reach the end of the trail before the other.

With Jazzlyn in the lead, Stacie kicked up her pace—the drumbeat of her heart accelerating, her legs aching for reprieve, and air rushing from her lungs in ragged, uneven gasps. *Damn, Jazzlyn is a real speedster,* Stacie thought. *She wasn't kidding when she said she was a habitual runner.* Jazzlyn definitely had the build of a runner. However, no matter how fast Jazzlyn was, Stacie was determined to win the race.

Even in a friendly one-on-one competition like today's, Stacie's competitive spirit burned to the utmost degree. She *refused* to even entertain the idea of losing. And this drive didn't simply stem from ego, but from a history of underestimation and belittlement.

Stacie's parents, before their deaths, were members of the Eight Elite—the wealthiest of Edenites. They provided her with anything she wanted. But over time, she became fed up with being labeled as just a privileged Elite "princess" by society. The notion of her being a silver-spoon heiress who had a leg up over everyone, because of family connections and assets, began to seriously grate on her nerves. Therefore, in her late teens, she had resolved to escape the gilded cage her parents had built for her. She wanted to prove to herself and her critics that she could achieve success without relying on her privileges.

To make her point, she instilled in herself the ambition to be an overachiever in every endeavor she pursued, from athletic challenges to being a Guardian—a soldier—in the prestigious Commonwealth Defense Force. That ambition was fueling her drive to come out on top in today's race between her and Jazzlyn.

Right now, her body was begging her to slow down—to just let Jazzlyn win this one. But the hurtful remarks from her peers at Cadwell Institute of Higher Learning spurred her on:

> *"No way you got those stellar evaluations by your own merits. Your parents finagle them for you or something?"*

> *"Probably got those high evals by sleeping around with your professors."*

> *"Spencer doesn't have to work nearly as hard as the rest of us. She knows her mommy and daddy can buy her graduation for her."*

Stacie wasn't sure why past insults *still* niggled her. What was she trying to prove to herself? She was now the queen of Spencer

Enterprises. She had taken over her parents' criminal empire and purified it into an instrument for positive change. But her parents' organization was an inheritance, not a venture she had built from the ground up herself. Sure, she had served as a Guardian in the CDF and earned the mantle of Warrior Extraordinaire during BCT, but it was all thanks to the support of her significant other, Randal Scott.

Her mind holed up in the past, another memory hijacked her thoughts as she trailed Jazzlyn, falling behind on the uphill stretch . . .

> *Stacie sat on the grass, nursing her injured knee after a rough fall during track practice. "Damn it," she muttered in frustration.*
>
> *One of Stacie's teammates extended a hand to help her up. "Here, let me help you," she said. Just as Stacie reached out, her teammate withdrew the offer and chuckled. "Try getting up on your own for once, princess."*

Harnessing the voices of her detractors into adrenaline, Stacie willed her exhausted legs into a sprint—overriding the ache in her tendons and the voice in her head telling her not to overexert herself. Momentum growing stronger and stronger, she overtook Jazzlyn like a lioness—long, silky blond ponytail billowing behind her.

Maintaining her pace, she pushed her cardio to the limit. *Faster,* she told herself, diaphragm contracting rapidly, metatarsal bones pounding the earth. *Faster!* A fallen twig snapped under her footfall.

She steadied her breathing: in, out, in, out.

She could hear Jazzlyn's sneakers gaining traction and closing the distance.

Motivating herself, Stacie repeated over and over in her mind, *Dominate. Be the fucking best. Win.* She and Jazzlyn were nearly neck and neck, but she held on to her slight lead, and they followed the trail into the lush park beyond the woods. Winner: Stacie.

Totally spent, both women slumped onto a white bench, resting their now rubbery legs.

All around, people were enjoying meals at the bench-tables and taking strolls. Birds twittered from their perches in the green trees. Amphibious creatures dwelling in limpid freshwater ponds bobbed.

"You're fast, Spencer," Jazzlyn huffed, pulse dropping to normal. Strands of sable hair clung to her clammy forehead. Her athletic wear, like that of her running partner, was drenched in perspiration, and the run's afterburn made her quadriceps and calves sting. "I thought I had you."

Stacie drew air into her breathless lungs. "You *almost* did. Good run." She peeled her shirt from her midriff and wiped her face with it, uncovering suntanned washboard abs glistening with sweat.

"I'll beat you next time." Jazzlyn glanced down at the engagement ring on her finger and sighed. The run proved to be a pleasant distraction for her, but the safety of her fiancée constantly pecked at her mind.

Stacie said, "I know you're worried about him, but I'm sure he's alright."

Unlike Stacie, Jazzlyn had her doubts. "Jarius should've returned from his assignment *five days* ago." She tugged at her hair, twisting it around her fingers.

Stacie squeezed Jazzlyn's shoulder reassuringly. "That was an *estimated* end date, right? I'm sure that as a Commonwealth ambassador, brokering peace deals and negotiating settlements can sometimes encounter unexpected hurdles. Mission completion dates are 'subject to change,' aren't they?"

Stacie's encouraging words weren't quite enough to quell Jazzlyn's unrest. An uneasy feeling lingered. She remained fearful that something terrible might have happened to Jarius. Thoughts of him stranded somewhere injured or being tortured by an enemy ran rampant in her mind. "Yeah, you could be right," she admitted, lips quivering. "That's got to be it." Though there was now optimism in her voice, her troubled heart found no solace.

"Yeah, I'm sure he'll be back on Eden any day now."

A vendor golem was scouring the park for potential customers. When its optics landed on the two tired, sweat-drenched young women, it rolled up to them. From the lens at the center of its ovoid head, it projected a hologram of a plastic bottle branded with a green thunderbolt logo. The golem then launched into a sales pitch. "Velocity Water, by VoltLife, is enriched with minerals and electrolytes that will—"

"We'll take two," Stacie interrupted, cutting short the bot's sales pitch.

The golem extracted two plastic bottles from the refrigerated storage compartment of its boxy midsection.

Stacie accessed the holotouch interface of her wristcom, opened a payment app, and tendered four credits.

The golem's circular eyes blinked, confirming receipt of payment. Then it rolled away, searching for VoltLife's next customers.

Stacie and Jazzlyn uncapped their bottles and guzzled the water, wetting their parched throats.

On the bottles' labels, the digital promo text VOLTLIFE scrolled from left to right.

Stacie lowered her bottle from her lips and admired the intricate gold filigree of Jazzlyn's engagement ring. If the day ever came that she got married, she wanted a ring just as glamorous.

Jazzlyn noticed the impressed look in Stacie's eyes. "It's nice, isn't it?"

Stacie tipped her chin. "It's lovely."

"I've gotta say, Jarius has good taste." Jazzlyn playfully nudged Stacie's shoulder with her elbow. "When are you and Mr. Scott gonna tie the knot?"

"Oh, um—" Stacie forced a wan smile, concealing her uncertainty. She groped for words. "Well, we just got back together, and I've decided I . . . wanna take it slow. I . . . just wanna be sure, I guess."

"Sure of what?"

Stacie reflected on the past. First, there was Randy's infidelity—his accidental entanglement with Kesley Whittaker, which sparked their breakup . . .

> *"Not only have you joined the enemy, but you sleep with them too! You betrayed your duty, but you also betrayed **me**! **Me**, Randy, the woman who dragged you out of your emotional withdrawal from society! The woman who broke you out of . . . being a loner! The woman who made you smile time after time since your mother's death by the very people you now ally yourself with!"*

And more recently, there were Randy's feelings for Akane Sugimori, the RISE member hellbent on killing Damien Sykes, even if it meant fouling DFI's painstaking investigation . . .

"This woman means a lot to you, doesn't she?" Stacie said to Randy.

*"Yeah, she's the first person to treat me like a comrade and a human being since I came back to the CDF from leave. She's my **friend**."*

"Did you two Link?"

"Yeah, so?"

"Well, I know you. You're not Linking with someone unless they're pretty special to you. Did you . . . sleep with her?"

Randy's forehead creased. "Yeah, we had sex, Stace. What's that got to do with anything?"

*"I'm saying your judgment might be impaired by your **feelings** for this woman."*

"Stacie?" Jazzlyn said, still waiting for an answer.

Stacie's brows lifted in response, her mind no longer adrift in recollection. "Huh? Yeah?"

Jazzlyn took another swig of water. "What is it you want to be sure about?"

"Oh, well, it's just—" Stacie dragged nervous fingers over her damp hair.

When she re-Linked with Randy during their mission to prevent Akane and Jay from killing Damien Sykes, she was exposed to the feelings he still had for her. Those feelings resurrected waves of nostalgic memories, from romantic outings to passionate nights in the bedroom. Yet, she couldn't shake the doubt that had crept in. Had she been too hasty in jumping right back into a committed relationship with him? Caught up in the initial dopamine rush from once again bonding through mental communion, she now questioned the wisdom of her decision. The potency of a Link never ceased to astonish her, with its potential to influence one's feelings and judgment.

The roar of atmospheric craft diverted Jazzlyn and Stacie's attention skyward, ending their conversation.

The craft's destination was outer space.

Side by side, Jazzlyn and Stacie watched the craft break the sound barrier, aft thrusters carving white plumes across the sky.

They exchanged curious looks.

"That's like . . . the third launch today," Jazzlyn said. Whatever mission the Air & Space Corps was mobilizing for had to be significant, she thought, with only a select few privy to it. As a lieutenant in the Reserves of the corps, she wondered if she'd be called up for duty. "Something big must be happening."

"Chief Amaechi announced that the Air & Space Corps would be conducting some orbital exercises for a few days. What else could it be?"

Jazzlyn continued staring at the sky pensively. Her intuition warned her that more than just space drills were in progress. "I don't know, Stacie," she replied worriedly. "It's like . . . a defensive perimeter is being established in geostationary orbit."

Stacie downed some water and wiped her mouth. "A defensive perimeter?" That pulled a laugh out of her. "Who'd be stupid enough to even *consider* attacking the Commonwealth? We're a member of the Interplanetary Union, and you mess with us, you mess with the other Union Worlds."

I hope to God I'm wrong, Jazzlyn thought.

Stacie curled an arm around her. "Alright, let's shift gears and steer clear of any depressing thoughts. How about we make our way to my mansion?" To ease Jazzlyn's anxieties about Jarius' well-being, she had planned a full in-home spa day to pamper her, which included appointments for manicures, massages, and beauty treatments.

Jazzlyn stiffly rose from the bench, her long, toned brown legs stretching to their full length. "Shall we?" she said with some cheer.

Stacie heaved herself up, standing a head shorter than Jazzlyn. She called an air-cab with her wristcom. "Are you watching the Executive debate tonight with friends?"

"I am."

Good, Stacie thought. She believed it wouldn't be wise for Jazzlyn to watch the debate alone, given everything she was dealing with.

"What about yourself?" Jazzlyn asked.

"Randy is due back from deployment today. We've got reservations at The Gourmet Oasis. Maybe we'll catch some of the debate while we're there."

"That sounds lovely."

After draining their water bottles, they tossed them into a nearby trash receptacle.

"I assume you're voting for Amaechi," Jazzlyn said confidently as they awaited their cab's arrival.

Stacie's face beamed. "*Abso-fuckin'-lutely.*"

"How was it growing up with her as your caretaker?" Jazzlyn asked eagerly, a huge Amaechi supporter herself. "She's such an *incredible* human being. When it comes to her values and what she believes in, she's like a firmly rooted tree that can't be toppled."

"Yeah, she is."

Stacie's parents, like all members of the Elite, the hegemonic criminal conglomerate, held themselves in high regard. Yet, they treated Oviereya, a colony immigrant, with respect as their domestic servant. They even entrusted their daughter to her care in their absence.

Growing close to Oviereya, Stacie adopted a mindset that diverged from her parents' and the majority of Eden's population. She believed that colonists were not inferior to AEGIS's "chosen." They were equals and deserved a chance at prosperity. They could be more than resource harvesters in the colonies, or industrial workers and housemaids as immigrants.

Stacie reminisced about the times Oviereya shared her wisdom while they strolled through the estate's flower gardens. Darlene Spencer would never have condoned Oviereya's teachings. Those teachings instilled in Stacie a profound respect for all the Commonwealth's people and taught her that the Commonwealth's classist society was a flawed one.

Nevertheless, during the civil war between the dissenting colonies and the Commonwealth Government, Stacie had viewed the insurrection as unjust, echoing the sentiments of most of Eden's population. And she had believed that so-called Independent Movement sympathizers were traitors. After all, according to the Commonwealth's constitution, a colony declaring sovereignty was treason—plain and simple. However, her perspective had since evolved.

Fond memories of her childhood with Oviereya livened Stacie's face. "Growing up with Oviereya was . . . enlightening," she said to Jazzlyn.

"I can only imagine." Jazzlyn envisioned what it might have been like to have Oviereya as a caretaker.

A yellow auto-driven air-cab descended on their location. Once its landing skids touched down on the grass, the overhead glass canopy snapped open.

Jazzlyn and Stacie climbed aboard, bound for Stacie's home.

◆ ◆ ◆

Expedition Task Forces Headquarters
Hangar Three

Task force Vanguard Alpha's ship, the *Nightingale*, rolled into the hangar, returning the team of Guardians safely to headquarters from their latest mission.

The drives shut off, hissing, and the ship coasted into its service station under a gantry.

Five technicians in gray jumpsuits, smeared with grease and oil, approached the ship to perform standard maintenance. They plugged charging cables into the ports on the ship's undercarriage to recharge the power cells, conducted diagnostic assessments, and inspected the exterior for any signs of structural damage or significant wear.

A stair-ramp extended from the portside of the vessel and made contact with the floor. Randy, in battledress, was the first to descend the metal steps.

He was relieved the Guardians killed by the Collective had finally made it home, giving their families a chance to pay their final respects. Still, his concern for Jarius persisted.

He thought about how loyal a friend Jarius had been. When Randy got captured by the Coalition, Jarius attempted a solo rescue mission, and even as Randy contemplated joining the Coalition, Jarius stood by his side. Eventually, Jarius followed his lead and joined as well. Randy was determined to do everything in his power to save Jarius, assuming he was still alive.

However, it wasn't just Jarius' well-being disturbing Randy's peace; the mystery surrounding the Collective weighed on him too, Zataldra's mention of retribution lingering in his mind. He suspected that her statement might have a connection to the Khanorian Campaign. It wouldn't be unexpected if Guardians had committed atrocities during it. He had seen for himself that the CDF wasn't always the virtuous force it was portrayed as. He intended to delve into the history of the campaign to uncover what he could.

As he reached the end of the stairs, Arturo came down behind him. Lieutenant Carl Breckenridge and the rest of Vanguard Alpha followed in tow.

Arturo went to Randy's side. "Hey, Scott, wanna join the team for drinks tonight and watch the Executive debate with us? It might help you unwind."

"I can't. I have a date tonight," Randy replied.

Arturo knew Randy was in a relationship with Stacie Spencer, one of the richest women in the Commonwealth. After seeing Stacie's beach photos online, he couldn't help feeling envious. She had a jaw-dropping body—marble abs, legs you could stare at all day, and shapely curves. "Well, maybe next time, then. Enjoy yourself tonight, hombre." He veered left, leaving Randy to himself.

With the Purists Paul Shaffer, Mark MaCallum, and Dan Maddox dead; Sam Guthrie transitioned by request; and Jamie Lister currently serving a minor sentence for his attempt to assassinate Damien Sykes alongside Akane, Vanguard Alpha had some fresh faces, friendly faces like Arturo. And Randy was grateful for that. He was also relieved that his rank promotion, which had been fettered by some Coalition-hating higher-up, was now underway. Many stressors had been lifted from his shoulders, but they had been replaced by new ones.

Randy made his way past technicians and Guardians conversing about tonight's Executive debate between incumbent Chief Oviereya Amaechi and centrist Darren Radcliff.

Most of the technicians and Guardians, who had gathered in

small discussion circles here in the hangar, were against reform. That meant they were against Oviereya. They were placing their bets on Daren to win.

He had surged to the top of the polls and emerged as Oviereya's political nemesis. And while not a Purist like a wannabe politician such as Damien Sykes, or at least not openly so, he wasn't a progressionist like Oviereya either. And for adherents of the status quo, who constituted the majority of Eden's population, anyone seemed preferable to Oviereya.

Randy's vote was unequivocally for the incumbent. Oviereya, the first colony-born Chief—a lottery beneficiary, an immigrant—had kick-started the first stages of true reformation in the Commonwealth. She had launched the Colony Restoration Initiative and set the groundwork for the establishment of the colonies' first university. She was phasing out unethical planetary-impact missions and had ordered an investigation into the CDF's questionable practices. Randy wanted this progress to continue. No one knew if the "Radcliff agenda" for the Commonwealth would discontinue Oviereya's reform efforts or sustain their momentum. Randy assumed the former.

"Randal Scott, I'd like to talk to you," came a woman's voice over the buzzing of electromechanical tools. It was strong and assertive—attention-grabbing. The woman stopped a few paces away from Randy.

Randy angled himself toward her.

She wore a russet-brown pantsuit, which contrasted with her tawny skin tone, and her hair was styled in a short updo of twisty jet-black curls.

Randy guessed her to be thirty-something.

"How can I help you?" he asked politely, turning fully to face her.

The woman replied, "I'm Maxine Lain, a member of Chief Amaechi's Truth Commission."

From the news, Randy had heard about the five-person commission assembled to investigate ethics violations within the CDF, specifically overly aggressive enforcement tactics and the mistreatment of enemy prisoners of war. But what did the commission want with him?

Maxine said, "I'm collecting testimonies from Guardians who were deployed to Satellite One during the civil war, to document any misconduct by comrades that they may have witnessed." She closed the distance between her and Randy, platform shoes clacking. "I'm particularly interested in Guardians who defected and sided with the Coalition—Guardians who, like you, have since rejoined the CDF. I'd love to get a statement from you, if that's alright."

Randy nodded. "Sure, I do have a date to get ready for,"—his eyes tracked between Maxine and his wristcom's time display —"but I can spare a couple of minutes." He was more than happy to contribute to the ethics investigation, to help the CDF course correct.

"Great, I'm pleased that you're willing to assist in the Chief's efforts to reform our military." Maxine opened her wristcom's holotouch interface and activated a voice-recording app. She then proceeded with Randy's interview. "Last year, you enlisted in the CDF and pledged to uphold the Oath—the oath to defend the Commonwealth from foreign and domestic threats. And you weren't, in the least, what's referred to as an Independent Movement sympathizer, correct?"

Randy casually slipped his hands into his pants' pockets. "That's right. And I was hellbent on eliminating my father, a man I believed had betrayed the CDF by siding with traitorous insurrectionists. Everything's kosher between me and my father now, but I, of *all Guardians*, had *absolutely* no reason to consider defection. The thought never even crossed my mind. It would've been blasphemy. I was a dedicated soldier, fully committed to the Oath."

"So what changed? What led you to neglect that oath and side with the insurrectionists, the Coalition?"

"A culmination of things." Randy's features twitched in discomfort. "Horrible things that I witnessed with my own eyes."

Maxine could see that whatever he had experienced truly disturbed him. "Like what?"

"Well, for starters, I watched a superior overstep his bounds and punt a defenseless woman in the gut, while she was *already* down," he said, referring to Kesley Whittaker's terrible treatment by Lars during their stop and frisk. "And the worst part? He was in a Shell. The woman had no way of harming him."

"And this action by your superior was unjustified?" Maxine clarified her statement, saying, "Meaning this woman didn't provoke the use of force."

"*No,*" Randy replied surely. "Backtalk doesn't warrant physical assault. My superior was just flexing his authority—demonstrating his power. *Abusing* his power." Randy's pulse pounded, the memory bringing back his anger from that day.

"Definitely an excessive-force violation. What else did you witness during your deployment to Satellite One?"

Randy snapped his eyes shut, fighting back the disgust. He withdrew his hands from his pockets and balled them into fists. Every sound in the hangar faded away, including the hum of a passing maintenance cart and the sharp honk of its horn. Those sounds were replaced by explosions, the crackle of energy blasts, and screams. It took all of Randy's willpower to block out the sounds of war.

After Randy remained unresponsive for a moment, Maxine said, "Are you alright? If this is too much for you, we can stop and —"

"No, it's okay." Randy opened his eyes. A series of expressions crossed his face, from revulsion to sorrow. "I'm fine. I wanna help the commission." His features relaxed. "To answer your question: I saw Guardians rough up a civilian simply because they questioned his allegiance. The poor guy didn't deserve to be manhandled just for talking trash about the Defense Force. Voicing discontent isn't a crime."

"Guardian misconduct, without a doubt," Maxine acknowledged.

"Yeah, but during Basic Combat Training, cadets are conditioned to perceive anyone who expresses negative sentiments about the CDF or the central government as a threat. No exceptions. A Guardian does not dare question the CDF's righteousness. Hell, my friend and comrade, Jarius Ford, was threatened with discharge by death just for wondering if colony citizens had valid reasons for protesting martial law.

"And if a Guardian showed *any* sign of sympathy or remorse for colonists or the Coalition, their peers slandered and stigmatized them, labeling them an Independent Movement sympathizer. The CDF silences objective voices by cultivating fear, specifically the fear of ostracism and social exclusion."

Maxine said, "And after you witnessed Guardian misconduct and your father provided you incriminating documentation on the highbinders within our government—the same father you had wanted to eliminate—you switched sides. You joined Operation Hammer Fall, the Coalition's mission to seize the Parliament Building and publish the corruption files on the net using its broadcast center."

"That's right." Randy now seemed abstracted. His mind was elsewhere, lost back in time. This interview with Maxine was shoveling up memories he wished would stay buried: images of him killing rebels and Guardians. He'd killed the former out of ignorance; the latter were collateral damage during the Battle of the Quad, unintended casualties.

"And did any of your rebel comrades have conversations with you about citizens being mistreated under military rule? Were there any former Guardians in the Coalition who spoke to you about injustices committed by the CDF?"

Randy tipped his chin in a quick nod. "Yeah, there were some former Guardians in the Coalition who recounted injustices they had witnessed. One of them was the Coalition leader himself, Arman Reza."

"Tell me more."

"Reza said that during his time as a Guardian, when he went by his real name Ahmed Hawsawi, he took part in the planetary-impact mission to intervene in the genocidal war between the Falgoah and Chalderat clans on planet Zelaforia. His squad, on the side of the Chalderat, was ordered to open fire on Falgoah clansmen who'd *already* surrendered. Because he refused to comply and denounced a needless, heinous act of violence, he was demoted to the Reserves."

Lead dropped into Maxine's stomach. *Punishment for standing up for what's right.*

Randy went on. "While in the Reserves, Ahmed was deployed to suppress the miners' strike in Colony Four, which was destabilizing the Commonwealth's economic security. His squad was ordered to open fire on some miners, the Commonwealth's *own* citizens. After he refused and assaulted his superior, he was dishonorably discharged.

"He later assumed a new identity, rechristening himself Arman Reza and reverting to digital activism as a means of taking a stand against government oppression. Eventually, he fathered the Independent Movement and later claimed the mantle of being the Coalition's leader.

"He had genuine aspirations to reform the CDF and the Commonwealth Government, striving for a fairer system. No more punishments for Guardians showing sympathy, and no more planetary-impact missions driven solely by avarice. Ethics before all else. Unfortunately, instead of collaborating with the public and uncorrupt government officials, he anointed himself the sole authority of the Commonwealth, and my father and I eliminated him."

Maxine said, "Then you took a brief hiatus from military life before returning to the CDF and transferring to the Expedition Task Forces. How was your experience in the CDF after coming back from leave?"

"Pretty damn bad." More recent events slid into Randy's thoughts. "Immigrant Guardians and defectors like me were being treated like shit by many of our comrades. Bitter superiors denied us promotions, pissed that the civil war had ended without repercussions for Coalition fighters. They took their anger out on immigrant Guardians and former defectors. We were their punching bags. And it was during my new start as a member of the Task Forces that I learned about an infestation of ultraextremists within the CDF and Eden's society."

"Purists," Maxine said to confirm.

"Yeah. They had infiltrated sectors of the government, the CDF, and the police forces. Some members of my task force, Vanguard Alpha, were Purists, but they're gone now.

"Since the CDF dismantled the largest Purist organization—the Brotherhood—and Chief Amaechi put all extremist groups on notice, the Purists within our institutions and throughout society have become more cautious than ever, and perhaps even more cunning and strategic. The hate epidemic hasn't ceased; we all know that."

Randy's attention shifted between the time displayed on his wristcom and Maxine. He obviously needed to go soon.

Maxine noted that Randy seemed anxious to leave so he wouldn't be late for his date. "I won't keep you much longer, but can you recall anything else that you'd want me to include in my report? Maybe experiences similar to your own that other service members shared with you?"

"One of the Guardians in my task force, Akane Sugimori, mentioned that during BCT, a fellow cadet and friend was punished with death by a drill sergeant just for voicing his opposition to the civil war."

Maxine exited the recording app. "Thank you, Randy. Your insights have been valuable. The compilation of all Guardian testimonies will prove beneficial in reforming the CDF. Once the commission completes its investigation, a report will be delivered to the Chief. Then the government can implement an action plan to better the CDF and gut the rot within it. Based on what I've heard, the cutthroat mentality of Guardians starts in BCT."

While in BCT, Randy never considered how relentlessly the cadre drilled into Guardians the tenet that they should never hesitate or question themselves before killing the enemy. The CDF demanded absolute unity of thought, and any second-guessing marked a Guardian as an outlier.

"Yeah, that's where the indoctrination starts. Assimilate or be disciplined. If you show sympathy for the enemy or stand up for what's morally right, then prepare to be reprimanded. Revising the CDF's training program would be a step forward, but we also have to acknowledge the existence of corrupt high-ranking service members who authorize and condone atrocities.

"I'm hoping the commission's report lands on Amaechi's desk and not Radcliff's." Randy suspected Daren would derail Oviereya's reform initiatives, stifling colony progression and cultural change within the CDF. Though not an extreme anti-reformist, or a Purist like Damien Sykes, Randy got the feeling he'd be another Jared Kerner—milquetoast when it came to reform.

Maxine said, "Oh, and by the way, don't fret about any backlash from your testimony. Your name will be redacted in the report, so you won't have to—"

"*No*, no need to redact anything. I don't scare easily. I want anyone who reviews that report to know I had a part in cleaning up the CDF." Randy believed in leading by example, and he wanted to encourage other Guardians to come forward and expose any atrocities they were aware of.

"Okay," Maxine replied evenly.

"I'm glad this commission was established. There are surely Guardians who've been too afraid to confess what they've witnessed or were forced to do. I hope many come forward to participate in the Truth Commission's investigation."

"Yes."

In preparing for the interview, Maxine studied Randy's service sketch and did her homework on him. He was the man who, out of a sense of morality, sided with the Coalition, risked being tried for desertion and treason, and set aside differences with his father to emancipate the colonies from systemic oppression. He was the man who charged into a building and put his life on the line to neutralize an active shooter—a Purist—to prevent him from murdering men, women, and children. Randy could've waited for the authorities to handle that dangerous situation, but that wasn't his nature.

Randy even stopped two members of the immigrant extremist group RISE, Akane and Jay, from assassinating Damien Sykes. Though Damien was a Purist and a human trafficker, Randy understood that killing him in cold blood wasn't right.

Maxine saw that Randy had a noble, heroic vibe about him. Though if anyone told him he had such a vibe, he'd likely just laugh it off—modest as he was. He didn't consider himself a novelty; he was merely a man striving to embody the ideal Guardian to the best of his abilities, a man who, like anyone else, was flawed and had fallen short at times, as evidenced by his rough patch in his relationship with Stacie. But deny it as he might, he did have a hero vibe about him—and a composed and collected demeanor.

Maxine said, "If I have additional questions, may I reach out to you?"

"Absolutely." Randy wouldn't hesitate in further assisting the Truth Commission if needed. "And it seems you already have the means to find me." He turned to depart.

Maxine stopped him mid-stride, saying, "Oh, just one last thing."

Randy looked over his shoulder. "What's that?"

"I'd like to interview the service members you mentioned, Akane Sugimori and Jarius Ford, right?"

"Well, Jarius is now a lieutenant in the Ambassador Corps. He was deployed on a mission and . . . hasn't gotten back yet." Randy had to keep the abduction of the ambassador delegation under wraps for the time being, in accordance with the Chief Executive's

53

decision not to disclose it to the entire CDF and the public. "And Akane took a leave of absence some time ago, needing some personal time. Right now, she's still on Satellite One."

"I see. At some point, I'll attempt to contact them to see if they'd be willing to take part in the investigation."

"Great." Randy resumed walking away.

"Enjoy your date."

"I will."

As Randy headed out, he thought, *Funny, the Commonwealth Defense Force makes fiends pay for their sins, but who holds us accountable for ours?*

Reaching the exit, he heard his wristcom chirp a message notification. Randy tapped the device. A holographic text projection then appeared above his wrist.

Akane: I'll be back on the job soon. I've maxed my leave extensions. No more freebies from Breckenridge.

A mingling of warmth and anxiety swept through Randy, from the depths of his gut to the core of his heart—fleeting yet strong. He pondered what it'd be like seeing Akane in the flesh after such an extended absence. The nineteen-year-old colony immigrant had made a positive impact on his life.

He'd be disappointed if Akane became involved in any more extremist organizations advocating for colony and immigrant equality. He understood that her feelings about her choices remained unchanged. She didn't resent murdering Skylar's harasser and the Purist Paul Shaffer, who killed her best friend, Simone. Both had despicable natures, but Randy believed that the proper authorities should have decided their fate. Nevertheless, at her core, Akane had a good nature.

Her behavior resulted from the marginalization and discrimination she experienced as a colony immigrant, amplified by

RISE's influence, which molded her into a disruptor of the system —a firebrand. Randy couldn't entirely fault her for her morally gray actions, and despite their divergent viewpoints, it'd be good to see her.

After taking a moment to formulate a response, he opted for brevity, typing a succinct message.

Randy: Cool. See you when you get back.

He left the hangar, his thoughts focused on his evening with Stacie. Her companionship offered a much-needed reprieve from the stressors troubling him: Jarius and the Collective.

◆ ◆ ◆

Zataldra approached Grand Elder Varanz, who was swathed in a crimson jacquard robe. His wizened, timeworn face and receding hairline showed he was several decades her senior.

Acres of grasslands surrounded the bucolic meadow designated for their meeting. To the north of the meadow were homes crafted from rough-hewn stone. Many of them were built into cliffsides, so they blended seamlessly into the natural environment. Though these were old-world dwellings, they weren't lacking the conveniences that modern science offered.

Snow-capped mountains rose to the south of the meadow. Zataldra's compound was nestled within those mountains, whose jagged, imposing peaks were a majestic sight to behold.

"It has been too long, Zataldra," Varanz said. Adhering to customary formalities, he clasped his hands and bowed in greeting.

After Zataldra reciprocated the gesture, she squared her shoulders and adopted a rigid posture. "What do you want, Varanz?" She had a strong suspicion that Varanz's intention for this meeting was to dissuade her from attaining vengeance on the humans. But she had already made up her mind.

Despite Zataldra's brusque tone, Varanz refrained from censuring her and remained composed.

Varanz's prolonged silence wore on Zataldra. "Go ahead; state your purpose," she said. "I'm pressed for time and have little patience for idle chat."

A rush of wind whisked by and tugged at Varanz's sleeves. "You have preoccupied yourself with the wrong pursuits, exploiting the pain and anger of vindictive, heartbroken Khanorians—training them to become instruments of violence at your mountain compound, with the assistance of ex-warmen. And for what? To serve as irregulars in a futile quest for retribution against an enemy that has long left our nation?

"These Khanorians should be on a path toward healing and recovery. Furthermore, I have heard you have become . . . dare I say, a mad scientist, constructing war machines in your laboratory?" The timbre of his voice matched the raw emotion written on his face. "You are a *councilwoman* now." He emphasized "councilwoman" to underscore his point. "Your focus ought to be on fulfilling your civic duties."

Following the Sorin's overthrow, a council was established to function as Khanoria's primary governing body. The goal was to prevent a resurgence of dictatorship by distributing leadership among an elected body of representatives instead of entrusting it to a single individual, a Sorin. Zataldra, being the well-liked daughter of a revered Grand Elder, easily secured a seat on the council.

In the face of Varanz's lambastes, Zataldra dug in her heels. "I haven't shirked my responsibilities as a councilwoman. What I'm doing in my personal research facility is developing weapons to retaliate against the beings who murdered innocent Khanorians, including my father."

Varanz persisted in trying to reach Zataldra and soften her

heart. "Your decision to use your gifted mind to construct war machines resulted in your expulsion from the Shaho'Gkodii, contravening the guild's commitment to employing science for nonviolent means.

"Your father took pride in witnessing your initiation into the Shaho'Gkodii. He would be ashamed if he were still alive today, as your aspirations once lay in using science to cure ailments—such as the one your mother succumbed to—and revitalizing fallow lands to yield a more bountiful harvest. You had wanted to leave the weaponization of science to the Protection Force's engineers, as I recall."

Regret flashed across Zataldra's face. She remembered how passionate she used to be about her work. "My nanomedicine research and terraforming project can wait. I have more pressing matters to invest my time in."

Varanz replied, "Do you truly place revenge above the noble aspirations you once cherished? Above curing illnesses and restoring vitality to lands?"

Zataldra shot back with, "Evidently, a third of the council shares my views and longs for revenge. That's all it takes to initiate a motion for war. And we'll see tomorrow if it passes or not."

"The odds of these contrarians within the council garnering enough votes to bring about war are minimal." The deep age lines etched into Varanz's face drew taut with disgust for violence. "What gain would come from a war anyway?"

"What gain would come from war?" Zataldra retorted. "Our nation operates under a system of laws that holds people responsible for injustices. No clemency is granted for wrongdoing.

"Tell me, Grand Elder, when offworlders upend our people's lives, commit acts of violence, and violate our rights, as the humans did, why should we allow them to escape punishment? Are you implying that if foreign powers commit transgressions on our soil, there should be no repercussions?"

Zataldra clenched her fists, her nails digging deep enough to leave imprints on her palms. "We reserve the right to hold foreign offenders accountable for all injustices they commit.

"Moreover, humans have inflicted harm on other races besides ours. Someone must rein them in. Someone must penalize this seemingly untouchable superpower. They cannot evade accountability." She jabbed a finger at Varanz. "Imagine if the criminals of our nation slew or assaulted or violated *your* children. What would happen then?"

A weary sigh escaped the Grand Elder's lips. "An Arbiter would administer the appropriate punishment to the perpetrators."

Zataldra pressed further. "Should justice not also be meted out to the foreign malefactors who murdered, assaulted, and violated Khanorians in the name of our deposed and executed Sorin?"

Varanz was hesitant to validate Zataldra's argument. Reluctantly, he said, "It . . . should."

"So, what inhibits us? Why do we cower before the humans? Imagine a foreign power arriving in our nation right now and bombing homes and slaying defenseless Khanorians. Would we simply give them a pass?"

"We would not," Varanz said. "However, the humans are not an active threat. They departed our nation many moons ago and have not returned. Engaging them now holds no worth. But do not mistake me for a fool, Zataldra. I see the devastation left in the humans' wake. I see the trauma they have inflicted on families. But . . . sometimes it is best not to rouse a slumbering beast. Besides, even though our military is stronger than ever, I fear it cannot best the humans'."

Zataldra's arms gestured vehemently as she countered. "But we need not confront them unaided. My forces have joined an alliance called the Collective. Its leader, Dafulton, has—"

Varanz snubbed her mid-sentence. "Yes, I heard that you have joined forces with this outsider, Dafulton, whom you follow so blindly. What do you truly know about him? How can you be certain that he is trustworthy?"

Defending Dafulton, Zataldra said, "He leads a loyal legion of followers dedicated to his mission of eradicating the humans, and he has supplied me with resources to expedite my research and weapons development. I have no reason to distrust him. In every sense, he is a unifier.

"He comprehends the suffering of the humans' victims across the galaxy, having seen it firsthand. He recognizes the injustice of allowing the humans to evade accountability. It was he who persuaded me to rally a third of the council in casting a vote for war."

"And if the war vote fails, then what?" Varanz asked. "Will you then abandon this ill-fated crusade and go back to using science for peaceful aims?"

"No, my troopers and I will continue to stand in unity with the Collective." Zataldra's single-minded goal of destroying humanity coursed through every fiber of her being. "Dafulton's plan to wipe out the humans will move forward with or without the National Protection Force. But, like he suggested, having them on our side would undoubtedly be advantageous."

"You confront the humans with this Collective, and should you perish in battle, what of Iya? Why deny her the only sister she has, especially after she has already lost her mother and father?"

"Iya is incredibly strong for her age," Zataldra replied. Iya had grown up fast, having witnessed things no youth should've had to: the Sorin's public executions, people being beaten in the streets by his National Protection Force and the CDF. "The risk to myself and my men is simply a fact of war. The humans' extermination is something that *must* happen."

"Keep your hands bloodless, Zataldra. Your father—my friend, my fellow Grand Elder—would have wanted that. He was, after all, a man of peace."

Zataldra said, "Prior to that, he was a warrior. He was a warrior who—"

Varanz stopped her from finishing. "Who fought to protect." The crow's feet at the corners of his eyes tightened. "He fought only when necessity demanded it. You fight solely to salve your grief with bloodshed. Control your anger, Zataldra. Do not let it control you."

"Yes, I fight for vengeance," Zataldra admitted. "And my science has become the weapon that I use to fight. However, you are mistaken about one thing: I fight to defend as well. I fight to defend other races from the humans' ruthlessness."

Sure that the war vote would fail, Varanz shook his head, pitying Zataldra. "There will be no ratification of war. Prepare yourself for disappointment." He spun away to leave. The tail of his robe caught the wind and fluttered. "Good luck, Councilwoman Gor'Ronn," he said over his shoulder.

Zataldra headed back to her aerial vehicle, but doubts about the war vote passing seeped into her mind.

◆ ◆ ◆

The clacking of footsteps outside Jarius' cell stirred him from his sleep. Since it wasn't suppertime yet, he wondered what his visitor's purpose was. Were they here to subject him to more mind-control experimentation?

"Human, are you in there?" came a gentle, adorable voice from behind the door.

Jarius recognized the voice as belonging to Zataldra's sister. "Yeah, I am." He wondered what she wanted with him.

Iya slid open the door's rectangular observation slot and peered into the cell's dark interior. "Earlier, you seemed unwell." The translator around her neck facilitated two-way communication. "How are you feeling now?"

"If I were free, I'd feel a hell of a lot better," Jarius said wearily.

On guard for deception, Iya crossed her arms. "I may be kind, and I may follow the Korahh'Havaell faithfully, but I'm no pushover. So don't think you can cajole me into setting you free.

"Now, according to the Korahh'Havaell, regardless of the sins you've committed, you can repent and receive forgiveness. You just have to choose the path of light. And no matter how grave your sins might be, you shouldn't have to endure torture or suffer needlessly for them. You should—"

Jarius' blood was reaching the boiling point. He hadn't harmed any Khanorians. "The problem, Iya, is that I didn't do a fucking thing to your people."

Wary, Iya knitted her silver brows together. "Then why did my sister imprison you?"

"Because your sister believes that all my people resemble the soldiers who came to your nation and wreaked havoc on behalf of your former Sorin, and maybe she has a good reason to believe that. The actions of the CDF caused a lot of harm here, and your people have also caught wind of atrocities committed by the CDF on other worlds. But I'm not like those soldiers. Tell me, Iya, what do you believe?"

Iya's instincts told her Jarius wasn't spoon-feeding her lies. "I hear the sincerity in your voice, but—"

"But what?"

61

"It's difficult to trust your word over my sister's. She insists you're a threat—you, a member of the race that took delight in harming our people. Regardless of the differences in our beliefs, Zataldra is my family."

"That doesn't mean your sister can't be wrong, does it?" Jarius realized Iya might be his ticket out of captivity. He needed her on his side. "Come on, do you truly believe that no human can be good?"

Iya pondered the history tomes that were mandatory in formal Khanorian education. These texts depicted humans as one of Khanoria's foremost adversaries, malevolent beings who had supported the Sorin's dictatorship and were to be shunned always. However, the teachings Iya had received within the Tograh'Dirkot, a Khanorian seminary, had ingrained in her the belief that anyone could purge evil from their soul.

She replied to Jarius' question, saying, "What I believe is that a society's principles and ideologies shape the upbringing, conduct, and mindset of its people. It's not uncommon for these principles and ideologies to be founded in elitism. This explains the existence of supremacist societies that perceive beings outside their society as inferior, akin to property or refuse.

"Perhaps your society is such. Perhaps your society has conditioned its people to see other beings as . . . lesser than them, and that's why your soldiers acted mercilessly, treating Khanorians as if they were beneath the basic respect that should be afforded to all living creatures. But, human, I believe that the teachings of the Korahh'Havaell can change anyone—"

Jarius had had enough of being preached to. "Listen, Iya, on my world, compassion toward other societies isn't a foreign concept. Of course, we have our fair share of scummy people. And yes, some Guardians deployed to this nation didn't give a crap about the lives they took, and maybe there were Guardians who were unrepentant defilers of innocent young women like yourself. But let me assure you, I'm nothing like them, and there are *numerous* upstanding Guardians in the CDF who are just like me —Guardians such as my friend Randy. The reprehensible behavior witnessed here in Khanoria would appall them if they knew about it.

"I'm sure many of the Guardians who came here had no intention of causing harm to anyone. They never expected to be ordered to kill—not in self-defense, but in cold blood."

"I . . . I must ascertain the integrity of your words to ensure they're not intended to mislead me," Iya stammered.

Jarius was making progress. "Okay, how? What did you have in mind?"

"Give me your hand."

"Alright." Jarius rose from the floor and eased his wrist through the observation slot. "What now?"

The skin atop Iya's wrist parted, and a spirally tendril wriggled forth.

Jarius recoiled and instinctively withdrew his hand from the observation slot. "Whoa, what exactly is that?"

Iya frowned at his reaction. "It's just a part of our anatomy. It's our Octakanai."

"Octa-what?"

"Octakanai," Iya repeated. "When two Khanorians join their Octakanai together, they bond deeper. Our Octakanai also enables us to draw sustenance from the earth itself, if needed."

Jarius processed what she said. "So, the conjoining of two Octakanai is like your people's version of a Link, but physical, I guess. Kinda. Sorta."

"What's a Link?"

"Never mind. But how is your Octakanai gonna confirm to you I'm not lying?"

"Though you don't have an Octakanai to conjoin with, I can coil mine around your wrist, allowing me to perform auscultation and measure the truth of your words. The rhythm of your heart, the beat of your pulse, and the flow of your blood will determine if I should believe you."

"Basically, your Octakanai can act similarly to a stethoscope."

Iya looked puzzled. "Huh?"

Jarius realized they were wasting valuable time talking. "Forget it, just . . . do what you need to do."

"Okay, give me your wrist, then."

Jarius stuck his wrist through the observation slot again, and Iya's Octakanai snaked around it.

Jarius felt the Octakanai's sliminess, but he hid his discomfort, keeping a neutral face.

"Now tell me, have you been lying to me?" Iya asked, her tone stern.

Jarius said, "No, I haven't. I swear on my birth father's grave."

Iya examined his breathing pattern, heart rate, and muscle tension. Every electrical impulse of his nervous system became an indicator of truth or falsehood.

Having completed her evaluation, Iya uncoiled her Octakanai from around Jarius' wrist.

"What's the verdict?" he asked anxiously, retracting his hand.

Iya's Octakanai curled back up, sealing beneath her skin. Her face displayed a new expression, one of trust instead of skepticism. "While my evaluation isn't infallible, I believe you're telling the truth. You are a good person."

"I appreciate your trust, Iya. I hope more Khanorians are as open-minded as you."

"It's difficult for my race to trust yours. During the reign of our former Sorin, your soldiers enforced his laws and regulations with harsh tactics. Their conduct is seen as a reflection of your entire race—malicious.

"In our educational tomes, humans are depicted as ruthless beings to be avoided at all costs, grouped together with the Great Evils—other enemies who've sought to disrupt our society and harm our people. Children are raised on these teachings from a young age so that the human race will always be despised."

The propagation of hatred using written and visual mediums, Jarius thought.

While it put a bad taste in his mouth to admit it, he knew the vilification of humans in Khanorian literature was understandable. The CDF served as the military force for humanity, and naturally, other intergalactic civilizations would perceive its conduct as a reflection of the entire human race. Regrettably, as evidenced by the Khanorian Campaign, the CDF's conduct didn't always cast humanity in a favorable light, providing ammunition for other civilizations' inhabitants to condemn humanity.

"By the way, what's your name?" Iya asked.

"I'm Jarius."

"It's a pleasure to meet you, Jarius. Now, we just have to convince my sister of your innocence and—"

"No! I can't wager my freedom—my fucking life—on your sister's rationality. You've got to get me out of here. I'm pretty sure Zataldra will dispose of me once I've outlived my usefulness."

Torn between loyalty to her sister and compassion for Jarius, Iya felt conflicted. "My sister isn't a bad person. She might listen to me if—"

"You don't know how ruthless your sister is. Has she explained what you saw in her lab, what happened to my comrades?"

"No, not yet, but—"

"Just listen." Jarius told Iya about Zataldra's mind-control weapon and about what she made Arlo and Cruz do to each other, as well as what she made him do.

Iya brought a hand over her mouth in muted shock. She held in her emotions.

Jarius informed her that Zataldra had joined forces with Dafulton, a former dictator, to destroy the human race, though Zataldra was most likely unaware of Dafulton's past.

Iya said, "I apologize for what my sister did to you and your comrades. Our father was killed by your Defense Force, and that's what underlies her obsession with revenge. That's why she's resorting to joining forces with this outsider she knows nothing about. I know that doesn't excuse what she did, though."

"Are you gonna let me out?" Jarius asked desperately.

Iya contemplated what to do.

There was an internal debate raging within her conscience. She wanted to help Jarius, but she also didn't want to betray her sister. She sorted through her feelings about the situation and said, "I don't want you harmed any further, but I don't want to jeopardize my relationship with my sister by going behind her back. She has always been there for me. She was even present when I was born. Let me speak to her. Let me try to handle this my way first."

Exasperated, Jarius flattened his hands against the door and leaned closer to the observation slot. "Damn it, she's not gonna listen, Iya."

Iya replied in an even voice, "You believe she won't; I differ. But if she refuses to free you, I promise I'll get you out of here. I won't let an innocent life perish." Cameras monitored the entire facility. Iya wouldn't be able to help Jarius escape without being seen. But she'd do it to save his life, even if it meant angering her sister.

"Iya, what are you doing here?" a voice said.

Shit, Jarius thought. *It's suppertime.*

Bingrew inched closer to Iya, a meal tray in his hands. His largeness dwarfed her petite form. "I said, What are you doing here?" There was noticeable disapproval in his tone.

Iya nervously tucked a strand of hair behind her ear. She clasped her hands behind her back and toed the floor. "I . . . just wanted to see the human up close."

"He is dangerous," Bingrew said. "You must stay away from him."

Iya rolled her eyes. "Even though he's locked away?"

Bingrew replied, "Your sister made it clear that you are not permitted to be near the human."

"Speaking of which, where is she? I'd like to talk to her about something."

"She has left for the evening to attend to important matters. She will be back in the morning."

"Thank you. I'll stay the night in the room she provided me and find her tomorrow." Iya left.

Bingrew slid the meal tray through the observation slot, and Jarius took it. The meal was the same crap as usual, a tasteless pap in a bowl and a sludgy drink. Though not appetizing, they gave him the nourishment needed to keep him alive.

Jarius knew Zataldra wasn't letting him out of her clutches. But once Iya failed to convince her to release him, he was sure she'd keep her promise to rescue him. And then he'd be able to hold Jazzlyn in his arms again, enjoy a proper meal, and share some laughs and drinks with his best bud, Randal Scott.

CHAPTER THREE

Oviereya Amaechi sat in the back of her executive limousine, en route to the convention center for tonight's debate against Darren Radcliff. Absorbed in her duties as the Commonwealth's Chief, she pored over the report displayed on her tablet. It informed her that the Task Forces' search teams had discovered the bodies of the fifteen Guardians who had been deployed with the ambassador delegation, but the three ambassadors remained unaccounted for, likely taken captive.

Oviereya silently prayed for the families of the deceased and crossed her heart before moving on to the next report. This one revealed the Collective had launched another assault, targeting Guardians assigned to a planetary-impact mission. With the Collective's aggression on the rise, Oviereya was confident she had made the right move by initiating the newly established Defense Protocols.

The attack on Eden soil during the Bhalkran War and the Coalition's successful takeover of the Quad underscored the need for a contingency plan against potential invasions. She was the first Chief to put such a plan into development and would still be called weak on defense by propagandists.

The Protocols had the Air & Space Corps erecting a defensive barrier around Eden's orbit and eventually Satellite One's. Apart from the Collective escalating hostilities against the Commonwealth, reports from DFI's network of foreign allies—which spanned galaxies—hinted at the strong likelihood of a major Collective attack on Eden soil. Oviereya couldn't afford to take any chances.

She would eventually have to inform the public why a defensive barrier was being erected in orbit. For now, she wanted to avoid causing unnecessary panic, leaving the public under the impression that the Air & Space Corps was just conducting drills.

Her wristcom chimed, signaling an incoming video call from Stacie. It was always a delight to hear from her. As Darlene's midwife, Oviereya had been present when Stacie was born, and even though Stacie was like a daughter to her and she a mother figure to Stacie, they were also close friends. They had even shared a Link before Oviereya became Chief. And both women had inherited messes to clean up: Stacie, a criminal family business; Oviereya, a corrupt government. So, they had something in common.

Oviereya accepted the call. Pixels crystallized into a hologram of Stacie's face. Her lips were colored bubblegum pink, magenta eyeshadow accentuated her eyes, and gold earrings dangled from her earlobes.

Stacie said, "I just wanted to wish you luck in tonight's debate."

"Thank you, Stacie. I appreciate it. How's your evening going?"

"Stellar. I'm off to meet Randy for date night at The Gourmet Oasis. We'll try to catch some of the debate from there, but I already know you'll kick ass. I'll talk to you later, okay?"

Oviereya nodded, and Stacie's image dissolved.

The limousine parked in the convention center's lot.

Disgruntled protesters—anti-reformists and perhaps even Purists—voiced their outrage at Oviereya's leadership. They belabored her for not delivering justice to former Coalition fighters and for her attempts to reform the CDF, accusing her of weakening it under the guise of an ethics investigation. They also opposed her decision to reallocate military funding from the exchequer to the Colony Restoration Initiative, viewing her as an anti-military pacifist.

Oviereya's executive protection detail emerged from the vehicles of the motorcade. One of the executive protection agents opened her door, and she stepped out of the limousine into the balmy night air.

"Stay close, Madam Chief," a male EPA instructed.

The fulminations of the angry crowd rose louder when they saw Oviereya.

"Coalition supporter!" a woman shouted.

A man brandishing a sign that said DETHRONE AMAECHI bellowed, "Go back to where you belong, Satellite One!"

Oviereya ignored the crowd's outpour of verbal bile and proceeded into the convention center.

◆ ◆ ◆

Navexira and Geznan stood atop a building that overlooked Cornerstone City's Terence Plaza. Zataldra had sent them to Eden to execute further trials of her mind-control weapon. They'd been to humanity's motherworld twice before, conducting recon and gathering intel on the Commonwealth's defense capabilities.

The sweeping view before them highlighted Cornerstone's boundless grandeur—architectural designs fashioned as helixes, cubes, and hexagons; trendy low-lying flats; towering residential complexes; and structures made of glass and steel.

Geznan and Navexira blended seamlessly into Cornerstone's crowds, as the metropolis attracted a plethora of intergalactic tourists.

Geznan reflected on the battles he, Navexira, and Zataldra had fought to overthrow the Sorin—both when the CDF was supporting the Sorin's regime and after the CDF's departure. He found satisfaction in knowing that humanity's judgment day was drawing near, and the mind-control weapon would play a pivotal role in the Collective's plan.

"Look at these people," Geznan muttered. He peered down at the densely populated Terence Plaza. Pedestrians, enjoying the nightlife, walked across and rode the slideways. Terence Plaza teemed with activity. "They happily turn a blind eye to the atrocities committed by their military forces against other races."

Hesitantly, Navexira said, "Yes, but during our brief missions here, I have also seen parents who genuinely love their children." Uncertainty seeped into her countenance.

"Even monsters cherish their own offspring," Geznan deadpanned. "And these humans *are* monsters," he tacked on, thinking about the Khanorians slain by the CDF. He also thought about the day Grand Elder Gor'Ronn was killed—a day that left Zataldra emotionally battered. The potent smell of Khanorian blood in the air that day remained vivid in his memory. "By wiping out the adults and steering the children down a different path than them, we would be doing the children a great service. Now let us proceed with the test and depart tonight. The more time slips away, the more I worry about getting past this defense wall the humans are fortifying in orbit, which suggests they may be aware of the Collective's upcoming assault."

71

"Well then, we should start getting the drone into the air."

◆ ◆ ◆

Within the shops, residential complexes, and restaurants that collectively made up Terence Plaza was the open-air restaurant The Gourmet Oasis. Under its awning, Randy sat at a table for two, waiting for his lover to join him. In the meantime, he mulled over the limited information he had gleaned regarding the Khanorian Campaign, before heading to The Gourmet Oasis for his date.

The files that were accessible to Guardians merely scratched the surface. He got the distinct impression that the true revelations were buried within the classified files he kept encountering during his probe of Defense Force records. And there were far too many of those classified files for one campaign. What was being hidden?

While conducting an online search, he found an interview that a Guardian had done for a news site. Displaying extraordinary courage, the Guardian confessed to being ordered to carry out cold-blooded executions of Khanorians. He detailed witnessing physical abuse and sexual violence. Sadly, the media and most of Eden's population, being staunch supporters of the Commonwealth Government, dismissed his accounts as baseless fabrication—a false exposé.

As he glanced at couples with other couples, memories of the fun-filled double dates he, Jarius, Stacie, and Jazzlyn had enjoyed together inundated his thoughts. He wanted to tell Jazzlyn and Stacie the truth about Jarius' abduction by the Collective. But that information was to be kept within the purview of the task forces selected to locate the ambassador delegation, until the Chief Executive authorized its disclosure.

To take his mind off Jarius, Randy tuned in to the debate on his wristcom, watching a holographic live stream.

Oviereya said to the audience in attendance at the convention center, "The Commonwealth, under my leadership, is progressing toward a future of equality for all its peoples. Such equality has been absent for too long. That lack of equality incited the Independent Movement and civil war. To avert history repeating itself, we must embrace change."

Daren retorted, "Achieving equality in the Commonwealth doesn't necessitate slashing the Defense Force's budget. Overinvesting in Chief Amaechi's Colony Restoration Initiative isn't prudent right now."

Defending her decisions, Oviereya said, "And when should the government finally prioritize the livelihoods of our fellow human beings on Satellite One?" She felt as if her opponent was rehashing the same redundant counterarguments prior Chiefs had made to impede colony advancement—rinsed and repeated.

Randy had much respect for Oviereya. Even when her approval ratings took a dive because of her unpopular positions, she stayed true to who she was. He turned off the live stream and checked the time on his wristcom. Stacie would arrive shortly. When he lifted his eyes, he spotted her entering the restaurant's awning from the street, her hair bumping about on her shoulders.

The twenty-two-year-old nubile blond reeled in leers from men as she sauntered across the restaurant's carpeted floor, her nails perfectly manicured from the spa day at her mansion. She sported an arresting bodycon dress that clung to her figure in all the right places and had a hemline that paraded her finely sculpted thighs.

Now at the head of the Spencer family's financial empire, she was recognized right away by several diners. She had been hitting the interview circuit, drawing public attention to her latest business ventures in technology and science, alongside initiatives dedicated to supporting colony restoration efforts. She was determined to dispel the negative image associated with Spencer Enterprises because of her parents' scandalous deeds.

Stacie strutted toward the linen-draped dining table where Randy awaited, and, happy to see her too, he matched her smile. His attraction to her was apparent, his eyes lingering on the pronounced curves and contours of her physique. He noticed her bustline bulged against the fitted dress nicely.

Stacie shifted her weight left, cocking a hip while gripping her chair's backrest. Her sex appeal was on full display. "Great to see you, babe."

Randy caught a whiff of her expensive perfume, a lovely floral scent.

Ever the gentleman, he stood up and pulled out her chair for her.

Stacie planted a smooch on his cheek. "Thanks."

Randy reciprocated, marrying his lips to hers in a lengthy kiss that she wished wouldn't end, as the gravitational pull of attraction bonded his hands to her midsection. The body underneath the gauzy dress felt solid.

Following Randy's affectionate gesture, Stacie settled into her chair and crossed a leg over a knee, her posture perfect.

Randy returned to his seat.

Amidst the chatter of dinner conversations, Randy asked, "How's the overhaul and rebranding of Spencer Enterprises coming along?"

"Pretty good actually," Stacie said. "I'd love to show you what I've been working on." Holographic blueprints of upcoming projects beamed from her wristcom. They included plans for humanitarian support in war-torn sectors of colonies.

Randy was proud of his lover; she wanted to help people in a big way, not just use her fortune to enjoy the finer things in life.

After discussing her vision for Spencer Enterprises' future, Stacie asked, "When's your next mission?"

"According to the rotation schedule, Vanguard Alpha won't deploy again for another two weeks."

"*Perfect*," Stacie exclaimed. She clapped her hands together and rubbed her palms up and down.

"It sounds like you have something in mind."

"As a matter of fact, I do. I was thinking you and I could go on a little intergalactic vacation. I've been working hard and so have you. Let's get offworld for a bit. We both deserve it."

Randy liked the idea of getting off Eden during Vanguard Alpha's downtime. "Yeah? Where to?"

"Glad you asked." Stacie jabbed her wristcom with her finger. "Check this out." A hologram appeared, depicting a shoreline under a dreamlike sky. "This is Kresnave III." Kresnave III was one of the Commonwealth's trading-partner worlds. Stacie flicked her finger over the beach scene, replacing it with cozy dining spots and quaint shops nestled among residential complexes. Another swipe started a slideshow of romantic destinations. "Lots of touristy hotspots, as you can see—the tropical kind." Her infectious enthusiasm got Randy stoked as well.

Her pulse racing, Stacie said, "Let's do it. Hell, let's leave tomorrow. I'll handle all the travel arrangements." She needed a brief escape from the pressures of leading Spencer Enterprises.

Randy's wristcom chimed, receiving a message. "Excuse me, let me see what this is about." He accessed the message. The contact name within the floating holotext identified the sender as Akane.

Akane: Hey, something's up. I was supposed to be headed back to Eden today. Suddenly, no flights allowed in or out of Satellite One for the next twenty-four hours. And the CDF's deployed a fucking armada of ships around Eden. What do you think is going on?

Stacie's mood dimmed. Her once joy-filled face was now fixed into a critical glare. *What the fuck?* she silently fumed, jaw tightening. Her nails drummed the table, and her lips pursed. After taking a sip of wine, which did little to quell her growing indignation, she tapped her foot while gnashing her teeth.

The dissatisfaction in her eyes spoke volumes.

Randy, quick to pick up on her mood shift, hurried up and composed a reply to Akane, the tips of his fingers darting over holokeys.

Randy: Hey, I'm actually in the middle of something right now. Get back to you later.

The holotext dissolved, and Randy refocused on Stacie, giving her his full attention. "Sorry about that."

Stacie looked testy. "That was from the girl we took down, the radical we stopped from killing Damien, right?"

"Yeah, and?"

"How long has *this* been going on?" Stacie griped, gesturing with her hands.

Her accusatory tone hit Randy like a blow to the gut. He felt like he was being interrogated. "How long has *what* been going on?"

"You *schmoozing* with the extremist who nearly screwed up DFI's investigation." *The extremist you decided to fuck,* Stacie didn't say aloud, biting her lower lip.

"We've exchanged a couple of messages here and there. Not many. Just check-ins, really. What are you getting at?" Randy held Stacie's gaze, his eyes never leaving hers.

"I'm just saying, I thought that when she left, this connection between you two would be over with."

Randy replied nonchalantly, "Akane went on a sabbatical to

clear her head; she's still a member of Vanguard Alpha. So we gotta interact."

Eyebrows high, Stacie said, "Yeah, on *duty*. You don't have to be *palsy* with her." Her voice carried a note of blatant discontent.

Akane had belonged to what was technically an extremist organization. Randy was obligated to report any terrorists or extremists he was aware of to the CDF. By making the conscious choice not to turn Akane in and keep their association secret, he was jeopardizing his career. If CDF Command ever discovered that he withheld Akane's involvement in RISE and his relationship with her, he could be court-martialled. To Stacie, it seemed like a considerable risk to take for just one woman. She wondered if Randy truly had no romantic feelings for Akane anymore.

Randy aimed an inquisitive stare at Stacie, his mind working to discern what this mood shift was about. "What's really bugging you, Stace?" He searched her guarded eyes. He was a straight shooter, and ambiguity annoyed him greatly.

Their squabble attracted unwanted glances from diners within earshot.

Stacie squeezed her eyes shut and stroked her face, calming herself. After a moment of introspection, she expelled a tiny huffing sound. She questioned whether she was blowing things out of proportion, reading too much into Akane and Randy's ongoing friendship. But then again, maybe not. "You know what? Just forget it," she said, shaking her head.

Resting his forearms on the tablecloth, Randy steepled his fingers. "If something's bothering you, you can tell me. It's better to get it off your chest and—"

"No, I'm fine." Stacie adjusted her tone. "We came here to have a good time, just the two of us, right?" Her lips imitated a smile, and, feeling uncomfortable with her own pretense, she fiddled with strands of her hair. "So, come on, let's do that." She didn't want to come off as being uptight or making unfounded accusations.

Stacie's microexpressions hinted she was still upset, leaving Randy unconvinced that she was "fine." He said, "Are you sure that you—"

"Yeah, I'm sure," Stacie cut in, perhaps tabling the discussion for a more appropriate time. Tonight was supposed to be about the two of them having fun.

Randy relented, dropping the conversation, at least for now. "Okay." Stacie's acting skills needed further refinement; the shift in her mood remained perceptible.

Randy wondered what might be nagging her. One minute she could hardly contain her excitement about traveling with him to an exotic corner of the universe, then the next she was getting worked up over his past relationships. What was the fuss about? Was she still bothered by his coupling with Kesley Whittaker? He had already issued numerous apologies for that. Maybe she was just apprehensive about his friendship with Akane. Or maybe it was both.

Randy had believed that their renewed relationship was on track, progressing well. But now there was this apparent withdrawal. He had earned the opportunity to try again with her but hadn't won back her heart yet? Was that it? He guessed it wasn't as easy for Stacie to let bygones be bygones as she had thought. What exactly did she want from him? Some kind of reassurance?

Outwardly, Stacie projected the illusion of being unperturbed. Internally, she was a jumble of emotions, including frustration, agitation, and restlessness.

The waiter arrived, bringing hors d'oeuvres to the table on a silver platter. The restaurant's owner prioritized creating a warm, personal experience for guests, opting for human waitstaff instead of server golems.

After the waiter set the platter down and left, a cacophonous ruckus erupted beyond the restaurant's open-air dining area, punctuated by angry shouts and frantic shrieks. It shattered the tranquility of Randy and Stacie's evening, which was already shaken by their uncomfortable conversation.

"What the hell's happening out there?" Randy said, mirroring Stacie's bewilderment. Brawls from the street spilled into the restaurant, a mob of people engaging in chaotic skirmishes that overturned tables and chairs and sent waitstaff scattering. "It's as if these people have lost their fucking minds."

Diners abandoned their tables, leaving behind half-eaten meals, and sought refuge from the escalating mayhem.

Stacie sprang up from her chair. "Time to go!"

Randy and Stacie ran outside and froze in disbelief, their eyes agape and blood thrumming in their ears. They couldn't find words to describe what they were seeing. Hundreds of people were inexplicably committing acts of violence against each other. Strangers, friends, and family alike were all beating the hell out of each other.

Randy took hold of Stacie's wrist. "Let's keep moving!" He could barely hear his own voice over the raucous growls, grunts, and snarls of people acting like animals.

Randy leading the way, he and Stacie pushed through the crowd.

Fists collided with faces. A stampede of people trampled grounded bodies, their footfalls inflicting gruesome injuries. Adding to the tumult were the staccato pops of gunshots from armed citizens taking aim at anyone in their line of vision.

A man twice Stacie's size jostled her, his shoulder sideswiping hers and breaking Randy's grip on her wrist.

She fell onto the phyocrete, landing hard.

Randy's voice rang out, "Stace!"

One of the frenzied citizens was about to drive a foot into Stacie's face while she was down. Randy tackled him, and their combined weight plummeted to the ground.

Randy subdued the crazy-eyed berserker, knocking him out with a well-aimed punch. A sizable lump would most likely be on his head when he woke up.

Stacie got her feet beneath her. Her flesh bore minor scratches; otherwise, she was unharmed.

Gasping heavily, Randy lifted himself off the man he had incapacitated.

The bedlam around Randy and Stacie escalated. A crescendo of shouts and screams made the hair on the back of their necks stand on end.

Taking Stacie's wrist once more, Randy set the pace, their feet thumping the phyocrete.

Wailing sirens of law enforcement vehicles and ambulances neared, offering a glimmer of succor.

As Randy and Stacie zigzagged through a throng of violent people, Randy accessed his and Stacie's Link. With their minds intertwined, their steps fell into perfect synchronization. Stacie could now anticipate Randy's directional shifts, him steering her with an unbreakable grip on her wrist. His unwavering courage and commitment to protecting her permeated her consciousness, via their Link, assuaging the frantic thoughts overrunning her mind.

<*Down!*> Randy's mental voice said to Stacie.

They both dropped low, a bottle flying overhead out of nowhere.

Winded, Stacie gasped. *<Nice call.>*

<Don't mention it.>

They pressed on and found safety in front of a clothing shop. Now that there was some distance between them and the violence, they detached from their Link. Both of them were exhausted and rattled.

"Are you okay?" Randy asked as riot police moved in to restore order.

Stacie inspected her hand. "Aside from a chipped nail and a few scratches, I'm fine, babe." She had been born a child of riches but shaped into a warrior by the CDF, so she could handle a few bumps and bruises.

Above, a police helicopter was hovering over the insanity, its propellers chopping the air loudly.

The pilot spotted Geznan and Navexira standing atop the roof they were using as an observation post. "Hey, what are those two doing up there?" he asked his colleague.

"No idea. But they might have something to do with what's going on down below."

The copter's spotlight illumined the rooftop and shone on the two Khanorians.

Geznan squinted upward and shaded his eyes with his hand. "It seems we've lingered here a bit too long, conducting our test."

"Indeed," Navexira replied. Her eyes were strained, too, by the pool of light. "Let us leave before we attract any more attention to ourselves."

The pilot's voice boomed from the copter's external loudspeaker. "YOU TWO, STAY WHERE YOU ARE!" He noticed Geznan was aiming some kind of techno-patterned orb at the copter. "What the hell's that?"

An energy beam shot out from the orb, blasting the copter's

rotor.

On the ground, Randy and Stacie watched the copter spiral out of control.

Realizing it was going to crash into a nearby building, Randy sprang into action. He enfolded Stacie in his strong arms and twirled around so that his back faced the building, shielding her from potential harm.

The copter exploded, tearing a chunk from the building and sending plumes of smoke into the sky. Debris and flaming fragments of the copter rained down onto the streets, burying parked vehicles.

Screams from civilians not under mind control merged with the crackle of fire coming from the wreckage.

After ensuring the danger had passed, Randy released his embrace of his lover.

Stacie's senses were on high alert. People going crazy? Helicopters being blown out of the sky? What was next? "This has been one hell of a date night."

"That's for fucking sure," Randy said.

Seven police officers converged on the building where the energy blast had come from. Others dispersed the crowd, throwing teargas canisters and shooting riot-dispersal rounds made of rubber. Some citizens appeared to be recovering from the trance-like state, shaking off the languor with unfocused eyes. Their sudden loss of cognitive control totally nonplussed them.

"What do you think could've caused all this?" Stacie asked Randy.

He shrugged. "I'm not sure. Maybe it was some . . . neural chemical agent?"

"Could be. But by whom?"

Randy knew the Commonwealth had no shortage of enemies,

but very few could've pulled off an attack on Eden soil. He tilted his head up at the roof of the building where the blast had come from. "The answer lies up there."

A new helicopter descended over the building.

Navexira and Geznan had recalled the drone used to transmit the mind-control signal and had just finished securing it in a metal trunk.

"We have to leave now!" Navexira hollered, the thudding of the copter's rotor blades drowning out her voice.

A canister ejected from one of the copter's cannons, landed on the roof, and dispensed a cloud of gas.

Coughing and disoriented, Geznan aimed his orb blaster at the trunk containing the drone. He fired and destroyed it, just before his and Navexira's limbs stopped working. Before they knew it, they were lying on the roof, unable to move. Darkness crushed everything in their sight, and their consciousness faded away.

The seven police officers who had entered the building now gathered on the rooftop to investigate the scene.

Randy, observing the building from below, wondered what was going on up there.

"Well, it seems our evening agenda is out the window," Stacie said. "Let's head back to my place. We can have dinner there."

"Sounds like a plan to me."

More sirens blared toward Terence Plaza.

Citizens stood bewildered and horrified by their violent actions —actions that would stay with them forever.

Randy curled an arm around Stacie. "Once we're a block or two away from here, an air-cab should be in the clear to pick us up."

They left, looking forward to having dinner without interruption.

The Commonwealth had an array of enemies, but Randy

couldn't shake the suspicion that the Collective was behind tonight's mayhem.

◆ ◆ ◆

Following news of the turmoil in Terence Plaza, Oviereya's executive protection detail quickly escorted her out of the convention center mid-debate. She sat in the back of her limousine, being briefed on the situation by her Secretary of Defense, Abeo Adasanya, on her wristcom.

Abeo's swarthy face bore a serious expression. "All we know is that citizens in Terence Plaza suddenly started acting erratically. We're uncertain about the specifics of the weapon used to cause this behavior."

Oviereya thought, *It's happened. Defense Force Intelligence's network was right. This was the expected attack by the Collective.* Not a conventional bomb, chemical agent, or active shooters, but an insidious weapon that humanity had never encountered before.

Oviereya asked Abeo, "What is the current state of those affected by the weapon?"

"Some are suffering from intense migraines, but who knows what other side effects there may be. All citizens who consented to an examination are being transported to medical facilities."

"Do we have any leads on who is responsible for this attack?"

"We do. A police helicopter came into contact with two potential other-world suspects. They are now in police custody, but they will soon be transferred to the custody of Defense Force Intelligence."

"Has it been determined where they came from?"

"They are Khanorian, the same race involved in the ambassadors' abduction."

"Ensure that Chief of Defense Force Intelligence Michael

Conlan keeps us updated on whatever he learns from their interrogation."

"Yes, Madam Chief." Abeo's image disappeared.

Remembering that Stacie and Randy were at The Gourmet Oasis in Terence Plaza, Oviereya audio-called Stacie to check on them.

Stacie's voice came through Oviereya's wristcom. "Hey, Madam Chief. It's been quite a wild night, hasn't it?"

"Did you and Randy get caught up in the chaos?"

"Yeah, but luckily whatever was used to cause all those people to go ballistic didn't affect us. We're safe and on our way back to my place."

"Good, I just wanted to make sure you two were okay."

"Thanks."

"I have to go now. Take care." The call ended, and Oviereya wondered, *What vendetta do these Khanorians have against us?*

◆ ◆ ◆

The violence in Terence Plaza had ruined Randy and Stacie's dinner plans at The Gourmet Oasis, but the evening continued with an equally sumptuous meal at Stacie's residence. Dinner wasn't the only thing the couple had planned for tonight, though.

Randy and Stacie lay in bed. Randy trailed his lips down the length of her neck to the upper swell of her breasts, which was accentuated by her push-up bra. Each peck of his lips ensured no bit of exposed flesh remained untouched.

Noticing the dull expression on Stacie's face, Randy asked, "What's the matter?" Then he kissed her lips.

"I . . . I'm just not feeling it tonight," Stacie replied listlessly. A strong air of detachment surrounded her.

"What's been up with you lately? You were acting

confrontational at the restaurant, and now you seem . . . distant."

Stacie twisted away from Randy and rolled onto her side. "It's just that—"

Randy leaned over her and kissed her shoulder. "Just what?"

Stacie sighed. "I've been wondering do you love me. *Only* me."

"What's this about? Kesley? Akane?"

Stacie allowed herself a brief pause to collect her thoughts. "If she were to show up tomorrow—Akane, that is—would you have any . . . feelings for her?"

"Are you afraid that . . . I might hurt you again?" Randy asked, trying to cut right to the point.

"It's just that—" Stacie turned onto her back and stared up at the ceiling. "I just . . . don't want my heart messed with. I don't want to be let down. And if you have any doubts whatsoever about whether I'm the right woman for you, then maybe—"

"Stace, stop," Randy said softly. "Whenever I'm away with Vanguard Alpha, all I think about is coming back to you. I didn't work so hard to get you back in my life just to lose you again."

Stacie continued staring at the ceiling, mind still unsettled. "You know, when we Link, I can feel you thinking about her sometimes."

"Yeah, it's called missing a friend, Stace."

"Are you *sure* that's all it is?"

"Yes."

Stacie wondered if she was being too paranoid. "Okay," she said. "Now, let's get some sleep." She snuggled into the covers. "I think we both need it after the night we've had."

Randy tried to hide the disappointment in his voice. "Yeah, sure." Sleep? That wasn't what he wanted right now, but it seemed sex wasn't in the cards tonight, after all.

Randy and Stacie closed their eyes. Though they lay beside each other, Randy felt as if Stacie were miles away. It was like he was sleeping alone.

CHAPTER FOUR

Zataldra was eager to receive Geznan and Navexira's report from their mission on Eden the day before. They were due to return to Khanoria tomorrow. She was confident that their test of her mind-control weapon had yielded the expected results. However, she was focused on her own test at the moment, as she continued to fine-tune her weapon.

She and three of her men held two handcuffed Guardians at gunpoint outside. The Guardians were fresh guinea pigs transported from Dafulton's ship. Once finished here, Zataldra would make her way to the citadel for the war vote. Then she'd find out if Grand Elder Varanz or she were correct about what direction the council would take.

Iya exited the main facility onto the rear grounds, where she had been told Zataldra would be. She wanted to talk to her about releasing Jarius and confront her about the murder of his comrades. When she saw Zataldra and her men aiming weapons at two Guardians, she ducked behind a power generator to observe. If Zataldra spotted her, she might command her to leave.

Her vision bleary from tears, the female Guardian said, "We

haven't harmed you. Please, just let us go. I have a son and a daughter." She was short of breath, her fear making it hard to draw air.

Zataldra retorted, "You humans are all alike: soulless killers, takers of life. How many of my people begged for mercy, only to be slaughtered? How many parents now lie buried in the ground because of your kind?"

The male Guardian had been half-starved aboard Dafulton's ship. The freezing cold only added to the misery of being malnourished. His impulse was to fight, but he knew Zataldra's men would shoot him on the spot if he tried anything, so he pushed the impulse down. "Whatever the hell happened here, my comrade and I weren't responsible for it."

Zataldra slung her fist into his jaw, knocking loose a tooth. "You're no better than *any* of the other soldiers of your military, so don't claim innocence with me."

The Guardian spat out blood. "You're fucking insane."

Zataldra poked her wristlet.

The Guardians' screams made Iya shudder. Their minds and bodies now belonged to Zataldra. She verbally commanded them to get down on their hands and knees. Instantly, they obeyed. At her next command, they bashed their heads into the ice-covered ground, killing themselves.

Iya gasped and held herself. Blood had splattered everywhere. Zataldra had killed two defenseless humans. And for what? The Gods would be irate.

"Another successful test." Zataldra's face was devoid of any feeling. "When Geznan and Navexira get back, we'll be able to confirm the weapon's emission range in its current state of development."

Iya stepped out from behind the generator. "Sister, was that necessary?"

Zataldra spun. "Iya, were you watching the whole time?"

"I was. What did those humans do to deserve to have their minds violated and control of their bodies taken from them? It's cruel."

"Not cruel enough."

Iya couldn't find so much as a hint of contrition in Zataldra's eyes. They were as empty as a black hole.

Zataldra was letting anger control her, transforming her into a different person. Iya believed that if Zataldra had followed the teachings of the Korahh'Havaell, like she and their mother, perhaps Zataldra could've found solace in the Gods instead of seeking revenge.

Iya said, "The human prisoner told me you violated his mind and the minds of the other two I saw dead in your lab. You need to stop these tests. They're *heinous*."

Zataldra frowned. "You spoke to the prisoner? You were supposed to stay away from him."

"Maybe he's not a bad person. Perhaps those humans you just killed weren't bad either. Isn't it possible some humans are good?"

"Good humans don't exist, Iya."

"And what do you plan to do with the prisoner, use him for more tests?"

"Yes, and once he has served his purpose, he'll be disposed of." Just as Jarius had said.

"After all the testing of your weapon is complete, then what?"

"Then I use my weapon to eradicate the humans—for our people, for *Father*."

"You must let go of the anger. It's corrupting your soul."

The vitriol living inside Zataldra spread through every part of her being. Memories of the CDF interrupting Jud'Zarr's final oration flooded her mind, trapping her in a time and place of unparalleled affliction. *You weren't there, Iya. You didn't have to watch Father die.*

Staring into the dark expression shaping her sister's features, Iya thought, *May the light lay your hurt to rest.*

"I have nothing more to say," Zataldra said, shutting down the conversation. Her demeanor was as cold as the mountains. "I'll be leaving shortly for the council citadel, so I may be gone for a while. Please stay away from the prisoner." To her men, she said, "Take those bodies to the furnace."

The men dragged the dead Guardians off to be incinerated, bloody trails marking their path.

Iya felt for the Guardians, currents of heartache stirring within her. After several seconds, she headed back inside. Zataldra was becoming unrecognizable, less and less like the sister she knew, but she believed Zataldra's heart could be healed. As for Jarius, he was facing certain death once Zataldra was finished with him. Iya vowed to rescue him before then.

◆ ◆ ◆

Randy awoke in Stacie's bed, morning sunlight slanting through the window onto his face. The frightening night they'd had still haunted his mind, the two of them surviving some sort of weapon that could make people go berserk.

He rubbed the sleep from his eyes. Stacie's side of the bed was vacant. She had already gone to shower.

Listening closely, he caught the tail end of a conversation coming from behind the bathroom door. Stacie was talking to someone on her wristcom.

"That's confirmed, right?" she said, speaking sotto voce so she wouldn't wake Randy.

A male voice replied from her wristcom, "Yeah, it's confirmed. The Six Elite will meet on Babylon Island on that day and time, for sure." Randy recognized the voice: Jason Mansford, second-in-command of Stacie's team of bounty chasers. "This is our chance to take them down. How do you want to proceed, boss?"

Stacie said, "I'll get back to you on that."

Randy's brow creased, and his lips compressed into a hard line. What was Stacie planning?

Stacie opened the bathroom door, swaddled in a turquoise towel wrap. When she saw Randy was awake, her body went rigid in the doorway, and her face blanched. "Oh, hey Randy, good morning." Her voice was jittery. She was worried that he had overheard her conversation, one that she clearly wanted to keep private.

Randy, in his sleeping shorts, scooted out of bed and stood on the red throw rug. "What was that about?"

Stacie brushed strands of her freshly shampooed hair from her face. "What was what about?" she said innocently, feigning ignorance. She stepped out of the doorway and strolled into the bedroom, a space with extensive square footage.

"I heard something about the Elite. I thought your mission to dismantle them ended after helping DFI get dirt on Damien's illegal operations. Oviereya warned you to stay away from them and stop taking matters into your own hands."

Stonewalling him, Stacie sidestepped Randy's remarks, picked up a hairbrush from her vanity, and began preening in the mirror.

After bearing the delay of a response for one second too long, Randy pushed Stacie to explain herself. "Are you going to say something?"

Stacie sighed, putting down the brush. After tucking stray wisps of hair behind her ear, she whirled around. "My parents were members of the Elite. They had full knowledge of *all* the families' criminal activities, and they were involved in such activities themselves." She went to her walk-in closet and deliberated about her attire for the day. From the sundry of outfits, she retrieved the clothing she wanted and began organizing it on the bed. "The day you provided me those files unveiling the Elite's corrupt dealings with venal officeholders here on Eden, I made a vow to stop them.

"When I traveled to Babylon Island to confront my parents, I saw some awful things there, including enslaved women from many worlds. I've been keeping tabs on the new Elite *(the children of the original family heads)*. They continue to run illegal operations on the island. Someone needs to shut those operations down *permanently*." She had planned to do that by eliminating the new family heads, whom she had been acquainted with during her youth, though loosely.

"Why not leave the Elite to the authorities and the Defense Force?" Randy asked.

Stacie crossed her arms and shook her head. "No. Since Earth Era, the original family heads were able to stay in business by flouting the law. They were exceptional at concealing their crimes to ensure their image as well-meaning entrepreneurs remained untarnished in the eyes of public perception.

"If it weren't for the Coalition revealing their crimes, no one would've known about them. My point is: I'm sure the new family heads learned all their parents' tactics. So, they know how to cover their tracks effectively too. I *seriously* doubt the authorities or CDF will be taking them down anytime soon. I have to be the one to do it."

Randy kept strong eye contact with Stacie, his stare an incredulous one. "You wouldn't know if the authorities or CDF are investigating the Elite, now would you?" Challenge thickened his voice. "They might be hot on their heels as we speak."

Stacie scoffed. "I *highly* doubt it. And even if they are investigating the Elite, they'd probably come up with *zilch*."

Randy continued to clash with her in a battle of words. "What about Damien? By the time you volunteered to go undercover for DFI, they'd already had eyes on him for a while, correct?"

"And it was only because of *me* that they gathered enough evidence to put him away, any evidence, really. So thanks for proving me right. And considering all the crimes the Elite have gotten away with lately, they'd be behind bars if the authorities or CDF were on to them."

Stacie then dropped a bombshell on Randy, informing him that some winners of the special Parliament elections—which had resumed after probes into suspected meddling by the Brotherhood and RISE—had ties to the Elite. The new family heads were adept at their parents' methods of political control.

Stacie also told Randy that the Elite had bought out judges, law-enforcement officials, and even high-ranking Guardians within the CDF, people who could aid in concealing their crimes if need be. This further bolstered Stacie's belief that the Elite were too powerful to be taken down by Eden's existing law-enforcement entities.

To reinforce her argument that she alone should dismantle the Elite, she said, "While probing my parents' files, I unearthed the origins of the Elite. Their unholy alliance didn't just happen on a whim. It was my parents who convened the inaugural gathering of the eight family heads during Earth Era. That meeting paved the way for the Elite to forge the empire they now reign over. It might seem absurd, but I feel it's my responsibility to slay the demon my parents helped create."

"And when were you going to tell me about this ongoing

pursuit of yours to thwart the Elite?" Randy asked, heat flaring in his eyes.

"I wasn't," Stacie confessed. "Because I know you. I knew you'd try to stop me."

"You doubt my love for you, and you were going to keep this covert mission of yours a secret. I need you to trust me, Stace."

Stacie's voice shrank. "I . . . I do trust you."

"It doesn't feel that way. It seems like you have trust issues, at least with me. I thought we were past this."

Yeah, maybe I have some trust anxiety, Randy, but I think it's warranted, Stacie kept to herself. The wounds of betrayal ran deep. Her trust in her parents crumbled when she discovered they were embroiled in a criminal conglomerate; her peers at Cadwell Institute exposed themselves as fake friends, jealousy and deceit poisoning those relationships; and Randy's entanglement with Kesley Whittaker lacerated her heart the most. "I'm . . . working on it," she said.

"Alright, I understand." Randy wasn't content, but he realized that rebuilding trust would be a gradual process, even if he wished for it to happen faster, so he decided not to press the "trust issue" any further. He was keen to avoid alienating Stacie and potentially losing her love forever, especially considering that he was responsible for the initial strain in their relationship.

And while he disagreed with Stacie's mission, he wouldn't press that issue any further either. It was futile to try to change her mind; she was a strong-willed woman who did what she wanted. And what could he realistically do to stop her?

As much as Stacie taking the law into her own hands bothered his "Guardian heart," he wasn't going to have his own girlfriend arrested for bringing down scumbags guilty of some of the vilest acts, such as human trafficking.

Stacie resumed organizing her outfit for the day on her bed.

Randy said, "Hey, moving forward, just . . . don't hesitate to share things with me. You and I are a team."

Stacie lowered her chin and reflected on her behavior. She considered that maybe she did need to be more open with Randy. After lifting her chin, she gave him a faint smile. "Okay, babe."

It wasn't the most convincing response, but Randy guessed there was nothing else he could do at the moment to alleviate her concerns.

"I should probably get dressed and head out now," Stacie said.

To lighten the atmosphere between them, Randy sidled up behind Stacie and wrapped his arms around her towel-covered midsection. "So soon?" he whispered, voice tinged with desire, then planted a kiss on her clavicle.

Stacie turned around and held Randy's cheeks in her hands. "Yeah, unfortunately. I have some business to take care of at the main office. And since I have to plan for my op on Babylon Island, we're gonna have to take a rain check on our intergalactic vacay." She leaned in and pressed her lips to his, but the kiss lacked the usual kick. To Randy, it felt bland and lifeless—no emotion, no love behind it. It felt like some conciliatory gesture meant to appease him. "Call me later."

"Yeah, sure," Randy replied dully, feeling like his relationship with Stacie was on shaky ground. His father once told him that all relationships go through their ups and downs, peaks and valleys. Randy was confident that he and Stacie would pull things together, but this definitely felt like a valley.

After getting dressed, he left the mansion. Crossing the walkway in the yard, he thought about the research he'd done so far on the Khanorian Campaign. He wasn't the type to start something and leave it unfinished. *What's in those classified files?* he wondered, passing by the angel-sculpture fountain. There was no way *he* could get authorization to access them, but he knew someone who could get it for him, the Chief of Defense Force Intelligence, Michael Conlan.

A long-standing friend of both Randy and his father, Conlan was the highest-ranking supporter Randy had within the CDF. Conlan was the one person who'd go the extra mile for him, as long as his request was within ethical boundaries.

Randy dialed Conlan's number on his wristcom's holotouch interface. FORWARDING CALL blinked.

◆ ◆ ◆

General Michael Conlan heard the chirp of his wristcom and glanced at the incoming-call notification. He'd love to chat with Randy, whether it was for catching up or if Randy needed a favor. Their last interaction was some time ago, when he, Randy, Arson, and Stacie were working together to bring down Damien Sykes and the Purist group the Brotherhood for Humanity's Salvation.

Occupied at the moment, Conlan ignored Randy's call and shifted his attention to the monitor within the glass-enclosed deck. The deck overlooked the detention pit below, where the alien terrorist Geznan—who had a hand in orchestrating the disorder in Terence Plaza—sat strapped to a chair.

Seated at the deck's control panel was the designated interrogator for Geznan.

Pumped with a concoction of hallucinogens and other mind-altering substances, Geznan was in a state of delirium, unable to distinguish reality from illusion. Before him was a lifelike hologram of Navexira bound to a chair, blood leaking from injuries. A Guardian held a knife to her throat, threatening to do more damage.

"Leave her alone!" Geznan shouted, his voice hoarse. His distorted senses had convinced him that what he was seeing was real.

The interrogator, who controlled the hologram, spoke into a microphone. "Please, Geznan, tell them what they want to know." Due to AI voice replication, Navexira's holographic likeness sounded exactly like her as it parroted the interrogator's words.

Hesitantly, Geznan said, "I—"

"Scare him some more," Conlan ordered the interrogator.

The interrogator upped the drug dosage, delivered via an intravenous tube embedded in the back of Geznan's neck. The feelings of terror overloading his mind were now amplified.

The holo-Guardian sliced his knife across Navexira's chest.

Blood doused her clothes.

"Please stop! I will tell you everything you want to know!" Geznan pled in distress.

Conlan's commanding voice reverberated through the detention pit as he questioned Geznan about the Collective. He inquired about who was in charge, the size of their forces, and their plans. He sought details about the mind-control weapon, but since Geznan had no involvement in its development, he had no pertinent information to provide. Finally, Conlan asked for the location of the abducted ambassador delegation, and Geznan disclosed the coordinates of Zataldra's mountain compound in Khanoria. Conlan then summoned two Guardians to escort Geznan back to his detainment cell.

Watching Geznan being removed from the detention pit by the two Guardians, Conlan thought, *Hopefully, our men are still alive.*

He made a mental note to return Randy's call, but he wouldn't tell Randy that DFI had learned the whereabouts of the captured ambassadors. Randy would find out once Vanguard Alpha and the rest of the task forces assigned to rescue them were redeployed, to complete the mission they started.

◆ ◆ ◆

Planet Khanoria
Council Citadel

Zataldra strolled down a hallway, its expansive windows maximizing natural sunlight. She was en route to the meeting chamber for the war vote. The pressure she was feeling was visible in her every movement. The Collective was counting on her.

She entered the chamber, ready to speak on behalf of the council's pro-war faction. The room was vast and had a stained-glass ceiling of prismatic colors. The council members sat in the tiered grandstands that encircled the tribune, the elevated dais at the center of the chamber.

The council's grizzled protocol magistrate, Korguzel, stood at the lectern on the tribune. His role was to maintain order and oversee the proceedings.

Zataldra crossed the walk bridge leading to the tribune. Once at the lectern, she clasped her hands together and bowed to Korguzel.

Korguzel then opened the session, saying, "Councilwoman Gor'Ronn now has the floor."

Zataldra took his place behind the lectern, while he stood off to the far right.

Zataldra's eyes traveled over her audience: men and women from opposite generations, their faces a mix of youth and age. Most council members regarded her with damning stares. She was determined to convince the pro-war faction's opposition that launching an attack on the humans was the right call.

She spoke into the lectern microphone. "I am not only a voice for the people's will, but also a representative for the Khanorians massacred by aliens who supported the previous—and final—Sorin's reign of fear, terror, and carnage. I speak for families torn asunder.

"There are men, women, and children who will never see their loved ones again because soldiers of the Commonwealth Defense Force took them from them. Irreparable trauma was inflicted on many lives. We *must* hold the perpetrators accountable for their crimes. What Khanorian doesn't want to see justice served to their loved ones' killers? Does any council member here not wish for retribution?

"The humans declared war on Khanoria when they sent their soldiers here. It's now this council's duty to punish them, to avenge the slain and prevent other races from experiencing the same suffering that we have.

"The victims of the Commonwealth Defense Force are many. Some have joined forces under an alliance called the Collective, including myself and my militia. While they couldn't be present here for this proceeding, three generals from the Collective have entrusted me with sharing their stories today."

A holofilm of the three generals she had mentioned projected from Zataldra's wristlet. One at a time, they recounted the damage done to their people by the CDF. They spoke about how Dafulton granted them the opportunity for vengeance by proposing they join his justice coalition, the Collective.

After the film ended, Zataldra said, "Do you see? Do you see how the humans foster terror across the galaxy? The Collective stands ready to obtain reparations not only for ourselves, but for all those wronged by the humans. The National Protection Force's help would ensure that the humans' malevolence doesn't resurface in our nation or spread to other worlds. Fellow council members, now is the time to act. Now is the time to make the humans pay in blood for their transgressions against us. I have presented my case."

Whispers and murmurs filled the chamber as the council members deliberated Zataldra's case for war.

Awaiting the verdict, Zataldra constantly wiped her sweaty palms on her pants. Her throat was parched, drier than a desert. She had done her best to persuade the council to join the Collective's mission, but was it enough?

The council members' mouths continued to move in quiet conversation.

Korguzel said, "Is there anyone who wishes to present a rebuttal?"

"I would like to speak," a voice announced from the rear seating of the chamber. It was Varanz. He had invited himself as a guest today, a privilege granted to all Grand Elders for council sessions.

Speech deserted Zataldra. She had no idea that Varanz would be here. *What are you doing, Varanz?* she thought. Her expression sharpened. She suspected his intention was to derail her efforts. "Objection!" she said. "The Grand Elder is *not* a member of this leadership council."

Korguzel's eyes swept across the chamber. "Does anyone oppose the Grand Elder's request to speak?"

Only the pro-war faction of the council raised their hands. They were afraid that Varanz might nullify any influence Zataldra had had with her well-crafted argument.

"It has been decided," Korguzel declared. "The Grand Elder may address the chamber."

Zataldra clenched her jaw and bit the inside of her mouth at this unexpected turn of events.

Varanz spoke. "While the desire for vengeance beats strong

within many hearts, plunging Khanoria into a war with the humans is unwise. Should their soldiers return, the National Protection Force would stand firm in this nation's defense. But to pursue retribution at the cost of our warmen's lives would only bring further anguish to Khanorians. Esteemed council members, I beseech you to not vote for war."

Zataldra's brow creased, and she muttered under her breath.

Korguzel said, "Is there anyone who wishes to offer a counterargument?" Silence followed his question. "Then let the vote begin. All those in favor of war, raise your hands."

Fifteen additional hands joined the pro-war faction's—council members persuaded by Zataldra's passionate argument. But their votes didn't equate to a majority consensus for war.

Korguzel said, "According to the yeas and nays, there will be no war."

Zataldra felt like the floor had just dropped from beneath her. "Cowards, every one of you!" Her temper had now reached a feverish pitch.

Korguzel stomped his staff against the floor three times. "Order!"

Zataldra ignored the protocol magistrate's command and continued her tirade. "You call yourselves leaders, yet you cower in fear, bowing to this Grand Elder as if he were a deity! We have the opportunity to avenge our loved ones and rid the galaxy of a threat! Instead, you spit on the graves of the fallen! All of you are gutless! You—"

Korguzel raised his voice over hers. "Councilwoman—daughter of Elder Jud'Zarr Gor'Ronn—I implore you to stop this instant!"

Zataldra got hold of herself. "I . . . I—" Her voice shook. Embarrassed, she sped out the chamber doors.

Korguzel cleared his throat. "This meeting is adjourned."

◆ ◆ ◆

Zataldra pulled up files on her desktop interface, immersing herself in councilperson work to distract her mind from the vote. She had informed Dafulton that her attempt to enlist the help of the National Protection Force had failed; however, its absence wouldn't be a complete hindrance to the Collective's mission. While having the Protection Force's backing would've significantly improved their odds, not having it wasn't a showstopper. The Collective still had their trump card, her mind-control weapon. And if they lacked the manpower for a direct assault on the Commonwealth, they could alter their plans for a more strategic one.

The sudden eruption of gunfire outside her office jolted Zataldra from her chair. *What's happening?* She rushed into the hallway and saw a male Guardian. He fired a blast from his energy gun that opened up the chest of a staff worker.

The staff worker crumbled, a simmering hole burned through his chest.

The Guardian's face looked stoic, emotionless, as if he were under the influence of one of Zataldra's mind-control devices.

Zataldra placed a hand over her fast-beating heart, afraid that what she was assuming was correct. *Did Dafulton—* she pondered.

Unfortunately, her suspicions were correct. After she had informed Dafulton of her failure, he had taken matters into his own hands and initiated his plan B: staging an attack that would pin the blame on the humans, the Khanorians' long-ago enemy. Using one of the mind-control devices Zataldra had delivered to him, Dafulton had manipulated one of the Guardians imprisoned aboard his ship, programming him to attack the citadel.

Zataldra wrestled with the ethical implications of Dafulton's actions. *This isn't right,* she thought, although she realized that this attack might serve as the ultimate catalyst for prodding the council into reversing their ruling on war. *Did Dafulton not conceive that someone may get hurt in this staged attack? Or was a casualty perhaps the intended outcome?*

Ignoring her completely, the Guardian's hollow eyes scanned past her. His mind had been programmed to dismiss her as a threat. He marched forward, his sights set on the council chamber.

Zataldra dashed to the staff worker, hoping against hope that there was something she could do to save him. Unfortunately, it was too late; he had already passed. Sorrow squeezed her heart as she whispered her condolences to his family.

Instincts screaming at her, she hastened toward the council chamber and burst through the entrance doors. Varanz, injured by a gunshot, lay on the floor. His assailant, the Guardian, stood over him.

Guilt suffocated Zataldra. *No!* she cried inwardly.

The other council members who were there were scurrying to safety.

At last, a security officer arrived. He bolted past Zataldra, who stood petrified in the doorway, and released a pulse of energy from his orb blaster, taking out the Guardian before he could kill again.

Zataldra's heart was heavy. *This . . . shouldn't have happened.*

The council members huddled around Varanz, some sending up prayers to the After.

Medics arrived, but the Elder was already gone.

Zataldra brought a hand over her mouth, suppressing a gag reflex. Her weapon had been used to murder Khanorians. Somehow, she kept the scream building up inside her sealed away.

◆ ◆ ◆

Zataldra sought solitude outside in the courtyard, moments after the tragedy inside the citadel.

Dafulton's image projected from her wristlet, the weak signal distorting his features.

Zataldra simmered. The air between her and Dafulton was growing contentious. "How could you?" she chided him, red-faced.

Dafulton, sitting aboard his ship, said, "The war vote failed. Now, the council may be inclined to reconsider their ruling. Isn't this what you desired?"

Zataldra's anger burned hotter. "Yes, but Varanz—my father's friend, *my* friend—was killed because of what you did. And a staff worker died as well. Your use of my weapon, meant for the humans, has disgraced me."

"You have my condolences. The deaths were not intentional, but they may encourage the council to support the Collective's mission. Tell me, Zataldra, are you still in this fight with me? Do you still want justice for your father's murder?"

Eyes downcast, Zataldra let out a barely perceptible sigh. "Yes, I do."

"Good."

Zataldra firmed her voice and squared her shoulders, refocusing. "The council is convening an emergency session tomorrow. Let us see how things play out."

"Use today's tragedy to hammer home the extent of their mistake," Dafulton urged.

"I will keep you updated," Zataldra said briskly before ending the transmission. She remained upset with Dafulton, but she also saw what had happened today as an opportunity.

◆ ◆ ◆

HOURS AFTER THE CITADEL ATTACK

A knock on his cell door startled Jarius.

"Jarius, it's me," came Iya's voice from outside the cell. "You were right. My sister refused to let you go. As promised, I'm here to help you escape."

"Thank you," Jarius said.

Iya pressed the unlock command on the door's keypad. After the clicks and clacks of bolts, the door creaked open, and she entered.

Freedom was so close that Jarius could taste it.

"Give me your wrists," Iya said. She picked his shackles' locks using a small metal tool.

One shackle fell away, followed by the other, clanging to the floor.

"Where'd you learn that?" Jarius asked.

"From my sister." Iya crouched to remove the leg shackles next. "These locks are antiquated, very easy to pick." Once finished, she stood up.

"Thanks again."

"Think nothing of it, but—"—Iya appeared troubled—"—something has happened. I think you should know about it."

Jarius saw her expression as a harbinger of bad news. He gripped her small shoulders. "Tell me already."

"My sister holds a seat on Khanoria's leadership council. This morning at the citadel, the council's headquarters, she set in motion a vote to declare war against your people. It failed."

"And?" Jarius prodded, urging her to get to the crux of the matter.

"Later, one of your military's soldiers attacked the citadel. He killed Grand Elder Varanz, who was a respected leader and close friend to me, my sister, and our father. The soldier also killed a staff worker. Eventually, a security officer dispatched him."

Jarius winced, befuddled. "A Guardian attacked the citadel? But that doesn't make any—"

"Here, let me show you," Iya said. The green lights flashing on her wristlet verified receipt of the instruction she inputted. Then the wristlet displayed holographic footage of the attack. "The public release of this footage has caused widespread panic and brought back horrid memories for many Khanorians."

Jarius watched intently. He recognized the Guardian attacking the citadel as one of the prisoners he, Arlo, and Cruz had been sent to rescue from the Collective. The Guardian's eyes were hollow of life and unblinking. It was obvious to Jarius that someone, perhaps Zataldra or Dafulton, had used mind control to make this Guardian an unwilling puppet of their will.

Iya said, "I'm sure you've come to the same conclusion as I: My sister's mind-control weapon was used to carry out this attack to convince the council that humanity is still a threat to Khanoria. But . . . even with her mind clouded by vengeance, it's hard to believe that Zataldra would deliberately endanger innocent lives."

"Maybe Dafulton used her weapon without her knowledge. Anyway, you can figure it out later. I need to get to this compound's ship hangar. The vessel confiscated from me and my ambassador colleagues should be there."

"I'll show you the way."

They exited the cell into the corridor.

"What is going on?" a voice said. It was Bingrew.

Shit, Jarius thought.

Bingrew's eyebrows shot up when he saw Iya and Jarius together. "Iya, you released him? What has gotten into you?"

Iya wrung her hands together, fingers intertwined. "Bingrew, please, *please* listen to me." Desperation colored her voice. "This human is no perpetrator of wrongdoing. He—"

107

"He has manipulated you," Bingrew interjected. "Out of the way, child!" He clasped Iya's arm and swung her aside, sending her stumbling backward. Activating his wristlet, he said, "Emergency in the holding area. The prisoner is loose."

Jarius lunged a fist at Bingrew.

Bingrew, faster than a man his size had any right to be, caught Jarius' fist with a grip as unyielding as forged iron. He then grabbed hold of Jarius' shirtfront, hoisted him off his feet, and hurled him across the corridor like he weighed nothing.

Jarius' back slammed into a wall, every bone in his body vibrating from the collision.

Iya shrieked, and she shrank back.

Jarius lay sprawled on the floor. *This motherfucker's strong.* He pushed away the mordant pain discouraging him from fighting on, telling it to take a hike. There was no way he'd give up now, not when he was so close to being reunited with Jazzlyn.

Bingrew stalked forward to snatch Jarius up and throw him back inside his cell.

Iya wanted to intervene, but what could she do?

When Bingrew was near enough, Jarius sprang to his feet. Instinctively, he tapped into his Land Combatant Corps training and executed a swinging hammerfist that connected with Bingrew's temple, knocking him for a loop. A follow-up knee strike to the kidney caused Bingrew to double over, clutching his abdomen. Seizing the opportunity, Jarius dealt a glancing elbow strike to the back of his thick neck, dropping him.

Jarius repeatedly stomped Bingrew's face. A paroxysm of anger possessed him, bringing out the violence inside. Each emotionally charged stomp was a visceral response to the memory of him blowing Cruz's head to pieces.

Iya shouted, "Stop it! That's enough!" She wrapped her arms

around Jarius' waist from behind to anchor him.

Jarius fought away the anger. "S-sorry." He paused for air. "Lost it there for a moment. It's been . . . rough."

Kneeling by Bingrew's motionless body, Iya checked for a pulse. "He's alive."

Zer'Katro's voice crackled over Bingrew's wristlet. "Bingrew, what is your status?" There was no response. "Are you there? Is the prisoner still on the loose?"

"I've gotta get the hell out of here." Jarius took the gun from Bingrew's holster.

"Let's go." Iya took off, with Jarius keeping up beside her.

They jetted down corridor after corridor.

"This way," Iya said, taking a left. She palmed the release mechanism on an exit door. It swiveled outward, and she and Jarius exited the facility into the freezing mountains.

A biting gust of glacial wind buffeted Jarius and chilled him to the marrow. "Damn it," he muttered, hugging himself. Iya appeared to be unaffected by the temperature. "Why the hell aren't you cold?" he asked, breath misting the air.

"Khanorians' bodies acclimate to their environment. Now come, follow me." A mix of snow and ice crunched under Iya's feet.

Jarius surveyed the various obstacle courses, shooting ranges, and simulated combat environments where humanoid drones functioned as interactive opponents capable of firing back. "Quite the training setup your sister's got out here."

"Indeed. Bingrew told me her militia has been using these grounds for training against your people long before joining the Collective. She built it up over time into what you see now."

Behind Jarius and Iya, Zer'Katro's voice bellowed from the corridor that they had left. "Stop!"

Jarius said to Iya, "I'm gonna need to play the role of the bad human and give the impression I'm using you as a living shield. That'll stop him from shooting."

"Do it."

Jarius stepped behind Iya and locked an arm around her throat. He then pressed his gun against her temple. "You good?" he whispered.

"Yes."

Zer'Katro dashed outdoors. "Stop!" He brought his gun to bear.

"Don't move!" Jarius exclaimed. "If you even think about pointing that weapon my way, I'll blow her fucking brains out!" Facing Zer'Katro, Jarius began backpedaling while drawing the back of Iya's head to his chest. "I'm leaving this frozen hellhole. And if you do anything, *absolutely anything*, to make me lose my cool, kiddo here is a goner, you understand me?"

Zer'Katro snarled.

"Don't doubt for a second that I won't follow through on my threat," Jarius warned. "What I want you to do now is drop the weapon and keep your hands up high. If you attempt to retrieve it or call for backup on your communicator, I do to her what you made me do to my friend. That means her head decorates the ground. Got it?"

Without a word, Zer'Katro did as told, the snow muffling his gun's fall. He then raised his arms aloft.

Jarius shifted. Iya now faced the hangar's direction while he gripped her collar from behind. "Lead the way," he said in a low tone. His body angled sideways, he kept his gun trained on Zer'Katro.

The hangar was just a few yards up, its dull-gray exterior contrasting the white surroundings. After Jarius and Iya made it there, Iya pressed the open command on an access panel.

The hangar's large door rumbled open, and the duo escaped the bitter cold. The interior was a cavernous space, where ships rested atop elevated docking platforms.

Once the hangar door closed, Zer'Katro said into his wristlet, "The prisoner is in the hangar and has Iya."

Jarius stuffed his gun into his waistband and scanned the hangar for his ship. "Damn it! It's not here! Fuck!" He stomped the floor.

Panic sparked inside Iya. "Your ship isn't here?"

"Yeah! Where the hell did they take it?" Jarius buried his forehead in his hands. "I can't pilot your people's craft. I don't know how." The odds of him escaping had just disintegrated.

"I . . . I will take you to your homeworld." Iya felt that was the right thing to do.

Jarius' brows leapt. "What?"

Iya nodded resolutely. "Let's go."

"Iya, I can't—"

"What other choice do you have?" Iya assumed a defiant posture. She wouldn't let herself be dissuaded. "If you stay, you will either be re-imprisoned or killed! The Korahh'Havaell and the teachings of the Tograh'Dirkot—not *you*, not my *sister*—make my duties clear: protect and save life whenever it's within my power!"

"Alright," Jarius said. Iya was free to make her own choices. And he'd prefer not to die.

"Come." Iya climbed a flight of stairs to the shuttle sitting atop the nearest docking platform. Jarius was in lockstep behind her.

The portside door of the fuselage opened via motion-sensor detection, and Iya stepped into the cabin first.

A moment later, the hangar door lurched open. A strong wind howled, carrying flurries of snow into the ship-filled space.

111

Standing in the shuttle's doorway, Jarius twisted around. Zataldra and company rushed into the hangar, brandishing weapons.

"Fire!" Zataldra commanded Zer'Katro and the two other men with her.

Blasts lanced in a trajectory toward Jarius.

Iya took her place at the shuttle's control chair. Everything Jud'Zarr had taught her about piloting came back to her. Each switch flicked and button pushed was a familiar echo of his instruction.

The shipboard scans checked all systems for optimal functionality: navigation, engines, power cells.

Iya knew it would take a few minutes for the shuttle's takeoff procedures to complete. A knot of tension grew in her chest. "We need time," she told Jarius.

"I'll keep them busy." Jarius stepped back out onto the docking platform and untucked his gun from his waistband.

Iya must be inside the shuttle, Zataldra thought.

Jarius fired back, his gun's recoil reverberating through his arm. His shots were deliberately off-target, aimed at suppression rather than inflicting fatal blows. Meanwhile, the shuttle's engines droned to life. He was almost there. He was almost free.

"Disable the shuttle's engines!" Zataldra ordered her men.

They redirected their aim. Small explosions rocked the rear of the shuttle, shattering Jarius' escape plans.

"It's over, human," Zataldra said. The shuttle's wrecked engines spurted smoke into the air. "Drop your weapon and come down from the platform."

Jarius let go of his gun. It clattered across the platform's metal floor.

Zataldra shouted, "Iya, come out!"

Iya stepped off the shuttle, standing behind Jarius. Shoulders sagging, she bore the look of defeat.

Both she and Jarius descended the stairs, Jarius with his hands raised in surrender.

Zataldra motioned for her men to hold their position while she went to meet Iya and Jarius at the foot of the stairs, gun in hand. Eyeball-to-eyeball with Iya, Zataldra spoke, the pitch of her voice rising sharply. "Sister, how dare you. I viewed the security footage. I know you set this human free."

Iya was shorter than Zataldra, but she stood tall—nerves steeled, chest puffed out. "This human is good, Sister, regardless of what you believe. And the Korahh'Havaell states we should—"

"Enough. I don't care about what the Korahh'Havaell says. *You* do, and so did Mother. But not me."

Iya held her ground. "Sister, you must listen to me—"

"I refuse to be lectured by a child."

Iya pushed back. "You speak of the humans' wrongs, but what of your own? That man who attacked the citadel was under the influence of *your* weapon. You're responsible for Varanz's death."

Zataldra glanced at her men. She wondered if they had caught any of what Iya had said. It didn't look like it. A period of silence stretched, her mind reflecting on the citadel attack. "I had no part in what transpired. The man who will lead me and my forces to victory, Dafulton, used my weapon without my knowledge."

"Jarius told me about this man and how cunning he can be." Iya's chastising stare impaled Zataldra. "Even after he has betrayed your trust, you still choose to follow him?"

A high level of cynicism permeated Zataldra's tone. "We all make mistakes, *don't we?* According to the *Korahh'Havaell*."

Iya placed her hands on her hips, anger climbing. "*Oh*, now you bring up the Korahh'Havaell."

"Enough. Go back to your room, Sister. We shall talk later."

Iya walked past Zataldra, chin held high. She'd never waver in her commitment to freeing Jarius. *Jarius, you and I will get you home. I have faith.*

Zataldra grabbed Jarius' arm. "Come."

Not budging, Jarius spoke up. "Dafulton is playing you for a fool. He uses lies and deceit to gain loyalty. The CDF rightfully removed him from power on the planet he ruled as a dictator. I can't even enumerate all the injustices he committed. The CDF saved people. I understand that may be difficult for you to believe, since you've only heard about the terrible things we've done. But I'm telling you, Dafulton is a first-rate shitbag.

"Iya told me your father was killed by the CDF. Dafulton is exploiting that pain. His only intention is to use you for his own selfish agenda. He doesn't care about justice for the CDF's victims or protecting the universe from the so-called 'evil human threat.' He's trumped himself up as a unifier and savior, but in reality, he's just a master manipulator. This war he plans to start is solely for his personal gain."

"Silence," Zataldra demanded.

Jarius wouldn't shut up just because she wanted him to. "Dafulton's hoodwinked you. He's got you wrapped around his fucking pinkie, and you don't even realize it. It was wrong of him to deploy your weapon against your own people. I'm betting he did it because the war vote Iya told me about failed, and he wanted to manipulate the council into supporting this clandestine agenda he's keeping from you, whatever it is. He's no different from your former Sorin."

"I said silence." Zataldra brought a hard slap down on Jarius' cheek. "You're obviously lying about Dafulton's ambitions. And your people's crimes far surpass his recent mistake of attacking the citadel."

Stubborn, Jarius thought, his cheek stinging. Zataldra and her men led him out of the hangar and back into the cold. He wanted to remain optimistic about his chances of being rescued by the CDF, but his supply of hope was dwindling fast.

CHAPTER FIVE

Expedition Task Forces Headquarters
Hangar Three

Vanguard Alpha had assembled aboard the *Nightingale* to execute ad hoc orders: strike Zataldra's mountain compound and secure the three ambassadors if they were still alive. Randy was glad that he and Stacie postponed their intergalactic vacation after all; he would've missed joining the rescue effort.

The team, clad in their sleeves, sat in the ship's conference room as Carl introduced the young woman standing beside him to the new members—a woman Randy knew well. "For those of you who don't know her, I'd like to introduce Private Akane Sugimori. She just got back from extended leave—refreshed and ready for a fight, I hope."

Full of invigoration, Akane pumped her fist. "Of course, Sir! When kicking ass is on the agenda, yours truly is always ready to rumble."

"Good." Carl introduced Vanguard Alpha's new members to Akane, gesturing to each as he called out their names. "Here we have Specialist Arturo de León, Sergeant Royce Thatcher, and Private Brayden Warnock."

Arturo adopted a chipper tone. "Pleased to make your acquaintance, Private Sugimori."

"Likewise, handsome," Akane replied, eliciting a smile from Arturo. "Welcome to the ETF's A-team."

Arturo whispered to Brayden, who was sitting beside him, "I'm diggin' this chick."

Brayden elbowed Arturo's shoulder.

Akane always had a presence that could brighten faces, Randy thought. However, she could also be a pain in the neck with her pertinacious attitude.

"Alright," Carl said, "now that the pleasantries are over, let's get down to business. Take a seat, Private Sugimori."

As Akane came Randy's way, warmth and nostalgia welled up in his chest. Though they had occasionally exchanged text messages, nothing compared to seeing her in the flesh again. Her lively, upbeat demeanor remained unchanged. She stayed true to herself despite the adversities that had plagued her life—the losses of Skylar Grace, Desmond Castillo, and Simone Conyers, and more recently, the destruction of RISE by the Brotherhood. She was undeniably tough.

Akane claimed the seat next to Randy. Sitting so close to him brought a glow to her face and a sparkle to her eyes. "Randy, what's up?"

"It's nice to see you, Akane."

"Ditto."

Using a single finger, Randy lifted a few of the purple-dyed strands streaking Akane's short black hair. "Trying out a new look, huh?"

Akane nodded. "Just felt like changing things up a bit." She rubbed a hand over her hair.

"Well, it suits you."

"Yeah?" A blush crept up Akane's cheeks.

"Yeah, it definitely does."

"Well, thanks. Mom and Dad weren't too thrilled about the dye job. They're very . . . old-fashioned."

Throughout their few text exchanges, Randy and Akane never touched on the night Randy disclosed RISE headquarters' location to DFI. Although the Brotherhood reached RISE before the CDF, Randy wasn't entirely sure whether Akane still harbored resentment over his decision. Since they were teammates and would be working together for the foreseeable future, he wanted to ensure there were no unresolved issues between them that needed to be smoothed over. But he chose not to broach the topic unless she did first.

Carl, starting the briefing, said, "By now, you've heard the announcement from the Executive Press Office this morning. If not, let me fill you in. In response to intel from DFI's intergalactic network, which implied a major Collective attack on Eden soil was imminent, Chief Amaechi activated the Defense Protocols a couple of weeks ago. That's why the Air & Space Corps has been engaged in space drills as of late and is securing a defensive perimeter around Eden and Satellite One.

"As feared, the attack happened—in Terence Plaza. The Collective executed the attack using a sophisticated weapon capable of bypassing cerebral implants' safeguards to manipulate our minds. They've perverted neurotechnology, designed to enhance human connection, into a tool for murder.

"The two shitbags charged with carrying out the attack were from Khanoria. Apparently, there's a group of Khanorians allied with the Collective. From one of the Khanorian terrorists captured, DFI learned the weapon used to transmit the mind-control signal in Terence Plaza was some sort of unmanned aerial system."

Randy was relieved that he and Stacie had escaped the weapon's powers of enslavement, presumably because its signal could only compromise a limited number of implants at once.

Carl said, "The prisoner also divulged the location of the three abducted ambassadors. They're being held at a mountain compound in Khanoria. That's where we're headed. And before it slips my mind, the prisoner also revealed that Dafulton holds absolute authority over the Collective. He's their leader."

Akane's posture shifted in alarm. "I studied up on him in the Academy's archives. He's a major big-time asshole."

"You'll brook no argument from me on that, Private Sugimori," Carl replied. "The CDF drove him and his minions off of planet Doagwar. But instead of fading into obscurity, he became a kingpin of intergalactic crime. He and his army of brigands have been pillaging and plundering."

Akane craned her head toward Randy. "Hey, your dad was involved in the operation to overthrow Dafulton, wasn't he?"

Snippets of Arson's story about Dafulton's last stand resurfaced in Randy's mind. "Yeah, come to think about it, he was." Randy remembered Arson saying that he had gone head-to-head with Dafulton and almost took him out for good, but he got away.

Carl said, "Based on the interrogation of the prisoner, Dafulton has been recruiting victims of the CDF's past atrocities, such as this group of Khanorians. He's absorbed them into his growing army of cutthroats and thugs, which he's now calling the Collective, apparently."

Sergeant Jenny Pines asked, "When we arrive at the compound, what's stopping these Collective Khanorians from using their special weapon against us?"

"Not a goddamn thing," Carl answered straightforwardly. "That's why we get in, find our people, and get the hell out as quickly as possible."

Arturo said, "Any chance our Shells can protect us from this mind-control signal?"

"No fucking clue," Carl replied. "We lift off in ten mikes. Let's get to the flight deck. After we reach orbit, you guys can do whatever you like until we're within Mabbeon's orbit. Any other questions?" There were none. "Alright, let's head out."

Randy got up and used his wristcom to send Stacie a message.

Randy: Leaving Eden now. Take care of yourself, love.

Stacie: You too.

Once the *Nightingale* reached orbit, Randy planned to grab a quick meal from the galley and then retreat to his cabin to catch a few winks. He hardly slept last night after receiving orders for Vanguard Alpha to deploy today to rescue the ambassadors.

He supposed that while eating his meal, he'd browse the classified Khanorian Campaign files Conlan had granted him access to. He had downloaded them but hadn't reviewed them yet. Surely, they'd shed some light on the atrocities that drove this group of Khanorians to relentlessly pursue humanity's annihilation, providing insight into Zataldra's mention of seeking retribution.

Securely strapped into a seat within the *Nightingale's* flight deck, alongside the rest of Vanguard Alpha, Randy watched the ship's ascent into space.

The Air & Space Corps' fleet came into view—a multitude of enormous ships called war frigates. Equipped with sleeping quarters and the facilities needed to sustain human life, they housed nearly a thousand Guardians each.

The implementation of the Defense Protocols was the geostationary equivalent—for the Air & Space Corps—of a long-term ground deployment for the Land Combatant Corps. The Guardians of the Air & Space Corps would remain on standby aboard the frigates, to protect Eden, until Chief Amaechi deemed it appropriate to lift the Protocols. Pilots would regularly launch from the frigates in fighter craft to patrol the distant fringes of the Commonwealth's sphere for any signs of Collective activity.

The Air & Space Corps was acting as Eden and Satellite One's shield, and Randy was grateful for every member's service. Knowing defenses were still beefing up under the Protocols, he suspected Jazzlyn might be called up soon, if she hadn't been already.

After soaring past the Air & Space Corps' defense barrier, the *Nightingale* and the other task force ships shifted into hyperspace travel. In eight hours, they'd reach Mabbeon.

◆ ◆ ◆

Randy sat alone at a small table in the galley, with the crumbs of his consumed prepackaged meal in the plastic container in front of him. Projecting from his wristcom were four of the files related to the Khanorian Campaign. To stay awake and finish his review of them, he took a swig from his can of orange-flavored energy drink.

The testimonies of Guardians within the files were shocking and never made it to Command. Instead, they were concealed and labeled classified.

Drowsiness hazing his lucidity, Randy folded his forearms on the table and rested his head on them.

The doors to the galley swished open, and Akane strolled in. "Randy, you okay?"

Randy lifted his sagging eyelids and straightened his back against the chair. He could barely keep his head up. "I'm fine," he said as Akane scoured the cupboards. He chugged down the last of his drink, its acidity washing over his tongue. The flood of more stimulants into his system perked him up a bit.

"Liar." Akane grabbed a meal bar from the cupboards and settled into the second chair at the table. In case the ship lost power, and therefore gravity, the furnishings and dishware were all magnetized. "Let's try this again: What's up?"

Randy answered truthfully this time. "I've been reading some classified files on the Khanorian Campaign that a friend of mine gave me access to. Guardians deployed to Khanoria were tasked with aiding the Sorin's National Protection Force in suppressing a civil uprising. I don't know all the details about what was happening in Khanoria at the time, but I'm guessing the rebels were in the right; that usually seems to be the case.

"There were Guardians who disregarded ethics and morality. Some took advantage of the lack of consequences for harming innocent citizens, committing acts of sexual violence and other atrocities. Mission leaders ordered unnecessary shows of force. It's similar to the iniquity I witnessed from certain Guardians during my deployment to Satellite One."

"Yeah, I know some pretty fucked up shit went down in Khanoria," Akane said.

"How did you find out?"

"Simone." Akane's voice slightly cracked from bringing up her deceased bestie's name. "She was deployed there near the end of the Khanorian Campaign, before joining Vanguard Alpha. She said the stuff she saw broke her heart—almost made her lose faith in the CDF and resign. Guardians even confessed to her about injustices they saw comrades commit. Some said they were forced to participate in public executions of noncombatants."

Randy nodded grimly. "Maybe the Truth Commission's investigation will make Guardians who thirst to misuse their power think twice. And once the commission's final report is released, the CDF's training curriculum will be revamped to instill a new mindset in Guardians—one that promotes compassion and respect for civilians and doesn't shun Guardians for reporting misconduct.

"I also hope this report leads to the removal of higher-ups who've been covering up their own crimes and encouraging the use of detestably harsh tactics against 'the enemy,' based on the misguided belief that fear and brutality will discourage resistance and protect the Commonwealth. Such tactics only tarnish the respectability of the CDF and humanity when other worlds' people learn of them or become victims of them, like these Khanorians we're about to face."

Akane bit into her meal bar. "It's good Guardians like you and me—like who Simone was—that are gonna become the next generation of leaders and change the CDF. That's what . . . Simone used to tell me."

Randy felt hopeful for the future. "Yeah," he agreed, ready to be a part of the change.

Randy and Akane continued to chat casually for a while, reconnecting.

Akane talked about how pleasant it was to spend time with her parents and friends in Sector 07. Thanks to the Colony Restoration Initiative, living conditions were improving in the sector. New tenements were being constructed and existing ones upgraded.

Randy told Akane that one of the captured ambassadors was his collegemate and best friend. He shared with her how he and Jarius met during their final year at Commonwealth University, along with stories of their time serving together during the civil war. With his only living relative on Eden—his maternal aunt Merriam Wells—estranged from him for siding with the Coalition, as well as many friends cutting ties with him, he emphasized how much Jarius and Stacie meant to his well-being.

The stimulants from the drink were wearing off now. His mind was going numb from his lack of sleep. He rose, the whites of his eyes red. Akane stood up as well. "I should get some rest," he said, finally caving to his body's demand to shut down. "It was great catching up with you, Akane."

"Same."

They stared at each other for a long, wordless, companionable moment in reminiscence of past times.

While on her sabbatical, Akane candidly disclosed her involvement in RISE and its less-than-legal strategies for achieving equality to her parents. She had no regrets about joining the organization or killing the immigrant haters that she did, even up to this day.

Her parents were displeased to learn that she had put her career in the CDF at risk. Nevertheless, they understood the emotional toll RISE's demise took on her. To help her move forward, her father shared a valuable insight: If you live in the past, you'll never be able to step into the future.

Her father also posed a thought-provoking question to her: Beyond championing equality and endeavoring to reform the CDF, what did Akane want for her life?

Lately, she had been giving that question a lot of thought. As she gazed into the eyes of Randal Scott—the man who was still one of her heroes for emancipating the colonies—she thought about the prospect of settling down with someone like him. Someone who stimulated her intellectually and romantically. Someone she deeply respected.

The sting of betrayal, from Randy divulging RISE headquarters' location to DFI, had ebbed away during their text messaging. In this moment, as they locked eyes, it was clear why she admired him so much: his heart. He had a genuine desire to make the Commonwealth better and sought to back up his intentions with action, like providing a testimony for the Truth Commission. And moved by compassion, he felt compelled to take action in relieving people's suffering, rather than staying idle. That was why he joined the Coalition.

Randy hugged Akane briefly and then stood apart from her, ending their silent reverie. "I'll see you when the mission starts."

While he walked back to his cabin, his cerebral implant evoked feelings, emotions, and sensations from his past involvement with Akane—which remained ingrained in his subconscious. Flashbacks of his and Akane's night of intimacy consumed his mind.

He was acutely aware of a Link's potential to foster a profound rapport between two people, especially two people who had a sexual history. He was also aware of its duality. Linking could be a double-edged sword, with its upsides and pitfalls. Randy's recollection of grappling with Cerebral Attachment Syndrome after he and Stacie split was a poignant reminder of this.

Though his and Akane's past had been on his mind today, it wasn't necessarily a sign that he was experiencing a relapse of the syndrome. He hadn't shared a Link with Akane long enough for that. Yet, traces of their erstwhile longings for each other were persistently badgering him, courtesy of the cerebral implant's mnemonic power.

Stifling a yawn, Randy stepped into his room and redirected his thoughts to the mission at hand, getting Akane out of his head. If he kept dwelling on her, his implant would continue feeding his mind more memories of their short-lived but passionate romance.

125

After Randy lay down on his bed, sleep quickly overtook his consciousness, but phantom sensations conjured by the mental imprint of Akane's touch lingered on his skin—palpable tingles and pinpricks, remnants of physical exultation.

◆ ◆ ◆

Akane lay submissively sprawled on Randy's bed, her body clad in a pair of velvety panties. Randy, already unclothed, took the pleasure of easing her panties down her limber legs and discarding them on the floor. There was no point in deceiving himself. He'd been waiting for this opportunity since Akane returned from leave. The Nightingale would be coming up on Khanoria soon, so time was running out. They'd have to be quick.

Randy knelt between Akane's legs, his erection elongated to its fullest extent. He swayed his hips in a ceaseless rhythm, pumping her. As his hurried thrusts chiseled away at her coherence, her head thrashed from side to side, and her mutters of sedition grew even less intelligible. Not letting up, he drilled into her inner recesses until stars speckled her vision. Finally, the inevitable moment of release arrived with vehemence, and he . . .

Randy jolted upright in his bed as the *Nightingale* descended onto Mabbeon, a planet of green-toned landmasses, swirling white clouds, and cerulean-blue oceans. The dream was fresh in his mind. *What the hell?* he thought. He covered his face with his hands and centered his thoughts. *No, that's not what I want from Akane,* he told himself.

Stacie's words entered his mind: *"If she were to show up tomorrow—Akane, that is—would you have any . . . feelings for her?"*

Randy assured himself that the dream was merely a manifestation of bygone longings and lusts for Akane, reawakened by his implant. Presently, he had no romantic feelings for her.

Akane had entered his life post-separation from Stacie, and they had bonded emotionally because both of them could relate to the feeling of being marginalized—she as an immigrant, and he as an ex-Coalition fighter. But that chapter of his life was closed. His and Akane's relationship was strictly platonic now. It could never be anything more. His heart belonged to Stacie, and it always had. That's why he had fought so hard to win her back.

Carl's voice came over the intercom. "Vanguard Alpha, we're approaching Khanoria. Get shelled and proceed to the drop bay."

Shrugging off the dream, Randy got up from the bed and made his way to the ship's armory. He entered it and hastened to his Shell's docking pod. Jenny, Brayden, Arturo, and Royce were already shelled and headed out. It was just him and Akane, who was directly next to him.

Explicit images from his sex dream took over his thoughts, and he eyed Akane's svelte figure up and down—his imagination undressing her.

Akane arched a quizzical brow. "*Uhhh*, that's some *in-depth* anatomy studying that you're doing. Something on your mind?" Suspicion laced her voice.

Randy pried his eyes away from her, redirecting them to his pod. "Um, no. I'm good," he mumbled, forcing out the lie.

Akane wasn't the type who could be easily fooled. "Dude, you are such a *terrriiible* fucking liar. Back in the galley, you said 'I'm fine' and were bullshitting me then, and it's obvious you're bullshitting me now. Just be real and keep it one hundred with yourself."

Randy brushed off his attraction to her. "If I wanted something, I'd say so." He tapped the pod's control module, and its glass door sighed open.

Akane, ever persistent, wasn't backing down. "Oh, so that 'I wanna fuck you' look was actually nothing but pure disinterest? *Pfft*, yeah, right." A small part of her believed that Randy still desired her. "What's the deal? You and the girlfriend not getting it on?"

Randy cursed himself for igniting this conversation by failing to keep his eyes in check. If given an inch, Akane would take a mile.

Akane said, "I'd say you're—"

"Drop it, Akane," Randy said firmly. This was the pain-in-the-neck side of Akane that he knew well, the side that wouldn't let up until she got what she wanted. "Mission first. Chitchat later."

"Agreed." Akane opened her pod's door.

Randy pressed another button. His pod's sliding tracks extended, delivering his standing Shell to him. After he stepped behind the suit, its torso, arms, and legs opened up, and he entered the padded interior. Then the suit sealed, locking him inside.

Randy retrieved the helmet from the magnetic catch on his armored hip, lowered it on, and spoke the Shell's activation code.

The suit's fibers adjusted—some expanding, others tightening—to accommodate his frame. Electromechanical whirs blended with the chinking from slats of armor shifting and compressing.

Superimposed pop-up messages and ideograms flashed on his HUD. Then the words SHELL FULLY OPERATIONAL scrolled across it. He disengaged his mechboots from the sliding tracks' footholds, stepping out of them.

Akane, having finished suiting up as well, came up beside him. Together, they exited the armory.

◆ ◆ ◆

In the drop bay, Vanguard Alpha was shaking off the pre-battle nerves.

Randy, his faceplate retracted, lowered his chin. Reluctance took root. He dreaded having to go to battle with these Collective Khanorians.

On one hand, the ambassador delegation needed to be rescued, and he had to follow orders, even if it meant killing. On the other, a strong sense of empathy tugged at his conscience. From the files he had read so far, Randy got a good understanding of the devastation brought upon innocent lives. There had been families torn apart and communities left in ruins. Each Collective Khanorian that Vanguard Alpha was about to face embodied a tale of pain and loss, having suffered because of the CDF, either directly or through their loved ones.

Randy felt a twinge in his chest at the realization that he was now perpetuating the cycle of humanity versus Khanorians.

Carl said, "Why so glum, Scott? We're about to save your friend."

Randy replied, "I did some digging into the Khanorian Campaign, Sir, and secured privileged access to some classified files. They paint a damning picture. Guardians committed unpardonable acts of violence. I have a strong inclination that these Collective-affiliated Khanorians are just seeking revenge for what the CDF did to their people."

"I understand where you're coming from. Hear me out. There are undoubtedly bad actors in the CDF. If there weren't any, there'd be no Truth Commission. These Khanorians may indeed be out for blood because some despicable Guardians abused their power. Yeah, there were probably fuckheads in charge who authorized unnecessary shows of force to suppress resistance, which pissed off a lot of Khanorians. Some of those angry, hurt Khanorians are most assuredly part of this militia we're about to confront. Unfortunately, the CDF's controversial actions have spawned vengeance seekers like them.

"But when you kill fifteen Guardians and abduct an ambassador delegation who came to you in good faith, when you use mind control to compel people to commit murder and they're left traumatized by mental violation, you've gone beyond seeking justice. That crosses the line into true evil.

"What happened in Khanoria was tragic. I get it. And while the CDF's misconduct played a role in sending these Khanorians down a dark path, their evil now needs to be snuffed out to protect the Commonwealth's people. It falls on us, the CDF, to safeguard the lives of those we care about.

"Refusing to listen to reason, this Khanorian militia wants to rationalize the blanket extermination of the *entire* human race under the pretext of 'justice for the fallen.' Did they explore diplomatic channels for obtaining restitution? Did they take into consideration that the Commonwealth Government might be under new leadership? Was our ambassador delegation given an opportunity to be heard? Nope.

"In my opinion, they've chosen a path of violence and bloodshed instead of civil resolution. They've essentially become the very thing they despise. That make you feel any better, Scott?"

Randy understood his point. Basically, people could become evil, and it wasn't always entirely their fault. However, once they had crossed that line and there was no turning back for them, someone had to stop them. Still, he couldn't help but condemn the CDF's bad actors more than he did these Khanorians.

Randy said, "Thanks, Sir. I feel somewhat better." He thought about Jarius. "But no matter how I feel, I'll do what I need to do to save my friend. And I'll always have my teammates' backs."

"Good."

The helmsman's voice broadcasted over the intercom, "We are now approaching the drop zone."

Vanguard Alpha would be the first to airdrop onto the compound, followed by the Guardians of the other task forces.

Randy relaxed his muscles and cleared his mind, mentally preparing himself for the fight. The Collective Khanorians had blindsided the ambassador delegation and their bodyguards, ambushing them and outnumbering them. Now, the CDF would get the jump on them.

◆ ◆ ◆

At the dining complex of Zataldra's compound, she and Iya sat across from each other at a table with their meals. An undercurrent of unease had been coloring their interactions all day.

Breaking the somber quietness, Zataldra said, "I hear you've been helping with Varanz's funeral arrangements."

"Uh-huh," Iya responded in a morose tone. She absentmindedly prodded at her meal with her utensil, showing little interest in eating.

"Is something troubling you, Iya? You've barely touched your food."

Iya decided not to bite her tongue about what was disturbing her any longer. "The human, do you still plan on disposing of him?"

Zataldra casually forked meat into her mouth. Without feeling, she said, "Of course. Why wouldn't I?"

The fact that Zataldra still intended to kill Jarius knifed Iya to the core. Hurt and anger pooling, she shot to her feet. "He has done nothing wrong! You must release him!" The rebuke in her voice was sharp and strong.

Zataldra jumped from her chair, slapping her hands down on the table. "Don't raise your voice at me, little sister!"

Iya *had* to try again to convince Zataldra to let Jarius go. She couldn't give up—not yet. Doing so would be the mindset of a defeatist. "The Korahh'Havaell—"

"Stop it," Zataldra said. "The human has poisoned your mind. He manipulated you into freeing him. Believe nothing he told you. Bingrew nearly died because of him."

"That was . . . in self-defense. You should let Jarius go, yet you keep him here like an animal in a cage." Imagining Jarius being executed, Iya almost broke into a sob.

"You speak his name as if the two of you are friends," Zataldra sneered.

"We . . . are friends," Iya insisted.

You delude yourself, Sister. "Even if I allowed him to go back to his homeworld, his life would eventually end during the Collective's invasion. Once the council convenes today for the emergency session, I'm confident they'll reverse their decision on the war vote, especially since Varanz was killed in the citadel attack. And with the Protection Force and Collective united, the humans' destruction is assured, and thus the destruction of your friend too, if I were to send him home. Either way, he is dead."

Angry, Iya looked like she was physically burning up. "Yes, the *fabricated* attack on the citadel by Dafulton—the man who *lords over you* and used your weapon—just might make that union a reality."

Zataldra ignored her sister's chastisement, continuing to eat.

A Khanorian man's voice crackled over the intercom. "Emergency! Aircraft are approaching. We believe they are CDF aircraft."

Jud'Zarr had said to Zataldra "Guard your sister well until I return"—a day that would never come. His words spurred her into big-sister mode. "Quickly, lock yourself in your room. Don't come out until you hear from me."

◆ ◆ ◆

The *Nightingale* banked downward from the sky, lowering its altitude.

The floor doors of the drop bay parted, and Vanguard Alpha peered down at the tundra below. In sight was Zataldra's compound: the main facility, blocky prefabricated buildings, equipment sheds, outdoor training courses, and the ship hangar.

Carl said, "It's go-time, people. Let's bring the thunder." He leapt out. The rest of the team was right behind him.

Wind lashed at Vanguard Alpha's armored forms as they descended in a free fall. One by one, each Guardian landed, ice and snow crunching beneath their mechboots.

Instantly, a hail of gunfire from waiting enemy troopers greeted them.

"Take them down!" Carl shouted.

The *Nightingale* climbed back into the sky, its silhouette standing out against the white cumuli above.

Other task force ships moved in to disgorge more Guardians onto the battlefield.

A string of blasts hammered Randy's Shell. His Oracle located the attacker, an arrowhead-like pointer on his HUD's aim assist directing him left. He discharged a counterblast from his wrist gun that missed its mark, sailing past the target. *Damn it.* Randy traded shots with his attacker, the glacial crags offering cover for both of them.

More troopers poured out from the main facility's entryways, prepared to fend off the Guardians. Four of them flanked Randy, joining his assailant to gang up on him.

Time to end this, Randy declared. At his mental command, a launcher unfolded from the back of his Shell, locking in place over his shoulder. He blazed away with his right arm's wrist gun while gripping the launcher's foregrip with his left hand.

Tilting the launcher skyward, he mentally ordered it to fire. A metal sphere boomed from the barrel, screaming upward. It erupted in a loud airburst, dispersing a quartet of mini rockets. They hurtled down and exploded, cratering the ground and dispatching Randy's attackers—blowing them to oblivion.

From the bellies of the task force ships high above, more Guardians free-falled onto the battlefield.

Randy scanned for any teammates in need of help, but all of them were holding their own.

Illuminations from enemy gun barrels flashed endlessly in his peripheral, and blasts whizzed past him. He'd have to stay vigilant. He and every Guardian were in constant danger out here.

Khanorian troopers in bronze exo-armor glided down from the air. It was the same exo-armor that had defeated the ambassador delegation's protection detail. As the troopers touched down, their armors' jetpacks sputtered out. Then the troopers surged forward, weapons roaring.

To ensure the enemy couldn't monitor communications, Carl spoke to Vanguard Alpha using C-comms. *<<Looks like the heavy hitters have arrived.>>*

Carl remained undaunted despite the troopers' arrival. According to the information from Geznan's interrogation, the Khanorian suits' weapons were activated by voice instruction, manual inputs via wrist controls, and gesture recognition. In contrast, cerebral interface was what triggered a Shell's arsenal, allowing for lightning-quick reaction times. The ambassador delegation's protection detail was only bested because their opponents outnumbered them. The reputation of Shells as the most lethal combatwear of the Interplanetary Union was well-founded, and these Khanorians were about to experience it for themselves.

Randy set his sights on the main facility. *Jarius, I'm coming.* The banging of weapons from friend and foe resonated all around him. He crossed his fingers that Jarius was still alive. <<*I'm heading for the objective,*>> he alerted his teammates.

Carl replied, <<*Copy that. Akane, back him up. The rest of us will help hold the line out here.*>>

<<*Gotcha,*>> Akane said. <<*Randy, let's do this.*>>

Randy dashed toward the facility, his mechboots crunching, squishing, and flinging ice and snow. Akane fell in behind him, keeping pace with his strides. A dozen Khanorian troopers without exo-armor stood as a barrier in the duo's way, firing wildly to keep them from advancing.

Randy ignited his plasma saber, the purple blade of energy flashing out from his right wrist. In a burst of acceleration, he maneuvered around incoming shots and closed in on two of the troopers. He struck them down, his blade sweeping and arcing through the air. One soldier was beheaded. Just as quickly as his corpse crumbled, the other collapsed to the ground, a smoldering gap in his chest courtesy of Randy's saber skills.

Two of the ten remaining troopers in Randy and Akane's path boldly charged at them, while the rest laid down cover fire.

Akane propelled herself into the air, bounding over Randy. In mid-jump, she unleashed a torrent of blasts from her wrist guns, felling both troopers. They lay dead, searing holes riddling their bodies. Descending from the air, Akane landed in a kneeling position, sinking into the snow.

Driven by his determination to save Jarius, Randy dispatched four more troopers, alternating between wrist-gun blasts and saber strikes. Akane contributed to the body count, arm and shoulder-mounted weapons cutting down the other four.

Once they made it to the facility, Randy cocked back a fist and slammed it into the metal door, knocking it ajar from its hinges. A kick from his mechboot finished the job, caving the door inward.

"Let's move," Randy said and went inside.

Before following Randy, Akane glanced back at the members of Vanguard Alpha. Her visuals zoomed in on the ongoing skirmish between the Task Force Guardians and Khanorian troopers. Blasts were flying back and forth between the opposing sides. Assured that Vanguard Alpha was faring well, Akane proceeded inside, trailing Randy.

Further down, the empty corridor they were racing through branched off to both the left and right. Footsteps clanked in their direction from the left, going from faint to loud as whoever was coming got closer.

Randy halted. To conserve his Shell's power after using so much plasma-based weaponry outside, he instructed his CPU to equip him with his sidearm. The compartment on his armored thigh hissed open, presenting the weapon to him. Drawing it from the securing clips, he took aim as the silhouette of the unseen figure slunk across the wall.

The person coming turned out to be a Guardian. "Whoa, don't shoot!" he said, palms extended. Another Guardian appeared behind him. They were from one of the other task forces. Just like Randy and Akane, they had breached the facility to secure the package. "I'm Corporal Horace Gill." He gestured to his comrade. "And my buddy here is Private Arthur Dacey. We're from Task Force Iron Sentinel."

"No time to waste. Let's keep moving," Randy said. He motioned for everyone to follow him into the corridor on the right. "Might as well try this way."

Randy, Akane, Horace, and Arthur rounded a corner. There was an unarmored Khanorian trooper dead ahead. Randy and the trooper leveled their handguns at each other, but Randy was quicker on the trigger. His gun bucked once, firing a shot that punctured the trooper's throat, ending his life.

One of the equidistant doors along the right wall of the corridor glided open.

"Careful," Akane cautioned. She positioned herself next to Randy and lifted her arm horizontally, readying her wrist gun.

Iya, who had heard the gunshot, peeked out the doorway. Her interspecies translator hung securely around her neck, vital in case she needed to speak to any human soldiers who entered the facility. "Please, don't shoot." She tentatively stepped into the corridor from the relative safety of her room.

Randy restrained Akane's wrist, lowering her arm. "Easy. She's just a kid."

"You're here for Jarius, aren't you?" Iya asked.

Randy's heart skipped a beat at the mention of his best friend. "How do you know Jarius?"

Iya replied, "He's . . . my friend. I can take you to him. I want him freed, just like you."

She sounded sincere to Randy, but he needed to ensure this wasn't a trap. He instructed his Shell's CPU to analyze the voice data from the stored footage of his visual feed. The CPU replayed Iya's words, examining the modulations in her tone. Unable to arrive at a perfect conclusion, it deduced that there was at least a seventy percent probability she was being honest.

Randy said, "According to my CPU, there's a seventy percent chance she's telling the truth. That's good enough for me."

Horace pointed out, "That still leaves the chance we're walking into a trap."

"Then we proceed with caution," Randy replied. "Is everyone on board with that?"

Akane said, "Trap or not, I'm not fucking afraid. Let's do it."

Randy's eyes came back to Iya. "Lead the way." He sealed his handgun back in its compartment.

Iya took in the sight of the trooper Randy had shot. Unspoken grief passed. "Come." She ran forward. *The Gods have answered your plea, Jarius. Freedom is near.*

"By the way, what's your name?" Randy asked, huffing as his mechboots pounded against the floor.

"Iya." She guided the four Guardians to the brig. "He's in there." She pointed to Jarius' cell.

Randy rapped the door with his knuckles. "Jarius, it's Randy! You in there?"

Jarius perked up. He rose from the floor and shuffled to the door, his ankle shackles' chain dragging behind him. "Boy, am I glad to hear your voice, buddy."

Relief flooded Randy. "Step back. Let me know when you're clear."

After a brief silence, Jarius' muffled voice confirmed that he was out of the way.

Randy channeled plasma energy into his fist and smashed the door down. It hit the floor, and Jarius emerged from the cell.

"Man, it feels good to see you guys," Jarius said. When he noticed Iya, gratitude softened his expression. "You led them to me, didn't you?"

"I did," Iya replied.

"Thank you."

Randy said, "Let me take care of those shackles for you." He yanked apart the shackles binding Jarius' wrists and ankles. Then he retracted his faceplate. "Are you alright? Do you need medical attention? And . . . what about the other ambassadors?"

The images cycled through Jarius' head: Arlo being bludgeoned by Cruz's knuckles, followed instantly by the moment Jarius took Cruz's life. "They're dead, used as test subjects for a mind-control weapon. And I could be better, but at least I'm alive and on my way home, thanks to you guys."

"We know about the weapon. I'm sorry about your fellow ambassadors."

Akane stayed alert, keeping her eyes peeled for enemy troopers. "Alright, we need to haul ass and get the fuck out of here pronto. Before they decide to test that mind-control weapon on us, or the task forces outside."

A series of thumps echoed from around the corner down the corridor.

"Heads up, everyone," Randy said. "We've got a hostile coming our way."

Zataldra appeared in a gilded mechsuit. It was a fearsome-looking war machine that boasted reinforced armor and a trove of weapon compartments. "As I thought, you humans have come to save your envoy."

Where have I heard that voice before? Randy wondered.

The face shield of Zataldra's helmet opened on her command, splitting apart. "How you humans discovered my compound's location is beyond me, but none of you will walk out of here alive." She saw Iya, and feelings of betrayal hardened her features. "And you, Sister, you led them to the prisoner? You've once again taken my trust and thrown it away. Have you no loyalty to Khanoria?"

Iya retorted, "I told you, Zataldra, it's the Gods who guide me. My loyalty lies solely with them, a truth I've made abundantly clear."

Randy's eyes narrowed. *Zataldra?* He said, "You're the leader of the Collective's Khanorian contingent—the woman who headed the ambassadors' abduction and the creator of the mind-control weapon—according to your associate." Randy had been wondering where he'd heard her voice—on the footage he'd downloaded from Harlow's Shell.

A flicker of panic spread from Zataldra's chest to every nerve ending in her body. "My associate? You're referring to Geznan or Navexira, aren't you?" She realized the reason they hadn't arrived on Khanoria yet was that they had been apprehended. "What did you people do to them? Did you hurt them? Did you torture them?" She gritted her teeth as rage boiled within her.

"No," Randy said. "I realize this might be hard for you to believe, but your operatives are unharmed. Psychotropic drugs and virtual illusions coerced the man into giving up information. It's the most harmless form of interrogation the CDF has. He has sustained no physical injuries—of any kind."

Conlan could have dosed Geznan with pain analeptics, but going to such an extreme wasn't his style. But with Oviereya calling for more humane treatment of prisoners and with the CDF under investigation by the Truth Commission, that may not have been a wise move anyway.

Zataldra's mauve complexion flushed red. Did this human expect her to take his word at face value? "I have no reason to trust you." Her mind conjured a horrific image: Navexira and Geznan enduring the same barbaric torture the CDF had inflicted on Khanorian rebels—electric shocks, brutal whippings that left raw welts, and the cutting of flesh with blades.

Randy understood why Zataldra couldn't place her trust easily. "The CDF has brought tragedy into your life. I feel for you and—"

Zataldra cut Randy's show of sympathy short. "I will hear no more!" Her countenance darkened.

Appeals to reason had reached a dead end.

Jarius said, "Randy, don't waste your breath, man. I tried talking to her already and got nowhere. She's a total ice-queen."

Zataldra advanced closer, her menacing steps thudding. "The Collective will annihilate you humans. We are gracious enough to exempt the children from our wrath, though. They will be spared and guided toward righteousness."

Randy saw Zataldra had a frigid air about her, as if there weren't even an ounce of warmth in her heart. "So the Collective's intention is to wipe out every adult human in the Commonwealth. And you have no reservations about it, *do you*, Zataldra?"

"That's right," she replied.

Randy realized Carl was correct in his assessment of this Khanorian contingent of the Collective. Zataldra embodied their beliefs to a tee. She had convinced herself that the human race needed to be eliminated, except for the children. She was already a party to mind-control terrorism, and she apparently had no qualms about murdering innocent people who had no involvement in what happened in Khanoria years ago. That included people Randy held dear, such as his father and Stacie. She didn't even *consider* the possibility that there might be humans who'd condemn the tragedy in Khanoria if they knew about it.

Peering into Zataldra's callous eyes, Randy saw she was beyond reason, and unfortunately, she needed to be put down.

He said, "Horace, Arthur, Akane, get the lieutenant ambassador to the *Nightingale*. I'll handle her." Dafulton was the Collective's leader, commanding all its contingents, but Zataldra was the Collective's scientific genius. She was the mastermind behind the mind-control weapon, and who knew what other instruments of destruction she might have in the works, to defeat the CDF and accomplish humanity's annihilation. Knocking her off would be a major win.

"I'm not going anywhere. I'm staying with you," Akane said.

Horace grabbed Jarius' arm. "Come on, Lieutenant, let's get you out of here."

Iya said, "I'll join in escorting you to your escape craft, Jarius." She'd be risking getting caught in the crossfire outside. That didn't matter to her, though. She wanted to see her friend make it to safety with her own two eyes and say her goodbyes, or else she wouldn't be able to rest easy tonight.

"Don't get killed, bro," Jarius said to Randy. He ran away with Horace, Arthur, and Iya.

Randy watched them go. *The only one about to meet their end is Zataldra.* His faceplate slid down and locked in place.

Zataldra had no need for Jarius, so she let him escape; she had more test subjects aboard Dafulton's ship. Besides, she didn't want to risk hitting Iya with friendly fire. The two Guardians facing off against her were what she needed to concentrate on. "It's time to do the universe a favor and cleanse it of two humans." Her face shield snapped back together.

Akane said, "Come on, let's shut this bitch up."

Weapon lockers on Zataldra's suit opened up, and explosive projectiles belched forth.

Randy and Akane's barrier shields sprang to life, bathing the corridor in a shimmering wash of blue light. The shields rippled as the projectiles smashed into them and exploded. Randy and Akane then deactivated the shields. Before they could launch a counteroffensive, Zataldra's suit unleashed an onslaught of wayward gunfire from the cannons perched atop her arms and shoulders.

One blast tore a rip into the metal husk of Akane's Shell, exposing internal hardware and throwing Akane off her feet.

"Akane!" Randy shouted. He flared up his plasma saber and sprinted toward Zataldra. His aim was to confront her at close quarters to prevent her from using long-range weaponry. But Zataldra wasn't having it. A missile streaked from her shoulder cannon.

Randy jinked out of its path, and the missile detonated against the far wall behind him. He hurled himself at Zataldra, targeting her chest plate with his saber. Just as the tip of the blade was about to make contact, the fight took a downturn for Randy. Four appendages snapped out from the back of Zataldra's suit, and their metallic pincers plucked him out of midair.

Zataldra laughed as she manipulated the four spidery limbs, squeezing Randy's torso.

The shriek of strained Kryoplaste filled the air, and a stream of damage reports flashed in the right-hand corner of Randy's HUD.

Akane got back on her feet, her Shell's damage sparking. *<<Randy, I'm on my way,>>* she transmitted over C-comms, rushing to his aid.

Zataldra burst into action, hurtling Randy at Akane. Their Shells collided and crashed to the floor, vibrations thrumming through the Kryoplaste armor.

Randy and Akane rose, mechanical joints whining.

<<We need more room to fight,>> Randy said.

<<Then make us an exit.>> Akane stepped in front of Randy and erected her barrier shield to protect them both from a wave of gunfire.

A shoulder launcher extended from Randy's Shell and ejected a missile at the ceiling. The explosion showered debris over the floor. Exit made.

<<To the roof,>> Randy said.

The duo jumped up onto the roof, and Zataldra pursued them.

Winds gusted, howling fiercely.

From her vantage on the roof, Zataldra saw that many of her troopers were no longer among the living. They lay dead on the snow-covered terrain. She felt her heart writhe in her chest. Pain had become a constant unwelcome companion in her life.

The remaining troopers fought on against the task forces, which were now pulling back, having secured the package. Unfortunately, that package only consisted of Jarius, as the other two ambassadors had been killed.

Zataldra seethed at the loss of her troopers. Loyal men had perished today, men brave enough to stand with her against the humans, unlike the council. In honor of their sacrifice, she would destroy the two Guardians going up against her.

She fired her shoulder and arm cannons at full blast.

Randy and Akane split up—Randy darting left, Akane right.

They delivered a blitz of plasma saber strikes, cutting through Zataldra's armor. Rip after rip, sparks popped. Exposed wiring crackled. The double assault was overpowering Zataldra. Perfectly coordinated, Akane and Randy's moves mirrored each other, their blades working together in harmony.

Swatting at the duo with the four appendages extending from her suit's back, Zataldra got her licks in. One hit sent Akane slewing dangerously close to the edge of the roof. Another whipped Randy in the side of his helmet, staggering his feet.

Randy jumped and spun in a full circle, slicing apart the topmost appendages. Then, one slash followed by another, he severed the bottom two in half. Ending the fight, he blasted the knee actuators of Zataldra's suit with his wrist guns, causing her to crash face-first onto the roof's floor.

"Nice moves," Akane said.

Over C-comms, Randy and Akane received a scolding from

Carl. <<*Randy, Akane, where the hell are you? Exfil is underway. Get your asses to the Nightingale ASAP.*>>

Randy replied, <<*We'll be there shortly, Sir. Just tying up some loose ends.*>>

<<*Well, tie them up faster, damn it,*>> Carl barked.

Randy trained his wrist gun on Zataldra to finish her. *Sorry.* Before he could trigger his gun, agony wracked both his and Akane's heads. It was as if a thousand scalpels were stabbing their brains.

Akane screamed, nearly blowing out her vocal cords. Her pain endurance was being tested to the max. "Can't . . . take it." She bared her teeth. Everything in sight was a wavy mess. The sky, rooftop, and Zataldra and Randy's forms stretched, bent, and warped in crazy ways. Akane couldn't distinguish between up and down, left and right. Senses warring with each other, her own voice sounded distorted to her.

On impulse, she scrabbled at her helmet. She wished she could burrow into her temples to excavate the pain, which was building to an unbearable intensity.

Zataldra shambled to full height on her shaky knee actuators, pistons screeching. At her command, nanofilament spread over her suit's damage—a temporary fix. The sinister smile on her face grew wider.

Randy's will was gradually slipping away, his implant's firewalls failing him. He knew what was happening: Zataldra was transmitting the mind-control signal from her suit. Dazed, he said to his AI Combat Assistant, "Oracle, there's . . . an electromagnetic signal compromising my implant. Can you detect it and neutralize it?"

"Working," the Oracle responded. Randy fought against the controlling force. Time seemed to crawl while he waited for the AI to finish. After what was an eternity for Randy, the Oracle said, "Signal detected. Developing countermeasure." It went into learning mode, analyzing the signal to manufacture a solution.

"Hurry, goddammit," Randy rasped, though he knew his words wouldn't speed up the process. He sent a message to Akane via C-comms. <<*Akane, your Oracle can suppress the signal, but . . . you need to trigger the process. Akane, do you hear me?*>> No response. He wasn't certain whether his words had reached Akane, her mind in the clutches of the mind-control signal.

Just as Randy was on the cusp of losing control of himself, his Oracle succeeded in its task. "Countermeasure developed. Scrambling the signal now," it said.

The distress in Randy's mind dissipated. He took another shot at reaching Akane. <<*Akane, can you hear me?*>>

She was unresponsive to Randy's voice. She stood motionless, now under the thrall of mind control.

Zataldra said to Randy, "Impressive. It appears you've devised a way to counter my signal. Unfortunately, your friend wasn't as quick to react." She tapped a sequence on her arm, commanding Akane to attack Randy.

Akane's plasma saber materialized. She lunged at Randy, swinging the blade. Though he evaded the full brunt of the attack, the blade had left a gash on his chest.

"Akane, snap out of it!" he shouted.

Akane hoisted the crackling blade overhead. Conscious of everything happening, she mentally yelled at herself to stop. She felt violated and helpless as her body moved against her will; the experience was like being in a nightmare she couldn't wake up from. She was completely powerless—a slave.

The blade descended. Randy seized Akane's wrist with his left hand. Outpacing her reaction time, he followed up by walloping her helmet with his right elbow, reeling her one step back. In less than a breath, he fired a blast from his wrist gun that jerked her shoulder sideways. Fragments of armor broke off. Amplifying the power output of his weapon, he discharged another blast before Akane could rebound, aiming center mass. The resounding clang of her back hitting the rooftop reverberated.

Task force ships in the distance ascended into the sky, leaving the compound.

Carl said over C-comms, *<<Randy, Akane, the Nightingale departs in fifteen mikes. What the hell's the holdup?>>*

Randy replied, *<<We've got a bit of a situation going on right now, Sir.>>*

<<What the fuck does that mean?>>

Akane rose to her feet.

Randy said to Carl, *<<Can't explain right now. If we don't make it in time, do what you've gotta do. >>*

Akane's fists flew in a flurry of punches, each blow thudding against Randy's Shell.

"Stop it, Akane!" Randy's voice boomed. No matter how loud his pitch rose, Akane couldn't tear free of the mind-control signal.

Randy kicked her shank, buckling her knee. She fell forward, hands slamming down to buffer the fall. Randy punted her in the side of her torso, sending her barrel-rolling to the other side of the roof. He said to his Oracle, "Can you free Private Sugimori from the signal's control, like you did for me? Is there a way to transmit a countersignal?"

"Uncertain," the Oracle said. "I will endeavor to generate a solution."

The crackle of detonations sounded. Akane had discharged a pair of missiles from her Shell's shoulder launchers.

Randy power-leapt over them. But they u-turned, zeroing in

on him. They were homing missiles. Randy thought, *In that case—* His barrier shield flickered to life, intercepting the missiles. Two fiery flashes bloomed.

The power readout on his HUD's suit-status display beeped. The warning indicated his Shell's power cell was running low. Not cutting back on employing energy-intensive weaponry was putting a substantial drain on the cell. But it wasn't like conventional bullets would be of any use against Zataldra's exo-armor. Sustaining the fight at this rate wouldn't be feasible for much longer.

It's taking my Oracle too long to find a way to free Akane. Think, Scott. The answer to his dilemma came to him quickly. A light seemed to come on in his eyes. *Of course! If you can't neutralize the signal, you disable its source.*

Randy ran toward Zataldra at top speed.

Zataldra braced herself for the impending clash. *Coming for me, are you?*

Akane caught up to Randy and flung herself at him, rear-ending his Shell with her shoulder, and both of them went sprawling across the rooftop. In a heartbeat, they were on their feet again.

The two traded blows, their fists, knees, and mechboots slamming into each other's armor—producing distinct indentations.

Randy dipped under a swinging punch from Akane. Then he closed his arms around her and body-slammed her onto the roof. Seizing the advantage, he dropped a plasma-charged knee down on her helmet, cracking her visor and disorienting her.

Akane was temporarily down. It was now time to deal with Zataldra. Her suit had sustained a lot of damage, but she stood prepared for battle.

A bevy of weapons popped out from compartments on Randy's Shell. Instead of confronting Zataldra head-on, Randy aimed his weapons at the surface beneath her and triggered a salvo of blasts. Caught off guard, Zataldra had no chance to react before the surface gave way, sending her plummeting down into the facility.

Randy approached the edge of the newly created hole. Peering down at Zataldra's vulnerable, prone form, he launched a missile. The resulting explosion further demolished her suit.

The weapons extending from Randy's Shell retracted.

Akane groaned and rose. Disorientation unbalanced her legs. The cacophonous sounds of her fight with Randy replayed in her mind while his voice called out to her in real time. He was screaming for her to let him know she was okay.

She removed her helmet, the cracked visor hindering her vision. The morass of sounds and voices ping-ponging throughout her mind, turning it into an echo chamber, died. She was back in control of herself. Randy had succeeded. He had damaged Zataldra's suit enough to render it incapable of transmitting the mind-control signal.

Randy fast-walked over to Akane. He lifted off his helmet and inhaled the chilly air nipping his face. "You okay?" He let loose a tired breath.

The winds picked up, tousling Akane's hair. Her body trembled, and the tension in her head didn't seem to want to leave. Finding her voice, she said, "That was . . . horrible, a complete fucking nightmare." Emotions caught in her throat, and warm tears rolled down her face. "I could see and hear everything. I was conscious of what my body was doing, but—"

Randy placed a hand on her shoulder. "Hey, it's all over now."

Akane sniffled and wiped her eyes, the wet streaks on her face nearly freezing in the cold.

Randy said, "Once we get back to Eden, make sure you visit the med unit at HQ for a complete psychological workup. We don't know all the aftereffects of this mind-control weapon."

Akane nodded as the tension in her head subsided. "'Kay," she said, her voice barely audible.

The Nightingale should be gone by now, Randy thought. The fifteen minutes had expired. *Wait, what's that?* It sounded like a ship coming.

The *Nightingale* soared down from the sky and hovered over the rooftop. The portside door slid open, revealing Carl. "I figured we'd swing by to pick you guys up," he said over the swishing winds. "No one gets left behind on my team. Come on." He made a hurry-up gesture and stepped back to make room for Akane and Randy to jump in.

Face getting windburned, Randy slipped his helmet back on, and Akane did the same. They both leapt into the open doorway, Akane going first.

On her walk back to the compound, Iya saw the *Nightingale* departing, the ship she had helped escort Jarius to with Task Force Iron Sentinel's two Guardians.

She thought about Jarius' last words to her before they hugged each other goodbye: *"You're kind, Iya. Never change."*

As the *Nightingale* receded into a speck in the sky, Iya hoped the Gods would align her and Jarius' paths again in the future. It was definitely a bittersweet parting for her.

Shifting her eyes to the dead Khanorian troopers, she dropped to her knees—her heart heavy—and joined her palms together in silent prayer.

The sky was now beginning to sleet.

Zataldra limped out of the main facility, having ditched her battered exo-armor. Her body ached from bruises and sores.

One of her men said, "You're hurt. Do you need medical attention?"

"All I need are some pain relievers and healing bandages and I'll be fine," she replied dismissively.

The man produced a compact medical kit containing what Zataldra requested and handed it to her.

Zataldra observed Iya praying for the souls of the dead Khanorian warriors to find peace in the afterlife. *You are much like Mother.* This second act of betrayal from Iya didn't sit well with Zataldra. But alongside her ire was a sadness—a yearning to restore the closeness they once had, which was now slowly dissolving. It hurt to think about them becoming estranged.

The remainder of the troopers gathered around Zataldra. She instructed them to attend to the fallen while she made her way to the citadel for the emergency council session, a sense of purpose guiding her every stride.

◆ ◆ ◆

In the galley of the *Nightingale*, Randy pulled Jarius into a hug. The rest of Vanguard Alpha was there too, relaxing after a successful mission, while the ship traveled hyperspace back to Eden with the other task force ships. All of the team, having docked their Shells, stood or sat in their sleeves.

After Randy stepped back from him, Jarius asked, "How's Jazzlyn been?"

Randy replied, "Worried sick. But she'll be okay as soon as she hears you're safe. How are you holding up, after all those days in that hellhole?"

"I . . . I don't know. Zataldra put me under her control. She forced me to . . . kill Cruz. Being used as someone else's playtoy was just—" His hands clenched and unclenched, an amalgam of anger, sorrow, and revulsion all roiling inside him. "I've been having nightmares about what I did. I—"

Randy said, "Get some rest. You deserve it, Sir."

"No need for formalities, so none of that 'Sir' stuff. I know what rank and file says, but for you, man, it's always just 'Jarius.' And though you're not an NCO or officer yet, you're just as much of a leader as a Guardian who holds those ranks. That's why I followed your lead and joined the Coalition during the civil war."

Randy nodded, and Jarius proceeded to his assigned cabin to bathe, finally take a shave, and sleep.

Randy didn't know if he had killed Zataldra. Only time would tell. But whether she was dead or alive, the Collective possessed the mind-control weapon. Inevitably, Dafulton would launch another attack on Eden soil using it. A Shell's Oracle could manufacture a blocker, so that meant Guardians were protected. The question was, Could the CDF develop a transmittable countersignal to protect civilians?

Arturo approached Randy, a canned drink in hand. "Is your pal gonna be okay?"

"Not entirely sure," was the best response Randy could give. He looked over at Akane, who had been sitting alone in silence, dark circles under her eyes. She got up from her table, head bowed, and left through the doors. She was clearly distraught from being Zataldra's killer marionette. "I'm gonna go get some rest," Randy said to Arturo before walking out of the galley. Whatever aftereffects there were to mind control, psychological or otherwise, he'd stand by Jarius and Akane's side until they beat it.

◆ ◆ ◆

Akane mumbled in her sleep. A nightmare had her head thrashing against her pillow. "No!" she screamed, opening her eyes. Gasping for breath, heart sinking, she brought herself upright. The grotesque images of her nightmare were still fresh. She saw herself under Zataldra's control, using a plasma saber to chop Randy into a bloody, limbless corpse.

"Damn it," Akane muttered, massaging her temples in a futile attempt to deflate a growing migraine.

She brushed her bangs out of her eyes before getting out of bed and going to the bathroom in her cabin. After activating the faucet, she slammed her eyes shut and splashed cold water on her face. "Leave me alone," she said to the images from the nightmare that refused to vacate her mind.

When she opened her eyes, Randy's reflection—head and shoulders—was in the mirror instead of her. Suddenly, a steel knife carved a path across his jugular. A fountain of blood gushed. He fell, revealing his killer standing behind him. That killer was none other than Akane herself, complexion cadaver-white, hand holding the murder weapon.

Akane lurched back from the mirror, terrified, and blinked the hallucination out of existence. In its place was her real— bloodshot-eyed—reflection staring back at her. Her mind was playing tricks on her. Zataldra had subjected her to a traumatic experience, making her another victim of this war—just like the citizens in Terence Plaza.

She swallowed hard and took a deep breath, wondering how many more nightmares were in store for her and what other symptoms might upend the quality of her life.

Being alone with her thoughts wasn't helping. She needed someone to talk to and confide in, so she left the bathroom and grabbed some blankets and a pillow from one of the wall lockers before leaving her cabin.

Restive and clutching the blankets and pillow in her arms, Akane lingered outside the door of Randy's cabin. Having had enough of pacing, she shed her hesitation and pressed the talk button on the control module beside the door. "Randy, it's Akane. Can I come in?"

Randy's voice came from the module's voicebox. "Yeah, sure."

The door chirped open, and Akane went inside.

Randy sat up on the side of his bed. Akane's troubled expression worried him. "Hey, what's up?"

"Just couldn't stay asleep. I had a nightmare about what happened, about my mind being enslaved by Zataldra's mind-control weapon. In it, I killed you. That mind-control shit is something I never want to experience again. I don't want *anyone* to go through that shit." Akane paused, looking at the floor sheepishly. "I don't wanna be alone right now." She lifted her chin. "Could I just stay in here with you until we get back to Eden? That's why I brought the blankets. I'll sleep on the floor."

Randy gestured for her to join him on the bed. "Drop the blankets and sit with me for a minute."

Akane dumped the blankets onto the floor and settled beside Randy.

He said, "I can't imagine what it was like being under that weapon's spell, but I do know something about dealing with mental anguish. After all, I killed Guardians during the Battle of the Quad—even if they were few in number—and also killed Coalition rebels who were my enemy at the time. And then there's the trauma I experienced from being Linked with my mother as she was killed. Stay as long as you want. I'll offer whatever comfort

I can."

Akane rested a hand on his thigh in appreciation, and a pleasant tingle rippled over his flesh. "Thank you," she said. She placed her hand back on the bed. "And . . . hey, I just wanna make sure that I clear any bad air between us." Randy locked his eyes on her sincere gaze. "I get how upset I was when you disclosed RISE's location to DFI, but the Brotherhood took down RISE, not you.

"Sure, I felt betrayed back then. That said, I don't hold any grudge against you. While visiting my family during my sabbatical, my dad said something to me: 'If you live in the past, you'll never be able to step into the future.' I don't wanna live in the past. RISE is behind me now, a closed chapter, and . . . I'm a hundred percent cool with you. I . . . just wanted to make sure that you knew that, 'cause time is finite, and we can't take it for granted. You never know when you might see your last sunrise, have your final kiss, or make love for the last time." Akane felt better, no longer pestered by words she'd needed to say.

Randy flattened a hand to her back. "Thanks for letting me know that." His fingers wandered as if they had a mind of their own, beginning a slow, gentle stroke down Akane's spine. He remembered the feel of her bare flesh.

Akane scooted closer to Randy, her thigh now flush against his. "And in the spirit of confession, I also wanted to say that the night we spent together in my bed was one of the most radical nights of my life. There, now all of that is out in the open."

Randy's eyes flitted away from Akane. He fished for something to say. Finally, he settled on, "That night meant a lot to me too."

Akane's voice, tinged with seduction, flowed into Randy's ears. "After the hell I endured today,"—her lips brushed against his, teasing a kiss—"I wouldn't mind experiencing that night again."

Their implants flooded their minds with the physical sensations from their previous coupling.

At seventeen, Akane snuck away from home and had sex for the first time with a man. He was handsome and in his twenties, like Randy. She could barely recall his name now, but that night had felt revelatory then. She'd had other partners since, men and women whose touch had left impressions, which included her bestie Simone. But Randy was different from them all. The chemistry and connection they shared the night they had sex had rewritten her definition of intimacy.

She ached for the hard contours of his muscles against her body.

Desire stampeded over Randy's self-restraint. He lowered Akane onto the mattress, his firm grip steadying her shoulders.

Fireworks went off inside her as she reached up, winding her fingers through his wavy hair, and brought his lips within kissing distance of hers.

Randy struggled against the pull of sexual attraction. After an underwhelming night in bed with his girlfriend, making love to Akane right here and now was tempting.

He pulled down on her sleeve's zipper, exposing a slit of flesh. The invitation had been made. All he had to do was take it. But Akane wasn't the woman he truly wanted. He wanted the woman who had stood by him and brought sanity to his life during one of its lowest points—the days after his mother was killed. He wanted the woman with whom he'd survived BCT and graduated as a Guardian.

"We can't do this," Randy said, his and Akane's breaths tickling each other's faces. He fortified his will and withdrew from her waiting lips, slamming the door on his urges.

Akane straightened, pulling her zipper back up to her neck. "Right, because of the girlfriend."

"Yeah, because of Stacie. I'm not going to ruin my relationship again. Short-term satisfaction for long-term loss isn't something I'm interested in. And like you said, we can't live in the past; I want to focus on the future." And he was sure, more than ever, that that future was with Stacie. "You'll always be significant to me, Akane, but we can only have a platonic relationship. What we had before is over."

"I respect that," Akane said. A pocket of emotion wedged itself chest-deep—heartbreak. She got up, arranged her makeshift bedroll on the floor, and tucked herself into the blankets. "Thank you again for letting me stay."

Randy lay back down. "No problem. You're my teammate and my friend, and no matter what, I'll be there for you in whatever way you need to help you overcome this ordeal. I promise."

"That means a lot to me."

They both closed their eyes. As Akane fell asleep, a mantra repeated in her mind: *Let there be no more nightmares.*

◆ ◆ ◆

Standing at the lectern on the tribunal in the council chamber, Zataldra addressed her colleagues. Korguzel faced the lectern, his hands clasped behind his back, as he presided over the session.

Zataldra said, "Yesterday, Grand Elder Varanz fell victim to an attack orchestrated by our old enemy, the humans. And today, the Commonwealth Defense Force unexpectedly assaulted my compound." She projected holographic footage of the battle from her wristlet. "Men of honor lost their lives," she said.

The council members cringed at the gruesome images of dead bodies—some of them headless, missing limbs, or charred to a crisp.

A skeptical councilman said from the grandstands, "And what

did you and the Collective do to provoke this attack?"

"We did nothing!" Zataldra proclaimed. Her voice carried a false conviction that was top-notch. In reality, the CDF had assaulted her compound to rescue men the Collective had abducted. "Just like no provocation led to the attack that killed Grand Elder Varanz."

Another councilman said, "I do not believe that we should call into question Councilwoman Gor'Ronn's integrity. The humans are our enemy, not her."

"Thank you, Councilman Al'Gerow," Zataldra replied. "I had been preparing my troopers to aid the Collective in eradicating the humans once and for all, before they could someday resurface. Unfortunately, my fears came to fruition: The humans struck first.

"Their motivations remain a mystery. Our planet had already provided them with valuable resources as part of their compensation from the Sorin. Perhaps they crave those resources again; I don't know. But we must act quickly before they attempt to repeat the destruction they caused in Khanoria years back."

A councilman rose from his seat. "My fellow councilpersons, I was present when Grand Elder Varanz was shot and killed. I saw the murderer's cold, lifeless eyes as he pulled the trigger—the eyes of a devil. I also personally knew the staff worker who lost their life. Until yesterday, I scoffed at Councilwoman Gor'Ronn's suggestion that we join forces with this Collective. But now, I believe retaliation is in order, before the humans strike again. And if they do, who is next to die: women, children, your husbands and wives?"

A councilwoman's voice echoed from the grandstands, "I second Councilman Bor'Roth. We cannot let the humans bring violence and destruction to our nation again." The woman was livid, the scar on her face and the ones beneath her garment serving as reminders of the beatings and sexual abuse she had endured.

Zataldra said, "Then we need to be proactive. Reevaluate the war vote. Extend the support of the National Protection Force to the Collective. We have a plan—a weapon that will guarantee victory. If the National Protection Force and Collective work together, we cannot lose."

Korguzel panned his gaze around the chamber. "If no one has words for Councilwoman Gor'Ronn, then let the re-vote begin."

Sweat beaded down Zataldra's forehead from nervousness. This was her final push to gain the council's support.

One by one, hands went up until every council member had voted in favor of war.

Korguzel declared, "It is settled. The National Protection Force will unite with the Collective."

Zataldra couldn't contain her smile of triumph. She had succeeded. The assault on the humans' homeworld would now have the full support of Khanoria's military. Dafulton's plan could move forward, and Zataldra hoped that Geznan and Navexira could be rescued.

CHAPTER SIX

Jarius Ford knew it wasn't every day a man received a personal audience with the Chief of the Commonwealth. Clean-cut in his dress uniform, lieutenant bars gleaming, he entered the Chief's office with the EPA who was escorting him.

The EPA announced, "Madam Chief, Lieutenant Ambassador Jarius Ford."

Oviereya stood up from behind her desk. "Thank you. You're dismissed." The EPA took his leave. Oviereya motioned for Jarius to join her in the seating area. "Come sit." She settled onto one of the couches, and Jarius sat across from her. "I remember seeing you inside the Parliament Building during the Battle of the Quad, as a Coalition rebel. And I know that you're close with Randal Scott and Stacie Spencer, having served together in the same unit at the time of the civil war. It's a pleasure to formally make your acquaintance."

"The pleasure is truly mine, Madam Chief," Jarius replied.

"How has your recovery from mind control been going?"

"I've been dealing with symptoms similar to everyone else's. I'm visiting medical today to see what the next steps to healing are."

"Good. Care for some tea?"

"I'd love some."

Oviereya lifted the self-warming kettle from the coffee table and poured tea into two mugs. "Enjoy," she said, setting the kettle down.

Jarius tilted his mug to his lips. "It's good."

"Yes, a taste of home." Oviereya took a measured sip. "When I was a colonist, I picked the very leaves this tea is made from."

A thrill ran down Jarius' spine. He felt as if he were in the presence of greatness. Oviereya's life journey was iconic. She transitioned from a field worker on Satellite One to a well-compensated domestic aide for the Spencer family, then ascended to the Parliament before ultimately becoming Chief. And Jarius admired her for her fierceness in championing equality.

He said, "My fiancée and I have gone out with Randy and Stacie a few times, and Stacie always speaks highly of you. And rightfully so. You hold such significant distinctions. You're the first immigrant member of Parliament, *and* you're the first immigrant Chief, even though you assumed the Chief Executiveship by default. Above all, you symbolize hope.

"During the civil war, I followed Randy's lead and joined the Coalition because I saw colonists being oppressed, witnessed living conditions that demanded change, and faced threats from my superiors for merely wondering if colonists' grievances had some legitimacy behind them. You're the first Chief who's taken major action to help the colonies, reform our military institutions and government, and remove the malfeasants and wastrels. Now, I can personally say, 'Thank you.' I really hope you win the election so progress can continue."

Jarius' words touched Oviereya's heart. "Thank you as well, Lieutenant. I commend you for your service to the Ambassador

Corps. I understand that fostering peaceful relations with interplanetary nations and rectifying the wrongs of our Defense Force is no simple task."

"No, but I'm up for the challenge."

Oviereya drank some more of her tea. "I requested this meeting with you not only to express my gratitude for your service in person but also to get your direct input on the Collective, specifically this Khanorian contingent."

Jarius said, "Normally, I'd debrief with my chain of command, and the information would then be elevated up to you."

"Consider me unconventional," Oviereya replied. "I cannot afford to wait for bureaucratic processes. The Commonwealth is in danger."

Jarius nodded gravely. He recounted the nightmarish experience of having his mind violated and controlled, describing how he had been forced to kill Cruz. He told Oviereya about Zataldra, his friendship with Iya, and the citadel attack orchestrated by Dafulton to gain support from the Khanorian council.

Oviereya said, "You've interacted with Zataldra several times; do you truly believe she's incapable of seeing humanity in a . . . more favorable light?"

Jarius took a moment to ponder before responding. "It'd be ideal if she could, Madam Chief. She'd be able to help us counter her weapon, and she could tell the Khanorian council the truth for us—that it was Dafulton who planned the citadel attack, not the CDF. Unfortunately, I don't think there's any way to win her over. But I stand ready as an ambassador to uphold any peace initiatives and liaise if ordered to."

Oviereya let out a sigh. "The Commonwealth now teeters on the brink of war, a war involving good people conned by a ruse—

mere pawns in some self-serving scheme by Dafulton. It seems the CDF has no choice but to harm these pawns to get to the puppet master himself."

"Seems that way." Trained in nonverbal communication analysis as a lieutenant ambassador, Jarius deciphered subtle cues in Oviereya's body language that would have gone unnoticed to an untrained eye. "You're way beyond nervous about protecting the Commonwealth's people, aren't you?"

Oviereya thought she had been doing well in disguising her emotions. "The Ambassador Officer Candidate School trained you well."

"I understand. We're facing a weapon that we don't know how to defend against. But implementing the Defense Protocols was a great first move."

"Well, the Commonwealth won't fall on my watch," Oviereya asserted.

Jarius was just as nervous about the upcoming attack as Oviereya. This time, the Commonwealth wasn't facing a Coalition-style invasion. The Coalition's mission was to commandeer the Parliament Building without taking any Guardians' lives, though that proved to be impossible, as expected. The purpose of this enemy invasion was to destroy the entire human race. Jarius supposed all he and Oviereya, or anyone for that matter, could do was hope for the best while preparing for the worst.

Oviereya got up, bringing the discussion to a close. Jarius followed suit, and they shook hands with mutual respect for each other.

Oviereya said, "Thank you for the briefing, and once again, I appreciate your service."

"And thank you for all you've done, Madam Chief." Jarius

departed.

◆ ◆ ◆

Randy sat at his desk in his condo, reading an email that Stacie left him earlier this morning. It had been late last night when Vanguard Alpha returned to Eden from rescuing Jarius, so he had waited until morning to let Stacie know he was back. He wanted to meet her for lunch today, but she hadn't been answering his calls. By the looks of the email, she'd probably be superbusy all day.

> **> From: Stacie Spencer <**
>
> Today is the day, Randy. The Elite are gathering on Babylon Island for their convocation. My team and I are going to put an end to them once and for all. I wanted to keep you updated so you're not left in the dark. Don't worry about me. I'll be okay.

After reading the email, Randy tried calling Stacie on his wristcom. She didn't answer. For the third time today, he got redirected to her voicemail.

Since he couldn't express himself directly, he left a message, finally giving release to the sentiments accumulating in his chest. "Stace, you asked me that if Akane came back into my life, would I have any feelings for her. Well, she's back. We had some alone time during Vanguard Alpha's recent deployment, but nothing happened between us. Nothing. Because she and I are simply friends and comrades. She's not the woman I want to build a future with; you're that woman." He paused, shaping his next words. "There's no doubt in my mind about us. I'm not conflicted.

"I love you with all my heart, and . . . I want you to marry me, Stace. I'm not saying this just to placate you or make you trust me more; this is me baring my soul to you. I want us to be together forever. I hope this message conveys the depth of my devotion to you. I love you. Call me back when you get this message." Randy ended the call. He trusted his words would reassure Stacie of his love for her.

♦ ♦ ♦

While Stacie was briefing her team at her mansion, her wristcom beeped, yanking her eyes to the blinking notification light. Randy's message had been received. She'd have time to listen to it later. Right now, she was focused on her mission: destroying the Elite. That's why she had been ignoring his calls this morning. If he had read the email she left him earlier, he'd intuit that.

She concentrated her attention on the holographic touch-responsive projection displaying schematics of the Elite's gathering place—the building they called the Spire. She had obtained the schematics from her parents' archives. Using a stylus, she sketched out her plan for approaching and infiltrating the Spire.

"Alright, team, let's take a quick break." She sank onto one of the cushioned seats around the dainty coffee table that the projector sat on. "Feel free to grab some food from the kitchen."

Jason, Eli, and DeShaun got up. They climbed the three steps of the conversation pit and went to the kitchen.

Stacie leaned forward and tapped the projector. The Spire morphed into a rendering of the Elite—men and women of privilege and power who were entwined within Eden's criminal underworld. To the Commonwealth Government, they claimed innocence and ignorance about their parents' illicit activities, but Stacie knew it was all lies. And their promises of reforming their families' criminal enterprises were nothing but a facade. If everything went as planned, the Elite's lives would end tonight, and then the foundations of their criminal enterprises would eventually crumble.

Jason walked back into the sunroom from the kitchen. "Do you mind if I join you?" he asked, holding a styrofoam cup of coffee.

"Not at all," Stacie replied.

Jason sat beside her and took a sip of his coffee. The rich flavor titillated his taste buds. "These six, do you know them like you knew Damien?" he asked, looking at the images of the Elite.

Stacie crossed her legs. "I wasn't particularly chummy with the other Elite children. It's not like all of us hung out every week. We might have seen each other . . . two or three times a year at most, at family gatherings, but that's about it. Damien and I only got close because of our . . . flings. Besides him, I'd say I'm most acquainted with"—she pointed to the freckle-faced, ginger-haired woman in the upper right corner—"her, Charlotte."

Jason asked, "Why's that?" He sipped some more of his coffee.

Stacie explained, "There's a . . . preparatory school that the Elite owned. Maybe they still own it; I don't know. The super-rich enroll their seventeen-year-olds in it to prepare them for college, adulthood, and success in life. Girls learn *'lady's etiquette,'* balance and coordination, and a bunch of other nonsense. Since the Elite owned it, they used its two-month program for their kids.

"The campus is expansive, so I didn't run into any of the other Elite children who were there at the same time—except for Charlotte. We coincidentally stayed on the same floor."

"So did you two become gal pals?"

Stacie chuckled. She and Charlotte, friends? Yeah, right. "Hardly. Let's just say we didn't get along."

"I see." Jason downed the last of his coffee and set the empty cup on the table.

Stacie remembered some of Charlotte's mean-spirited antics at

Elite family get-togethers. There was the time Charlotte had intentionally spilled her drink on Stacie's dress, leaving a stain. One time, Charlotte had convinced the other Elite kids to hide Stacie's shoes, forcing her to wander the yard barefoot. When they both attended the special preparatory school at seventeen, Charlotte would do things like "accidentally" bump into Stacie in the crowded hallways, causing Stacie to drop her books. Or she'd sit just close enough in the library to mutter snide remarks under her breath, making it hard for Stacie to concentrate on her studies.

Jason remarked, "So all the family heads trained their children in their criminal ways. But you found out about your parents' activities from the files given to you by your boyfriend. Why weren't your parents prepping you to take over their organization?"

Stacie said, "Well, the family heads indoctrinated their children at varying ages, some in their early or late teens. My parents probably planned on indoctrinating me when I reached my early twenties because I was a bit more of a . . . problem child compared to the other Elite children.

"The older I got, the more rebellious I became toward my parents and their overbearing nature. When I started at Cadwell Institute of Higher Learning, I fully embraced the party scene and engaged in . . . some deviant behavior. I was determined to unshackle my life from the path my parents wanted me to go down —being the family business's successor. I didn't know the business entailed illegal activities; I just . . . wanted to do something different, at least for a while.

"I was hardly shaping up to be the golden child my parents envisioned. They were probably at a loss on how to handle me, as they realized that their criminal philosophies would be rejected if they tried imposing them on me.

"They must have thought I needed more grooming before fully

introducing me to how Spencer Enterprises generated our wealth, instilling their philosophies in me more gradually. But it wouldn't have worked anyway. I give credit to Oviereya Amaechi for that. Her teachings during my childhood, unseen by my parents, instilled values in me that would've clashed with their philosophies."

"Yeah, you're not the type to conform to what someone else wants you to be," Jason commented.

Stacie scoffed at the thought of her bending to someone's will. "Definitely not."

Jason changed the subject. "Do you ever miss . . . being a Guardian? I mean, it was a big part of forging your own path in life, from what I understand."

Stacie shrugged nonchalantly. "Sometimes I miss it. What made you ask?"

"I've been thinking about the impact I had as a Guardian, and with another attack on Eden lurking, I find it difficult to just sit on the sidelines and be a helpless civilian." The fiery glint in Jason's eyes made it clear that being unable to contribute to defense efforts was frustrating him. Jason's days as a Guardian were over, yet the oath to protect the Commonwealth continued to resonate in his heart.

Stacie enlisted in the CDF to defy stereotypes associated with her privileged upbringing and chart her own course in life. Though patriotism wasn't her sole motivator, she comprehended its significance. "I understand patriotism. I understand wanting to defend the Commonwealth from its enemies. But we *are* defending it, by putting an end to the Elite. Now, let's get back to work."

Switching gears, Stacie called Eli and DeShaun back from break. After wrapping up the strategy session, she dismissed the team. They were to regroup at sundown to head to Babylon Island.

◆ ◆ ◆

As the time approached for Stacie to leave, her eyes rose to the portraits lining the foyer. Nearby, housekeeping golems dusted and tidied the common room.

She homed in on a portrait of her eight-year-old self standing between her parents, holding their hands. The irony wasn't lost on her; the daughter meant to carry on their legacy would ultimately be the downfall of the criminal conglomerate they had brought into existence, and would be the catalyst for sanitizing Spencer Enterprises. She was going to redeem her family name.

While gazing at the portrait, good memories of Patrick and Darlene caused a lump to swell in her throat. At the same time, their disgraceful actions, along with her recollections of Darlene's cruelty, riled up her anger. *Mom, Dad, if only you had—* She wondered what could have been if her parents had made different choices. But dwelling on an alternate future was pointless. They had died as criminals, and redemption was never on their agenda. Spencer Enterprises was founded on illegal practices, and her parents were determined to stay on that path. There was nothing Stacie could've done or said to make them turn over a new leaf.

She left the foyer, determined to make amends for her parents' crimes by eradicating the Elite tonight—their creation. She walked down the hallway and stopped at the door to her mother's private study. It was a place she had been avoiding. This time, curiosity got the better of her, and she entered the room. Its opulence mirrored the rest of the mansion, from the expensive carpet to the luxurious curtains draping the floor-to-ceiling windows.

Her gaze fell on the tablet sitting on the desk, and she instantly recognized it as her mother's diary. She had often seen her mother with this tablet. Fighting her apprehension, she powered it on and scrolled through the dates of entries. There was an entry from the day Arman Reza's kill squads murdered her parents. Intrigued, she opened the entry and read her mother's last words:

> *When my daughter finally reestablished our mother-daughter Link after years, she somehow sent all her pent-up anger and resentment rushing into my mind. She may have been recalcitrant toward me, but I never realized she harbored such emotions to that extent. I have never been one to apologize for my actions, but I now see that I have been too harsh on my daughter. If only I had been a tad more gentle, perhaps she would have been more receptive to me during her teenage years and early womanhood, and not disregarded so much of my counsel. I apologize for everything I have done to hurt her, all the punishments I inflicted on her for disobeying me.*

Darlene's apology was a pleasant surprise for Stacie. The lump returned to her throat, and she read on:

> *In spite of what I have done, I still hope that my daughter will listen to my advice and leave the Commonwealth Defense Force. Common careers are beneath us, the Elite.*

A spark of annoyance rinsed away any stirrings of heartbreak, and the lump in Stacie's throat went away. Her mother *never* would've understood why she wanted to be more than just the heir to the family business.

Stacie's eyes skimmed the rest of the text:

What is the benefit of her being a Guardian? What does she hope to achieve by prolonging her education in leading Spencer Enterprises, the organization that will be hers after her father and I are no longer here?

Stacie sighed heavily and shut off the tablet. One benefit of her time as a Guardian was learning to be strong and resilient. She had also adopted principles that went against those of her parents'. And being a Guardian had equipped her with the skills needed to take down the Elite tonight. And that was exactly what she intended to do.

While she was exiting the study, she heard her wristcom ring. Randy was trying to reach her, but she rejected the call. *Sorry, babe, I have to get going.*

◆ ◆ ◆

Couldn't Stacie at least text him to let him know she was okay? Patience was truly a virtue. To distract himself as he awaited his guest's arrival, Randy watched a live interview playing out between Oviereya and a prominent commentator. The commentator lashed out at her with acerbic remarks, saying that the recent attack in Terence Plaza was a consequence of her being lax in defense.

He claimed that cutting back military funding to finance the Colony Restoration Initiative reflected poor judgment. He accused Oviereya of establishing the Truth Commission solely to vilify and weaken the CDF by calling their tactics too harsh, given her pacifist nature. Additionally, with Oviereya advocating for postponement of the election because of another Collective attack being on the way, the commentator accused her of attempting to salvage what he considered to be a failed administration.

To Randy, the conservative, pro-war commentariat was more

united than ever in casting aspersions on Oviereya's character, but it was election season.

The door buzzer interrupted his thoughts. His guest had arrived. He shut off the TV, rose from his armchair, and opened the door. Akane stood waiting, a duffle bag slung over her shoulder and a paper bag of takeout in her hand.

She had asked if she could join him for the evening and perhaps spend the night, still grappling with the trauma from mind control. Akane needed someone to be there for her, and Randy was the person she was closest to on Eden. When she had stayed in his cabin on the *Nightingale*, he had promised to support her in any way he could, and he wasn't about to break that promise.

"Akane, please come in," Randy said.

"Thanks for everything."

Randy gave Akane a hug, and she took off her shoes, leaving them at the door.

Akane and Randy sat at the kitchen table. The large window beside them offered a view of the city below—cafés, coffeehouses, retail boutiques, trendy apartments, and office buildings. The streets were alive with people carrying on the best they could. They were trying to maintain a sense of normalcy in the face of imminent peril and enjoy the days leading up to the announced Eden-wide lockdown.

Staring out the window, Akane wondered what was going through their minds. A lot of them were obviously shaken up, an impression she had gleaned from the nervous energy of the people she'd passed while on her way to Randy's condo. She hoped that the Air & Space Corps' defensive barriers would be strong enough to repel the hostile incursion, sparing both Eden and Satellite One's inhabitants from losing loved ones—and sparing them from the horror she had suffered under mind control.

She retrieved two wrapped sandwiches from the take-out bag and passed one to Randy.

"Has your . . . condition gotten better?" Randy asked, unwrapping his food.

"Nah, still having nightmares, and . . . I've experienced two panic attacks."

Randy's every muscle was on edge. Panic attacks could mean the symptoms were worsening. "What did the med unit at headquarters advise?"

"Glad you asked. Dealing with the psychological impact of mind control is uncharted territory. I was told victims may require tailored approaches to recovery. The med unit assigned me a therapist named Vanessa Berwick. I told her all about these nightmares where I'm hurting you, like I'm still stuck under Zataldra's control in them. After chatting with Vanessa, she suggested Linked Trauma-focused Cognitive Therapy, with your involvement, since these nightmares always feature you."

Randy would contribute to Akane's recovery in any way possible. "So what's my part in this . . . Linked Trauma-focused Cognitive Therapy?"

Akane said, "Well, first, the three of us—you, me, and Vanessa—would establish a Tri-Link. We'd enter a dreamscape together, where I'd conjure up the memory of me being controlled. Not exactly thrilled about reliving that moment, but Vanessa swears it's necessary." Just thinking about the powerlessness she felt in her own body was unnerving. "You'll be by my side, though, helping me rewire my thoughts and confront the memory head-on. Cognitive restructuring is what it's called, I think. I'm not entirely clear on *all* the details of this procedure, but that's the gist of it."

She paused and shrugged casually before continuing. "No promises this'll work wonders, but Vanessa thinks it's our best shot at kicking this trauma of mine to the curb. And yeah, it's possible to conduct the therapy without you, but your presence just might bump up its success rate, if it works at all. So, you on board?"

Randy said, "Do you even have to ask? Of course I am."

"Awesome."

They ate and chatted, distracting Akane from her hardships. Randy was happy to see Akane smile and laugh. There was a gleam in her eyes that hadn't been there when she came in, as a result of his company.

Akane pondered what it would be like to share meals with Randy and enjoy each other's company forever. What-ifs racked her mind. She imagined how their romantic relationship could've blossomed under different circumstances. Her parents wanted her to find a life partner, and for her, it was difficult for anyone to measure up to Randal Scott. He remained one of her heroes. He was someone she deeply respected and admired. He was an inspiration to her. And his decision not to report her as an extremist to DFI allowed her to remain a Guardian. She owed him.

Randy checked his wristcom for the hundredth time. No message from Stacie yet. His foot incessantly drummed the floor. The anxiousness on his face was plain to see.

Akane, chewing on her sandwich, asked, "What's wrong?"

"Nothing." His composure marred by Stacie's lack of communication, Randy adjusted his posture—again.

Akane swallowed her food. She saw past Randy's facade. "Like I said before, you are a *terrible* liar. You've been there for me; let me be there for you. It's only fair. Reciprocation, y'know." She gently rested a hand on top of his.

Randy wrenched his hand from underneath hers. "Not much you can really do. It's just that I've been trying to reach Stacie all day, but she hasn't responded to any of my calls or texts. I understand she's busy with something important and probably doesn't want to get distracted, but it would've been nice to *at least* get a message back by now. On top of that, our relationship has gotten . . . rocky."

Hearing that made Akane feel as if there was a possibility that she and Randy could have another chance. Her dream scenario would be that Randy and Stacie's relationship just naturally crumbled apart, allowing her to step in and fill the void. It was wishful thinking, maybe foolish thinking—an abstract idea that clung to the back of her mind. She knew she needed to let go of the past, but emotions didn't always follow logic. The heart had a way of feeling what it wanted to.

"I'm sure you two will figure things out," she said.

"Yeah." Randy sighed. He hoped Stacie would accept his marriage proposal. She had become unsure about their future together. He thought maybe his proposal would reconcile their issues.

He stood up from the table, crumpling his wrapper in his hand. "Are you staying overnight?"

"Gave it some thought; I think that'd be for the best," Akane replied.

"Fine by me. When you're ready to call it a night, you can take my bed. I don't mind sleeping on the couch."

"No, this is your place. I'll crash on the couch."

"You sure?"

"Positive."

"Okay."

Akane yawned. "Bedtime for me."

"Make yourself at home."

Akane spread out the blankets from her duffle bag on the

couch. "Thanks a bunch, Randy."

Randy took one last glance at Akane. During dinner, her voice and body language intimated the feelings she still had for him. He believed they'd eventually fizzle out. Before closing his bedroom door, he said to her, "Wake me if you need anything."

"Thanks," she said. After the door clicked shut, she tucked herself into her makeshift bed. If she had nightmares tonight, Randy would be there to comfort her. That put her at ease as she closed her eyes.

◆ ◆ ◆

Stacie and her team were en route to Babylon Island in a transformable all-terrain vehicle in submersible mode. She clasped her seat's armrests, the knuckles beneath her gloves turning white —a sign of underlying stress. There were only thirty minutes remaining until the team reached their destination. If everything unfolded as planned, they would infiltrate the Spire, kill the Elite, and leave the island without a trace, becoming anonymous heroes for the Commonwealth.

While Stacie had fears of potential casualties among her team during the mission, they had been well aware of the risks since the day she recruited them to fight her private, albeit illegal, war against the Elite. To them, the reward—pay that surpassed what they were making as Guardians—was more than worth the danger.

As the vehicle neared the island's shores, Stacie's mind fixated on the unsettling truths in the corruption files. Human trafficking networks, money laundering schemes, and bribery of influential figures were just a few of the Elite's crimes.

Even if her parents hadn't partaken in the worst of the crimes, their knowledge, tacit approval, and support of them placed them on par with the family heads who did. Tonight marked the end of it all.

Seated next to Stacie, Jason said, "You've been quiet. Everything okay?"

"Just getting my head in the game." The Elite dead meant Stacie would no longer have to balance running Spencer Enterprises with trying to thwart their operations. It would be a weight off her shoulders. "Hey, Jason."

"Yeah?" he responded.

"After tonight, the team is yours if you want it," Stacie said. "I'll officially sign over leadership to you. Even though I wouldn't be in the field anymore, I'd still provide financial support for the team. Whatever you need, I would take care of it."

The bounty-hunter registration had served as a cover for Stacie's true intentions: gathering weapons and resources for her fight against the Elite. She imagined that after tonight, the team could concentrate on fulfilling its intended purpose, which was hunting down criminals harming the Commonwealth.

"I'd like that," Jason said. He had been unsure if Stacie would disband the team or keep it in service once the Elite were eliminated. By leading his own team of bounty chasers, he could continue serving the Commonwealth without being a Guardian.

Stacie glanced down at her wristcom. She still hadn't listened to Randy's message, wanting to keep her mind zeroed in on the mission. She promised herself she'd listen to it once she got back home. Maybe she'd even call Randy; he deserved that much, after she had ignored his attempts to reach her.

Upon reaching the western coast of Babylon Island, the vehicle surfaced and transitioned from submersible to land mode. The drooping fronds of reedy trees scraped against its roof as it parked along the shore.

Despite her close calls with death, Stacie preferred the

177

excitement of the field over the tedium of corporate meetings in stuffy boardrooms. Right now, a thrill was coursing through her solar plexus. Not something she ever felt in the dull world of mergers, acquisitions, cutting deals, and cinching contracts. She was proud of everything she had accomplished with Spencer Enterprises, though—despite the work being boring and mundane.

"Let's move out," she said.

The team put on their smart-helmets, filed out of the door into the windless night, and circled to the rear of the vehicle.

Their helmets' night-vision visors allowed them to see well in the dark.

Stacie tapped her electronic bracer, and the flip-up cargo hatch clicked open. Inside, there were hoverbikes for each team member. After they retrieved the bikes, Stacie tapped her bracer again to close the hatch and send the vehicle back into the water in submersible mode. The team then mounted the bikes and proceeded inland, following a discreet route to the Spire that took them past empty guest bungalows.

The island's quietude suggested the team's intel was spot on: The Elite didn't have any patrons or guests on the island tonight—consumers of their slave-provider services and other illegal commodities. This worked to the team's advantage. It meant fewer eyes to avoid.

Once they were close to the Spire, they dismounted their bikes. They had made it unimpeded as planned.

Looking at the Spire, Stacie recalled her last argument with her mother—the last time she had seen either parent alive. Darlene's apology, written in her diary, came to Stacie's mind. Sealing away the memory of their last argument, she got down to business. "Alright, everyone, stealth mode."

The team touched the button on their belt clips. A ripple

shimmered outwards. Their forms were now blended into the environment by their individual camouflage fields. The mission was on.

Navigating the trees, Stacie coordinated the team's approach with subtle hand gestures. They crested an incline with military tact and reached the treeline, grass padding their steps.

Under the spotlights beaming down from the Spire's roof, five uniformed guards patrolled the manicured lawns.

Stacie arced her hand, ordering the team to spread out. They melted into the shadows, using the trees and foliage for concealment. Their camouflage fields immediately adjusted.

One guard broke off from the others. "Smoke break. I'll catch up." His companions vanished around the corner of the building.

Mindful of the sign prohibiting smoking near the building, he walked to the treeline to make sure that he was at a suitable distance. Stacie skulked up behind him with calculated steps. Just as he reached into his pocket for a cigarette, she jammed a plasma knife into his back and covered his mouth to muffle his cries. Carefully, she guided his squat body to the ground and dragged it into the foliage.

One of the four remaining guards doubled back. "Hey, Dutton, quick question. Did you happen to . . . Where the hell did he go?" Inklings of foul play set off an alarm in his mind. "Hey, Dean, Liam, Tobias, something ain't right! Dutton's missing!" The other three guards hurried to him and cautiously approached the treeline, handguns drawn.

Jason, Eli, and DeShaun emerged from behind the trees. By the time the guards caught a hint of their camouflaged forms in the darkness, silenced gunshots were piercing their skulls.

After the team deactivated their camouflage fields, Stacie said, "Get the bodies out of sight and let's get inside. There may be more guards on perimeter security duty." As her team dragged the guards' bodies into the foliage, she said, "Jason, the backpack."

Jason unslung the black gear bag on his back and gave it to Stacie. He then went back to helping with the bodies, while maintaining situational awareness.

Stacie took a lightweight drone from the backpack. She punched in a command on her bracer, launching the drone into the air. It transmitted a signal that would temporarily disrupt the Spire's alarm system and video surveillance long enough for the team to reach the Elite's dining suite and take them out.

Once the bodies were well-hidden, the team hustled to the loading dock. Eli plugged a cable from his bracer into the dock door's access panel to hack the lock. Everyone else kept vigil for security patrols.

"Got it," Eli said after the lock clicked. His skills at hacking never failed.

The door slid into the wall, and as a cohesive unit, the team entered the loading dock. Moving stealthily past boxy containers and orange safety cones, they reached the service elevator from the schematics. It would take them to the first-floor vestibule.

They rode the elevator one floor up. The receptionist at the front desk jumped from her chair when she heard the elevator doors ding open. No one was supposed to be here tonight except the Elite.

The team emerged into the lavish setting of red carpet and neatly arranged furniture.

When the receptionist whirled around, the color drained from her face. She saw the team's darkly clad figures rushing forward threateningly. Trepidation anchored the receptionist's feet.

Before she could scream, Jason fired a stun dart into her arm from his handgun. Her body numbed, and she fell to the floor, knocking over her chair on the way down.

The team scanned the vestibule with eagle-eyed precision, sweeping their rifles in all directions. The couches surrounding coffee tables and the seats at the bar were empty; no other personnel besides the receptionist was here. All was quiet for the Elite's private gathering.

Jason became suspicious. For him, things seemed to be going too well. Perhaps it was just his military mind always expecting the worst.

"This way," Stacie said, leading her team to the vestibule's elevator bank. Her heart raced with the anticipation of finally getting rid of the Elite.

The team made it to the elevators unchallenged and stepped into one. They ascended to the fifth floor and bolted across the lengthy catwalk, their hands gripping their weapons tightly as they braced themselves.

Stacie thought, *This will all be over soon.* A feeling of fulfillment had already sunk in. Her mission's end was now just moments away.

The team burst through the doors of the dining suite, weapons rattling. Shockingly, no one was there.

"What the hell?" Stacie said.

Jason organized his thoughts, contemplating what went wrong. "Our intel was solid. I don't get it. How could—"

From an unseen intercom, antagonizing laughter from multiple voices flowed into the suite, cutting Jason's words short. The team's heads whipped upward, their eyes searching a blank ceiling.

Jason surmised that the Elite must have had a secret escape route inside the suite, something not on the schematics. The Elite were supposed to be trapped in here. The only way off this floor was supposed to be the elevators on the other side of the catwalk.

A man's jaunty-sounding voice said, "Kudos. You came close; I'll give you that. A little too close for our comfort."

A new voice chimed in—a woman's. "Yes, quite impressive. However, your intrusion into the Spire didn't go undetected as you had intended. Tsk, tsk." Stacie recognized the voice as Charlotte's. "If anything remains of your corpses, we *might* be able to identify you—the ones who nearly succeeded in assassinating us."

If anything remains of our corpses? Stacie's body tensed. "Go! Fucking run!" she shouted.

The team had only seconds to spare and barely made it out the doors before the entire suite exploded into a fireball.

Feeling the heat on her back while running, Stacie summoned the team's vehicle using her bracer. A 3-D rendering showed the vehicle waking up from its hibernation cycle. It transitioned from submersible to land to aircraft mode. It was now headed to the Spire to retrieve the team and would pick up the hoverbikes on the way.

Once the team was midway down the catwalk, four armed guards shot out from the elevators and opened fire. The team's rifles blazed in retaliation. One of Stacie's bullets pierced a guard's throat. Then she stitched his body with more bullets. The other three guards were cut down by chestfuls of hot lead from Jason, Eli, and DeShaun.

Stepping over the bloody aftermath of their handiwork, everyone entered the center elevator.

Jason mashed the button for the first floor. His breaths were labored, and sweat trickled down his forehead as he steadied his nerves.

Stacie seethed. *How the hell did this op become a clusterfuck? Everything was on point.* Coming to terms with failure, she ground her teeth and swore silently. Anger razed her from the inside out.

The elevator decelerated to a stop at the first floor.

Jason said, "Expect hostiles, everyone. Rifles up."

The doors chimed open.

Jason, Eli, and DeShaun dashed out of the elevator, with Stacie close behind them. The team peeled away from each other, dodging incoming bullets from more guards and taking cover behind the vestibule's furnishings and pillars. They answered the guards' onslaught with streams of rifle fire.

Jason, behind a pillar, took aim at an advancing guard and put a bullet in his eye. He fired a second shot that instantly dropped another guard. Then he lobbed a grenade. The explosion jettisoned five guards off their feet and sent their scorched bodies slamming into couches and tables.

Stacie aligned her rifle's iron sights and fired two rounds, picking off two guards with head shots. Then she crouched behind an overturned table.

On her bracer, she checked the ETA for the vehicle. The holographic display showed it was seconds away. *Should be here right about . . . now!* The vehicle barreled through the wall, breaking apart wood, masonry, and plaster.

Stacie inputted a command on her bracer, and the vehicle's AI targeting system spun up the gun turrets, unloading a volley of bullets that mowed down the last of the guards and trashed the place.

The scent of expended rounds hung in the air.

"Everyone, inside!" Stacie ordered.

The team double-timed it into the vehicle and seated themselves, buckling up. Wheels squealed in reverse, pulverizing debris from the demolished wall beneath them. Outside, the vehicle converted into its aerial configuration and elevated into the sky, aft jets glowing.

Stacie pressed a button on her bracer, and the drone used to disrupt the Spire's alarm system and video surveillance detonated, leaving no trace of Spencer Enterprises.

She unsnapped her helmet's clasps, flung the helmet against the wall, and broke into a furious cry.

Jason, sitting next to her with his helmet off, said, "Relax. I know things didn't go our way, but at least we made it out of there alive." Crestfallen, Stacie flattened a palm to her forehead. Jason gently rocked her shoulder. "Hey, you good?"

Stacie muttered, "Yeah . . . don't worry, I'll manage." There was a bitter taste in her mouth. Failing was eating her up.

"Okay," Jason said, "but don't keep shit bottled up inside. Talk to your boyfriend or something. If you want, talk to me."

"Thanks."

◆ ◆ ◆

Her shower finished, Stacie sat on a sofa with her second glass of wine, recuperating her mind and body. Exhaustion clung to her like the silk of her robe. She had been waiting for the chance to end the Elite. Finally, she got it, and it ended up being a fiasco. Failure was intolerable to her. Always a high performer, she expected success in everything she attempted.

A disquieting sense of mediocrity disturbed her relaxation. She graduated as a Guardian largely because of Randy's support. Her parents' fortune and enterprise weren't a product of her own efforts. Jason Mansford's endorsement was why she achieved the rank of sergeant in the CDF. Her first mission to sabotage Damien Sykes' trafficking operation resulted in her team's capture by Jacob Kilbourne and their subsequent rescue by Vanguard Alpha. And though today's assault on the Spire wasn't about self-validation, it served as a stark reminder of her perceived inadequacies.

The echoes of her detractors at Cadwell tortured her mind again:

"Why bother getting a degree? Just mooch off your parents."

"We're not like Spencer. We have to work to get ahead in life."

"Spencer's a pampered princess. She's not made to handle life's rigors."

She quaffed all her wine in a single gulp. Her failure to eliminate the Elite, combined with the voices of her Cadwell detractors, was alienating her beyond measure. If only she could switch off her mind.

She hurled her wineglass across the room. It shattered into shards as it crashed into the hardwood floor.

"Damn it!" She pounded the sofa's arm with a drop of her clenched fist. "Fuck!"

She palmed her face, doing her best to stop the self-loathing. She told herself to get it the fuck together. Throwing helmets and wineglasses wouldn't help. Reverting to old smoking habits wouldn't help either. She expelled a huff of air and sank her head into the sofa's cushioned backrest. Then she remembered Randy's message. Grabbing her wristcom from the side table, she accessed her voicemail.

From the wristcom came Randy's sincere confession. "Stace, you asked me that if Akane came back into my life, would I have any feelings for her. Well, she's back." Stacie's face cringed. "We had some alone time during Vanguard Alpha's recent deployment, but nothing happened between us. Nothing. Because she and I are simply friends and comrades. She's not the woman I want to build a future with; you're that woman." Butterflies fluttering in her stomach, Stacie felt her pulse quicken. "There's no doubt in my mind about us. I'm not conflicted. I love you with all my heart, and . . . I want you to marry me, Stace." Stacie's heart was beating at a thousand times per minute, her doubts about Randy's commitment fading. "I'm not saying this just to placate you or make you trust me more; this is me baring my soul to you. I want us to be together forever." Emotions flooded Stacie's mind. "I hope this message conveys the depth of my devotion to you. I love you. Call me back when you get this message."

Stacie remembered facing BCT's challenges with Randy, the graduation banquet, teaming up with him to stop Akane and Jay from killing Damien, and their recent outings with Jarius and Jazzlyn. *Randy, I love you too,* she thought.

◆ ◆ ◆

Randy sped toward Stacie's mansion in his sports cruiser. She had texted him, asking him to come over as soon as possible with little explanation. She said she'd tell him more when he arrived.

It was the first communication he had received from her since returning to Eden from Vanguard Alpha's mission. He wondered what could be so pressing for her to reach out in the dead of night. Despite how late it was, he wasn't going to tell her to wait until morning. He had quickly thrown on a T-shirt and jeans and rushed out the door, careful not to rouse Akane from her sleep.

The security system of Stacie's mansion recognized his vehicle and permitted it to land on the carport. He shut off the engine, hopped out of the cruiser, and hurried down the walkway to the veranda.

He pressed the comm button on the door. "Stace, it's me.

Open up." Stacie opened the door and let him inside. After closing it, she remained mysteriously silent. "So what's—" Before Randy could finish, Stacie's tongue was in his mouth, and her fingers were in his hair. He guessed that the message he had left her had been enough to ease her worries about his commitment.

Wrapping his arms around her, he drew her tighter against him. The feel of their pressed-together bodies tingled his flesh.

Pausing to catch their breath, they stood apart, chests heaving.

At a loss for words, Randy asked, "Does this mean everything . . . is . . . you know . . . back on track between us?"

Stacie's smile suggested they were only just getting started. Her teeth playfully nipped Randy's lower lip, a promise of what was to come. "Yeah, everything's good," she said softly. She took his hand, guiding him toward the staircase. "C'mon."

They scaled the stairs, pausing for brief, frantic kisses until they reached the bedroom.

Randy parted Stacie's robe and ran his hands over her sculpted body.

Stacie slipped out of the silk and stood clad in designer lingerie. She tugged Randy's shirt up over his muscled abdomen until he yanked it off and tossed it aside. Eagerly, she unfastened his belt. Then he unzipped and stripped down to his briefs.

Locked in a tangle of limbs, they crashed onto the bed.

As Stacie lay against the sheets, Randy blazed a trail of kisses up her midriff. When their faces met, she gripped the back of his head and pulled his mouth to hers. The electricity between them pulsed.

Randy unclasped Stacie's bra—freeing her perfect breasts—and closed his mouth around her nipples, devouring them until they stiffened.

The pad of his thumb glided over one of the sensitive peaks.

Stacie released a breathy sound. Enthralled by her beauty, Randy continued toying with her her nipples, drinking in her every facial expression.

She answered in kind, sliding a hand into his briefs to fondle his cock. Her firm, demanding grip made his hips jerk against her palm.

Desire burned hotter between them as they gave and received in a frenzy of touching and kissing.

Dying to satiate his urges, Randy wrestled Stacie's panties off and shed his briefs. Stroke after stroke, he drove into her, his body grinding against hers.

Stacie's hips lurched repeatedly, colliding with his relentless rhythm.

Caught in the heat of the moment, he went on a quick pounding spree between her legs, each uncontrolled thrust hammering moans out of her.

Enraptured in the throes of orgasm, Stacie completely came undone.

Just when Randy's release was about to explode, he dislodged his cock, spurting jets of cum over Stacie's stomach. Any longer and he would've come inside her.

Shallow gasps escaped Stacie as the afterglow of their coupling washed over her.

The two lovers spent the rest of the night entwined in passion, looking forward to a promising future—if they survived the enemy invasion.

CHAPTER SEVEN

Stacie awoke to morning birdsong outside her window and sat up from beneath the bedcovers, naked. Randy was still in slumber beside her.

She instructed the mansion's virtual assistant to depolarize the windows. Sunlight warmed her bare skin as she closed her eyes in rumination, her mind dissecting last night's failed mission step by step. She was trying to understand where her plan had gone wrong.

Randy stirred. He registered the contemplative expression on her face and sat up. "What's bothering you?" he drawled.

Stacie surrendered a sigh and got her dilemma off her chest. "It's . . . It's just that lately I've been feeling . . . unaccomplished."

"Why?"

Stacie rubbed her eyes, shaking off the morning grogginess. "I've faced many detractors in my life, particularly at Cadwell and even during Basic. They all assumed I had a charmed life and acted as if my parents could simply snap their fingers to get me anything I wanted. It's not like they were totally wrong, but as a woman who embraced individuality, I didn't want my entire life handed to me by my parents.

"My detractors' doubts, criticisms, and scathing remarks motivated me. I wanted to prove to them, and myself, that I could become an accomplished woman without relying on my parents or anyone else. Just me."

Randy said, "Yeah, you told me all this before, and?"

"Well, I've been wondering, Just what have I accomplished?" Inquisitiveness creased Randy's brow. Stacie elaborated, saying, "I survived BCT and earned the accolade of Warrior Extraordinaire, but it was your helping hand that carried me through my trials. Before ending my service as a Guardian, Jason Mansford recommended my promotion to sergeant, something I really wasn't qualified for. My parents' organization was something I inherited. And my mission to take out the Elite yesterday just . . . went to shit. So, have I . . . accomplished much of anything?"

Randy did the best he could to not bust out laughing, but he couldn't help himself.

Stacie grabbed a pillow and playfully bopped him on the back with it. "Hey, *buster*, this isn't a laughing matter."

Randy held in the rest of his laughter. "Stace, during BCT, I may have provided a shoulder for you to lean on, but it was *your* perseverance and grit that got you through its physical demands. That refusal to give up on yourself—that inner strength—didn't have a damn thing to do with me. And without you, DFI's investigation into Damien's operations may not have turned up anything. Plus, you took your parents' criminal enterprise and transformed it into an entity that helps people. In my eyes, those are all major accomplishments."

A weight lifted from Stacie's chest. "Yeah, well, that is true." Randy had a knack for offering a grounded perspective.

"And don't forget, we're just twenty-two damn years old.

You've got plenty of time to achieve whatever you want."

A bright smile blossomed across Stacie's face. "Thank you, Randy."

Randy relaxed his head against his pillow and tucked his hands behind his head. "Hey, it's what I'm here for." Looking up at Stacie, he said, "Can I ask you something?"

"Yeah, sure. Shoot away."

"You told me your mom was strict, always trying to mold you into the ideal 'Spencer woman.' Straight A's, impeccable behavior, never falling short at anything. From what I understand, at no point was failure acceptable to her. Ever since I've known you, you've had a drive to be the best. Is it something that genuinely comes naturally to you, or are you still just trying to live up to your mom's standards?"

Stacie said, "Yeah, Mom definitely set the bar high for me. If I failed to meet her expectations, there were *severe* consequences. That pressure pushed me to be the best at everything I did, no matter what. But as I encountered criticism and envy from people who saw me as just a spoiled, entitled rich brat, proving them wrong became this whole obsession. I *had* to be number one at everything, just to spite them.

"Now, when things don't go as planned or blow up in my face, I can't help but beat myself up. Any time I think I could've done better, feelings of inadequacy bubble up inside. It's hard to break that cycle."

Randy said, "This drive to be the best started because of outside pressure, and then it just . . . stuck with you?"

"Yep."

"I totally get it. Just remember, setbacks don't define you. You're not a failure or inadequate because things don't go perfectly according to plan. Do you think you're now over this whole 'existential crisis' you were having?"

Stacie crossed her arms defensively. "It *wasn't* a crisis."

"Sure looked like it."

Stacie asked in a more lighthearted tone, "Oh, by the way, when can I expect my engagement ring?"

Randy's countenance stiffened. "We need to survive what's coming first."

His foreboding tone hardened Stacie's features. "Another attack from the Collective, you mean. Like the one in Terence Plaza?"

"Yeah, you can bet it's coming soon." Randy had never felt this unnerved in all his time as a Guardian. The lives of every human being were at stake. "We're most likely facing a full-scale assault on the Commonwealth. And right now, we don't have a way to defend against the Collective's mind-control weapon. We also don't know exactly when this assault will happen. It could take place any day now."

"Do you think the Collective is strong enough to breach the Defense Protocols?"

"Don't know."

"Would the Interplanetary Union back us up?"

"That's another uncertainty."

Stacie planted a soothing grip on Randy's shoulder. "Hey, let's do something fun tonight. It'll take our minds off our troubles."

"Agreed. How about we do dinner with Jazzlyn and Jarius tonight?"

Stacie's eyebrows soared. "Jarius is back?"

Now that Jarius had been rescued, the Executive Press Office was going to release a statement today about what had happened to the ambassador delegation. Randy felt it was now okay to level with Stacie. He told her the Collective had imprisoned Jarius and that Vanguard Alpha's recent ad hoc mission was to rescue him. He also shared that Jarius had been under mind control and had been forced to kill a comrade.

Stacie said, "I'm glad he wasn't severely injured, physically, anyway."

"So, you're good with the four of us going out for dinner tonight?"

"Yeah, that would be nice." Stacie hesitated before telling Randy the last thing he wanted to hear right now. "Hey, even though yesterday's operation flopped, I'm not giving up on going after the Elite. They have to be stopped. Maybe not today, maybe not tomorrow, but eventually."

Randy was worried that Stacie's mission to topple the Elite might put her in danger. He believed she should leave them alone, as Oviereya had advised. Criminal empires were always going to exist. Evil wasn't going anywhere. But Randy knew that once Stacie set her mind on something, you'd have to kill her to stop her. "I don't agree with you going after them, but do what you feel you have to."

"Thanks."

An idea struck Randy. "Maybe you've been going about taking them down the wrong way."

"What do you suggest?"

"Instead of trying to attack them directly, why not hit them where it hurts the most—their finances?" He added, "Just a thought."

Stacie considered the idea and acknowledged its potential. "Interesting. You might be onto something there."

Randy took a reflective pause. Since Stacie had shared that she was going to continue pursuing the Elite, he felt it was only fair to be open and honest with her as well. "I want to be upfront with you about something. Akane's having a tough time. I've made a commitment to be there for her. After losing RISE—her family here on Eden—she went to Satellite One to visit her parents and heal. But now she's back on Eden, dealing with the aftereffects of being mind-controlled during Jarius' rescue in Khanoria. She doesn't have much of a support system here, so I've decided to step up and be as much of a support system as I can.

"After my mom died, having you around was a lifesaver. I want to be that person for Akane. Is that okay with you?" Randy didn't necessarily feel that he needed Stacie's approval to support Akane, but he wanted to address any potential objections she may have. Just as Stacie wouldn't give up pursuing the Elite, he was determined not to abandon Akane.

Stacie, understanding Randy's compassionate nature, calmly replied, "That's fine with me. I've got no problem with you helping a friend." She didn't want to keep being paranoid about Randy's friendship with Akane.

Randy then added, "And . . . just so you know, she spent last night at my place. She needed some company."

A trace of agitation crept into Stacie's voice. "Ah, okay. It was just . . . a onetime thing to check in, right?"

"No, not exactly. She's been having nightmares and panic attacks. She's staying over again tonight. I don't know how many more times there will be."

"Whoa, hold the phone!" Stacie's brows dipped, and she mashed her lips into a stern line. *One step forward, two steps back,* she thought. "So you two are *cohabitating* now?" Her facial expression revealed how she felt, and it wasn't positive. She didn't have a problem with Randy providing emotional support to Akane, but overnight stays were a bit suspect to her, even if it was a temporary arrangement.

"I've only got eyes for you, Stace. Akane's not some . . . side chick. There's nothing for you to worry about."

Stacie knew she needed to trust Randy if their relationship was going to work. "Alright, take care of your friend."

"Thanks for being cool about it."

◆ ◆ ◆

Planet Khanoria

The Sanctum of Farewell, an octagonal outdoor terrace, was the setting for Varanz's funeral. At its center was a multi-floor shrine housing the tombs of Khanoria's prominent leaders, from Elders to Sorins. Hundreds of Khanorians had gathered on the terrace. Many more were watching the funeral from their homes via a live feed from aerial drones.

The eulogist said, "We have assembled to honor and commemorate the life of Grand Elder Drosaide Varanz, a man who will forever be revered in history and whose legacy will transcend time. He brought healing and enlightenment to those in need, and he worked tirelessly to improve Khanorian society.

"Although he may no longer be with us in physical form, his spirit will always remain in our hearts and minds. We will never forget all he did for Khanoria."

Zataldra stood shoulder to shoulder with the others who had come to honor the Grand Elder. She wore a white ceremonial vestment that had interlacing designs and tiny gold bells that hung along its hem. The garment was reserved for the most important occasions—such as today—and had once belonged to her mother.

Inside the shrine was her father's sepulcher. This sacred mausoleum wasn't just a resting place for the dead; it was also a historical archive chronicling the lives of the esteemed public servants interred within it. Interactive displays, like windows into the past, showcased their achievements.

Zataldra had never ventured inside to see her father's tribute; neither had Iya. Someday, she'd find the strength to face his memory.

Thinking about Varanz, she plastered a hand to her chest as if to stop her heart from breaking. Varanz had helped her and Iya cope after their mother and father's deaths. His absence would be felt for a long time.

She recapped what had happened at the citadel over and over again in her mind, each iteration deepening her anger over her weapon's use in facilitating the attack.

Iya, standing three bodies down from Zataldra, also mourned the loss of Varanz and wore a similar garment. Since the CDF's assault on Zataldra's compound, they hadn't spoken. The rift between them was widening amidst disagreements over Jarius and Zataldra's collaborations with Dafulton, the man who had shattered their world by taking Varanz away.

Stealing occasional glances at Zataldra, Iya intuited that she was just as bothered as she was about their relationship turning ice-cold.

As the eulogist continued, the crowd buzzed with curious susurrations at the unexpected appearance of Khanoria's new ally, Dafulton.

Zataldra stilled. *What are you doing here?*

Iya, blinking away the sting in her eyes from crying, reared back at Dafulton's arrival. Her forehead creased. She fought to suppress the impulse to lash out at him verbally. Nerves practically vibrating, she repeated a calming prayer from the Korahh'Havaell in her mind. It did little to help.

Dafulton strode to the front of the gathering, not in a showy or boastful manner, but quietly and respectfully. Understanding the importance of gaining the trust of these people, the CDF's victims, he wanted to ensure that he made himself visible. Attending the funeral of a Grand Elder was a calculated move to maintain his facade of compassion toward them. Skilled in deceit and manipulation, he was wielding these tools to his advantage, as he always did.

The eulogist finished.

A woman sobbed in her hands. Varanz had obviously touched her life.

Varanz's three adult children—two sons and one daughter—embraced each other.

The eulogist's two aides each seized a handle of the casket and began rolling it indoors. The attendees chatted, sharing memories of Varanz. The attendees ranged from ordinary citizens to council members and Grand Elders.

Dafulton engaged in cordial conversations with some of them. Having studied up on Khanorian language, he knew enough to communicate well. He promised the attendees retribution against humanity for their suffering and Varanz's death.

Conflicting emotions warred within Zataldra—reproach toward Dafulton clashing with her disgust for humanity. Dafulton bore responsibility for the tragedy at the citadel, but, convinced by his assurances that the deaths were accidental and needing the National Protection Force's help, Zataldra upheld the narrative that blamed the tragedy solely on humanity. Her parents had always taught her that lying was wrong, though.

The Sanctum of Farewell started to clear out, attendees descending one of the stairways flanking the terrace's eight sides. They moved forward with their day, fighting sorrow's choke hold on them.

Iya left, whizzing past Zataldra without so much as a "hello." Zataldra wanted to speak to her sister, but the expression on Iya's face made it clear that now wasn't the time for any attempts at reconciliation.

Zataldra approached Dafulton, and he greeted her with faux warmness. "Ah, there you are," he said. "I was hoping to see you."

"What are you doing here?" Zataldra's tone came off confrontational, as today's funeral was caused by Dafulton's cockeyed plan.

"I came to offer my condolences to these people. The loss of Varanz was not intentional, and it grieves me deeply," Dafulton explained, his performance nearly perfect.

Zataldra stared daggers at Dafulton, wordlessly chastising him for using her weapon without her consent. "I'll see you later today to discuss war preparations with the Protection Force's generals."

"Of course, I will be there," Dafulton replied. His true intentions lay hidden beneath the layers of charm and false sincerity. Once the National Protection Force fulfilled its purpose in his grand scheme, he'd have no further need for them—or Zataldra.

◆ ◆ ◆

National Protection Force HQ

Zataldra stood on the exterior deck of National Protection Force HQ. Looking out at the airfield, she watched ships from Dafulton's fleet touch down. This hour marked the commencement of war preparations. Still depressed from Varanz's funeral, Zataldra had to push herself to carry on with her responsibilities as the new intermediary between the council, Minister of War, and Dafulton. But what she wanted was to escape to a peaceful retreat to cope, such as the glades that Jud'Zarr had often taken her to for leisurely strolls.

The sliding doors opened, and Dafulton appeared. "I was told you were here. You must be pleased that revenge is finally within your reach."

Zataldra faced him, offering a silent nod. Pivoting back toward the ships, she saw a throng of his thugs and cutthroats disembark.

At Varanz's funeral, Dafulton had sensed that Zataldra hadn't gotten over his use of her weapon to attack the citadel. But he didn't care about her *feelings*; he had successfully enlisted the Khanorian Protection Force for his agenda. Varanz's life was a necessary sacrifice, a means to an end goal. And as long as Zataldra continued to fall in line, she could be upset with him all she wanted.

Zataldra turned to Dafulton. "Who are these men of yours, the ones who do not belong to any of the contingents?" She eyed them with suspicion, finding them to be quite enigmatic.

Dafulton said, "Why do you ask now, after all this time?"

Zataldra replied, "The warmen of the Protection Force need assurance that whoever fights alongside them is trustworthy. I am the designated liaison for both the Minister of War and the council; it's my duty to convey their reservations to you. What measures do you take to ensure these men are of noble character?"

Dafulton's eyes narrowed. *Now she develops a backbone.* Their working relationship had already taken a downturn, and now there was Zataldra's new inquisitive attitude to bear. He hoped it wouldn't be too much of an inconvenience to him. He hid his irritation behind a level tone. "Rest assured, these men can be trusted. Their goal is the same as yours and mine—to end the humans." He delivered his lie expertly. In actuality, he and his men were only interested in plunder.

Zataldra accepted his response for the time being. "Very well. Also, the council has formulated rules of engagement you and your men must adhere to, if you want to keep their support. Now that the Protection Force has united with the Collective, this war is a collaborative effort. You will not be able to make unilateral decisions."

"I understand the concept of alliances, where power is shared among all involved and decisions are made collectively," Dafulton shot back, his words slapping Zataldra in the face. He preferred having complete control of the Eden invasion. He was a dictator and despised sharing power with anyone. "What are these *rules of engagement?*"

Zataldra explained, "The council does want retribution, but if they can spare the lives of warmen and prevent unnecessary hardship for their families, they will. Their intent is to give the humans an opportunity to surrender before resorting to a full-scale assault."

"*Ha*, we all know the humans will never kneel to us," Dafulton said.

"In that case, we follow the existing plan: striking the defense infrastructure identified by Geznan and Navexira's reconnaissance missions." Zataldra thought about her friends. According to Randy, they were unharmed, but what was a human's word to her? "The one caveat to the plan is that if the humans decide to surrender during our attack, all forces are to halt combat and seize control of their lands. Personally, I would prefer to exterminate the humans regardless of surrender."

Although Dafulton desired revenge for his previous defeat, wiping humanity off the galactic map wasn't his endgame. It was a calculated ploy to rally those scarred by the CDF's brutality. His true aspiration was to occupy Satellite One, humanity's resource hub. "And what about the spoils once we are victorious?" he asked eagerly, perhaps too eagerly for Zataldra's liking.

Her glare, a silent reprimand, cut the air. "You seem remarkably concerned about these so-called spoils."

"There is nothing wrong with reaping the rewards of your hard work," Dafulton argued.

"The so-called spoils will be used for reparations. After victory is achieved, we can address what you believe you're entitled to. Right now, the primary focus is war preparations."

Curious, Dafulton asked, "And if the humans surrender, what does the council plan to do with them?"

"The council will discuss that when the time comes," Zataldra replied.

"Any other rules of engagement?"

"No, there aren't."

"And how goes the mass production of the mind-control emitters?"

"Right on track."

A substantial quantity of emitters was rolling off the assembly lines of the Protection Force's manufacturing facilities. Once affixed to vessels and hooked into their power supply, the emitters would have their signal range extended far and wide for the invasion.

Dafulton said, "And are you not concerned about the CDF's combat suits being able to disrupt the signal? What if the humans conceive a way to shield their race altogether?"

"Admittedly, the humans' soldiers being protected is a wrinkle in our plans. But how likely is it that the humans will mass-produce some kind of helmet blocker for their *entire* population before we arrive? Take into account time, resources, distribution . . . It seems improbable. And developing a wearable signal blocker is one thing, crafting a counter-signal is quite another. That's something they never have and never will achieve."

"Confident, are you?"

"I am."

The doors slid open. Korguzel stepped onto the deck. "Councilwoman Gor'Ronn, may I have a moment of your time?"

Zataldra said to Dafulton, "I will see you at the war prep meeting."

Dafulton passed by Korguzel and left.

"Korguzel, what is it?" asked Zataldra.

"I heard that you will be joining the invasion force. Knowing you ever since you were a child, I wanted to speak with you before you deploy. I can only imagine how Varanz's death has affected you. How have you been managing?"

"Varanz is missed, but—"—Zataldra grappled with the hidden truth—"he, like my father, fell victim to the humans' aggression. The alliance forged between the Collective and the Protection Force guarantees they will answer for their crimes."

Korguzel moved closer. "The humans returning after so long is shocking." He reflected on the lives lost during the CDF's Khanorian Campaign and then added, "Have you spoken to Iya recently?"

Zataldra shook her head, a flicker of something unreadable crossing her features. "No, I haven't," she said, her voice whispery and tight.

"Not even during the funeral rites?"

"Iya and I have been . . . at odds lately."

"I see," Korguzel said. Hearing that there was a rift between the Gor'Ronn sisters was disheartening. In this crucible of war and grief, their bond was more important than ever.

"Is there something wrong with Iya?" Zataldra asked, feigning apathy. But her subtle nonverbal cues were telling.

"She seems troubled. Perhaps she has misgivings about Khanoria plunging headlong into a war with the humans. I certainly have mine. Losing any of our brave warmen is saddening."

"This invasion is the only path to ending the human threat," Zataldra declared. "I'll speak with Iya before I leave with the invasion force. Farewell, Korguzel." She exited the deck, leaving Korguzel alone.

Korguzel silently watched the sky. A metallic swarm of Collective ships descended onto the airfield. The empty feeling in his stomach was a reaction to his disdain for conflict. He headed back inside.

♦ ♦ ♦

In his flagship's cavernous hangar, Dafulton surveyed the array of mining equipment and vehicles acquired for his audacious plan—some obtained through theft, purchase, or other shady methods.

Cruk, who'd been one of Dafulton's trusted lieutenants since his regime's rule over planet Doagwar, approached him. He briefed Dafulton on the preparations, informing him that the final batch of mining equipment was on its way.

As Cruk updated him, Dafulton mentally choreographed his plan. He calculated that five days of mining on Satellite One should be sufficient to extract enough of its treasures without drawing suspicion from his new allies, the Khanorian Protection Force. It was a tight timeline, but he'd have to make it work. His plan was: While the Protection Force waged their battle to invade Eden—the primary target—he and the bulk of the Collective would set their sights on capturing Satellite One—the secondary target.

Because Eden was humanity's motherworld, he expected the CDF to prioritize its defense. Better to have the Protection Force suffer the most casualties. However, he envisioned his forces would still have quite a fight in store for them to get to Satellite One. And of course, to maintain appearances and not raise doubts among the Protection Force's generals, he planned to allocate a minute amount of his forces to aid in the Eden invasion.

He scoffed at the Khanorians' mission to annihilate all of humanity. He had effectively sold them the promise of victory.

Having clashed with the CDF in the past, he foresaw heavy losses for the Khanorian forces. However, he acknowledged that there was a slim chance of success due to Zataldra's weapon. Indifferent to whether or not the Protection Force achieved victory, he viewed them merely as a distraction to keep the CDF occupied while he pursued his own agenda. Without their assistance, seizing Satellite One would be highly difficult, if not impossible. Fortunately, orchestrating an attack on the citadel had swayed the council in his favor.

In Dafulton's assessment, there were two potential scenarios. One: the Protection Force triumphed. Two: the Protection Force was repelled, but with his forces entrenched on Satellite One, they'd fall back there, using the colonies as a strategic foothold for continuing their attacks on Eden, thereby complicating the war beyond initial expectations.

Regardless of which scenario unfolded—victory or retreat—Dafulton stood poised to amass the resources needed to make him quite a wealthy man. The risks and routine of piracy were becoming wearisome, but the riches obtained from Satellite One would allow him to scale back his reliance on such practices.

By manipulating Zataldra, recruiting the CDF's victims, and obtaining the council's support, Dafulton had successfully set the stage for his Satellite One heist.

Cruk finished his report.

Dafulton nodded in acknowledgment. It was time for him to convene with the Protection Force's generals and Zataldra to talk strategy.

◆ ◆ ◆

In the empty chapel of the Tograh'Dirkot, Iya sat on her heels, hands clasped together. Her deteriorating relationship with Zataldra and the council's declaration of war disturbed her mind. Prayer, a familiar comfort within these walls, offered no solace this time.

The first and second waves of the Khanorian Revolution left a trail of death in Khanoria. Night after night, Iya had been afraid that Zataldra would fall in battle. She didn't want a repeat of that emotional roller coaster. This time, Zataldra might get killed. She had equal concern for her human friend, Jarius. *What can I do?* she asked the Gods.

Humans weren't entirely bad people. Her sister's weapon might be the end of them. It wasn't right. Her inner voice spoke to her. A plan crystallized in her mind. She'd gather as much data as possible on her sister's weapon and deliver it to the humans on their homeworld. By doing this, she'd be choosing sides, wouldn't she? Giving the humans a better fighting chance seemed like the right thing to do. Overall, she wished the war would be called off. She didn't want her sister or Jarius to be killed. She didn't want any Khanorian or human to die.

Iya pepped herself up, thinking, *I must do this. I must help the humans.* The voyage to Eden terrified her. Would the humans trust a Khanorian? Would they attack her on sight? No matter the reception, she had to try to help them. Inaction was unthinkable.

The data she needed was at Zataldra's mountain compound. She'd go there immediately.

She stood up and whispered a thank you to the Gods for guiding her toward a course of action, no matter how fraught it was.

◆ ◆ ◆

At a rooftop restaurant in Cornerstone City, Randy and Stacie came up to Jarius and Jazzlyn. It was a reunion long overdue after the Collective had taken Jarius captive. Stacie, dazzling in a backless gold diamanté minidress, hugged Jazzlyn, who was looking dynamite in a navy-blue cocktail dress. Randy and Jarius, both dressed to impress in sharp tuxedos, shook hands.

The four settled around a table under the moonlight.

"Great to see you, Stacie," Jarius said warmly.

"Likewise. I'm so glad you're okay."

Jarius took a reflective pause. "Man, feels like a lifetime ago when you, me, and Randy were at Basic together and then flown off to Colony Four to fight in that damned civil war."

"Yeah, it does," Stacie concurred. "It's amazing how far we've all come since then. You're a lieutenant, I'm running Spencer Enterprises, Randy's about to be promoted to sergeant, and—"— she announced cheerfully—"we're all getting married."

Jazzlyn gaped at the news. "Oh my gosh, you and Randy are tying the knot?"

Stacie bobbed her head. "Yes."

"I remember you . . . had some doubts about that before."

"I did, but not anymore." As long as Randy and Akane's interactions stayed platonic.

"That's great to hear."

Stacie got up and excused herself to the ladies' room. "Be right back."

Jazzlyn got up to join her.

Randy noticed a hint of angst in Jarius' demeanor. "Something up, buddy?"

Jarius replied, "Jazzlyn received orders to deploy to the Air & Space Corps' geostationary blockade. I'm afraid for her life."

Akane's words came to Randy's mind: *You never know when you might see your last sunrise, have your final kiss, or make love for the last time.*

Randy said, "There's no guarantee what the future holds. We can't control the outcome of this war or the number of casualties. All the more reason to make the most of the time we have."

Jarius nodded and picked up his wineglass. "A toast to the future, to marriage, and the many years to come."

Randy lifted his glass and clinked it against Jarius'.

The inevitability of wartime casualties—Guardians and maybe civilians too—burdened Jarius. His thoughts turned to those already killed by the Collective, Guardians on Mission Worlds and those, like Cruz and Arlo, who Zataldra used as test subjects. Suddenly, he was thrust back into the moment when he ended Cruz's life. The memory struck him with such visceral force that his hand spasmed and dropped the glass.

Wine sloshed over his tux as the glass hit the rooftop, bursting into shards.

The instinct to help nearly jolted Randy from his chair. "Jarius, hey, are you okay?" Jarius relaxed and steadied his shaking hand. "Hey, you good?"

"I . . . Yeah, I'm good now."

A cleaning golem wheeled over to the table and sucked up the shards with its vacuum hose. It then asked Jarius if he wanted another glass of wine. He said he did, and the golem whirred away.

"What happened?" Randy asked. "You spaced out for a second."

"Yeah. I started thinking about Cruz and then—"

Randy said sympathetically, "I understand what you're dealing with. Akane's having a hard time too. Have your symptoms worsened at all?" He thought about Akane's condition and then asked, "Any hallucinations or anything like that?"

Jarius shook his head slightly. "No, but . . . the nightmares are relentless. And sometimes, like now, I just . . . lock up, tremors wracking my body whenever I think about what I did, what Zataldra *made* me do."

"What did the med unit you visited say?"

"They suggested—"

"Linked Trauma-focused Cognitive Therapy," Randy finished for him.

"Yeah."

Jarius' symptoms didn't seem as severe as Akane's, but they were still affecting his well-being, which made Randy's stomach tighten. "Don't worry, we'll get through this together. All four of us—you, me, Stacie, and Jazzlyn."

"Thanks, man."

Stacie and Jazzlyn rejoined the table. Everyone continued the evening with good food and delightful conversation. But war's unknowns cast a shadow over their enjoyment. In the back of their minds, they were wondering if this would be the last time all four of them were together. Would their group be incomplete after the war?

◆ ◆ ◆

Iya traversed the corridors of Zataldra's main facility, footsteps echoing in the unnerving quiet. The entire compound was deserted. All of Zataldra's remaining troopers—now mobilizing for the invasion—were at Protection Force headquarters. There wasn't even a skeleton crew left behind.

She crossed the scarred corridor where Akane and Randy had fought Zataldra, passing under the gaping hole in the ceiling. When she arrived at Zataldra's science lab, the automatic doors parted. She stepped inside, and the ceiling lights flicked on. The large humming computer console was where the data was stored.

Running her fingers across the keypad, Iya booted up the console. Screens came alive. She navigated multiple menus until she found what she came for—blueprints for the mind-control weapon.

She plugged a memory stick into the import slot and tapped the copy-data key. A green status bar appeared, tracking the download's progress. While waiting, she deleted all camera footage of her inside the facility, just in case someone, namely Zataldra, viewed the surveillance recordings.

Her wristlet chirped, a voice transmission coming in. She accepted it. "Iya, where are you now?" said Zataldra.

"I'm . . . at the Tograh'Dirkot," Iya lied. "Why?"

"I would like us to talk before the invasion force sets out. I know we have different opinions about this war, but I believe some time together would be good for us. It's what Father would've wanted."

"Oh . . . alright. I'll come to you. Where can I find you?"

"I'm at my mountain compound. There are some things I need to retrieve from my laboratory." Iya's eyes widened. "Why don't we meet at the Gra'Jahorne for a late meal?"

High-strung, Iya glanced at the progress bar. The download was only halfway done. "Um, come to think of it, let's just meet there in the morning." She could use some rest after bidding farewell to Varanz at his funeral, praying at the Tograh'Dirkot to lift her melancholy, and escaping the building without being seen by Zataldra.

"Iya, are you okay?" Zataldra asked, perplexed by her quivery voice.

"Yes, I'm fine. I'll see you tomorrow morning." Iya ended the transmission and brought up a camera feed on the screen to her left. It showed Zataldra walking down a corridor, closing in on the lab fast. Iya's body tensed up. The progress bar was now at eighty percent. *Almost there,* she thought, biting her lower lip. By some miracle, the download sped up. When the confirmation chime signaled "import complete," the tension in Iya's body slackened.

On the camera feed, Zataldra was seconds away from the lab. Iya shut down the computer console and jerked the memory stick from the import slot.

The doors slid open just as Iya had crawled under a table.

Zataldra's sharp mind immediately registered that the motion-activated lights were already on. Her mind jumped to the possibility of Guardians doubling back to steal data on her mind-control weapon. "If there's anyone here, reveal yourselves!" She snatched her handgun from its holster. "There's nowhere to hide!" She began checking under tables and searching every corner and storage room.

Iya sat with her knees drawn to her chest, trying not to make a sound. If she stayed where she was, Zataldra would find her.

Across from the table Iya was hiding under, there was a vent hatch set into the very bottom of a wall. While Zataldra's attention was focused in the opposite direction, she had a small window of opportunity. She crawled to the hatch, opened it, and slipped inside, shutting it as quietly as possible.

Zataldra thought she heard something and moved in Iya's

direction.

Please don't find me, Iya thought. Watching Zataldra pace past the vent, she wiped away a bead of sweat from her forehead.

Seeing no one in sight, Zataldra put away her gun. She powered on the computer console and accessed the camera footage. A few minutes were missing. She reasoned that a system glitch had prematurely activated the lights and paused the cameras. Not dwelling on the oddity any further, she grabbed items off several tables and stuffed them into a bag.

After Zataldra left and the doors swished shut, Iya released a deep breath and crawled out from the vent. Outsmarting Zataldra wasn't easy.

She had what she came for: the blueprints for the mind-control weapon.

Before leaving, she reactivated the console and set a twenty-minute delay on the cameras to mask her exit.

Tomorrow she'd depart for Eden. She hoped the blueprints would aid humanity in defending against Zataldra's weapon. And perhaps, by some twist of fate, she might see Jarius again, her friend. That would be a welcome bonus, she thought, smiling.

CHAPTER EIGHT

Iya was a few steps away from the outdoor cabana-like booth where Zataldra was seated. She, Zataldra, and their parents had enjoyed many family dinners here at the Gra'Jahorne. Sometimes after dinner, they'd walk down to the shoreline to stargaze and admire Mabbeon's three moons.

Servers moved across the sandy terrain, rolling capsuled food carts to the dining booths. Others were busy escorting patrons.

Iya felt grateful for the warm breeze coming off the ocean. It helped quiet her restless mind.

An attentive female server stopped Iya while en route to deliver a meal. She expressed her admiration for Zataldra's leadership in defending Khanoria. Zataldra had been proactive, forming a militia and uniting it with the Collective. And she was the one who created the weapon that would destroy the humans.

If only she knew, Iya thought. If only the server knew Zataldra had concealed the truth about the citadel attack and that the ambassador delegation's abduction had provoked the assault on her compound. Khanorian warmen were being sent off to war based on bogus information. Knowing this made it even more difficult for

Iya to chat with her sister.

Iya paused at the entrance of her and Zataldra's booth. Her nostrils widened as she inhaled, easing the nervousness from her system. She was about to sit down with Zataldra to clear the air between them, while also planning to go against her by delivering the mind-control weapon's blueprints to the CDF. She expected that this breakfast would be uncomfortable.

Iya pushed apart the curtain of beads and entered the private space.

Zataldra felt just as awkward as Iya. After all, Iya had helped Jarius escape and then led the CDF straight to him during their attack on her compound. Though Zataldra considered Iya's actions traitorous, she couldn't see her own sister as an enemy, and this morning was about putting aside their differences to just be family —no quarrels, no arguing. Really, there was nothing else Iya could do to offend her, she thought, not knowing that Iya was going to hand over her weapon's blueprints to the people she was at war with.

"Iya, I'm glad you accepted my invitation," Zataldra said. "I know things have been . . . edgy between us. It hurt me that we weren't on speaking terms at Varanz's funeral."

Iya sat down. Fidgeting with her ear, she said, "Yes, it hurt me too." Zataldra was partially responsible for this war that had every Khanorian living in fear of the human race once again. That was hard to get over, even for one meal. But Iya reminded herself of the Korahh'Havaell's teachings about redemption and forgiveness.

Zataldra said, "I want us to have a nice time together before I leave with the Khanorian Protection Force and Collective. If I don't survive, I don't want our last memory to be of us at odds with each other."

"Neither do I."

213

"So let's not talk about what has happened. Let's just enjoy ourselves and reminisce."

A waitress brought their food, setting plates down on the round wooden table between them.

The Gor'Ronn sisters spoke of their happy memories, times of togetherness as a family. But thoughts of unnecessary war and bloodshed remained a constant distraction for Iya. Her sister and the former dictator she had aligned herself with were the cause of it all. Khanorian warmen would die, leaving behind distraught loved ones, and for what?

Once they had finished breakfast, Zataldra presented a gift to Iya. "Go on, open it."

Iya took the small box and removed the lid. Inside, there was a pair of earrings identical in design to the ones their mother had been buried with. To Iya's amazement, they were made from the same nearly nonexistent gemstones.

Zataldra said, "I know you had always wanted a pair just like our mother's."

Affection washed over Iya. "You remembered."

"Yes," Zataldra replied. Iya put on the earrings. "You look so much like her, you know."

Iya closed her eyes, almost moved to tears. This was the good-hearted sister she knew and loved.

Zataldra stood. "I must go now. There's no guarantee that I'll survive. Just know that I love you, Iya." The two sisters shared a long hug. "Goodbye. Mother and Father would be proud of you." Zataldra disappeared through the curtain of beads.

For Iya, this morning had been a reminder of who her sister once was. But she remembered the corpses of Jarius' fellow ambassadors and of the two Guardians Zataldra had made kill themselves. She prayed for Zataldra to go back to the way she used to be, before rage had gotten hold of her soul. And she also prayed for an end to the war with no loss of life.

Oviereya sat at her desk in the Executive Office, her muscles rigid. Surrounding her were holograms of the other six Union leaders, all of whom had joined the virtual conference she had requested. She had delayed asking for their aid because she knew it would require airing the Commonwealth's dirty laundry. But with no way to defend humanity against the mind-control weapon and with a potential alliance between the Khanorians' Protection Force and the Collective brewing, she had no choice but to ask for the Union's help.

Secretary of Defense Abeo Adasanya lingered in a corner, intentionally out of sight of the office's transmission cameras.

Aware that dealing with the Union leaders—except for the Eminence of Taramassia, Pappalonie—would be challenging, Oviereya anticipated her request encountering pushback.

The Union leaders adhered to meeting etiquette, introducing themselves one by one.

Durgraso snarled. "What is the emergency? What crisis have you humans caused now?" he grumbled, ever skeptical of the human race.

"Let us not make assumptions," Pappalonie interjected, coming to humanity's defense. "Let the Commonwealth's leader speak."

Durgraso snorted, and the gills of his neck hissed his gall.

"We are listening," Baraphelis stated with guarded eyes.

Oviereya drew in her stomach and suppressed a rising prickle of anxiety. "A group calling themselves the Collective has attacked CDF freight ships, Guardians on planetary-impact missions, and Guardians traveling to or from deployments.

"They captured a team of Guardians who were returning from a peace-intervention mission. I ordered an ambassadorial delegation to be sent to negotiate their release. The agreed-upon meeting was actually a trap." She briefed the Union leaders on the mind-control weapon, what happened in Terence Plaza, the staged attack on the citadel, and Jarius' rescue.

Durgraso asked, "What did the Commonwealth Government do to anger the Collective?" The confidence in his tone suggested that he was certain the Commonwealth Government was at fault for provoking the Collective's hostility.

Oviereya was hesitant to reveal the dark parts of the Commonwealth's history, but transparency was crucial in obtaining Union support. "Over the years, the CDF carried out many planetary-impact missions. Details of several missions were withheld to secure your approval, and there were also missions purposefully kept off the record—all of them financially motivated.

"Regrettably, malevolent despots sometimes used the CDF's services. And—" She paused, uncomfortable with the truth, but she went ahead and confessed it. "And it has come to light that Guardians engaged in unethical behavior during some missions."

The veins standing out on Durgraso's temple and thick neck throbbed, the anger inside him growing. His words came out like he was breathing fire. "Are you saying that we were not fully informed about specific missions and that some were executed in secrecy to circumvent our approval?" Steam might as well have been coming from his ears.

"Yes, I'm afraid so," Oviereya replied somberly. "Dafulton, an ex-dictator who the CDF overthrew during a noble planetary-impact mission, leads the Collective. He's exploiting the CDF's past misdeeds to manipulate and recruit its victims for this false justice coalition of his. His true motives are most likely rooted in self-centered, nefarious objectives.

"Based on evidence, the Collective is preparing to attack the Commonwealth. Because of his staged attack on the citadel, it's highly probable that Dafulton has gained the support of the entire Khanorian National Protection Force.

"We regret that we have to cause further harm to the Collective and Khanorian soldiers who Dafulton has manipulated. The negligence of past Commonwealth Government leaders and corrupt service members has victimized these people enough. But we may not have any other choice; war is inevitable."

Durgraso's brow scrunched into a frown. "And you are requesting our assistance in your defense?"

"Yes," Oviereya replied. "Though it's true a Shell can protect a Guardian, it's been determined that we need the actual mind-control weapon to develop a countersignal. The CDF has no way to protect the Commonwealth's people from this weapon. We also don't know what other devices the Collective may have at its disposal.

"You have every right to be upset, but I'm pleading for Union military aid under our mutual-defense comity."

Durgraso chortled and flippantly said, "You want us to put our soldiers in danger because vengeful foreign powers are coming to hold the Commonwealth accountable? Once again, humanity's star nation has become embroiled in a conflict of its own making. Prior, it was your civil war."

Ziltilda's snake-like hiss expressed her frustration with the matter. "The Union is a place of peace, yet you humans continue to bring war to our doorstep," she accosted. "These people wouldn't be out for revenge if it weren't for the CDF's actions. This conflict is entirely humanity's own doing." Her reptilian eyes glared at Oviereya with enough intensity to cleave her in half. "Personally, I

217

will not risk my forces to prevent the Commonwealth from being impaled by its own sword."

Pappalonie, usually supportive of the Commonwealth compared to other Union leaders, was unsure if she should put her soldiers' lives on the line for this war. She tapped her chin, deep in thought. "Whether to intervene is not a straightforward decision for me to make. This coming war is a mess caused by the mistakes of Oviereya's predecessors, rogue Guardians, corrupt government leaders—the whole rotten bunch. Oviereya's leadership is the beginning of a new era in the Commonwealth, and I do not believe all humans should have to pay for the sins of others—the sins of before.

"In my heart, it feels wrong to let the CDF face the Collective and Khanorian Protection Force alone. Nonetheless, Tarmassaia's intervention requires careful consideration."

"Understandable," Oviereya acknowledged.

All the Union leaders except Pappalonie outright declined to aid the Commonwealth. They logged out of the teleconference stream, and their holograms dimmed until they faded away.

Lost in thought, Oviereya rubbed her arms in a self-soothing way. The Collective-versus-Commonwealth war was undoubtedly her greatest challenge in office yet. What made it even more taxing was that it was happening right in the middle of a reelection campaign.

Abeo came out from the corner and approached her. "Are you okay, Madam Chief?"

"To be honest, no. I'm not sure what else can be done to protect Eden and Satellite One. I only hope that the CDF is strong enough to prevail against our enemy's forces."

"Well, there is one more thing you could do," Abeo said hesitantly. "The one option you are not fond of could at least reinforce the CDF's ground defense capabilities."

Oviereya knitted her brows together. "No," she stated firmly. "I'm not reactivating Area 14, Cornelius Gould's darksite. Those weapons were unsanctioned and detrimental to the Guardians who operated them. I won't allow feelings of desperation to compromise my ethics and morality. Plus, the M-X03 Shell's development is coming along well and—"

"And will not be ready in time for the enemy's assault," Abeo said, cutting her off. "The reactivation of Area 14 should remain on the table. What if we could fix the weapons' flaws and—"

"Abeo, this isn't up for discussion," Oviereya asserted. "Now, please leave me."

Abeo acquiesced, tilting his chin respectfully before exiting the office. "At least think about it." The door clicked shut.

Leaning forward, Oviereya rested her face in her hands, her locs dangling around her. She was doing everything within her power to protect the Commonwealth. The question was, Would it be enough?

◆ ◆ ◆

There was a sense of hopelessness in the air on Eden. With war looming, Guardians of the Land Combatant Corps were being recalled from planetary-impact missions, the Reserves had been activated, and all the Task Forces' deployments were suspended. It was all hands on deck. Tomorrow, every Guardian on Eden was to remain at their base and conduct wartime drills, staying ready to defend Eden and Satellite One at a moment's notice.

Randy was going to be grounded at Task Forces HQ like all the other Guardians in the corps. It was uncertain if Vanguard Alpha would get any free time for him to visit Stacie, so they had been spending every waking hour of the day together.

They strolled through Cornerstone City, Randy in a T-shirt and jeans and Stacie in a backless yellow sundress.

Hanging on to Randy's arm, Stacie said, <*When we have kids—in the far, far future—we'll have plenty of stories to tell them, won't we?*>

His mental voice carrying a note of humor, Randy replied, <*Like the time when I beat their mom one-on-one.*>

Stacie's mind flicked to her and Randy fighting each other during the Battle of the Quad—him on the Coalition's side and her on the CDF's. She fake-punched Randy in the shoulder. <*You got lucky.*>

<*Not luck, skill,*> Randy said lightheartedly. Now that their relationship was on solid ground, he felt uplifted. He dreaded having to take the lives of people who'd been duped by Dafulton. When it came to Dafulton's own men, pirate thugs, he had no problem. While with Stacie, he found he could push aside thoughts of the war and have a day of peace before combat preparations were in full swing.

Flyers soared over a labyrinth of rooftops and around Eden's grandest skyscrapers. Honks from street traffic and the voices of pedestrians talking in pairs filled the air. Randy saw gloom on many faces. People weren't that confident that the CDF could hold back the enemy and prevent them from deploying their mind-control weapon on Eden.

As Randy and Stacie passed a colossal building, Stacie paused. It was the headquarters of a weapons manufacturing company owned by one of the Elite—Charlotte.

Stacie realized the war would likely be a boon for the Elite. Mergers and acquisitions had given them a stranglehold on the private defense industry, and war meant huge profits. Whether the CDF won or the war dragged out, the demand for weapons and military equipment would spike. If Stacie could have it her way, the Elite would be dead before they could enjoy this windfall.

Even amid all the despair surrounding the war, and despite the excitement of getting married, she hadn't forgotten about her mission. The Elite thought they had the Commonwealth in their pocket, but she was about to show them. She had already set into motion a plan that would compromise some of their businesses. If everything went well, they'd wake up to a pleasant surprise tomorrow. She wished she could see their faces.

Randy said verbally, breaking Stacie's silence, "That's one of the Elite's companies, isn't it?"

"Yes." Stacie's eyes narrowed. She'd had her degenerate phase while attending Cadwell; thankfully, she clung to her morals and didn't become a hedonistic asshole, unlike the Elite, whose consciences had been diluted by greed and power. She remembered that even as children, there was something sinister about them.

"Anything you wanna talk about?" Randy asked.

Stacie shifted her mind away from what awaited the Elite tomorrow. "No, let's not talk about the war, the Elite, or any other bullshit. Let's just enjoy ourselves."

"That's alright with me."

Wrapping both her arms around Randy's right arm, Stacie leaned on his shoulder, and they continued their evening stroll.

Though Randy was savoring every precious second with Stacie, he was worried—not so much for his own life. He didn't fear death; what he feared was what might happen to Stacie.

When the enemy arrived, he'd be in a Shell, defending Eden; Stacie wouldn't. She'd be vulnerable to the mind-control weapon if any enemy forces breached the defense barrier and deployed it near her home. However, the enemy would likely target vital infrastructure and heavily populated urban areas before spreading elsewhere. Stacie's mansion was in the countryside. Still, the thought of Stacie falling victim to the mind-control weapon bothered him.

Stacie snapped her fingers—once, then again. "Hey, get out of your head," she said warmly, as Randy drifted further into the dark imaginings distracting him. "Stay in the moment."

"Yeah, sorry. Come on."

Randy and Stacie stepped onto a slideway to give their legs a break, heading to a rooftop garden. There, exotic plants, artificial waterfalls, and hovering platforms offering panoramic views of the city would provide a serene atmosphere for them to relax.

◆ ◆ ◆

In sweatpants and a tank top, Akane moved around her home, packing to be stationed at Task Forces HQ tomorrow with the rest of Vanguard Alpha. Her parents were on the floating holoscreen that was following her.

"Do you have everything you need?" Akari asked.

Akane zipped up the last bag. "Yeah, Mom. I'm all packed and ready to go."

Benjiro said, "And what about these trauma episodes you've been having? When's this special treatment supposed to start?"

"When I get it scheduled, Dad," Akane replied. First, she needed to coordinate with Randy to find a time that would work for him, since he'd be involved in the procedure.

Benjiro said, "Then why haven't you—"

"Mom, Dad, I know you're superworried about me, but I'll be fine."

Akari had fought her emotions to a standoff, but they finally broke loose in the form of tears. "We love you, Akane." Akane was a Task Force Guardian. She had been risking her life for a while now, but what was coming would differ from anything she had faced on missions with Vanguard Alpha. Akane was going to war, even if that war only lasted a day, and Akari knew wars brought death. "We just don't want anything to happen to you."

Akane forced her lips into a reassuring smile. "I love you guys too. With any luck, the bad guys won't get past Eden or Satellite One's defense barrier. I've gotta go. I'll stay in touch." She instructed her home's virtual assistant to end the stream, and the holoscreen receded and winked away.

Akane plopped onto her bed and tucked her hands behind her head. She was terrified for her parents' lives. It was a given that some enemy forces would slip past the Air & Space Corps and that there'd be some serious fighting on Eden and Satellite One. To do her job, Akane had to beat the trauma so she could be in peak mental and physical condition.

She closed her eyes for some rest and tried to forget about what had happened to her in Khanoria. Her cat, Bubbles—whom a neighbor had taken care of while she was on leave—jumped onto the bed and perched itself next to her.

Akane *was trapped in a claustrophobic glass cube. She pounded on it with her fists. "Let me out!"*

Cornerstone was a war zone. Bodies, charred and mangled, littered the ground. Akane slapped her hands against the glass wall. "Someone help me!" She kicked at it repeatedly. The glass wouldn't break, mocking her attempts to escape.

Randy, in battledress, was running from Khanorian troopers' gunfire. He stumbled and fell.

Akane banged on the glass. "Come on, get up! Get the fuck outta there!"

Randy muscled himself up to his feet. The gunfire had stopped, and the Khanorian troopers had disappeared.

Steeped in shadows, an Akane with hellish glowing red eyes began walking in his direction, a gun in her hand.

"Akane, stop!" Randy shouted, extending open palms.

The real Akane continued to pound on the glass. "Randy, move!"

The trigger clicked, and the gun flashed.

Randy howled.

Zataldra's laughter echoed.

Akane gasped awake in a cold sweat, bottom lip twitching. Fear danced inside her. *Calm down, Akane,* she told herself. *It was just a dream.* She needed to stop thinking about Khanoria, stop thinking about the mind-control weapon altogether.

She groped for her earbuds on the bedside table. After putting them in her ears, she instructed her home's virtual assistant to play some soft music to relax her mind and lull her back to sleep.

As the music flowed from the earbuds, she once again closed her eyes. *Okay, let's try this again.* To prevent her sanity from going off a cliff, Akane needed Linked Trauma-focused Cognitive Therapy to work.

She wished Randy were there to snuggle with, but Bubbles' company would have to suffice.

◆ ◆ ◆

Jarius and Jazzlyn were outside the gate of Fort Pittman, where the headquarters of the Air & Space Corps was located. Jarius had flown her there in his flyer so she could report for duty and deploy to support Eden's defense barrier.

He kissed her cheek. "Hey, be careful up there, flygirl."

Jazzlyn said, "After I get settled, I'll reach out." Jarius looked uneasy about her departure. She squeezed his hand in hers. "Don't worry, I'll be okay." She moved along to the gate.

Jarius got back into his flyer and took to the air. Once a Guardian in the Land Combatant Corps, he understood what it was like to be in a theater of war. His respect went out to all the Guardians who'd be fighting in space and on the ground. He almost wished he could be fighting too, as part of Eden's ground defense. But he wouldn't trade being a lieutenant ambassador for anything.

As a lieutenant ambassador, he had traveled to different worlds to broker peace between the Commonwealth and people who had been mentally, emotionally, and physically wounded by the CDF. He wondered if apologies and condolence payments would've been enough to quell the rage of the Collective's contingents, especially the Khanorian contingent. He had seen Zataldra's hatred. Not even her own sister had been able to help quell it.

Iya, he thought. He missed Iya. The workings of the heart were strange. He and Iya had known each other only a short time, yet that time was enough to bond. How was she doing? How was she feeling about Khanorians being dragged into war? If only his thoughts could reach her.

◆ ◆ ◆

Randy couldn't get enough of the narcotic that was Stacie's lips. They stood kissing in her bedroom, quietly concluding a long day.

Randy ran his hands through Stacie's hair, over the exposed flesh of her back, and under her dress—his favorite place.

Stacie's loins jerked in satisfaction at his touch. Contraceptive capsule already taken, she was ready for a night of raw sex.

Caught up in making out with Stacie, Randy almost forgot

about his surprise. He pried his lips from hers. "I have something for you."

"And what would that be?" Stacie replied, her lips edging closer for another kiss.

Randy retrieved a small case from his pocket and presented it to Stacie.

Her heart boomed. She took the case and opened it. Inside was exactly what she thought, an engagement ring. Her eyes sparkled. The words LOVE YOU ALWAYS ~ RANDY were engraved in the ring. She couldn't wait to show Jazzlyn.

"Wanted to make things official," Randy said, unable to keep from blushing. "You like it?"

Stacie couldn't stop staring at the ring. "Totally!" She snapped the case shut and set it on the vanity. Then she jumped into Randy's arms, winding her legs around him. He planted one hand across her spine and the other on her backside, keeping her flush against him.

Stacie's mouth clung to Randy's like a magnet to steel.

During the Civil War, Randy's lust for Kesley Whittaker caused him to stray from his relationship covenant with Stacie. But while testing the waters with Kesley after the civil war, his attraction to her eventually faded. They went their separate ways, remaining friends. A relationship between them wouldn't have worked out anyway, since he chose to stay on Eden. While still broken up with Stacie, he met Akane and had a short-term amorous relationship with her. Neither Kesley nor Akane could truly compare to Stacie.

Holding Stacie in a viselike grip, Randy laid her down exactly how he wanted—her legs dangling over the side of the bed. He had every intention of surviving the coming war, but he'd seen too many Guardians carried home in body bags to trust promises of tomorrow. If this was his last night with his fiancée, he'd spend it fucking her for hours on end.

His cock sprang to life, straining against the fabric of his pants. He hurriedly took off his clothes, every inch of his solid frame stripped bare in seconds.

His pulse thundered as he bunched Stacie's dress up to her waist and removed her panties—something he'd never tire of.

Before she could even undress, he shoved her thighs apart and, with his hand, guided his cock halfway into her socket. A primal urge consumed him instantly, and he slammed the rest of the way in, burying his cock to the hilt.

Randy's ragged breaths and the squeal of bedsprings drowned out Stacie's mewls as he hammered her, testosterone blazing in his veins. On instinct, she arched her body to meet him stroke for stroke.

Each thrust from Randy sent tremors up her spine. And each cry from her lips fueled his merciless pace.

Stacie's body convulsed, orgasm after orgasm leaving her panting and making her claw at the sheets.

At last, Randy pulled out, his cock dripping and chest heaving. He wasn't done—not even close. He just needed a moment to catch his breath.

Stacie stripped her dress off, sex drive skyrocketing. She craved the feel of her fiancée's flawless physique pinning her to the mattress.

Going all out, Randy and Stacie Linked.

Their love, lust, and joy engulfed each other's minds and bodies. It was an experience that transcended mere physical touch. This was the purpose of a cerebral implant: to deepen human connection, to let lovers truly know one another's hearts. Neither Randy or Stacie could have imagined this technology being used as a weapon to cause harm.

They pleasured each other in multiple ways, changing positions until Stacie was straddling Randy, riding his upward thrusts.

She leaned in and pressed her lips against his—with his cock still firmly rooted inside her.

Through their Link, Randy's emotions bound Stacie to him, and Stacie's emotions bound Randy to her.

Breaking their kiss, Stacie sat upright atop Randy, fingers finding purchase on the headboard. She rolled her hips with brutal abandon. Randy closed his eyes, absorbed in the sensation.

He grabbed handfuls of Stacie's gorgeous ass as he bucked beneath her, matching her ferocity.

"Oh, shit," Stacie huffed in exhilaration, wisps of hair grazing her shoulders as she moved. "Fuck." The word exploded from her lungs breathlessly.

Randy reached up and squeezed Stacie's breasts. An orgasm then tore through her, wracking her entire body. Still pounding her, Randy climaxed as well.

Stacie, covered in a veneer of sweat and gasping for air, dismounted.

Lying next to each other, they rested in contented silence, but the Link between them still hummed with echoes of their connection.

Randy awoke to the sound of clicking.

Stacie, still naked, worked her fingers across her computer's keyboard. The glow from the screen illuminated her body, spotlighting every curve and dip.

Randy stared fixedly at her posterior sticking out as she leaned forward in concentration. He bet that most men would give anything to be that office chair.

Stacie's gaze almost burned a hole through the screen. Dedicated to her mission, she read the latest emails from the men she had paid to execute tomorrow's plan against the Elite. She didn't want any more failures, like the disaster at the Spire.

Randy said, "Hey, what are you doing? Come back to bed."

Stacie absentmindedly brushed a tendril of hair out of her face. "I'm just checking on something. Be there in a minute, babe."

"Checking on what?"

"I'm making sure the people I've got working on my plan aren't encountering any complications that they need more resources to handle." A hundred thoughts raced through Stacie's mind.

Randy noticed how tense she looked, her shoulders hunched over as she typed. He sighed and slid out of bed. Earlier, Stacie had told him not to think about the challenges ahead and to enjoy the day, but here she was, obsessing over whatever plan she was trying to execute.

He jabbed the power button on the keyboard, shutting off the computer.

"H-hey, I wasn't done," Stacie protested.

Randy closed the laptop and took her arm, gently insisting that she get up. Reluctantly, she conceded. He stood behind her, arms around her midsection. "Relax and follow your own advice," he said. "Forget about the Elite." He kissed the side of her neck. "And whether things go right or don't go as planned, remember it's not the end of the world."

Randy kneaded Stacie's left breast, gripping it like he meant to brand her with his touch. He wiggled the perfect orb of flesh in circles before sliding his other hand down between her thighs, where he found her already slick. As he inserted two fingers inside her, she melted against his chest.

Her body was a masterpiece—athletic, statuesque, curved in all the right ways. Touching her felt dangerous, forbidden. She was a fucking goddess. His goddess.

He drove his fingers deeper, circling and stroking. Stacie's nipples hardened, and her breath caught. She was completely at his mercy, hardly able to breathe or form a single word.

Randy let go of her breast and skimmed her ab muscles. Then he cupped her right breast and fondled it, while he rubbed her clit with his opposite hand. Every touch was an act of worship, every caress a tribute to Stacie's beauty and sensuality.

She felt the fingers inside her move in and out until she was weak at the knees.

Randy angled her over the side of the bed before she could collapse and shoved himself inside her, his cock hitting home base.

Stacie whimpered broken sounds. Her mind was now completely off the Elite.

Randy doubled his pace, his scrotum slapping against her ass. There was nowhere else he wanted to be tonight than between his future wife's legs. To him, bending her over and taking her from behind was intoxicating.

The clap of Stacie's rippling ass cheeks filled the room. She ground back against Randy's every thrust and surrendered a keening wail, the kind of sound that could make any man drool.

They transitioned to the bedsheets, where their lips and bodies continued to mingle.

Randy drilled his cock into Stacie again. She wrapped her legs around him, bringing him even closer, and her nails clawed his back.

As Stacie took each feral thrust, her mind swirled. *<More,>* she begged. She wanted the very summit of her lover's passion. *<Faster.>* Their bodies moved as one, synced to a feverish rhythm that was only possible through Linking.

Randy plunged harder, knocking the breath from Stacie's lungs. Sparks burst behind her eyes, and her nipples pebbled beneath his chest.

This is what she craved—all of Randy's passion and desire fully unleashed.

Minds connected, they entered a state of ardor and sexual hunger.

The faster Randy thrust, the more animated Stacie's breasts became, jiggling incessantly. It was a sight that turned him on.

Spent, Randy slowed to an easygoing pace. Then he withdrew his cock and collapsed onto his back. However, his thirst for Stacie's body hadn't waned.

A hypersexual woman, Stacie wasn't done, not by a long shot. She draped her body over Randy's, kissing him in a haze of delirium. She adored every inch of him—his trim, muscular build; his smoldering gaze; his handsome face. She could swear he was made just for her.

The feel of Stacie's body reinvigorated Randy. He rolled her over and fucked her with renewed fervor.

Their Link amplified their sensations, so every stab of Randy's cock jolted Stacie. Randy was working her over good.

Sweat drenched their bodies as they constantly shifted positions, both of them unwilling to separate for even a microsecond.

Stacie's hands wandered over Randy. She loved the feel of his steely pecs. She loved the way he moaned and gasped as she took him in her mouth, sucking and licking until he was on the brink of coming.

Randy hooked Stacie's legs over his shoulders. Each downward thrust traveled deeper than the last. Consumed by his addiction to her, Randy drove her to the edge and toppled her over it. Spasm after spasm of intense euphoria overtook her, her body trembling as every nerve vibrated.

They climaxed together, Randy emptying himself inside Stacie in abundance. Yet he didn't stop. He dropped all his weight, folding her beneath him even more. He went into overdrive, spearing her without pause.

The amount of neohuman cum pouring from Stacie's entrance spoke to how much Randy enjoyed fucking her. There was so much of it that his thrusts were accompanied by faint squelching noises.

Once he was done, he extracted his cock.

Sparks danced along Stacie's skin. She was on cloud nine.

Randy twined his fingers in her hair and tipped her head back. His lips hovered a breath away from hers, then closed the distance.

After the kiss ended, Randy devoured Stacie with his gaze. She was beautiful—too beautiful. And she was his.

He massaged her right breast. The nipple sticking up from its areola beckoned to him. His mouth seized it, the suction audible.

Stacie's mind barreled into a tailspin, and at that point, Randy gave her a moment.

Lying beside her, Randy whispered, "I love you." His fingers rubbed lazy patterns across her shoulder. Life without her was unimaginable.

Stacie gathered herself. "I love you too," she replied, emotion thick in her voice. "Always."

Their lips met unendingly as they leaned wholly into each other's presence.

That night, they made love more times than ever before. Their bond would endure until death tore them apart, hopefully not soon.

◆ ◆ ◆

Iya had spoken to the Headmaster of the Tograh'Dirkot about borrowing one of the shuttles used for interplanetary missionary work. It wasn't standard practice to lend shuttles to apprentices for personal use. Iya didn't tell him all the details but stressed that she had been called to do something important.

Because she was the daughter of a Grand Elder and one of the most dedicated apprentices the Headmaster knew, he trusted her and permitted her to use a shuttle.

Iya opened the door of the compact craft and drew her legs inside. She flipped switches, pulled levers, and tapped buttons. The engines hummed to life, and displays lit up.

Even with the blueprints in humanity's possession, the outcome of the war remained unpredictable.

A message flashed on the instrument panel's screen that said ENGINES READY.

Iya hesitated to take off. By going to humanity's corner of the universe, she'd be entering hostile territory. What were the odds of humanity trusting a Khanorian? What were the odds of the CDF not killing her on sight? She had to be brave. She had to do this. Doubt was testing her, but courage won out. Sometimes doing good meant risking your life.

She punched the launch button and took the controls, navigating the shuttle into the night sky. The earrings Zataldra had given her dangled from her ears. Zataldra would be deploying with the Collective—deploying into war. Just like during the Khanorian Revolution, all Iya could do was pray for her sister's survival.

The shuttle emerged into space. Iya found the silence to be a relaxing change from the mind-numbing commotion in Khanoria. Everyone, including the media, was talking about the war.

She set a course for the Commonwealth, unsure if her choice to help humanity would prove to be a fatal or promising one.

CHAPTER NINE

Jazzlyn was conducting a routine patrol of the outer fringes of the Commonwealth's sphere in her interceptor space jet. Her wingman, Aeronaut First Class *(lower enlisted)* Jonah Barton, flew adjacent to her. It was too bad that Jarius had just gotten back to Eden and now she was the one away, stationed at the war frigate *Star Phoenix*.

She expected to hear a positive update on his condition during their scheduled video chat today. She was optimistic that the mind-control symptoms wouldn't persist for long.

Checking the time on the instrument panel, Jazzlyn figured she and Jonah had time to make another round. A warning beep came from the radar. She said to Jonah, "Aeronaut First Class Barton, incoming craft." He responded with a "roger." "Prepare to intercept," she said. She thought it could be a Collective ship. But sending only one ship seemed odd. Maybe it was a scout ship. But even for a recon mission, sending just one ship was dicey.

The interceptors rocketed toward the lone craft.

When the craft came into view, Jazzlyn queried her computer's index to identify it. It was a Khanorian craft.

Inside the craft was Iya. Over the translation system, she heard, "I'm Lieutenant de Medici of the Commonwealth Defense Force. Power down your engines immediately, and do not resist."

"I . . . I, um, mean you no harm," Iya stammered. Had she just given herself a death sentence? "I come as an ally."

Jazzlyn remained skeptical. Was this a ploy by the Collective? "Explain," she demanded.

Iya replied, "I bring you blueprints of the mind-control weapon used against your people."

Jazzlyn's suspicions grew. She believed Iya could be a saboteur. "And why would you do that?"

"Even though your Defense Force has hurt Khanorians in the past, I don't hate all humans. I met one of your ambassadors, Jarius, and he showed me that not all humans are malicious. He's a good man, and I don't want him to perish."

Jazzlyn thought, *She knows Jarius?* She wondered if this was the same Khanorian girl that Jarius had told her about. "What's your name?" she asked. Iya answered, confirming she was the Khanorian girl who played a pivotal role in helping Randy rescue Jarius. Still, exercising caution was essential. Jazzlyn said into the comms, "Iya, I know the ambassador you mentioned. I want to trust you, but I have protocols to follow. Please shut down your engines so I can transport your craft back to my command ship. We'll sort things out there."

Iya weighed her options. She had come too far to reverse course now. "Okay." She powered down her engines.

A tractor beam from Jazzlyn's interceptor grabbed Iya's craft.

Jazzlyn said, "Aeronaut First Class Barton, let's return to base."

"Roger, Lieutenant," she heard back.

With her wingman alongside her, Jazzlyn dragged Iya's craft back to the *Star Phoenix*.

◆ ◆ ◆

Jarius never imagined he'd find himself being escorted into the Chief's office again, especially *this* early in the morning. He wondered what she wanted. Entering the office, he could hardly believe his eyes. "Iya!"

Iya rushed to him and squeezed him in a hug, her face lighting up. She was grateful to Oviereya for facilitating their reunion. Their star-crossed friendship was entering a new chapter.

Oviereya said, "Iya was stopped and detained by a security patrol. After I learned she was the girl you mentioned from your rescue, I had her transported to me."

Jarius looked nonplussed. He said to Iya, "It's great to see you, but why are you here?"

Iya replied, the interspecies translator around her neck making her words understandable, "The Gods have spoken to me. I'm called to help defend humanity against the coming invasion."

Jarius opened his eyes a little wider. "And how are you gonna do that?"

"Well, for starters, I brought the blueprints for the mind-control weapon."

Hope pulsed in Jarius' chest. He asked Oviereya, "Have the blueprints proven useful to Defense Force engineers?"

"The blueprints have been thoroughly examined, but a countermeasure to the mind-control weapon remains elusive. Since the Oracle of Randal Scott's Shell developed a defense mechanism, I remain optimistic."

Jarius turned to Iya. "When are you headed back to Khanoria?"

"I'm not leaving. I told Oviereya that I want to try to reason with my sister when she arrives with the invasion force." It was a decision Iya had made while en route to Eden, her soul begging her to try once more at getting through to Zataldra.

Jarius could barely believe the words coming out of Iya's mouth. He eyeballed her as if he were evaluating her sanity. "You tried reasoning with Zataldra before, to free me from captivity, and it didn't work. What makes you believe you'll get any results this time?" Her thinking was an enigma to him.

Iya's chin fell, then lifted, her will not to give up impervious to anyone's protests. "I'm doubtful, but I have to try. I have to try everything I can to convince her to leave the Collective and admit the truth to the Protection Force about the citadel attack. It's all I *can* do." Her resolve was firm, as solid as Kryoplaste.

"Are you sure Zataldra is even gonna be joining the invasion force?"

"She told me so herself," Iya confirmed. "Her thirst for humanity's destruction has been brewing for a long time; she wouldn't miss out on it."

"Well, I'd say the odds of Zataldra listening to anyone are zero. But if you believe it's worth a try, then go for it."

Oviereya said, "We shouldn't leave *any* diplomatic stone unturned. With no Union support and no way to defend against the mind-control weapon yet, all ideas are on the table."

Jarius nodded understandingly. "If Zataldra *can* be brought to her senses, she might be able to stand down the Khanorian Protection Force by—like Iya said—disclosing to them that it was Dafulton, not the CDF, who was responsible for the citadel attack that killed Varanz. That would remove the Protection Force from the invasion equation. Then we'd only have to deal with the Collective." *That'd be a miracle,* he didn't add aloud. But Oviereya was a pacifist, and he knew she was resolute in exploring all possibilities for preventing the war or weakening the enemy's military strength, no matter how far-fetched they may seem. She owed everyone in uniform at least that much.

"I will do my best," Iya promised.

Jarius remarked, "Just know, when the invasion—the war—starts, you may not be safe here on Eden. It's more than likely some enemy ships will get past the defense barrier." He really wanted Iya to go home.

Iya glared at Jarius with unflinching courage. "I *already* know that." Oviereya, too, had warned her of the risks of remaining on Eden, not wanting her to get hurt. But when Oviereya realized she couldn't persuade Iya to leave, she accepted her help. Iya wasn't going anywhere.

"Okay," Jarius said, resigned. Though he was pretty sure of the answer, he asked Oviereya, "Where will she be staying while on Eden?"

"The Executive Guesthouse. And I want you to stay there as well."

Jarius quirked a brow. "What do you mean?"

"With the invasion drawing near, I would like to appoint both of you as my special advisory team."

Iya was honored to be given such a privilege. "I accept."

Jarius said, "Madam Chief, I'm not sure how much help we can be—"

"Nonsense," Oviereya interrupted. "You've had encounters with Zataldra during your time in captivity. And being a former Guardian of the Land Combatant Corps and now a lieutenant ambassador, I trust your judgment on matters of war, civil resolution, and de-escalation. And Iya knows her sister and the Khanorian Protection Force better than anyone."

Iya had learned the ins and outs of the Protection Force from Jud'Zarr. "As a former warman, my father taught me a great deal about how the Protection Force operates," she said to Jarius.

Jud'Zarr even took her to visit the War Camp, where Khanoria's warmen underwent training.

Oviereya said, "Please accept my appointment, Lieutenant Ambassador Ford. No matter how small your contributions may be, they will be beneficial. And I can ensure your therapy sessions are moved to the guesthouse, if that's something you wish."

Jarius nodded. "Okay. I'll help you out in any way I can." And with Jazzlyn deployed, he welcomed Iya's company.

Oviereya contacted an EPA to escort Jarius and Iya to their rooms in the guesthouse, which was behind the Manor. Once the agent arrived, he introduced himself as Brendan, and Iya and Jarius left with him.

They strolled along the walkway in the back lawn, the sun beaming down on them and the birds perched on the treetops.

Iya said to Jarius, the enthusiasm in her voice childlike, "I've seen a bit of Eden during my commute to the Executive Manor. This world is *breathtaking*. But tell me about this second world, Satellite One."

Jarius replied, "Satellite One is vastly different from Eden. The colonies there are desperately in need of modernization. Their living conditions are crappy compared to Eden's cities."

"Why are they so different?" Iya asked, perplexed.

"It's a complicated situation. In the aftermath of a self-induced apocalypse on our primordial homeworld, Earth, humanity had to divide itself between two future homes: Eden and Satellite One. Eden received the lion's share of resources from Earth's governments and the intergalactic partnerships they'd forged. Satellite One was the less favored of the two planets.

"An AI called AEGIS cherry-picked people for maximum survival potential. Those with the highest health, intelligence, skill quotients, and top genetic pedigree got the golden ticket to live on

Eden. The belief was that they'd be humanity's future visionaries and innovators—leaders who'd shepherd humanity into its next chapter. Basically, they were considered to be the VIPs of the New Humanity. So, their survival was prioritized. The powers that be sent the rest of Earth's population to Satellite One, where things were a lot less, well, idyllic."

A muscle in Brendan's jaw clenched, and his brows twitched beneath his sunglasses. A comment burned in his throat, but he forced himself to hold his tongue and stick to his escort duties rather than join the conversation.

Jarius went on. "With Eden having only one continental landmass and humanity's resources in short supply, there was no way both planets could be top tier. Tough call, but the suits decided that a selection process was the only way to play it. Unfair? Yeah, but the best solution anyone could come up with. And I certainly don't have any bright ideas about how humanity could've been partitioned differently during those trying times. AEGIS just might have been a necessary evil.

"Eventually, Satellite One was *supposed* to be leveled up to Eden-quality, but progress there . . . let's just say has been lagging."

"How come?" Iya questioned.

"There are various reasons, some valid and others not so much. Wars have drained resources, and the New Humanity's financial meltdowns have made budgets tight. To make matters worse, some officials, along with most of Eden's population, developed a serious superiority complex. They see colonists as nothing but low-rung laborers, beneath them in every way.

"Progress on Satellite One became an afterthought for the Commonwealth Government. Politicians were busy sending Guardians to support and prop up tyrants like that Sorin of yours

—making bank on those operations.

"Chief Amaechi is all about shaking things up. She's pushing for change in the colonies and is weeding out corrupt politicians. She's been a fierce champion of equality ever since she smashed the glass ceiling and became the first immigrant chairwoman in the Parliament. And she's the first immigrant to become Chief, even if it wasn't through a typical election."

"What are immigrants?" Iya asked.

"They're Satellite One inhabitants who've been granted Eden citizenship," Jarius answered. Elaborating further, he supplied, "Years ago, millions of colonists were brought to Eden as laborers. They were the first immigrants. Later, an immigration lottery was instituted. But honestly, the lottery was just a way to keep colonists feeling like progress was moving forward. Not saying the lottery is a bad thing. It's how Chief Amaechi came here."

"I see." Iya was grateful for the education she was getting on the Commonwealth's history.

As Brendan led Jarius and Iya forward, he kept his ears tuned to the conversation. The words bubbling up inside him clashed with his professional poise.

Jarius said, "Many Edenites treat immigrants as second-class citizens, just as they treat colonists. But hey, not all of them act high-and-mighty. Take me, my future Mrs., Stacie, and Randy, for example. We're all chill. Well, Randy technically qualifies as an immigrant since his dad won the lottery and brought him to Eden as a baby, but Randy grew up here his entire life."

Brendan couldn't restrain the thoughts bothering him any longer. He snapped to a stop. "Hey, I just want you two to know that I don't believe colonists or immigrants are inferior to anyone. My parents taught me to see everyone as equals. We're all flesh and blood. We're all deserving of a good life. Unlike most folks here on

Eden who are glued to their comfy-ass chairs, I've been to Satellite One, on a travel pass, and seen for myself how colonists live. The experience opened my eyes for sure. Ever since, I've been rooting for colonists to have a better life.

"And when the Collective comes knocking, they won't be picking who to kill. They'll target *all* of us. We're in this together, colonists and Edenites alike. Here's to hoping people spoon-fed superiority all their lives finally wake the fuck up and see the bigger picture. All of humanity's on the line. Extinction doesn't discriminate.

"I just wanted you guys to know I support societal change in the Commonwealth." Brendan was out of breath from speaking with such passion.

"Thanks for letting us know that," Jarius said.

Iya remarked, "Every civilization, no matter how grand, grapples with its demons." There was a knowing glint in her eyes. Khanoria wasn't perfect. "Tyranny, shortsighted leadership, and prejudice weave their webs across many societies. I'm able to overlook humanity's flaws and the past sins of its Defense Force to see its true light. I'm committed to stopping the Collective and Khanorian Protection Force."

Brendan nodded. He then took Iya and Jarius through the grandiose doors of the Executive Guesthouse. Polished mahogany floors shined under the glow of recessed lighting. Ten identical guest rooms lined the hallway, and a spacious lounge—furnished with inviting armchairs and sofas—promised relaxation. There was also a well-stocked kitchen at the very end of the hallway.

The layout upstairs mirrored the ground floor's, offering the same ample accommodations.

"Enjoy your stay." Brendan left Iya and Jarius to settle in.

Stepping toward a doorway, Jarius was eager to steal a nap.

"I'm a little tired," he said to Iya. "How about we reconvene in two hours?" He stifled a yawn. "I'll show you some of Cornerstone City's finest sights, and, of course, we can get some food."

"Sounds like a plan." Iya was tired herself.

Jarius retreated into his room, the door clicking shut behind him. He sank onto the gel mattress of his bed, and a familiar warmth washed over him at the thought of Jazzlyn. He eagerly awaited their scheduled video chat, picturing her surprise at learning about his reunion with Iya. Little did he know that Jazzlyn and her wingman were the very security patrol that had intercepted Iya—fate intertwining their lives in unexpected ways.

CHAPTER TEN

Stacie's fingers danced across her computer's keyboard, the casual comfort of a bustier and jeans her attire of choice this morning. On the bottom toolbar, a scrolling news alert snagged her attention. BREAKING NEWS FROM THE EXECUTIVE PRESS OFFICE. TEENAGED KHANORIAN-FEMALE OUTLIER DELIVERS BLUEPRINTS FOR MIND-CONTROL WEAPON TO TIP THE SCALES OF WAR.

Jarius had group-texted Stacie and Randy about Iya's arrival on Eden today, a text that also told Randy that Zataldra was alive. Stacie knew it was a smart move for Oviereya to release a public statement regarding the blueprints. People were in a panic; they needed a morale booster. And Stacie was glad that the Parliament had voted to postpone the election. It would've been idiocy not to. Allowing the Chief to focus on military readiness was the sensible thing to do, even for Oviereya's critics in the Parliament.

Stacie cut off her news-alert notifications and got back to business. She typed up an email. I'VE CONFIRMED THAT YOUR ATTACK WAS SUCCESSFUL. I WILL BE IN TOUCH WITH NEXT INSTRUCTIONS. She smiled as she pressed the send button.

Following Randy's advice, Stacie had successfully hit the Elite where it hurt them the most—their finances.

She had recruited a pair of hackers who had past dealings with her parents. Overcoming obstacles, the hackers executed a cyberattack targeting several of the Elite's financial accounts. They siphoned off a substantial sum of credits before encountering a complex security wall that booted them out, blocking their unauthorized entry. Disrupting the Elite's finances was a sweet addition to Stacie's overall takedown strategy. Her hackers also successfully implanted malware into the systems of select Elite-owned enterprises, resulting in operational setbacks. A more calculated approach over sheer aggression had its benefits, though Stacie still smarted over her failed attack at the Spire.

She leaned back in her chair. *Thanks for the strategy idea, Randy.* Randy had set off in the wee hours of the morning for Task Forces HQ. She missed his presence already. She'd be thinking about him at all hours.

She glanced at the time on her computer. Jason Mansford would arrive soon for them to discuss and iron out her next plan for the Elite.

A sudden crash downstairs caused her to jump to her feet. *An intruder,* was the first thought that slammed into her mind. She had a top-of-the-line home security system, yet someone had infiltrated her property.

She suspected this wasn't a run-of-the-mill trespasser and took a guess at who might have sent them—the Elite. That would mean they had concluded that she was behind the cyber onslaught on their financial accounts and businesses' systems.

She hurriedly yanked open a drawer and retrieved a firearm and magazine. She slapped the magazine in, racked the slide, and crept downstairs, holding the gun at the low ready. Reaching the bottom of the stairs, she saw that someone had smashed in one of her windows. The opening was definitely large enough for an intruder to have come through.

She scanned for the perpetrator as she moved away from the staircase. *Where*— she thought.

A masked figure sprang up from behind the wet bar. By sheer luck, Stacie caught a glimpse of him from the corner of her peripheral vision and twisted away just as a dart blasted from his weapon. It whizzed past her shoulder, missing it by the tiniest margin.

"Damn it," the intruder blurted, irritation showing in his coal-dark eyes.

Stacie squeezed off several rounds, her gun bucking in her grip. Bottles on the wet bar exploded in a shower of glass, and the rounds peppered the wall. Undeterred, the intruder returned fire. This time, his dart found its mark, embedding itself in Stacie's shoulder. An icy cold spread through her veins. She gritted her teeth, ripped the dart free, and flung it aside. Numbness bum-rushed her, legs now barely able to support her weight. The edges of her vision blurred.

The intruder grabbed her arm roughly. "You're coming with me," his gravelly voice declared.

The world tilted around Stacie, and holding her eyes open became challenging. She had to muster all of her willpower to stay standing. *Can't let myself. . . black out.* She kneecapped the intruder with a kick.

He yowled and crumpled to one knee. "Fuck!"

Gotta get out of here. Stacie dragged her lumbering feet toward the door. As her strength abandoned her, her legs stopped working. Lying prostrate, she registered one final sound before everything went dark: the menacing thump of the intruder's footsteps getting closer with each heartbeat.

Just as the intruder's shadow stretched over Stacie's unconscious body, he heard a yell from behind him.

He swiveled around just in time to see Jason Mansford's knuckles. The left-hand punch struck him square in the face, and he staggered backward. Momentum carried Jason's opposite fist forward in a knockout blow.

Jason crouched at Stacie's side. "Hey, Stacie! Stacie, are you okay?" He checked her pulse. It was steady. Before securing the intruder, he lifted Stacie off the floor and set her on the living room couch.

◆ ◆ ◆

Randy stood inside the gate of Fort Kenmore, the base that housed Task Forces Headquarters. The next shuttlebus was ten minutes away.

He was freaking out about Stacie. She hadn't answered his calls in over an hour. He assumed she was just swamped with work. While waiting for the shuttlebus, so he could get to his assigned on-base housing, he dialed his father.

The news of Randy's proposal to Stacie thrilled Arson. He told Randy that his mother would've been overjoyed. After they concluded their call, more Task Force Guardians landed outside the gate in air-cabs. By the end of the day, the rest of Vanguard Alpha would have arrived. Tomorrow morning, the team would assemble to be briefed by Carl on what the next few days would entail for them. Obviously, daily drills would be incorporated into their war prep to keep them sharp.

Akane's voice rose over the chatter coming from Guardians entering the gate. "Randy!"

"Hey, Akane," Randy said.

The autonomous shuttlebus pulled up. Randy, Akane, and eight other Guardians filed in. The shuttlebus could only accommodate ten bodies, so the rest of the Guardians had to wait for the next one.

Akane snagged a window seat, and Randy sat next to her.

The shuttlebus whisked by barracks, shopettes, a commissary, and other facilities on base, headed to the west-side living complex.

"How are you feeling, with this invasion force on the way?" Randy asked.

"I'm scared for my parents. The enemy targeting *both* Eden and Satellite One is stretching the Defense Force thin, and according to the Chief, the Union is still MIA on support. What's the point of being in this fucking Union if they won't back us up? Totally lame."

"For them, the risks of aiding us are high, and the justification is thin. But we'll prevail, regardless. We have to. The Commonwealth *won't* fall." Randy thought about Stacie. "And after all this is over, I look forward to marriage and a happy future with Stacie."

Hearing that Randy intended to marry Stacie, Akane was shaken. She remembered her beloved friend, Skylar Grace, saying: *One day, Akane, you and I are gonna meet the loves of our lives, get married, and live happily ever after with them.*

Unable to stop the words from rolling off her tongue, Akane blurted, "So this is like . . . official? You two are really getting hitched?" The echo of her father asking her what she wanted for her future pestered her mind.

Randy saw a hint of sadness in Akane's eyes, a silent confession of her unrequited feelings. Time, he assumed, would heal her sore heart. She'd eventually move on and find another lover. "Yeah, I proposed."

Akane turned to the window, hiding from Randy the dejected expression she couldn't stop from appearing on her face. Every part of her rebelled against the idea of just forgetting about what they once had. Whatever she was feeling right now—bummed out, regret, nostalgic—she hated it.

Shifting gears, Randy asked, "So when's your therapy session with Dr. Berwick? Vanguard Alpha needs you firing on all cylinders before the invasion. No room for trauma episodes in the middle of a firefight, right?"

Akane shriveled up the hurt in her heart and discarded it, composing herself. "Vanessa said she could fit me in today. If you're okay with that, I'll get us scheduled for our therapy session."

"Do it. Let's get this done," Randy said without hesitation.

"Good, I'll make the call."

Randy and Stacie had agreed not to Link with anyone of the opposite sex outside of family, but Randy considered this situation an exception—a means to alleviate a friend's suffering. Following the tragic explosion that killed his mother, he had to cope with immense trauma. Being Linked with her during her demise resulted in psychological scars that took time to heal. If he could prevent Akane from having to endure long-term trauma, his relationship agreement with Stacie wouldn't stand in his way.

Speaking of Stacie. He tried calling her again, to no response. She often had a hectic schedule, leading Spencer Enterprises and all, but he wondered if her covert mission to dismantle the Elite had put her life in some kind of danger. The disquiet in his chest grew. His concern for Stacie's safety added another layer of stress while he was engaged in war preparations.

◆ ◆ ◆

Stacie regained consciousness and found herself on the couch in her living room. Jason, Eli, and DeShaun looked in her direction after hearing her wake up. They were standing around the intruder, who was bound to a chair.

"Hey, how are you feeling, boss lady?" asked Eli as Stacie got to her feet.

Stacie's hardening eyes locked on the intruder. "Fine." Obviously, Jason had arrived for their meeting just in time to save her. "Thanks, Jason." She went up to her team. "The Elite sent him, right?"

"Yeah," Jason said. "That's all we've gotten out of him so far. I had a background check done on him. His name's Ryker Gibbons. He's a hit man for hire."

Stacie gripped Ryker's shirtfront. "The Elite discovered I was behind the cyberattacks, and they sent you to nab me, is that it?"

Peeved, Ryker turned red. "Go fuck yourself."

Stacie's eyes dropped to the gun holstered on Eli's hip. Jason had instructed the team to come armed in case more hired thugs showed up. "Can I borrow that?"

"Sure can." Eli unholstered the gun and handed it to her.

Stacie jammed the barrel against Ryker's temple. "Start answering some questions, or your head goes 'splat.' Your choice."

"Okay, okay," Ryker said. "What do you wanna know?"

"You tried to capture me; why not just kill me?"

"The Elite want you alive and brought directly to them. They got proof you worked with DFI to convict Damien Sykes. They also know you're the one behind the assault on the Spire and that you stole a shitload of credits by having their accounts hacked.

"They're still locked out of some of those accounts, and several of their businesses' systems are crawling with bugs and crashing, thanks to your fancy malware attack.

"The Elite are confident they can eventually track down the stolen credits and fix that malware mess, but in the meantime, their immediate business transactions are being impacted. They figured, Why drag this out? They want you to return their money and point 'em to your hacker accomplices so they can force 'em to undo the damage they've done and hold 'em accountable. Saves the Elite a lot of trouble, wouldn't you say?"

Stacie asked, "And where were you supposed to take me?"

"Some place they call the Sanctuary, I think. I was supposed to just drop you off, get paid, and then scram. Easy."

Stacie opened her wristcom's holotouch interface.

"What are you up to?" Jason inquired.

"I'm accessing my parents' files to see what I can pull up on this Sanctuary."

Stacie touched a few more holokeys. A 3-D schematic of the Sanctuary appeared. It was a nondescript, windowless phyocrete building surrounded by land collectively owned by the Elite. The subterranean level was like a heavily fortified bunker, one with living arrangements and a workstation hub. The Elite had the Sanctuary built for times of crisis, like the upcoming invasion. It allowed them to continue to live luxuriously while overseeing and managing their operations. The attack on Eden during the Bhalkran war, which had exposed vulnerabilities in the Commonwealth's defenses, was what caused the Elite to establish this emergency shelter.

Eli asked, "Those schematics say anything about that place's security?"

"Nada." Stacie tapped her chin thoughtfully. An idea took shape.

DeShaun said, "I can see those gears in your head moving. What are you thinking?"

Putting together a plan, Stacie played out scenarios in her mind. "I think we have another chance to take out the Elite while they're all in one place. I'm going to let Ryker take me to them."

"Then what?" Jason asked. "Security will search you once you're dropped off, so you won't be able to get a weapon inside that place."

Ryker scoffed. He had no incentive to help Stacie. "And what do I get for my cooperation?"

Stacie pressed the muzzle against his cheek. "We let you go, and we don't hand you over to the authorities. But to ensure you don't double-cross us, you're getting chipped before we leave. If you deviate from the plan, I'll trigger the self-destruct. That means your head goes"—her arms made an expansive gesture—"kaboom."

Ryker grumbled. He had no choice but to comply. "Fine. Looks like I'm backed into a fucking corner here."

Stacie said pointedly, "Yes, you fucking are." This time, the Elite wouldn't escape like they had at the Spire, Stacie thought.

She saw Randy had been trying to get in touch with her while she was unconscious. She'd call him and then contact who she needed to get Ryker chipped.

◆ ◆ ◆

In an all-white room, Randy and Akane sat facing each other in sapphire-blue chairs. Akane rubbed her palms against her thighs, trying to center herself. Vanessa Berwick would arrive in a minute or so, and the unpredictability of the effectiveness of the scheduled therapy session had every atom in her on tenterhooks.

Randy gingerly took both of Akane's hands in his. "Hey, with any luck, this will make a difference, and you'll be better."

The swishing of the doors announced Vanessa's arrival. Dressed in a cerulean uniform and holding a tablet, she entered the room. "Akane," she greeted, adjusting the square glasses perched on her nose.

"Hey, doc," Akane said.

Randy stood and shook Vanessa's hand. "Doctor, I'll help in any way I can."

Vanessa replied, "I appreciate your willingness to get involved." She held out the tablet. "I just need your signature on this consent-to-participate form."

Randy took the tablet and skimmed over the text. Way too much to read for him. To get straight to the point, he asked, "Any danger to my mind with this procedure?"

"There's a possibility. I can't say how unearthing Akane's traumatic experience will affect you—or me, for that matter. It's within my sole discretion as a CDF therapist whether to offer Linked Trauma-focused Cognitive Therapy. In this case, I've chosen to. Are you having second thoughts?"

Randy had a future with Stacie to consider, and he wanted to be the healthiest partner possible for her, but he wasn't going to wimp out now. "No, no second thoughts."

He pressed his thumb to the digital form's signature box and handed the tablet to Vanessa. She placed it on a nearby table and then parked herself in the chair positioned between him and Akane.

Vanessa began by explaining the procedure. She reiterated what Akane had told Randy, that the three of them would Tri-Link and enter a dreamscape manifested by Akane. There, Vanessa would guide Akane in accessing the memory, addressing any fears and reservations that may arise. Once the memory surfaced, Randy could help Akane confront and overcome the trauma.

Randy said, "So what exactly am I expected to do inside the dreamscape for this . . . cognitive restructuring?"

"I can't give you a definitive answer," Vanessa replied. "We can't predict how Akane's trauma will manifest itself in the dreamscape. But as a soldier, you know how to fight. Help her fight the trauma."

"Have you performed this type of therapy before?"

"I have. This is a unique circumstance, though. You were directly involved in the events surrounding Akane's trauma. Having a trusted comrade who was present during the event increases the likelihood of the procedure's effectiveness compared to any solo efforts by me, although it's still possible to succeed without your presence."

"Thanks for the clarification, Doctor. I'm ready when you ladies are."

Vanessa shifted in her chair, getting comfortable. "Let's get to it."

"Ever Tri-Linked before?" Randy asked Akane.

"No," was her immediate response.

"Neither have I. I guess there's a first time for everything."

Linking allowed a maximum of three people to connect cerebrally at once. The experience was fundamentally similar to a dual Link.

Akane took a deep breath, attempting to ground herself. She sent a Link request to Randy and Vanessa. Once they accepted, their cerebral implants verified the connection with a simultaneous, resonant mind-ping. Closing their eyes, the trio allowed their consciousnesses to slip into the dreamscape Akane was crafting, leaving their physical bodies behind in suspended animation.

Inside the dreamscape, the trio stood in a vast expanse of nothingness.

Vanessa said to Akane, "I need you to revisit Khanoria. Take us back to that battle on the roof."

Reluctantly, Akane closed her eyes, steeling herself. A torrent of horror was about to engulf her mind. *I have to be brave.* She mustered the courage to dredge up from her subconscious what had happened to her in Khanoria.

"You can do this, Akane," Vanessa said.

Shuddering from the icy tendrils of fear gripping her, Akane pushed herself and conjured up the heartrending experience Zataldra had forced upon her. A circlet of fire shot up around her, a vivid manifestation of the trauma clawing its way back to the surface.

Randy, outside the flames with Vanessa, stepped forward to intervene. "Akane!"

Vanessa said, "Hold on. Let her continue. She's facing her fears head-on, still drawing forth the memory."

The dreamscape flickered and warped, followed by what sounded like a crash of thunder. The crown of fire surrounding Akane sputtered and leapt higher. An aperture opened in the white void, a window into the pivotal moment of her struggle against Zataldra's control. Overwhelmed, Akane sank to her knees as she watched the scene unfold again. The chilling sensation of her body being used as a murder puppet, a weapon to kill Randy, yanked her back into the throes of powerlessness and terror.

The whiteness of the dreamscape darkened to black.

Through the window in the void, Randy watched his rooftop battle with Akane in Khanoria. He imagined what it must have been like to be the one on the other side—to be Akane. He bravely stepped through the flames and knelt next to her. "It's okay, Akane, I'm here."

Akane rasped out, "I . . . I can't stop Zataldra's control." Her mind was stuck in a replay loop, the fight with Randy repeating itself over and over.

Randy placed a hand on Akane's trembling shoulder, his touch a comforting anchor amidst the chaos in her mind. "I know it feels overwhelming, Akane, but you can beat this."

Akane turned her tear-streaked face toward Randy. Her pain-filled eyes pled for reassurance. "But how? How can I escape this never-ending nightmare? It always . . . comes back to haunt me, invading my dreams, attacking my body in my waking hours."

Randy's gaze softened. "You're so much stronger than you realize. It took a lot of strength to endure unjust treatment as an immigrant and to go on living after losing friends like Skylar and Simone. So you've got what it takes to conquer any challenge life throws at you, including this trauma."

Vibrant beams of light cracked the darkness. The flames that once encircled Randy and Akane transformed into ethereal wisps of color, swirling and dancing like luminescent fireflies. Booming thunder faded into a distant rumble.

"You're not Zataldra's toy, Akane," Randy said. "You're not a puppet to be enslaved by a mind-control weapon, and you're too fucking strong to let the trauma you've been dealt keep you down." He stood up and extended his hand. "Come on, get up."

Akane clasped his hand and rose to her feet, gratitude and affection shining in her eyes.

An unseen force slung Randy onto his back. A double of Akane formed behind her, solidifying from a ghostly outline into a physical form. The double coiled one arm around Akane's waist, the other around her neck. This doppelgänger had the same blank expression and bottomless eyes as the one Akane saw in her bathroom mirror on the *Nightingale*.

The double's arms tightened, constricting Akane.

Akane writhed, her flailing limbs striking out in all directions. "Lemme go!" Her muscles labored, every sinew straining to free her. She was putting forth all her might and then some.

Randy got up. "What the hell's happening?" he asked Vanessa.

"That lookalike is a new manifestation of Akane's fear," she explained. "Her fear of being controlled by the weapon again."

Akane yanked and pulled on her double's arms. No success. She felt like her bones were going to crack under the pressure of her double's hold.

Randy's voice bellowed, "In our Shells, we're now protected. You don't have to worry about being controlled! That will never become your reality again!"

Her soul set afire by Randy's words, Akane stopped struggling like a helpless animal and stood tall, back straight. She had always had a resilient spirit, unbroken by setbacks. She had faced insurmountable challenges as an immigrant and come out on top. This stored-up trauma wouldn't be any different.

Akane unwound the viselike grip from around her neck easily, now feeling ten times stronger than her double. Then she snapped free from the arm around her waist. "I refuse to be haunted by you any longer!" Her eyes were steady, showing no fear.

Glass-like cracks spiderwebbed Akane's double. She began to disintegrate, particles of her floating away. An obsidian cube materialized overhead, rotating. It sucked Akane's double into it as if to signify the extraction of Akane's nightmares and trauma from her mind. In a spectacular explosion, the cube shattered into rainbow-colored fragments.

Returning to the physical world, Randy, Akane, and Vanessa opened their eyes.

Akane, disoriented, caught herself before she could fall out of her chair. "Feels like a whirlwind swept me up and slung me halfway across the fucking planet."

Randy sought Vanessa's expertise. "Did the therapy work? Is Akane's trauma . . . gone for good?"

Vanessa replied, "Facing her fears and the trauma was a significant step. As for whether she'll have more nightmares or if any remnants of the trauma will respawn, I don't know."

Randy helped Akane stand up from her chair and steady herself. "Easy does it."

Akane nodded appreciatively. "Thank you, Randy. I think I need some rest now. Let's pray that this ordeal is truly behind me."

"I'll accompany you to your quarters when we get back to the living complex," Randy said.

"You don't have to do that. I think I can make it to my room without passing out or anything."

"Yeah, but I want to, just to be sure." Randy would take no chances.

After thanking Vanessa, he and Akane left to take a shuttlebus back to the living complex.

◆ ◆ ◆

Akane lay on her bed and stared at the ceiling. Minutes ago, as she walked down the hallway with Randy toward her quarters, they'd had light conversation, and before they parted, he told her to hit him up if she needed anything, no matter the time. That was Randy, always doing what he could to help someone in need.

He served as a tether to a normalcy Akane didn't have on Eden with RISE gone and her parents and friends living on another planet. Every interaction they had made her ache for something deeper, things she could no longer have—his touch, his affection, the physical intimacy she craved. Ironically, she was the ex-lover now, not Stacie. Desiring someone whose heart was already taken felt like chasing shadows in the dark.

Her mind spun, replaying moments with Randy. Did she ruin their chances of being together by persisting with the Damien Sykes assassination after Randy had told her to stop?

Frustration building, Akane pushed herself upright, raking a hand over her hair. She thought some fresh air might help—anything to escape the prison of her thoughts.

She swung her legs over the side of the bed, went to the window, and threw it open. A soothing breeze brushed her face, and she inhaled deeply, trying to get her emotions in order. She had to let go of the sliver of hope that kept her chained to these one-sided feelings. Her and Randy's romance was relegated to the past tense. He was going to be with Stacie forever, and she needed to accept that.

Right then and there, she made a decision. No more dwelling on what could have been and what would never be. She wished Randy and Stacie a happy future, and she'd be there for him in whatever way she could, just like he had been there for her, putting his own mind at risk in the dreamscape to drive away her trauma.

◆ ◆ ◆

In the back of Ryker's panel van, Stacie sat next to Jason, Eli, and DeShaun, who wore masks to pose as Ryker's hired muscle. They were on their way to the Sanctuary, where they'd finish the Elite once and for all.

Though her wrists were bound by handcuffs, making her look every bit the prisoner, Stacie knew the release mechanism would free her in seconds.

Once they arrived at the Sanctuary, Ryker would fake a vehicle malfunction after dropping off Stacie. The team would then wait for her signal to create a disturbance, hopefully drawing most of the interior security personnel outside. Relying on her hand-to-hand combat skills, she would overpower her captors, secure a weapon, and eliminate the Elite.

Jason had reservations about the plan but acknowledged it was the best they could come up with.

Eli looked up from the newscast he was watching on his wristcom. "It seems like this invasion has everyone super-spooked."

Thanks to Iya's more precise estimate of the enemy's arrival, Oviereya moved the Eden-wide lockdown to an earlier date. As a result, citizens were stripping store shelves bare to stockpile food and supplies before the lockdown. It was as if humanity's next apocalypse was coming. Fear of the mind-control weapon had driven some people to undergo dangerous implant removal procedures, which sometimes resulted in death. Everyone on Eden felt like a doomsday clock was ticking.

Even in the colonies of Satellite One, hysteria spread like wildfire—even though colonists, lacking cerebral implants, were immune to mind control. It was an ironic twist that the Commonwealth's biased society, which had initially excluded colonists from humanity's evolution, inadvertently granted them a significant advantage in facing this unprecedented threat.

"I wish we could lend a hand in defending the Commonwealth," DeShaun said.

"Our focus is on our own mission right now," Stacie reminded him.

Ryker eased the van to a halt outside the Sanctuary's gate. He was pissed off at being forced to go along with Stacie's plan. But she and her team had put him under anesthesia and had a chip implanted beneath the nape of his neck, giving him no choice but to be their accomplice. Stacie had meant it when she warned that any resistance would result in his head going *kaboom*.

A hawk-nosed guard exited the security booth.

Ryker lowered his window halfway. "I'm Ryker Gibbons," he said. "Delivery."

The guard's eyes flitted to his tablet. He searched his log to confirm the delivery. He gave a curt nod and disappeared back into the booth.

The rolling gate creaked open, and Ryker steered the van forward. He drove it into the Sanctuary's loading dock and braked, stopping in front of two armed men. They stood stoically, awaiting the hand-off.

Ryker stepped out, went to the back of the van, and flung open the doors for Stacie to hop down.

Jason took one last glance at her before Ryker closed the doors. He was hoping the plan wouldn't go to shit like before.

Ryker, playing his part, manhandled Stacie toward her two escorts. She offered a token resistance, maintaining the illusion of a struggle.

"My work is done," Ryker said.

The escorts aimed their rifles at Stacie.

"Keep your hands above your head, do as we say, and don't try anything funny," one of them ordered.

Stacie grimaced, keeping up the act.

The other escort touched a finger to his tablet, and a chime sounded. He informed Ryker, "I've transferred your payment to your account. Now leave."

Ryker got back into the van and backed out of the loading dock.

Stacie silently assigned nicknames to her escorts. The blond guy became Escort One. The brown-haired guy became Escort Two.

"I'll frisk her for weapons," Escort One said. His fingers probed Stacie in inappropriate places through her formfitting black jumpsuit. *This dishwater-blond cunt is a fine piece of ass.* He ran his grabby hands down her flat abdomen and then lower still.

Stacie frowned in disgust, heat rising in her cheeks, but she kept her cool. She'd get her comeuppance on this asshole later.

Escort One copped a feel one last time before telling his partner, "Okay, done. No weapons." He smirked, visualizing himself bending Stacie over a table. He wished he could take her clothes off right now.

Escort Two nudged his rifle's muzzle against Stacie's shoulder blade. "Move it!" he barked.

Escort One, taking point, pushed open a service door leading into the Sanctuary's interior. Stacie followed. Escort Two stayed behind her, a constant reminder of the bullet waiting at her back if she tried anything foolish. Sneaking glances at her rear end, he definitely didn't mind the view.

The hall beyond the door had a level of extravagance that seemed out of place for an emergency shelter. Opulence was the Elite's calling card, even in a place built simply for refuge. Apparently, they couldn't tolerate staying anywhere that carried even a hint of common-man vibes.

While following her escorts, Stacie took stock of her surroundings and mentally logged every turn. A set of ornate double doors was ahead, likely the gateway to the Elite's presence.

She covertly pressed her right index finger to her left cuff, signaling Jason to begin the first stage of the plan.

The escorts' radios came alive, the muffled voice of the exterior security team's captain coming through. "Alert, this fucking guy, Ryker, says he's having a vehicle malfunction. Needs to fix it to leave the premises."

"Copy that," Escort One replied.

Stacie's plan was unfolding like clockwork.

Behind the doors, she could hear voices talking about her. Once her escorts opened the doors, she saw the Elite sitting around a mahogany table, supercilious grins on their faces. Charlotte North, Gabriel Prosser, Alistair Gantry, Elijah Benjamin, Miles Russo, and Caspian Legler.

"Well, well, so nice to see you again, Stacie Lynette Spencer," Charlotte drawled with a sardonic edge.

"Wish I could say the same," Stacie replied.

Elijah dismissed the two escorts, waving his hand.

Charlotte gestured to the chair directly across from her at the opposite far end of the table. "Please, Stacie, have a seat."

"Guess it's not optional, huh?" Stacie sat down with her old acquaintances, for what she intended to be the last time.

Charlotte said, "We understood you wanted to leave the conglomerate for personal reasons. But fighting us? We never fathomed that." She listed Stacie's offenses, saying, "Working with DFI to expose Damien. Orchestrating an attack on the Spire. Stealing from our coffers."

All of the Elite scowled.

Stacie said, "Okay, what's the point of this little chitchat? Shouldn't I be strapped to a torture table or something?"

"Torture will come soon enough if you don't cooperate," Charlotte guaranteed, "but we're *genuinely* curious. We want to understand what drove you to betray us."

"*Aw*, did I hurt your *feelings*, Charlotte?" Stacie pretended to wipe tears from her eyes.

Charlotte's contempt for Stacie bubbled over. "Hardly."

Elijah said to Stacie, "The Elite are a family. Our parents forged a pact through the ashes of the Earth Era apocalypse, securing dominance in the New Humanity. It is the Elite who built Cornerstone City, and our defense companies supply the

CDF with invaluable weapons—weapons you yourself used as a Guardian. Even now, our companies collaborate with the CDF on the M-X03 Shell project. Why turn your back on such greatness? Why forsake your parents' legacy, your very birthright?"

Stacie scoffed. They were actually confused. The concept of a conscience, of rejecting profit built on suffering, was alien to them. Their parents instilled in them a ruthless pursuit for wealth, by any means. Stacie was different, largely because of the influence of Oviereya Amaechi.

Stacie said derisively, "Let me break it down for everyone. There's a clear distinction between right and wrong. While our parents survived the Earth Era apocalypse through morally ambiguous means, which allowed us, their offspring, to even be born, I refuse to walk that same path. I refuse to hurt others just to aggrandize my bank account."

Charlotte countered, a shrewd glint in her eyes. "You disdain the origin of your wealth, at least the portion that was ill-gotten, yet enjoy its benefits—living comfortably." She cackled. "My, you are such a *fucking* hypocrite, Spencer."

Stacie met Charlotte's challenge head-on. "True, I don't know the exact source of every credit. But whatever the source was, I'm using those credits to make amends—to help others. I'm repurposing them for good. It's redemption, not hypocrisy. And I intend to dismantle this very machine my mom and dad built."

Charlotte laughed. "You can't do anything locked up."

Just you wait till I get my hands on you, Stacie thought.

Caspian's disapproval toward Stacie hardened his expression. To him, life was a brutal game of survival of the fittest, and profiteering was the ultimate sport. "Trying to destroy us was a boneheaded move, Stacie. The Commonwealth is on the verge of war, and if this invasion force penetrates the defense barrier, there

265

may be mass destruction. Our construction companies would then be poised to rake in a fortune.

"And don't forget the defense-industrial complex. The aftermath of this war will bring a skyrocketing demand for weapons, combat vehicles, aerospace tech—the whole nine yards. War equals obscene wealth, and you could've been at this table with us, capitalizing on the opportunity that's staring us right in the face. Instead, you decided to attract our ire."

Stacie said, "Sit at a table with people who kill their own when they see fit?"

"Damien defied our bylaws by running for Chief Executive. We gave him plenty of time to rescind his candidacy. Just like him, you're too stupid to know what's best for you."

"Oh, drop dead, Caspian."

"You first."

Stacie's patience had worn thin. "Enough talk. Let's just get to the damn torture already."

Charlotte chimed in. "Agreed. Unless, of course, you're willing to cooperate and give us the information we want."

Stacie's response was a resolute, "Nope."

The Elite exchanged glances and nodded assent for Stacie's torture to begin.

Charlotte pressed a button on the table and spoke into the intercom transceiver, her voice cold as she ordered Stacie's escorts to come get her. Stacie endured five uncomfortable minutes before they finally arrived.

"Wolcott, Orson, take her away," Caspian said. Wolcott was the one Stacie had dubbed Escort One, and Orson was Escort Two.

Orson grabbed Stacie's arm. "Come on."

Her eyes delivered a pointed warning: Hands off. "I can stand on my own." She lurched out of Orson's grip and rose.

Both men led her out into the hall, flanking her like grim shadows.

She discreetly tapped her left cuff to transmit the next signal to Jason. He, Eli, and DeShaun would launch their assault on the Sanctuary in any second—the fabricated van malfunction a smokescreen to buy time for the signal.

Halfway down the hall, a voice crackled over the escorts' radios. "Those guys who dropped off the woman have opened fire! Initiate lockdown! Sanctuary under attack!"

"Shit!" Wolcott shouted. "I knew somethin' was up!"

A red-alert klaxon blared, shattering the Elite's illusion of safety.

Stacie decided the time was ripe for her to make a move. She pivoted sharply and rammed her full weight into Wolcott, pinning him against the wall.

Orson, on Stacie's right, reached for his shock baton—but Stacie was quicker. She delivered a frontward kick that caved in his stomach and knocked him on his ass. Before she could turn back to Wolcott, who had recovered, his bodybuilder arms were squeezing her waist from behind.

Orson scrambled back to his feet, stomach throbbing. He cocked back a fist, itching to lay waste to Stacie's pretty face. "Keep her still," he said to Wolcott.

Once Orson was within proximity, Stacie kicked him in the groin. Using Wolcott's hold for leverage, she pushed her feet off the floor and slammed them into Orson, sending him falling down. Struggling against Wolcott's grip, Stacie whipped her head back into his chin. He recoiled, and his hands released her waist.

"Damn it!" he said, cupping his chin. "Fucking bitch!"

Stacie tapped her left cuff. It popped loose. She then secured it around her right hand, using it as an impromptu knuckle-duster. Wolcott, still reeling from the head-to-chin blow, was too slow to avoid the metal cuff. It caught him in the forehead, splitting skin. That was payback for him getting too handsy while frisking her.

Blood welling from the gash, he was out for the count.

The electric sting of a shock baton struck Stacie in the back. She swung around with her knuckle-duster extended. Orson ducked and speared her with his broad shoulder, slinging her to the floor. Enraged, he drove his shock baton down on her prostrate body repeatedly.

Stacie clenched her jaw, bearing through each electric shock.

Orson paused his assault. "Give it up, sweetheart."

Stacie kicked him in the back of the knee, yanking his footing from underneath him.

After jumping back to her feet, she discarded both cuffs. Then she threw herself into a forward roll and grabbed the baton that had slipped from Orson's hand. When he got up, the last thing he saw was Stacie braining the front-center of his head with the baton, taking him out.

Stacie heaved for breath, sweat staining her jumpsuit. She relieved Wolcott of his handgun. There was no time to waste. She needed to make sure the Elite didn't leave the Sanctuary. They weren't going to get away like they had at the Spire.

The popping of gunfire echoed in the halls. Her team had made it inside. They'd be at her location soon. But by the time they got there, she planned to have already pumped the Elite full of bullets.

Stacie raced back down the hall, her staccato footfalls blending with the rhythm of her heartbeat. The doors to the Elite's meeting suite burst open. Charlotte emerged, her pistol spitting bullets. Stacie darted into the hall that was to her right as Charlotte emptied her payload and clapped in a fresh magazine.

Stacie peeked around the corner and fired back. Her bullets found no purchase. Caspian came out of the suite, adding his gunfire to Charlotte's, to keep Stacie pinned where she was.

Shit, not how I thought things would go. Stacie had expected an easy kill, but the Elite obviously had a weapons stash in their suite.

Charlotte shouted, "You're a clever one, Spencer! You've concocted some scheme to get the upper hand on us, unlike on Babylon Island! But you won't be leaving here alive!" Her gun's muzzle flashed.

Stacie didn't back down, returning fire. "It's over!" she said above the deafening gunshots. "My team has breached your security. They're already inside. Once they get here, you're all as good as dead!"

"You'll be a corpse by the time they arrive," Charlotte retorted.

The other four members of the Elite emerged from the suite with pistols, taking up positions on either side of Charlotte and Caspian. They had Stacie severely outgunned.

Stacie said, "Just give yourselves up. Expose *all* your crimes to the justice system and be held accountable. This is the only mercy you'll get from me. You'd better take it."

Bullets from the Elite's guns pinged off walls. That was Stacie's answer. Surrender was out of the question.

A bullet grazed Stacie's shoulder. She grunted, gritting her teeth. Blood slicked her fingers as she clamped her nongun hand down on the wound. She winced at the pain as she yanked her gun's trigger again and again.

The corner of the hall, her only shield, was becoming pockmarked by bullet impacts.

Suddenly, Jason's voice boomed from within the building, barking tactical commands to Eli and DeShaun.

"Stacie!" Jason shouted, running to her rescue. Eli and

DeShaun were in tow. Jason's rifle spewed a stream of death the Elite's way.

Eli passed by Jason and slid up to Stacie's side. "You okay, boss lady?"

"I'll live."

Eli handed Stacie a heal patch. She slapped it over the wound.

DeShaun appeared next to Jason, his twin pistols bucking in his hands. One bullet hit its target, taking down Caspian. The tide was shifting in Stacie's favor.

Running from behind the cover of the wall, Stacie and Eli joined Jason and DeShaun. The Elite crumbled from the team's combined gunfire.

"They're down. Cease fire," Stacie said.

The clicking of triggers paused. The air smelled of the metallic scent of expended shell casings.

Stacie's ears picked up Charlotte's faint breaths as she walked up to her. Charlotte was just barely alive.

Stacie aimed her gun at her. "It's over, Charlotte."

"Please, Stacie . . . don't—" She gasped for air, her terrified eyes staring down the barrel of Stacie's gun. After a bang, she was finished.

Stacie took a silent moment. It was over. She had just toppled the most powerful criminal empire in all the Commonwealth. But there'd be time for victory laps later; she and her team needed to wrap up business here and go.

"Good work, guys," she said, voice hoarse from emotion, then firming as she continued. "None of you had to do this. None of you had to help fight my battle against the Elite. But you did. You stood beside me every step of the way, even when I made mistakes. I can't thank you enough. My gratitude—" She trailed off, searching for what to say. "It runs deeper than words can describe."

Her team stood proud. "Now, let's plant the explosives, blow this place to hell, and head back to my home for drinks. We've earned it."

◆ ◆ ◆

Stacie, Jason, and Eli were in the back of Ryker's van, while DeShaun sat at the wheel. Ryker himself had fled during the fight outside the Sanctuary.

The destruction of the Elite was a goal Stacie had doggedly pursued and finally achieved. She should've been rejoicing, but a dark threat was on the horizon, so it was difficult to be in a celebratory mood.

Eli's eyes were glued to an address by the Chief, the live stream projecting from his wristcom.

"Hey, turn that up," Jason said to him.

"Sure."

"Effective tomorrow," Oviereya said, "we enter full lockdown. I won't mince words. Your homes may offer physical shelter, but they won't shelter your minds from the enemy's weapon. Although our Khanorian ally has provided blueprints, we haven't been able to develop a countermeasure. However, do not despair. The Guardians of the Air & Space Corps stand ready to defeat the enemy. *Should* they breach the geostationary defense barrier, the Land Combatant Corps, Task Forces, and all the CDF's courageous warriors are prepared to sacrifice their lives for you."

Randy, Stacie thought.

Oviereya said, "And yes, this is a hell of the Commonwealth's own making. As I've previously mentioned, our prior enemy Dafulton manipulated the minds of the CDF's victims to amass this invading army. Nonetheless, we mustn't assign blame to the *entire* CDF. A number of Guardians have sullied the CDF's image and, by extension, humanity's standing among other civilizations. But the CDF, at its core, remains a force for good. Once the Truth Commission completes its investigation, the government will implement reforms to prevent such an abuse of power from ever happening again.

"Even though the enemy is formidable, my faith in the CDF remains unshaken. They have weathered battles that tried their mettle at every turn. The Phazharian and Bhalkran wars serve as testaments to their resilience and skill. Above all, the New Humanity was forged from the crucible of adversity—the collapse of the Earth Era and our arduous resettlement in our new habitats. We will overcome this challenge, just as we have overcome others."

The urge to defend the Commonwealth against the invaders infused Stacie's veins. But she was no longer a Guardian. She had left the CDF and chosen a different mission—dismantling the Elite and reforming Spencer Enterprises. Unable to join the fight, she could only pray—a hollow comfort amid the encroaching doom.

She dreamed of marrying Randy, of seeing her friends Jazzlyn, Jarius, and Cassie thrive. She envisioned Jazzlyn as her bridesmaid and herself as Jazzlyn's. But the coming war cast a shadow over her hopes. Too often, war stole the lives of loved ones. Perhaps a celebratory toast at home with her team, in honor of today's victory, could offer a temporary reprieve from her fears.

CHAPTER ELEVEN

This was a doomsday years in the making, Zataldra thought. On the bridge of Dafulton's flagship, she occupied the second command chair. Beside her, Dafulton sat in the primary.

Today, she wore a cape that had belonged to Jud'Zarr, paired with a leg-baring one-piece armored outfit. Wearing the cape felt like carrying a piece of her father's spirit with her into battle.

Humanity's Commonwealth would be in view soon. As the ship flew closer, harrowing memories of the Khanorian Revolution fractured her concentration. Today, she would fulfill the vow she made after her father's final moments of life: Make humanity pay for his death, for her own anguish, and for every Khanorian they had beaten, raped, or killed.

Perhaps after the battle was over, she'd resume the nanomedicine studies and terraforming project that held so much promise. It was what her father would've wanted, as well as . . . Varanz. His untimely death still saddened her. In all but blood, he was family.

Fond recollections of time spent with Varanz, Jud'Zarr, and Iya took hold. Remorse coiled itself around her heart. *Varanz, I deeply regret what happened.*

Warning chimes and the alert messages popping up on screens snapped her into a war-ready state of mind.

The exterior camera zoomed in, and the CDF's defense fleet filled the mother screen.

The sheer size of the fleet tightened Zataldra's chest. Her breath hitched. In the beginning, she thought the Collective stood a decent chance without the Protection Force if she failed to secure their backing. Now, she wasn't so sure about that.

Brushing aside the shock, she set herself, relaxing her knotted muscles. The combined forces of the Collective and Protection Force, the Alliance, would be victorious. Humanity was going to end here and now.

She tapped her chair's armrest and brought up a holographic display of the Alliance's fleet. A worrisome detail grabbed her attention: More Collective ships than designated were converging on Satellite One.

She swiveled her chair toward Dafulton. "Why are so many Collective ships being distributed to Satellite One?"

"Just a minor tactical adjustment," Dafulton said coolly.

Zataldra pushed back. "I believe an explanation for this *minor adjustment* is in order."

"This is the right move. Trust me. I'm speaking from experience."

Zataldra regarded Dafulton warily. Then she returned her eyes to the holographic display, brow wrinkled with suspicion. This unexplained maneuver felt like a violation of her trust, another discordant note in their working relationship, just like his use of her mind-control weapon. She wondered if he had a hidden agenda, as Jarius had said, perhaps something to do with the spoils he was so concerned about. Right now, she had to clear her mind of any distracting thoughts and focus all of her attention on the battle ahead, but she'd look out for any additional "minor tactical adjustments" that might suggest Dafulton had another plan at play.

◆ ◆ ◆

The CDF had been alerted that Alliance ships were nearing the defense barrier. All Guardians on Eden were mobilizing for action.

Members of Vanguard Alpha were in their armory at Task Forces HQ, preparing to get shelled for deployment.

Randy, in his sleeve, stood in a corner, talking to Stacie over his wristcom.

"We did it," Stacie's hologram said. "My team and I took down the Elite yesterday. It's finally over." For someone who had just accomplished a longtime goal, Stacie's voice lacked enthusiasm.

"You don't sound too thrilled."

"I know, I know. I should be *superoverjoyed*." She sighed. "It's just that . . . part of me is dying to be out there on the front lines like you and Jazzlyn. Instead, I'm stuck under lockdown like everyone else. I feel so . . . damn helpless."

Akane zipped into the armory and saw Randy conversing with Stacie. She smiled for him, glad that his relationship with Stacie made him happy.

Carl, about to step into his Shell, hollered, "Scott, can the social call! Time to move!"

"Gotta bounce, Stace," Randy said.

"Just . . . promise me you'll be careful," Stacie pled. "Marriage plans fall through when you're six feet under."

"I'm not dying today. We're getting married. Nothing's stopping that."

Stacie blew Randy a kiss, and he ended the call. Her image

buckled and then disappeared.

Protecting Eden, protecting Stacie—that was Randy's mission. He wouldn't let anything stand in the way of his future with her.

He ran up to his Shell's docking pod.

A hand touched his shoulder—Akane's. "Ready, Randy?"

"As ready as I'll ever be. How's your mental state been since the therapy?"

"No trauma attacks, no nightmares . . . yet."

"That's a good sign. But if the symptoms ramp up again and you feel you need to be dismissed from the mission, let Breckenridge know, okay?"

Akane's posture telegraphed zero anxiety. Nothing but confidence emanated from her. "I'm in this fight to the end. I'll be fine."

After everyone had been shelled, Carl said, "Hey, before I forget, quick team huddle." Vanguard Alpha gathered around him. Their faceplates slid up. "Good news, someone's rank promotion finally got approved." He looked at Randy. "Congratulations, Scott." Vanguard Alpha clapped, cheered, and woo-hooed. "Let's get the ceremony done quickly so we can get to our BUS."

Randy stepped forward to face Carl, and everyone else assumed parade rest.

Carl proceeded with the ceremony. "Specialist Randal Eugene Scott, in recognition of your outstanding service, bravery, and dedication to duty, CDF Command has promoted you to the rank of sergeant."

Randy unfastened the rank insignia from his Shell's chest and handed it to Carl. Carl then inserted the new one in its place.

Arturo said, "After all this war shit is over, I say official rank party for Scott. Who's in?"

"If there's gonna be plenty of booze, you can count me in,"

Jenny said, her accent thickening.

The rest of the team seconded her.

Randy had to admit, finally being promoted felt good.

"Let's move out," Carl ordered.

Vanguard Alpha went to the motor pool to board their BUS.

The CDF had been divided into two forces: Infrastructure Protection Force (IPF) and Civilian Protection Force (CPF).

The IPF's mission was to defend vital installations like military bases, communication hubs, and power plants. The Alliance would surely make these sites their top priority.

The mission of the CPF—which Vanguard Alpha and other task forces had been assigned to—was to patrol city streets to maintain order, safeguard civilians, and minimize property damage from enemy infiltration. If the Alliance breached the defense barrier and deployed the mind-control weapon, civilians would be turned against each other and Guardians, complicating the CPF's mission. One saving grace for the CPF was that children were immune to the weapon because they had no cerebral implant.

Meanwhile, Reserve Guardians on Satellite One had already established ground defenses at the planet's key infrastructure. However, given Eden's importance as the presumed primary target, it received the highest level of protection.

◆ ◆ ◆

The ships of the Alliance reached comms range with those of the CDF. Both sides held their positions, ready to duke it out.

On the bridge of Dafulton's flagship, a priority transmission from the CDF's flagship war frigate, the *Valor*, came in. Over the comms, a stilted voice said, "This is Admiral Victor Collins of the Commonwealth Air & Space Corps speaking. I am the commander of this fleet. You have trespassed into Commonwealth domain. Leave immediately. This is your only warning."

Dafulton nodded, authorizing Zataldra to respond.

She said, "My name is Zataldra. We are the Alliance, an army that comprises the Khanorian National Protection Force and the Collective. We demand humanity's surrender. Face judgment for your crimes—by those you wronged, those who lost loved ones to your cruelty.

"On this comms transmission, I'm joined by three Collective generals, each one representing peoples scarred by humanity's actions. They thirst for justice.

"Listen to their stories and understand that their suffering fuels our resolve to see your downfall. But know this: Their people are but a fraction of the ones you've harmed. We stand for them all."

The first general's voice crackled over the comms, a raw echo of past injustice. He spoke about how the Yarlbrat exiled his people, the Kaldragg, from their shared territory after they lost the battle against them. The CDF tipped the scales in the Yalbrat's favor by training their soldiers and supplying them with materiel. Now, fences and checkpoints barred the Kaldragg from their homeland, relegating them to living in wastelands.

Fury laced the second general's words. He recounted how the CDF betrayed his people, the Forrac. During the Bhalkran War, the Commonwealth struck a deal: to use the Forrac's small community as a temporary staging ground. When the CDF's welcome expired, they refused to leave. The corrupt commander of the operation fabricated charges against the Forrac, reporting to CDF Command that they attacked his forces first. Using the charges as a pretext for violence, the CDF forced the Forrac from their own land. Women were violated. Lives were shattered.

The third general, leader of the Collective's Nozzkatari contingent, spoke with quiet pain. Guardians were on a mission to protect miners sent to drill on a faraway world. When the crooked commander of the operation discovered the land being drilled on belonged to the Nozzkatari, he disregarded their cease-and-desist order and pressed on. Needless conflict ensued. Innocent Nozzkatari citizens were mass-murdered in nanogrenade bombardments from CDF strike drones. The general would never be able to lay his pain to rest, but retribution would give him a sense of closure.

After Zataldra told the Khanorians' story, she said, "These are the sins for which the human race is being punished. Judgment day has come."

Admiral Collins replied, "I cannot dispute nor confirm the validity of your claims. But the CDF does not yield."

"You have the authority to deliver a message to your leader, do you not?"

"I'll see to it that any message reaches the right ears."

"Then inform your leader that the Alliance presents two demands. First, the immediate release of our comrades, Navexira and Geznan. Second, the unconditional surrender of the Commonwealth. Your leader has twenty-four hours to comply."

"I'll deliver your message, but I have a feeling that you're going to be disappointed."

As expected, Zataldra thought. She was just following the council's rules of engagement.

The ship-to-ship transmission cut off.

Dafulton grumbled, "Giving the humans more time to fortify their defenses irks me, but we're stuck following *your* council's *rules of engagement.* All we can do right now is sit and wait for the humans' *inevitable* rejection."

Zataldra stood up from her chair, not liking having to wait herself. "I require rest. Inform me the moment we have word from this admiral about his leader's response." She exited the bridge, her tresses a tide of silver gleaming against her black cape.

◆ ◆ ◆

Iya and Jarius, Oviereya's special advisors, had been called to her office. She told them about the electronic missive downlinked from the *Valor* by Admiral Collins to CDF Command and the Executive Office: the release of Geznan and Navexira and the twenty-four-hour deadline to surrender.

"What do you think?" Oviereya asked.

"I say we comply with demand number one," Jarius said. "Let's do a trade: our prisoners for theirs—if our people are still alive, that is." He was referring to the prisoners he, Cruz, and Arlo had been sent to secure the release of. "Who knows, returning their prisoners might serve as an olive branch. We don't need them anyway."

Iya curled a finger around her chin, thinking. "I agree. But we should propose that Zataldra be present for the exchange. This would grant me the opportunity I was hoping for. I can accompany the detainee retrieval team and attempt to reason with her. Perhaps I'll be able to convince her to stand down the Protection Force."

Iya knew Zataldra would be shocked beyond belief when she saw her. They had a pleasant meal at the Gra'Jahorne, avoiding any mention of the war with humanity and instead focusing on fond memories. It was a moment of reconciliation for their strained relationship. And yet, here they were, butting heads as enemies on opposite sides of the war.

"I'll go too," Jarius volunteered. "Negotiation and conflict de-escalation is my wheelhouse. Maybe I can help you get through to her." In truth, he still didn't think Zataldra could be convinced to stand down the Protection Force. And at this point, that might be beyond her call to make, especially with Khanorian leadership already invested in humanity's annihilation, but who knew, she might have some sway.

Oviereya said, "Does this mean you're starting to believe that reasoning with Zataldra is possible?"

"No, but I'm an ambassador. This is my job."

Iya said, "It may not be wise for you to go with me, Jarius. My sister imprisoned you and forced you to kill another ambassador. Seeing her may bring back those uncomfortable memories and trigger your trauma. I can do this alone."

"I—" Jarius' glazed-over eyes drifted away from Iya, staring at nothing in particular. The vivid memory of Cruz's gruesome end surged into his consciousness. He remembered the chilling feeling of being mentally enslaved. Snapping himself out of the memory, he pounded his knuckles together as if he was psyching himself up for a fight. "I'll be fine, Iya," he said surely. "My therapy sessions have worked wonders. Talking to Zataldra shouldn't be a problem. I won't lose my cool or anything because of what she did to me. I'm a trained professional."

Iya's fingers kneaded the tense muscles at the back of her neck. She didn't want Jarius, her friend, to put himself in a position that may cause him unnecessary mental anguish. "Well . . . okay."

"Then it's settled. Both of us will go to orbit with the detainee retrieval team." Jarius set aside his doubts about Zataldra's willingness to reason. There was no point in being pessimistic and dampening everyone's spirits. "We'll do our best to talk some sense into Zataldra—you and me, a human and a Khanorian side by side. Maybe that will show her that us humans aren't all bad. If we were, you'd be dead. I'll let you take the lead, though." Jarius turned to Oviereya. "Is all that okay with you, Madam Chief?"

Oviereya said, "It sounds like a plan to me. Bringing you two on board as special advisors was a good move.

"I'll have Admiral Collins informed of the plan. He'll relay our proposition to the Alliance. Once it's confirmed they agree with it, I'll get the logistics of your travel sorted out. You'll receive notification from me after everything has been arranged; then you can head straight to CDF HQ's airfield for departure to the *Valor*, with the retrieval team."

"Yes, Ma'am," Jarius said. "Come on, Iya. Might as well go back to the guesthouse for a quick bite while we stand by."

Iya nodded, and they left.

◆ ◆ ◆

Stacie fixed her eyes on the TV screen. Media drones broadcasted Guardians flooding Cornerstone City's vacant streets. News reports informed citizens of the Alliance's twenty-four-hour surrender deadline. There were also reports that a peace delegation was being sent to orbit.

Helplessness gnawed at Stacie. It sucked that all she could do was stay glued to a TV screen for war updates. A longing to be out there, defending Eden, twisted her gut.

She thought about Randy. *Stay safe, babe.*

Stacie knew that, if Alliance forces got past the first line of defense in space, Randy would give his life protecting Eden's citizens. He'd take a deathblow for any man, woman, or child. She also knew that if the CDF was victorious and he survived, heavy burdens would weigh on him. While harming Dafulton's pirate thugs wouldn't faze him, harming the Khanorians and others Dafulton had manipulated would likely wound his conscience. During the battle, he'd steel himself, compartmentalize the hurt. But later, the emotional fallout could be devastating and take time to recover from. And she'd be there for him, his pillar of strength.

Juggling her fluctuating emotions, she was relieved that she didn't have to sit through the invasion alone. Jason, Eli, and DeShaun were there. She certainly had enough rooms in her mansion for them. Together, they'd stay updated on the war through the news media. It felt like she was hosting a watch party for the end of the world.

◆ ◆ ◆

Vanguard Alpha arrived in the streets of Cornerstone in their BUS. Guardians of the CPF were everywhere. They had to watch the sky for enemy ships and any aerial systems that might be used to emit the mind-control signal. The last thing they needed was thousands of civilians turning on themselves and attacking them—all part of the Alliance's plan to sow chaos.

Vanguard Alpha disembarked from their BUS. They were responsible for securing several city blocks. Randy had hoped for the development of a countersignal, but it didn't happen.

Akane scanned the deserted streets, as members of Vanguard Alpha dragged the team's hoverbikes from the BUS to start their patrols. "Wow, the city is so . . . so dead."

Cornerstone was eerily silent. The lockdown had left every street devoid of the usual hubbub. On a normal day, there would be intergalactic visitors mingling with citizens, all of whom were mandated to return to their homeworlds prior to the lockdown. The only sounds Akane heard were the hum of her Shell's systems and the mechanical clinking of Guardians' mechboots. Each sweep of her gaze revealed more of the same—a hollow, chilling silence.

Her senses hyperaware, she magnified her visuals and scoured the skies for enemy ships that might have slipped past the defense barrier. Every stray noise, a rustle or creak, set her on edge and amplified the surrounding emptiness.

"You weren't here during the Coalition's Operation Hammer Fall?" Arturo asked, getting onto his bike.

Akane shook her head. "Nah, Vanguard Alpha was away on a mission."

Carl said, "I'm sending everyone their patrol routes." Mentally, he sent the routes to their Shells' CPUs. "Remember, any enemy contact—drone, ship, or otherwise—relay it over comms."

Everyone said, "Yes, Sir!"

Randy jumped onto his bike and powered it on. Jarius' last text message to him said that he and Iya were being sent to negotiate with Zataldra. Randy hoped Jarius would make it back to Eden safely. Anything could happen. He also hoped that Jazzlyn, out in space defending Eden with other aeronauts, would survive the battle.

He revved up the bike's engine and sped away to go on patrol.

The transport ferrying Jarius, Iya, and four combat Guardians—all wearing spacesuits with helmets pulled back—steadily neared the defense barrier. The rear detainment compartment of the craft held Geznan and Navexira.

Engrossed in thought, Jarius stared at the holographic picture of Jazzlyn's face projecting from his wristcom. She was on his mind constantly.

Iya—who had learned of Jazzlyn's connection to Jarius during their talks at the guesthouse—said, "Your fiancée is so kind. While journeying to Eden, I feared encountering more humans like those who ravaged Khanoria and killed my father. Thankfully, my first contact was with Jazzlyn. Fate seems to put me in the company of wonderful humans like you, Jazzlyn, and your friend Randy— consistently showing me that not all humans are as described in

Khanoria's tomes."

Jarius clicked off the hologram. "Jazzlyn is an amazing woman. I'm scared for her."

Iya's chin dipped. "As I am for my sister," she said, voice somber.

The transport approached the *Valor*. It was a threatening behemoth of a war frigate. Its sternward deck boasted launch ramps for the rapid deployment of interceptor squadrons. Defense cannons dotted its surface, poised to repel attacking ships. At the *Valor's* prow, the bridge served as the nexus of its operations. There, Admiral Collins oversaw the battlefield and coordinated his fleet's maneuvers.

Jarius and Iya gazed at the large viewport screen. The scene outside was both breathtaking and terrifying. The CDF's impressive wall of ships stood stationary, facing off against their enemy's equally massive fleet. A vast gulf of space separated the two, marking the do-not-cross boundary between them. Both sides were ready to engage as soon as humanity's twenty-four-hour deadline to surrender expired.

The transport's pilot said over the intercom, "Prepare for docking, everyone."

The *Valor's* ship bay opened. The transport glided inside, and its hull vibrated slightly when the landing gear settled against the floor. Then the bay door lowered with a hiss of decompression, sealing shut. Now that it was safe for the team aboard the transport to disembark, the caution lights along the bay's walls switched from red to green and shut off.

"Docking complete," the pilot announced.

The transport's door opened. Jarius and Iya headed straight for the bridge to link up with Admiral Collins, while the rest of the retrieval team escorted Geznan and Navexira to the spacewalk

285

access hub, where they'd wait for the prisoner exchange to commence.

Walking down corridors of the *Valor*, Iya got goose bumps. She had visited the Protection Force's airfield with her father a couple of times and toured warships, but she had never been inside one this size.

Jarius asked Iya, "How well do you know Geznan and Navexira?"

"We're acquainted, but my sister knows them far better than I do."

The door to the bridge whistled aside. Iya and Jarius strode into the hums, warbles, and murmuration of the machinery surrounding them. Personnel at battle stations looked perturbed, their faces washed in light from screens. When these aeronauts joined the Air & Space Corps, little did they imagine they'd be the first line of defense against an invading armada.

Admiral Collins rose from his command chair to welcome the Chief's special advisors, who were taking the lead in the prisoner exchange.

"Hello, Admiral," Jarius said.

"Greetings, Lieutenant Ambassador Ford and Iya Gor'Ronn," Collins replied. "Now that you two are aboard, I'll inform the Collective flagship that we are ready to proceed. They've agreed to send a ship for the exchange. The ship will link with the *Valor* via our spacewalk bridge. You may head to the spacewalk access hub now."

A young purple-haired man, barely past his promotion to senior aeronaut, eyed Iya. He jabbed a finger in her direction. "How can we be sure *she's* not some kind of double agent?"

Jarius frowned.

Collins set straight the senior aeronaut, his tone firm. "The

Chief Executive trusts her. That should be enough assurance for you. Now, focus on your job."

Embarrassment reddened the senior aeronaut's face. "Yes, Sir. Apologies, Sir," he replied in a more pleasant tone.

Jarius said to Collins, "Admiral, before we hail the Collective vessel, I'd like to request a small favor."

"What can I do for you, Lieutenant Ambassador?"

"My fiancée is stationed on the *Star Phoenix*. If it wouldn't be too much trouble, I'd love to say hello."

"Of course."

Collins ordered an aeronaut first class to relay Jarius' request to the *Star Phoenix*. Soon, word reached Jazzlyn that her fiancée was on the line.

A comms module transmitted Jazzlyn's voice. "Jarius."

Jarius' heart fluttered. He leaned closer to the module's receiver. "Hey there, flygirl."

"What the hell brings you out here?" The joy in Jazzlyn's voice was clear even through the comms.

"Iya and I are heading the detainee retrieval team. Not much time to chat. I just wanted to hear your voice. Be careful out there, alright?"

"You too, lover. I'll see you when this mess is over." After a faint click, the connection cut out.

Jarius doubted that this war could end peacefully. And casualties were inevitable. He just didn't want Jazzlyn to be one of them.

Collins said, "Lieutenant Armentrout, inform the enemy flagship we are ready to make the exchange."

"Yes, Sir."

Though nowhere near the size of a CDF war frigate, the Collective ship sent to rendezvous with the *Valor* was not small, and it carried enough firepower to defend itself in case of deception. The ship paused at the prearranged distance. From the portside of the *Valor*, the spacewalk bridge extended, connecting to the Collective ship's starboard airlock.

Iya and Jarius stood inside the spacewalk access hub, waiting for the hatch to unseal. Geznan and Navexira, spacesuited as well, stood behind them in silence with their wrists cuffed. The four combat Guardians took their positions behind the prisoners.

Iya's explanations weren't enough for Geznan and Navexira to understand how she could side with the people who had terrorized Khanoria.

Geznan said to Iya, "Your father would be ashamed of you."

Iya spun around to face him. "My father valued peace above all else. He would never endorse sending soldiers to die needlessly for Dafulton's war—Dafulton, the man responsible for Varanz's death."

Navexira gasped. "Grand Elder Varanz is dead?"

"Yes," Iya replied. "Dafulton, your so-called leader, orchestrated an attack on the citadel using the mind-control weapon and pinned it on the humans to drag the Protection Force into this war he lusts for. Varanz was killed in the attack, though not intentionally targeted. My sister knows the truth, yet she touted Dafulton's lie to secure the Protection Force's support for the Collective.

"Dafulton has some clandestine agenda. He cares nothing for the people victimized by the Commonwealth Defense Force. And he most likely expected fatalities during his citadel attack."

Iya's words gave Geznan pause. "You lie, child."

Iya put him in his place, saying, "An apprentice of the Tograh'Dirkot *does not* lie."

Over the intercom, the *Valor's* helmsman said, "Anti-gravity field engaged."

Jarius and Iya glanced at the overhead monitor, which displayed an external view. They saw a green energy field envelop the bridge. If the field went down for some reason, the spacesuits' magnetic boots would keep them anchored.

Jarius harbored no illusions about Zataldra's cooperation. After her inevitable refusal to stand down the Protection Force, he and Iya would return to Eden to wait out the remaining hours of the Commonwealth's surrender deadline. Though surrender was never an option, the CDF's fighting men and women could use as much respite as they could get before all hell broke loose.

"Nervous?" Jarius asked Iya.

"A tad." Questions swirled in her mind. How would Zataldra react when she saw her with Jarius? Could she convince Zataldra to stand down the Protection Force?

Jarius said, "Are you sure you don't wanna carry a weapon, for precaution?" He pointed to the gun holstered on his belt. "Even we ambassadors carry a sidepiece when the situation calls for it. Like now, when we're in the middle of full-on wartime operations."

Iya glared at Jarius' gun with distaste. "An apprentice of the Tograh'Dirkot cannot carry a weapon." Her dedication was unshakable—steadfast and true.

"And if attacked?"

"If we're attacked, we may use anything at our disposal to defend ourselves, but we're forbidden to carry a weapon willingly. And this is just a prisoner exchange, not a firefight."

Jarius didn't rule out any possibilities. *Yeah, a prisoner exchange that could go sideways.*

Over the intercom, the helmsman said, "They're ready to make the exchange. Hatch opening now. Best of luck out there."

Jarius and Iya gripped their suits' pullover helmets and drew

289

them forward, locking them to the suits' upright collars.

The circular hatch unsealed.

Jarius glanced back at the prisoners. "Let's go."

He and Iya exited first, the green glow of the energy field reflecting on their suits. Geznan and Navexira trailed behind them, flanked by the four Guardians keeping a watchful eye on them.

Zataldra approached, her stride purposeful. Five Guardian prisoners, hands bound, walked behind her, flanked by three imposing figures serving as her personal guard. They all wore spacesuits.

Both teams met at the bridge's halfway point.

A pang of grief resonated within Jarius. There were supposed to be eighteen prisoners. The rest, test subjects for Zataldra's twisted experiments, were dead.

One of the Guardians behind Jarius clenched his fists, anger flaring.

Jarius said to him, "Easy, Private Glosby. I know it hurts."

A muscle in Glosby's jaw jumped. "More than you know, Sir." He seemed to grow more irate by the second.

Seeing Geznan and Navexira safe and sound brought relief to Zataldra's troubled heart. *Thank the stars they're okay.* When she laid eyes on Jarius' face, she recoiled, startled by his unexpected presence. "You?" she spat.

"In the flesh," Jarius said. "And though you held me prisoner, I . . ."—he remembered blowing Cruz's head away, his body at Zataldra's beck and call—"I don't hate you."

"Your feelings toward me are irrelevant." Zataldra's eyes rested on Iya's visor, and a frisson of shock coursed through her. "Sister? But . . . what are you doing here?"

Iya said, "I came to the humans' homeworld to give them the blueprints for your weapon."

Zataldra recalled that the lights in her lab had already been on when she arrived. She realized it must have been Iya who was there. "How could you?"

Iya ignored the question. "You must help end this madness. Inform the Protection Force that Dafulton, not the humans, was responsible for the citadel attack.

"Not all humans are malicious. Yes, some of their soldiers committed unforgivable acts in Khanoria. But the actions of a few humans should not condemn their entire race. I know you want to avenge Father. I share your anger. But you must allow your heart to heal. I agree we Khanorians deserve some form of restitution. We should work with the Commonwealth's leader to achieve that. I've met her. She's a compassionate woman and—"

A tremor entered Zataldra's voice as she interrupted Iya. "No. Why do you persist in siding with humans over your own kind?" Disappointment flickered in her eyes. She and Iya had had a lovely time at the Gra'Jahorne. It felt like their relationship was getting better, but now this? "Why?"

"Because I walk the path of righteousness. The Korahh'Havaell itself instructs us to—"

"Enough!" Zataldra's sharp command silenced further discussion.

Iya stepped closer, shrinking the distance between her and Zataldra.

"Hold! Maintain your distance!" barked one of Zataldra's men.

Iya froze, her momentum killed.

Jarius said to Zataldra, "If we were the monsters you say we are, would we be returning your two friends unharmed? Would Iya be standing beside me, a human, if that were the case, huh?"

Her voice icy, Zataldra said, "We've offered clemency—the opportunity to surrender and face judgment for your crimes.

Perhaps you should accept it, rather than peddling empty platitudes and a false narrative of human benevolence."

"But it's the truth!" Iya insisted. She edged closer, her hand reaching for her sister. "Please, you have to—"

"No more talk. It's time we completed this exchange."

Iya had failed, which didn't surprise Jarius. He never expected Zataldra to fold. "Very well, let's get on with it." He waved Geznan and Navexira forward after his Guardians removed their cuffs.

The five prisoners on the other side began walking forward too.

Private Glosby whipped his rifle up. "Murderers!" he screamed, his blood hot.

Suddenly, the tension in the air thickened.

Jarius reacted instantly. "Whoa! What the hell are you doing? Stand down, Private Glosby!"

Glosby, ignoring the order, fired his rifle.

Zataldra's men, ready for such eventualities, shot back with orb blasters. The other three Guardians of the retrieval team sent a volley of rounds flying across the bridge. What was supposed to be a civil prisoner exchange had gone to hell, weapons roaring.

A blast from one of Zataldra's men struck Iya, and she fell. Gasping hard, eyes wide, she felt death creeping in.

Zataldra felt like her heart had just plummeted from her chest and splattered across the bridge. "Cease fire!" she yelled at her men. Their weapons stopped.

"Hey, knock it off!" Jarius demanded his Guardians.

Private Glosby, the instigator of the firefight, continued shooting even as his comrades lowered their weapons as ordered.

Jarius snatched the rifle. "Damn it, I said knock it the fuck off!" He shoved Glosby forcefully. "I'm your fucking superior! What the hell is wrong with you, Private?"

Glosby shouted, "My brother is one of the prisoners who ain't here! It's their fault he's dead! Heads need to roll, Sir! Someone has to—"

"Shut the fuck up!" Jarius thundered, his throat dry. "You will be disciplined for insubordination."

One of Zataldra's men lay lifeless. Another was clutching a wound, still standing, though. On the CDF's side, one Guardian was down, his fate uncertain.

Jarius knelt beside Iya and assessed the wound in her midsection. "Hey, you alright?" Her ragged gasps were his only answer, the next weaker than the last. He took a healing patch from his belt and applied it to the wound. "Hang in there, Iya. Don't you fucking die on me. You hear me?" Gently, he scooped her up into his arms.

Zataldra lurched forward, a snarl twisting her features. "Unhand my sister!"

One of her men grabbed her shoulder. "We have our people. We should fall back to the ship."

One Guardian of the retrieval team lifted the downed Guardian into a fireman's carry. He was alive, barely.

Zataldra unholstered a gun and aimed it steadily at Jarius. She wanted to get Iya back, but Iya was in the crossfire. She couldn't risk taking the shot.

Geznan hoisted the fallen Collective soldier onto his shoulders. "Let's go, Zataldra."

Both sides retreated to their respective ships. With one Collective soldier dead, Jarius had a feeling the surrender deadline —a mere formality—was now effectively void.

The retrieval team and rescued prisoners rushed back inside the spacewalk access hub. Medics were already there on standby, as Admiral Collins had seen everything that went down from his monitoring station on the bridge.

The medics placed Iya and the shot Guardian on gurneys and hooked life-support equipment up to them. Others checked on the health of the rescued prisoners.

The medics' words were a blur of jargon to Jarius, yet the mounting dismay in their voices told him everything—Iya's condition was critical.

The medics began wheeling both gurneys to the infirmary. Jarius kept pace behind the medics, his eyes locked on Iya's unmoving form. *Please, hang in there, Iya,* he thought.

◆ ◆ ◆

Back from the disastrous prisoner exchange, Zataldra strode onto the bridge of Dafulton's ship. She sank into her command chair. It once again adjusted to fit her specific proportions. Then she buried her face in her hands, worried about Iya.

Dafulton spoke from beside her, forced sympathy lacing his voice. "I witnessed the entire thing. Are you alright?"

Zataldra was a hysterical mess inside. "This . . . this shouldn't have happened. It's all my—" She broke off mid-sentence, unable to get the rest out.

"It's all the humans' fault, that's who. Iya should not have been out there. But they manipulated her. The waiting is over. We attack now. I'll inform the Protection Force commander."

Uncovering her face, Zataldra revealed an expression of pure despair. "But Iya . . . she's on their flagship."

"Then we will have to be meticulous in our offense."

On Dafulton and the Protection Force commander's orders, Alliance ships moved into attack formations.

◆ ◆ ◆

Jarius paced back and forth in the infirmary. Medics huddled around a glowing screen, their faces grim as they studied Iya's X-rays and anatomical data to assess the severity of her wound. Khanorians were very human in appearance, but their internal makeup was quite different.

One medic was monitoring Iya's vitals on the console beside the bed, a quiet beep signaling weak readings.

Jarius thought, *Iya, hold tough. You've got this.*

"Attention," came Admiral Collins over the ship-wide intercom, "we are receiving a transmission from the Collective flagship. I'm patching it through."

Dafulton's voice filled the room as the medics continued working. "Fleet of the Commonwealth Defense Force, an Alliance soldier now lies dead. We consider this act of aggression your official refusal to surrender. Today, you will face the consequences of your sins. We will have retribution for every life you humans have stolen and every wrong you have inflicted!"

Jarius scoffed, knowing Dafulton was a wolf in sheep's clothing. *This asshole cares nothing about retribution.*

Dafulton said, "Prepare for battle."

The comms line closed.

Jarius watched the medics operate on Iya.

His unease deepened.

He and she were supposed to be on their way to Eden. Instead, they were stuck on a ship about to go to war, and Iya was on her deathbed—her life hanging in the balance.

CHAPTER TWELVE

The first salvo of gunfire flared from Alliance craft. War frigates of the Air & Space Corps countered, their cannons thundering as interceptors launched from their decks.

Charged with adrenaline, Zataldra tapped at the keys of her chair's module. She activated a holographic tactical map displaying a crowded arrangement of color-coded ship markers. Blue for Alliance. Red for CDF. Tracking the enemy's maneuvers, she contemplated strategies. Never had she been involved in a battle of this scale, not even during the Khanorian Revolution.

In the raging tempest of space combat, where thousands of craft clashed, her mind clung to a single, fervent hope: *May my sister survive.* She felt her stomach tying in knots.

◆ ◆ ◆

For her safety, Oviereya remained in the underground bunker of the Manor. She sat in her secondary office, receiving updates on the battle in orbit. The CDF was putting up a valiant fight, but enemy ships had slipped past Eden's defense barrier. She was awaiting further updates on how well Satellite One's barrier was holding up.

Moments ago, she had tried reaching out to the Union leaders again—a final Hail Mary. There was no response, a sign that they hadn't changed their minds. The Commonwealth would have to weather this storm alone.

◆ ◆ ◆

The Guardians of the CPF and IPF received notification that Alliance ships had descended upon Eden.

Vanguard Alpha stood atop a building. In sight were two of the invading ships, hovering at a low, fixed altitude over rooftops. Below, mind control had dragged civilians out of their homes. Now, these innocent men and women were beating on each other in the streets.

Guardians were trying to subdue the civilians and restore order.

Carl said, "Those ships are definitely transmitting the mind-control signal. The larger the transmitter, the wider the range. The drone used in Terence Plaza was just a prototype signal-deployment method. These ships are the real one."

Randy synced his HUD to a network of street cameras. There was a swarm of Alliance ships stationed all over Cornerstone. The mind-control signal emitted by the ships had seeped into households, spilling out crazed citizens onto the streets, pitting neighbor against neighbor. Police forces had joined the fray alongside Guardians. They were using nonlethal weapons to try to stop the violence and avert a full-blown human-to-human massacre.

Randy watched the multiple windows superimposed over his HUD. *It's hell out there.* He accessed live newscasts, the media's drones broadcasting the pandemonium from a bird's-eye view while, in studios, commentators spoke over the footage. *The Alliance's utilization of mind control to instigate the slaughter of adult civilians perfectly complements their goal of sparing the children.* The Collective knew from Navexira and Geznan's intel that children had no cerebral implants.

Akane flinched. The sight of the citizens below attacking each other reminded her of her own experience.

Randy, beside her, said, "You okay?"

"I'm fine."

"If your symptoms start again, you should—"

"Knock it off, Randy. I'm good."

The sky thundered, jerking Vanguard Alpha's attention upward. Two more Alliance ships had infiltrated Eden airspace and were flying to a location beyond Cornerstone City. Despite the breaches, the defense barrier was holding most of the enemy at bay —the Air & Space Corps giving it their all.

Randy pondered the status of Satellite One's defenses, thinking about his father and the relatives from his father's side he hadn't met yet.

Arturo, staring at the two ships in sight, said, "Where's our air assets when you need them?"

Carl replied, "Air support can't do a damn thing. As long as those ships are hovering over the city, we can't blast them out of the air. They'd plummet right into civilians' homes. And the Alliance knows that."

Randy said, "So we gotta take them over and shut down the signal."

"You got it, Scott," Carl said. He had his CPU scan the CDF's database for any information on the ships. It turned out they were Khanorian vessels, which was a relief. The CDF had obtained specs and tutorials for the ships during the Khanorian Campaign— part of the Commonwealth Government's compensation package with the Sorin. The tutorials gave Vanguard Alpha instructions on how to maintain power to the engines while cutting power to the rest of the ship. And cutting the power would shut off the emitters transmitting the mind-control signal. "There are tutorials for the ships in the database. They'll tell you what you need to know to accomplish the task."

Randy poised himself for action, his posture confident. "Well, let's get to work, then."

Carl gave orders. "Two Guardians per ship. The rest of us will assist with restoring order to the streets." He then said to the mission commander of the CPF's Cornerstone forces, through comms, "Lieutenant Breckenridge of Vanguard Alpha here. We've confirmed the two enemy ships are the source of the mind-control signal. We are going to take control of them."

"Roger that," came the response.

Carl knew the mission to protect Cornerstone, Eden's capital, necessitated constant flexibility. Cornerstone's Guardian forces would have to be a two-headed beast, dealing with the immediate threat of mind-controlled civilians while scanning for any further airspace breaches.

The burden of leadership for task force leaders like him felt like a tightrope walk. Split-second decisions and continuous communication with each other and the Cornerstone mission commander were the keys to navigating this mess. It was essentially like leading within the throes of a waking nightmare.

Randy stepped up to the plate first. "I'll take one ship. Who's coming with me?"

Akane was quick to join him. "I got your back, Randy." Just like she had his back in Khanoria. It was the least she could do after he had helped her overcome her trauma.

Carl said, "Specialist de León and Sergeant Pines, you two take the other ship. The rest of us will stay out here to help on the ground."

Randy motioned for Akane to follow. "Come on."

They leap-frogged from rooftop to rooftop, mechboots thudding. Once they reached the rooftop directly above the ship they intended to infiltrate, they threw themselves into the air and landed on top of it.

Two auto defense cannons emerged from their housing.

"Well, no element of surprise for us," Randy said wryly.

Akane shrugged. "Looks like it."

The cannons spewed blasts. Randy dodged left while Akane dodged right, going after opposite cannons.

Mini missiles belched from their Shells and obliterated the cannons.

"Let's get inside," Randy said. He powered on his plasma saber and carved a circle into the ship's roof. The piece of hull crashed to the floor below.

Randy jumped down. Akane descended behind him.

Inside, an alarm klaxon blared and red-alert lights flashed across drab gray walls. Three of Dafulton's lackeys rounded a corner, weapons aimed at the intruders. In a flash of motion, Randy cut loose a volley of shots from his wrist guns, propelling the men against the walls before they slumped to the floor.

Randy was glad that these men were Dafulton's pirate thugs and not the innocent recruits he had duped. "Come on, let's find the control room."

He and Akane ran.

Another man appeared. He became frightened out of his wits as he stared down the barrels of Akane and Randy's wrist guns, eyes bugging out. For a moment, he forgot how to work his limbs. When he eventually managed to fire his weapon, his arm shivered so badly that he couldn't aim for shit. His shots went wide, gnawing holes into the wall instead of hitting their targets. Before he could compensate for his miss, Akane's wrist gun barked once, and he was down.

Adrenaline pumping, Randy and Akane blasted down doors in a mad search for the control room. Head or body shots reduced any of Dafulton's men who got in their way to lifeless corpses. Eventually, they hit pay dirt and stormed into the control room, where two men—alerted to their approach by security cameras—greeted them with energy blasts. No match for Shells, the men were taken out by Randy and Akane's wrist-gun fire.

The helmsman, hands raised in surrender, opened his mouth to speak, but a single, decisive head shot from Randy silenced him before he could utter his plea for mercy.

Randy noticed the controls differed slightly from those in the tutorials. The Khanorian Protection Force had upgraded this type of ship since the Khanorian Campaign. "This is a new model. The controls are a bit different. I'll have my CPU cross-reference the new controls with the old ones to find out what I need to do to shut off the power. It's probably pretty much the same." His CPU began processing.

Akane looked out of a window. Anarchy reigned in several streets across Cornerstone. Citizens trapped in a mindless rage were tearing each other apart with ruthless savagery. Akane, having gone through a similar hell under Zataldra's control, felt her heart mourning for them. Would they have to endure the same aftereffects she had experienced? "What's the status?" she asked Randy.

"My CPU is still working," Randy said. His HUD beeped: ANALYSIS COMPLETE. "Okay, got it." Randy toggled switches and inputted a sequence on the control panel. A chirp of compliance confirmed that he had cut the ship's power, while leaving the engines running.

After a droning sound, the room went dark.

Randy and Akane activated their helmets' lights.

Peering once more out the window, at the area directly below, Akane saw people regaining their senses and the police and Guardians standing down. She gave Randy a thumbs-up. "The emitters are off."

Randy said into his helmet's comm, "This is Sergeant Scott to Vanguard Alpha. Akane and I were successful."

Carl replied, "de León and Pines were successful as well. Now get back down here."

"Yes, Sir."

Randy and Akane went back into the corridor, where broken doors and dead bodies littered the floor.

◆ ◆ ◆

Iya's eyes peeled open as the effects of the sedatives wore off. She saw Jarius sitting by her bedside. "Jarius," she said weakly and tried to sit up.

"Take it easy. You're not fully recovered yet."

Iya sank back onto the bed. "Are we still on the *Valor*?"

"Yeah, and the war has started."

An explosion rocked the infirmary. The lights blinked off, and the life-sustaining equipment hooked up to Iya groaned. Then the lights flashed back on.

"Damn it," Jarius said. "We can't afford to have interruptions while you're healing."

"I'm scared," Iya confessed.

Jarius clasped her little hand tightly. "You and me both, kiddo." Jarius was as brave as they came, and he had fought in the civil war, but facing the possibility of death was still daunting. "I'm going to the bridge to see how the battle is going." He got up from his chair.

"I . . . I don't want to be left alone."

"I'll be back before you know it. I promise. And the medics should be returning soon." Jarius left the infirmary.

His thoughts dwelled on Jazzlyn. It was mentally overwhelming knowing the person he loved was in the thick of the battle.

He recollected the day they first met. Both were leaving a shopping mall when their paths crossed. Jazzlyn's beauty instantly struck him. Her arms full of overstuffed bags, she fumbled, dropping one. That was his cue. He swooped in to help gather her scattered items with all the smooth charm of a natural gentleman. A little harmless flirtation followed. Of course, she played hard to get, but he didn't let that deter him. They found out they were both lieutenants in the CDF—she in the Air & Space Corps Reserves, he in the Ambassador Corps. After lunch that day, it was a given that they were a match, their chemistry undeniable.

Jazzlyn, please stay safe, Jarius silently pled.

Jazzlyn weaved her interceptor amid a hail of laser fire. Blasts from the opposing sides crackled across the cosmic battlefield. Every corkscrew maneuver and near miss with enemy fire tightened the ball of anxiety in her gut.

Locking on to the enemy ship ahead, she opened fire and destroyed it, reducing it to scrap metal. Two red dots appeared on her radar, signaling that two more enemy ships were en route.

Jazzlyn's focus sharpened, and her piloting instincts took over. She dodged the enemy ships' fire, barrel-rolling out of the way. Then her own cannons roared, crippling the enemy ships. "Hell yeah!" she said, cheering herself on. Her victory was short-lived, a never-ending stream of targets appearing on her radar.

As more blasts whizzed past her interceptor, Jazzlyn remembered the day Jarius proposed to her. They were having a romantic picnic in a tranquil park surrounded by nature's beauty. The sun shone down on them, birds sang, and gentle breezes ruffled the trees' leaves. Near a sparkling waterfall, Jarius got down on one knee and asked for her hand in marriage.

Enemy fire hit Jazzlyn's interceptor. She retaliated and took down another ship before being struck again.

Alarms blared and controls malfunctioned.

"No, no, no," Jazzlyn blurted. Realizing her fate was sealed, she thought of Jarius, Stacie, and Randy.

This was it for her—her life was ending. No more runs with Stacie in the park, no more laughter-filled double dates. Jazzlyn's dream of her and Stacie serving as each other's bridesmaids dissolved. With the heaviest of hearts, Jazzlyn bid farewell to it all.

Silently, she apologized to Jarius for not being able to return to him as promised.

Tears wet her face.

Memories took her back to the moment Jarius slipped the engagement ring onto her finger. She sobbed, eyes puffy from crying, and then everything went dark, her interceptor shattering apart in the cold expanse of space. There was nothing left of Jazzlyn Rochelle de' Medici. Nothing but the memories her loved ones would forever hold on to.

From the *Valor's* bridge, Jarius watched the turmoil of interstellar warfare rage on. Unaware of his fiancée's death, he thought, *Jazzlyn, please come back to me.*

CHAPTER THIRTEEN

The situation in Cornerstone had worsened. More ships had gotten past Eden's defense barrier, and more Alliance soldiers had been dispersed onto the streets.

A thunderous explosion jettisoned vehicles into the air.

"Move!" Randy said to Akane.

They scrambled to safety as the vehicles crashed down around them, some cartwheeling before slamming into buildings.

The Alliance soldiers' mission was to eliminate Guardians and protect their ships. Civilians, their minds hijacked by mind control, now served as unwilling shields for their enslavers, the signal commanding them to attack Guardians.

Carl had dispatched Randy and Akane to a hot zone. They faced a double threat: enemy soldiers plus innocent civilians turned into weapons. Since their Shells had run out of knockout-gas projectiles, they had to find a way to neutralize the civilians without causing harm to them.

Randy's aim assist zoomed in on two enemy soldiers shooting at him. He couldn't risk firing back at them through the mob of civilians marching closer like a horde of mindless zombies. Instead, he commanded his Shell to launch the Predator Bomb. The airborne ordnance flew overhead, bypassing the civilians below. It banked downward and stopped right at its targets. By the time the enemy registered the bomb, they had no chance to get away. The bomb detonated, an orb of plasma energy ballooning until it exploded in a brilliant flash, tearing into the enemy's exo-armor.

Randy said into comms, "Lieutenant Breckenridge, how long until we can get some backup? Things are getting rough over here."

"Sergeant Pines and Specialist de León are en route to your location."

"Roger."

"Ugh!" Akane yelled in frustration. Three civilians were futilely whaling on her armor with their bare fists. "Sorry about this." She grabbed one by his shirtfront and tossed him aside. Then she shoved another to the ground. Before she could neutralize the third man, a blast from an Alliance soldier ripped through his back and struck her, knocking her down. She was unharmed, but the civilian was dead, sacrificed for a cheap shot. Enraged, she got up, aimed her wrist gun, and blasted the soldier's helmet until his head disappeared.

Arturo and Jenny descended from a rooftop, their Shells blemished from combat like Randy and Akane's. When they landed, they fired knockout-gas pellets that sent the civilians to sleep.

"Appreciate the assist," Randy said.

"Happy to help," Jenny replied.

The four Vanguard Alpha Guardians mopped up the remaining enemy soldiers, trading shots back and forth.

After the dust had settled, Randy wondered how well Eden and Satellite One's defense barriers were faring and who was winning the battle in space.

Over comms, Carl said, "Scott, situation report."

Randy responded, "Situation under control, Sir. Civilian hostiles subdued without harm. Enemy forces eliminated."

"Great. Now get yourselves to Orion Square. There's a heavy concentration of Alliance soldiers there, and Team Iron Sentinel could use a hand."

"On it," Randy said.

Arturo was hyped for the next fight. "You heard the lieutenant. Let's get over there and kick some ass."

Randy checked his Shell's power-cell gauge and weapons inventory on his HUD. The power cell was at twenty-five percent. His nonplasma-based weapons were nearly empty. "My Shell could use a recharge and restock."

"Mine too," Akane said.

Arturo and Jenny confirmed their Shells were in a similar state.

The team heard a faraway boom. More firefights were developing throughout the city.

Randy said, "Let's head to the closest mobile rearmament station and then get over to Orion Square."

The team ran past the scattered dead enemies and twisted remains of vehicles.

Akane caught sight of a young girl—peaches-and-cream skin, long brown pigtails, perhaps eight years old. She was standing alone in the street. "Guys, hold up!" shouted Akane. Everyone's mechboots clattered to an abrupt stop. Akane approached the girl. "Hey, kid, what are you doing out here?"

"Wow, a Guardian," the girl whispered to herself. It wasn't every day that someone got to see the Commonwealth's soldiers up close.

Akane asked, "Didn't your parents tell you to stay inside?"

The girl nodded nervously. "Uh-huh. Something . . . happened to them, just like they said it might. They started acting all weird and then just left. It was like they were in a trance or something."

Akane thought grimly, *They're out here somewhere, under mind control.*

The girl said, "I got scared being alone, and I wanted to go find Mommy and Daddy."

"What's your name?" Randy asked kindly.

"Mikayla," the girl answered.

"Well, Mikayla, you're a brave girl, but it's important that you stay inside like your parents told you."

"Will they . . . Will they be okay?"

"We're going to do everything we can to bring them back and —"

Blasts lanced down from the air and tore up phyocrete.

Arturo looked up. "Incoming baddies!"

Two exo-armored figures were gliding down toward the team.

One of them shouted, "Time to die, human filth!"

Arturo leapt and activated his plasma saber. The blade flickered out from his wrist at maximum power. He impaled the soldier in midair, bringing him down. As Arturo landed, the soldier's body clanged to the ground behind him. If the soldier wasn't dead, his armor was certainly out of commission.

"Sorry, death and I aren't on good terms right now." Arturo's saber fizzled out on his command.

Akane shouted at Mikayla, "Get behind me! Now!" Mikayla did as told.

The remaining Alliance soldier came soaring down with a kick that Randy ducked under. Summoning his plasma saber, Randy braced himself for a fight.

"For Khanoria!" the hulking Alliance soldier roared.

So, he's a Khanorian, Randy thought.

Just as Jenny and Arturo were about to step in to help Randy, he halted them by extending an open palm.

Randy said to the Khanorian Alliance soldier, "I'm Randal Scott. What's your name?"

"It's Torrallis, a name you'll remember in death."

"Torrallis, I know the CDF's actions in Khanoria were wrong. Your people deserve restitution. We don't have to fight."

Akane admired Randy's commitment to sparing Khanorian lives. *Randy, still aiming for diplomacy when he can. Still trying to do the right thing.*

Torrallis produced a handheld energy blade, just as long and formidable as the Shell's plasma saber. "This war was inevitable. I've trained for it, *craved* it." His and Randy's blades collided in a spray of sparks.

Randy disengaged and reared back. *He's just like Zataldra. Hatred eating him alive. Believing all humans must perish.* The atrocities in Khanoria had inundated many minds with rage, and Torrallis' mind was one of them. The only remedy for that rage seemed to be humanity obliterated.

Randy swung his saber, but Torrallis was quick on his feet. A shimmering energy buckler projected from his forearm, blocking the blow.

Torrallis said, over the sizzling of his buckler and Randy's saber pressed together, "I've fought in every major arena of Khanoria. I've suffered through wars, acquired many scars, and come close to death. I will not fall to you." His will was strong—unbreakable.

He pushed back Randy's saber with his buckler.

The sizzling of their pressed-together weapons loudened.

Randy grunted, saber fluctuating. The power in his Shell's arms allowed him to hold his ground in this tug-of-war.

Torrallis advanced, forcing Randy to retreat a step, their

weapons still locked. "As long as there is breath in my lungs, I will fight you people to the end!"

Randy jumped back while firing his wrist guns. The blasts dissipated harmlessly against Torrallis' buckler. Randy then released three miniature spherical drones into the air. They circled Torrallis and blitzkrieged his armor with laser beams.

When Randy saw Torrallis' armor in rough condition, he sent a mental command to the drones. They stopped shooting but remained hovering in the air on standby.

Desperation colored Randy's tone. "Don't make me end your life. I don't want to."

Deaf to Randy's heartfelt entreaty for a truce, Torrallis charged at full speed. His armor's mobility was noticeably lagging from the damage.

Since the conclusion of the CDF's Khanorian Campaign, a fire had started inside Torrallis, always burning for retribution, never dying. Torrallis surged every iota of strength into his next maneuver and aimed to kill. Randy parried Torrallis' blade, forcefully shunting it away with his own. He then riposted, attempting to exploit the opening, but Torrallis threw himself sideways. In an "oh, shit" moment for Randy, he saw Torrallis' blade coming at him fast despite the exo-armor's drop in mobility. He quickly jerked his saber up between himself and the blade. Wrestling with regret, he delivered the fatal stab, his saber piercing Torrallis' chest.

I'm sorry. Randy jerked his saber backward and turned it off.

Torrallis crumpled, lying at Randy's feet. He soon lost the ability to breathe, the jaws of death closing in.

Remorse asserted itself over Randy. The necessity of killing Torrallis didn't lessen the discomfort. Ending his life felt like a cruel twist of a knife into the heart. This was the brutal reality of war—good people on both sides forced to kill each other, just like in the civil war.

It was just as agonizing for Jenny as it was for Randy to have to kill people who didn't deserve to die. She wanted to give him more time to gather his bearings, but they were in the middle of fighting an invasion. "Hey, Scott, we'd better get to Orion Square. Team Iron Sentinel needs our help."

"Yeah," Randy said wistfully, recalling his zapper drones. He was weary of this battle's mental burdens already. By transferring from the Land Combatant Corps to the Expedition Task Forces to hunt cross-planetary criminals, he had sought to avoid the moral quandary of discerning whether his targets were actually good people or real bad guys. Yet, he had found himself ordered to fight another war where he had to do exactly that.

Randy would be in a slump after the battle, and if he needed an extra shoulder to lean on besides Stacie's, Akane promised herself she would be there for him. "I'll escort Mikayla back home and catch up with you guys at the rearmament station," she said.

Randy put the soldier-base back in his voice. "Alright, let's move out." He metaphorically rolled up his sleeves, getting his mind back in the game.

◆ ◆ ◆

Trying to ignore the pain in her heavily bandaged midsection, Iya walked onto the *Valor's* bridge to the sound of Admiral Collins barking orders.

When Jarius saw Iya, he got up from the computer station he sat at and left the holographic battle-displays he had been watching. "Iya, you shouldn't be up."

"I'm feeling stronger," she said. "The medics tried to stop me from leaving, but I couldn't lie idle any longer. I need to know how the battle is going."

"We're fighting hard, but some enemy ships have made it to Eden."

Explosions vibrated the walls, missiles pounding into the *Valor*.

A tremor ran up Iya's spine, and her eyes reflected a mix of fear and worry. The lives of both humans and Khanorians were being lost in this conflict. And it wasn't an unlikely possibility that her sister could be dead by the time this battle was over.

Jarius tenderly brushed a sweat-dampened strand of hair from Iya's face. "I know this is scary, and it's natural to fear for your sister's life. We can only hope that the Alliance surrenders, with Zataldra unharmed." *And Jazzlyn unharmed too,* he thought, still unaware of her death.

Collins said, "Lieutenant Armentrout, any updates from the Satellite One defense fleet?"

"Affirmative, Sir. The report shows another wave of enemy ships has gotten to Satellite One."

Collins pounded his chair's armrest. "Damn it."

A bone-jarring explosion rocked the bridge.

A woman's voice reported, "We've lost turrets five, eight, and nine."

Collins said, "Keep all guns firing at full blast. And power up the mega cannon."

The mighty roar of the *Valor's* turrets sounded like it could shake the very foundations of the cosmos. A squadron of Alliance ships erupted into balls of fire, none of them able to penetrate the barrage. The *Valor's* mega cannon began charging up, its barrel glowing and crackling. Finally, the cannon spat out a sphere of emerald plasma energy. It grew in size as it devoured the Alliance ships in its path before finally dissipating. This was no weapon to be used lightly; it sapped a significant amount of power from the

Valor's core.

Collins almost jumped from his chair in triumph. "Yes!"

"Oh, fuck yeah!" shouted a blue-haired Korean woman.

Crewmen cheered, but Iya wondered who inside those ships she might have known—warmen introduced to her by her father when she was little. What if Bingrew or Zer'Katro were inside two of those ships? There was no rejoicing in any Khanorian deaths for her. And if the CDF won and the Alliance retreated, would that end the war? Or would both sides continue plotting and attacking each other, entangling Khanoria in a long-lasting conflict?

◆ ◆ ◆

Randy, Arturo, and Jenny arrived at the rearmament station, a Maintenance Corps BUS.

A female shelled Guardian said, "Maintenance Sergeant Sigrid Falk at your service. My crew and I will take care of you. Whose Shell needs servicing?"

"All of us. We need a recharge and restock," Randy said. "And there's another member of our team on the way."

Randy, Arturo, and Jenny unsealed themselves from their Shells, mechanisms clicking and servos whining. They stepped back, exiting their Shells' interior.

Recognition dawned in Sigrid's eyes when she saw Randy. "You're Randal Scott, son of Arson Scott, right?"

"Yep," Randy replied tersely.

Sigrid retracted her faceplate so that Randy could see her sincerity. "During the civil war, I became skeptical of immigrant Guardians. I thought they might become 'Independent Movement sympathizers' and turn into traitors—like I thought your dad was, like I thought you were. After the war ended, I was furious. I wanted all former Coalition fighters to pay. And I became even more weary of immigrant citizens, thinking they might be members of extremist groups like RISE.

"But after witnessing former defectors like you and immigrant Guardians give their sweat and blood to protect the Commonwealth, I've changed my views. Your dedication is inspiring, Sergeant Scott. Thank you for not giving up on the CDF. And thank you for riding out any hardships you may have faced for being a former Coalition fighter and the son of an immigrant."

One of Sigrid's crew members added, "I used to believe all that fucking bullshit about Edenites being superior humans. But we all bleed and die the same. When you think about it, the term 'immigrant' is absurd, since both immigrants and original Edenites are citizens of the Commonwealth."

Randy appreciated their words. "Well, thanks for getting me all warm n' fuzzy on the inside. What you said means a lot to me—seriously."

Sigrid made a hand gesture to her crew. "Okay, folks, let's get to work." She and her team of five plugged charging cables from the BUS into the Shells and opened up the Shells' weapons compartments and lockers to restock them.

Arturo sat with Randy on the landing of a nearby building's steps. Jenny chose to stand, staying by the BUS and making small talk with the maintenance crew.

Randy rubbed a hand over his face, exhausted and still toting guilt from Torrallis' death. It was a shame he had to kill him.

He thought about Jarius and Jazzlyn, both of them in the midst of the heavy fighting going on in space—assuming they were still alive. Stress piled up inside him.

Arturo tried to lighten Randy's mood, saying, "Hang in there, Sarge. Once we kick these invaders' asses, we can all have a big celebration with plenty of food and drinks."

"Nothing like coming together for a good time," Randy replied in a monotone, a post-war celebration the last thing on his mind.

Arturo anchored his eyes on Jenny. Her sleeve outlined every bit of her physique, including her full chest. "Hell of a woman." His veins buzzed as he pondered her dimensions.

Randy playfully slapped Arturo's back. "Hey, keep your head in the game, soldier."

"Says the guy with the smoking-hot girlfriend. I broke up with my gal three months ago." Arturo's gaze raked over Jenny. "I think it's time for a new one," he said, Jenny's voluptuous backside holding his attention.

Having had a mutually agreed-upon one-night stand with Jenny before he got back with Stacie, Randy was well aware of how achingly attractive Jenny was. He was also aware of how encouraging she could be. The night they had slept together felt like ages ago now—a brief outlet for the loneliness he had felt while facing societal persecution and being separated from Stacie. But if Arturo could win Jenny over, Randy knew he'd be a very happy man.

Randy and Arturo chatted about their experiences as Guardians and their personal lives. They touched on family, the women they had been involved with, and hobbies—just two guys shooting the breeze.

Randy's mood became lighter. Both he and Arturo were temporarily distracted from the war.

"Let me get this straight, bro," Arturo said. "You and your girl are good with each other, she's filthy rich, and you wanna *continue* being a Guardian?"

Randy replied, "Yeah, I'm not the sort to live off his girlfriend. Besides, being a Guardian allows me to do some good in the

315

Commonwealth. I think it'll be a while before I hang up the uniform." His family had a long history of service. It ran in their blood.

"Just sayin', if I were in your shoes, I'd hang it up *tomorrow*. Don't get me wrong, I like what I do, but I'd much rather be gallivanting the universe with my rich girlfriend and fucking the living daylights out of her every chance I get."

"You'd get bored without the CDF."

"Nah, hell no."

The sound of a roar in the sky startled Randy and Arturo. They were on their feet in half a second. Another ship had slipped past the defense barrier and was headed to a location in Cornerstone.

Randy wondered how much longer it would take for the Shells to fully charge and be good to go. Maybe another fifteen minutes, tops. If an Alliance ship activated the mind-control signal close to their vicinity while they were outside their Shells, they'd be done for.

Jenny went up to the foot of the stairs and looked up at Randy and Arturo. "The Shells aren't at full power, but I think they're charged up enough to last a while. I say we head to Orion Square."

Six armored airborne Alliance soldiers jetted out from between two buildings.

"Shit, we got trouble," Arturo said.

The Alliance soldiers ignored the Vanguard Alpha trio and fired down on the maintenance crew from above with their guns, considering the shelled Guardians their primary threat. Caught off guard, the crew barely had time to react. The blasts chewed through three of them before they could retaliate.

A missile boomed from Sigrid's Shell and exploded against one of the Alliance soldiers. His smoldering armored form whooshed down from the air, crashed into a building's giant advertisement screen, and then plummeted into the phyocrete with a bloodcurdling crunch. Shards of glass from the broken screen rained down, tinkling against his armor.

The five Alliance soldiers landed, surrounding Sigrid and her one remaining teammate. Randy, Jenny, and Arturo made a break for their Shells. As the two Maintenance Corps Guardians were being mowed down, the Vanguard Alpha trio heard and felt their screams.

Randy, Jenny, and Arturo suited up, pulled away the charging cables, and separated as blasts now darted *their* way.

Arturo caught one in the torso. The damage was minimal. He pumped out countershots from his wrist gun, reverberations jolting up his arm.

An Alliance soldier's jetpack boosted him into the air. He strafed the ground with gunfire, attempting to kill the trio.

Out of nowhere, Akane leapt down from a building. Her knees smashed into the soldier's jetpack, sending him dive-bombing into the roof of the BUS. Akane landed on the ground in a forward roll, came up, and rushed at her next target while Randy, in a display of teamwork, power-leapt onto the BUS's roof and stabbed his plasma saber down into the soldier's sternum.

Akane slid under a spray of blasts, her armor grinding against the phyocrete. Staying low, she fired a grappling cable that coiled around the leg of her assailant. Then she shot to full height while yanking hard on the cable. The soldier's finger remained clamped on the trigger, sending stray blasts lancing skyward as he collapsed. Randy jumped down from the BUS, landing in a crouch and stabbing his saber through the soldier.

Sometimes it amazed Akane how well she and Randy worked together as a team.

When they turned to Arturo and Jenny, they saw the other

three Alliance soldiers lying defeated.

Randy got down to business, having no time to mourn the dead maintenance crew. He kept the emotion out of his voice and said, "Arturo, Jenny, you guys get to Orion Square. I'll stay with Akane while she recharges her Shell."

"You got it, Sergeant," Arturo replied.

Akane stepped out of her Shell and grabbed a charging cable, while Randy stood guard, keeping his eyes peeled for any more hostiles.

Akane fastened the cable to her Shell. She spoke the words swirling in her subconscious, saying, "Hey, Randy, I want you to know that . . . I'm happy for you and Stacie. I'm not clinging to the past or entertaining the idea of us getting back together. I was for a while, but not anymore. Invite me to the wedding, 'kay?"

"Thank you for letting me know that, Akane." Staying alert, Randy spotted a figure on top of a building. "Sniper! Get the fuck down!"

"Shit!" Akane quickly dove to the ground, a blast streaking over her head.

The sniper realigned his iron sights. Randy narrowly avoided the next shot, twisting sharply to the left.

"Get in the back of the BUS, Akane!" Randy commanded.

"But I can—"

"Just fucking do it!"

Akane hurried inside the BUS's trailer compartment, out of harm's way.

Randy couldn't wait for the M-X03 Shell to be completed. It would have flight capability that would allow Guardians to easily dispatch enemies who had the high ground. He launched a Predator Bomb. It burbled toward the sniper. Being an adept marksman, he blew it apart.

Randy switched to plan B. A missile launcher extended from his shoulder and fired. The missile struck the part of the building where the sniper was perched, and he went tumbling down in an uncontrolled descent, debris clanging against his armor. As the ground rushed up at him, he flared his jetpack and avoided becoming a splat of wrecked exo-armor.

Flying at maximum speed, the sniper rammed himself into Randy, catapulting him into a light post.

The sniper landed. He ejected the depleted power cartridge from his weapon and jammed in a new one. Before he could fire, Randy tackled him to the ground. While on top of him, Randy raised his fist and drove his plasma saber into the sniper's helmet. The hiss of material melting and the sniper's squeal fused into a gut-wrenching sound.

Panting heavily, Randy stood up and powered down his saber. "Akane, you can come out now."

Akane stepped down from the BUS. "I could've jumped back into my Shell and helped."

"He could've offed you while you were trying to suit up. Couldn't risk it. We'll move once your Shell is at fifty percent."

"Okay. I'll reload the weapons suite while you watch out for more hostiles."

Randy said into comms, "Arturo, Jenny, how are you guys doing?"

Arturo replied, "Sergeant Pines and I are almost at Orion Square. We'll keep you posted."

A rumble in the sky announced the arrival of three Alliance ships, flying in an organized formation.

Damn, Randy thought. *Does this mean Eden's orbital defenses are cracking?*

◆ ◆ ◆

Dafulton grinned deviously. Alliance forces were now securing a foothold on Satellite One. His men would begin taking control of quarry pits and shaft mines for their resources.

A warning chime erased his grin. "What is going on?" he asked his helmsman.

The helmsman's eyes darted across his monitor. "Incoming ships! A massive fleet!"

Zataldra craned her head toward Dafulton, alarm etched on her face. "Who are they? Where did they come from?"

"I do not know, Zataldra," Dafulton muttered.

"We have received a communication request," the helmsman announced.

Unease replaced Dafulton's earlier bravado. "Patch it through."

A voice boomed over the bridge, every word carrying authority. "This is the Eminence of Taramassia speaking, Pappalonie Valasirus Cetreon. You have attacked an ally of the Interplanetary Union. You will now have to face us as well."

The humans have allies I was unaware of, Dafulton thought. *This may complicate things.*

For the first time since the battle started, Zataldra saw Dafulton's confidence waver.

The Taramassian fleet opened fire, coming to the CDF's aid.

◆ ◆ ◆

Aboard the *Valor*, cheers rang out amongst the crew.

Iya was sitting beside Jarius' computer station. She asked him, "What's happening?"

A renewed sense of optimism blossomed in Jarius' core. "One of the Union members decided to help us." He monitored a holographic display, observing the ebb and flow of the battle. The

Taramassians' intervention had breathed new life into the CDF's defense. And though the CDF had been far from defeated, the Taramassians' arrival promised to limit lives lost, as the size of the forces protecting Eden had redoubled.

More Taramassian warships emerged from hyperspace in waves and joined the battle, their cannons unleashing blasts.

Pappalonie's flagship fired a barrage of precision strikes, crippling vital systems on enemy vessels.

The previously stalemated battle was tilting in the CDF's favor. But claiming victory would be premature. There was no room for complacency.

◆ ◆ ◆

Dafulton surveyed the battlefield. The monitors showed that the Alliance was losing ground. The chances of victory were decreasing by the minute. But he wasn't concerned. His true objective was to plunder Satellite One's resources. All he needed the Alliance to do was hold Satellite One long enough for his men to begin and finish mining operations. Afterward, he'd abandon the war effort entirely, leaving the Khanorian Protection Force and the other pawns he had manipulated into fighting for him to fend for themselves.

Feeling the winds of war shifting, Zataldra calculated the odds of success. "We might be in trouble."

"This is unexpected. All forces should fall back to Satellite One and establish a stronghold on the planet's surface. By leveraging humans as our shields against a direct attack on us, we can continue devising a winning strategy."

This wasn't the outcome Zataldra had wanted, but Dafulton's suggestion was the most logical course of action. By holding the colonies hostage, the Alliance would gain a strategic advantage, using the colonies as a staging ground to launch further assaults on Eden. "You're right."

Dafulton informed all Alliance forces about his proposed plan. The Protection Force commander concurred.

◆ ◆ ◆

"Enemy ships disengaging, Sir," a crewman said to Admiral Collins.

Jarius wondered what the Alliance's retreat meant. He doubted they were throwing in the towel. They might simply be regrouping. "Hold on." His eyes scanned a monitor bank. "They're heading to Satellite One!"

Dafulton said over the *Valor's* comms, "This message is for Admiral Collins. You have claimed victory in this encounter. However, the war is far from its conclusion.

"Stand down the planetary defenses of Satellite One so the rest of our ships may pass without interference. If you refuse, we will authorize our soldiers on the ground to execute civilians."

Collins had no choice but to comply. "Understood." He issued a stand-down order to all Air & Space Corps vessels.

◆ ◆ ◆

In the streets of Cornerstone with other Guardians of the CPF, Vanguard Alpha watched Alliance ships abort their mission, climbing in altitude and accelerating as they left Eden.

Akane said, "Is this it? Did we win?"

Footage from street cameras streamed across Carl's HUD. It showed Alliance soldiers withdrawing. "The battle, maybe. The war's another story."

Randy viewed newsfeeds. Reports said that enemy air strikes had damaged power plants, communication hubs, and CDF bases and artillery storehouses. Fortunately, there had been few civilian casualties in the cities that had been invaded. Randy expected the government's official reports, when made available, to reflect that. The true cost, he knew, would be borne by the brave men and women of the Air & Space Corps, who had held the line against the enemy's onslaught.

Exhausted from the battle, he thought about Stacie. All he wanted right now was to see her.

◆ ◆ ◆

Oviereya received communication from Admiral Collins. He informed her that Taramassian forces helped the Air & Space Corps win. Humanity could always count on Queen Pappalonie to be there for them when needed. But the Alliance had seized control of Commonwealth territory, something no other enemy in history had accomplished. Now the CDF's fight to reclaim Satellite One would begin, while they worked to thwart further attacks on Eden.

◆ ◆ ◆

Jarius, on the *Valor's* bridge, waited for confirmation of Jazzlyn's return to the *Star Phoenix* from Admiral Collins. His despairing thoughts plunged him deeper into a rabbit hole of angst. Iya, remembering how kind Jazzlyn had been to her, sat beside him, sharing his anxiety.

Jarius constantly adjusted his posture and tapped his foot against the floor. His entire emotional state was in disarray.

Collins approached Jarius to deliver the bad news, his expression already giving away the truth. Each step he took felt like a drumroll leading to the answer he knew would devastate the young man.

"I'm sorry, Lieutenant Ambassador Ford," Collins said. "Your fiancée's interceptor wasn't among those that made it back."

Because each interceptor's ID number was associated with its pilot, the frigates' systems didn't take long to generate the names of those who had and hadn't survived.

Jarius jumped from his chair and froze in place like a deer caught in the headlights. "What? There's . . . gotta be some mistake." The tightness in his throat made it hard to speak.

"I wish there were, son. Lieutenant de' Medici is no longer with us. I know this isn't what you wanted to hear." Collins walked back to his station, chin down. Losing people was the worst part of his job, and he had lost many people today—too damn many.

Jarius stifled a sob. He remembered Jazzlyn's infectious laughter, gentle touch, and beautiful smile. Everything about her made him feel like he was on top of the world. And now she was gone, without even a chance for him to say goodbye or tell her one last time how much he loved her.

Iya hugged him, her friendship providing some level of comfort. "It's okay, there's no need to keep your hurt bottled up."

The inner moorings that were straining to hold in Jarius' emotions snapped, and the floodgates opened, rivers of sorrow streaming from his eyes.

The crewmen looked at him with sad faces, their hearts breaking.

A loud wail tore out of Jarius. This was the most miserable he had ever felt.

Iya held him tighter. "I'm here for you." She sniffled and brushed away a tear with the back of her hand.

CHAPTER FOURTEEN

Oviereya stood on the stage behind the Executive Manor. The media had gathered to watch her address all of Eden via live stream.

She said, "For too long, there has been much debate revolving around the role of colonists in our society. Some people have, either implicitly or explicitly, advocated for their continued status as a subservient class. Thankfully, a growing number of Edenites recognize our colony brethren as equals deserving of prosperity. As Chief Executive, I've been fighting to give colonists a better life. But any debate about what colonists' role in our society should be is now more irrelevant than ever."

Her voice grew firmer. "The Alliance's attack has laid bare a stark truth: We are one people, Edenite and colonist alike. The enemy doesn't discriminate; they seek to annihilate us *all*. Your designation as a native Edenite, immigrant, or colonist doesn't matter. Labels such as Highborn and Lowborn do not matter. The epithet 'nadir' alludes to nothing. And what side of the political aisle you're on is unimportant. We are all under threat. We are all in this fight together. And it is together that we will prevail. We will free our brethren trapped within the enemy's claws."

A pause, then a call to action. "And to any former Guardians wishing to serve again—to honor our fallen Guardians and reclaim our land from the Alliance—we welcome you back into the fold, for one more mission. We need you." She ended the address, saying, "And if the Alliance is watching this broadcast, I have a message for you: Flee while you can."

A barrage of questions erupted from the reporters.

◆ ◆ ◆

Stacie shut off her TV, processing Oviereya's address. She had been powerless during the Alliance's invasion. All she had been able to do was be a spectator and fret over her fiancée's safety. She decided right then and there that she was going to answer the CDF's call for ex-Guardians to re-enlist for this one mission: crushing the Alliance and freeing Satellite One.

A message from Jason projected from her wristcom.

Jason: You joining the fight?

Stacie: Yeah.

Jason: Me too. So are Eli and DeShaun.

Stacie: *Thumbs-up emoji*

◆ ◆ ◆

DAYS LATER

Defense Force Academy

Randy, dressed in civilian attire, walked toward the auditorium to watch Stacie and other ex-Guardians take the Oath.

The Alliance's control over the colonies left Randy constantly worrying about his father. Randy had tried to contact him several times, but Colony Four's communications grid was obviously down

—maybe all of Satellite One's. That implied that the Alliance's invasion had decimated the Reserve Guardians deployed to protect vital infrastructure.

Randy hoped his father and Sariah were still alive. He was also concerned about the rebels he had fought with in the Coalition, the closest being Kesley Whittaker. Not knowing if people he cared about were okay was driving him nuts.

If Arson were alive and not trapped inside the Alliance's area of control as human shielding, he'd reunite as many former Coalition fighters as he could and mount a resistance. He had been a captain in the CDF, leader of a Coalition faction, and essentially Arman Reza's right hand. If anyone knew how to fight back against a hostile occupation, it was he. The Alliance was on Coalition turf, and Arson would give them hell, even if the odds were against him. But with no way to contact him, the best Randy could do was stay focused on the mission to liberate Satellite One.

His aunt Merriam happened to be coming in his direction. They stopped face-to-face. An awkward silence hung between them. Their discomfort was palpable, as their most recent conversations had been contentious.

"Aunt Merriam," Randy said in greeting.

Merriam replied, "Nephew, it's good to see you. Can we talk a moment?"

"Yeah, sure."

"There's no denying that things haven't been easy between us since you sided with the Coalition during the civil war. I had always believed the war was unjustified."

"And now?"

"While I still think colonies One, Four, and Six could have explored other paths to equality, I understand why their citizens wanted autonomy." Her voice softened. "And I hold nothing against you for siding with the Coalition. My sister wouldn't want animosity to fester between us.

"These dark times remind us that political divisions, disagreements about societal roles for segments of humanity, or debates over war justifications are insignificant. As the Chief said, we are all in this fight together."

There was a time Merriam had thought about jumping into the election scene and running against Oviereya, enraged that some bleeding heart who had sympathized with the Independent Movement and pardoned Coalition fighters was leading the Commonwealth. Now, those feelings were gone. She respected Oviereya's stance and her effort to improve colony life.

Merriam wasn't the only Edenite to come round; Randy could feel a shift in the atmosphere after the invasion. It seemed like a good deal of people were waking up to the fact that their political and ideological differences were becoming a hindrance to unity.

Randy said, "Thank you for telling me that."

"Where are you headed?"

"To watch my fiancée swear back in."

"The Spencer girl, Stacie, right?"

"Yeah."

Merriam imagined how happy her sister would've been for Randy. "I'd like to meet her soon."

"I'd like that too." This wasn't just politeness; Randy deeply meant it.

"Well then," Merriam said, "don't let me hold you up."

Before Merriam could leave, a Link request from Randy pinged her implant. She smiled warmly and accepted his request. Restoring their familial Link was everything to her.

Randy said, *<Let's talk again tomorrow.>*

<I'll see you then.>

Merriam and Randy had taken a significant step in repairing their relationship.

With the swearing-in ceremony about to start, Randy picked up his pace.

◆ ◆ ◆

Randy sat in the tiered bleachers of the auditorium, watching the returning service members, in their dress uniforms, get into formation. Last time he was here, he and Stacie had just completed Basic and MOS training and were swearing in alongside each other.

He was proud of Stacie. She was one of the wealthiest women on Eden. She didn't have to come back to the CDF to fight the Alliance, but she was anyway.

Stacie stood with her peers, her eyes watching the Master of Ceremony ascend the stage. Before, she had joined the CDF to step out of her parents' shadow and give purpose to her life. Now, her reasons weren't about self. She had already given purpose to her life through leading Spencer Enterprises, using its resources to benefit others. Her single motivation for re-enlisting was to protect the Commonwealth's people from the Alliance.

Witnessing the Alliance attack Eden and occupy Satellite One had ignited a new fire within her, especially as Spencer Enterprises had been working to improve conditions on Satellite One. She was determined to prevent the Alliance from undoing all her organization had achieved there, free its people, and stop further attacks on Eden.

The Master of Ceremony—the same one who had sworn in Randy and Stacie's class—positioned himself behind the lectern. "First, let me express my deepest admiration for your decision to rejoin the Commonwealth Defense Force during this pivotal moment in the New Humanity's history. Never have we faced such an indignity—an enemy occupation of our own soil!

"This adversary has seized Satellite One, turning it into their center of operations for waging war against us. This cannot stand!" He dropped his fist, hammering the lectern. "It is courageous men and women like yourselves who will rise to the occasion and crush this menace. We cannot allow a foreign power to control Satellite One and keep our people enslaved. Be they colony or Eden citizens, they are our compatriots.

"You weren't conscripted into re-enlisting. You rejoined the Commonwealth Defense Force because your hearts beat with the spirit of a warrior. And warriors never cower in the face of dark times. I commend you! Now, let the ceremony begin!"

Stacie and every enlistee repeated the colonel's words as he spoke the Oath. "I, Stacie Lyn Spencer, take this oath with no reservations. And I promise to protect the Commonwealth and its allies from all enemies, foreign and domestic. Till my final breath or till such time my commitment expires."

The group mirrored the colonel's swift movements, clapping a palm against their heart and then punching a fist outward.

The colonel concluded with, "Welcome back to the fight."

Stacie glanced down at the sergeant insignia on her dress uniform's jacket. When Command had awarded her that rank— thanks to Jason Mansford—it had simply been a boost to her ego. But she was a different woman now. That rank symbolized an opportunity to apply what she had learned while leading her bounty-hunter team, going undercover for DFI, and eliminating the Elite. These experiences had shaped her into a stronger leader, making her even more prepared for the rank of sergeant.

She never fully understood why Jason had recommended her for the promotion. He always insisted it was because he had seen potential in her—the same reason he made her a sub-leader in Fourth Platoon during the civil war—not because of his crush on her. In the end, everything seemed to align perfectly, and the CDF needed strong leadership right now. She was ready, more than ever, for the responsibility.

Jason took up a spot next to her and said, "Looking good, Sergeant Spencer. Maybe I'll see you out there on the battlefield."

"Same."

Eli and DeShaun, who had also sworn back in, spoke to Stacie too, and then they left with Jason.

Randy came down from the bleachers and wrapped Stacie in his arms.

"I never thought I'd be putting the uniform back on, but here I am," Stacie said as Randy let her out of his hug.

"The CDF definitely has a challenge ahead, freeing Satellite One. It could use you."

Stacie took one of Randy's hands in hers. "How's Jarius doing? My heart goes out to him." Jarius had been ignoring her calls and texts, likely needing breathing room.

"He's been hurting badly since Jazzlyn's funeral."

Stacie squeezed Randy's hand, knowing how rough it was for him to see his friend in such sorrow. "He's joining you today for that . . . meeting with the Truth Commission lady, Maxine, right?"

"Yeah, he and Akane."

"Well, tell Jarius I'm thinking of him."

"Absolutely. See you at dinner." Randy planted a kiss on Stacie's cheek before heading out.

◆ ◆ ◆

Cornerstone Park

Randy found Jarius and Akane already seated at the bench-table, waiting for Maxine Lain to arrive. Even though the lockdown had been lifted, few people were out. Everyone on Eden was afraid, despite a heavy Guardian presence remaining in the streets of every region state. The Alliance was planning their next attack, and no one knew when or in what form it would come.

Randy sat down on Jarius' left. Akane was sitting to Jarius' right.

From his expression, it was clear that Jarius was still grieving Jazzlyn's death.

"Let me know if there's anything I can do for you," Randy said.

Akane echoed his sentiment. "Me too."

Jarius said, "And the same to you guys. It's the least I can do for you rescuing me in Khanoria, and I know these are difficult times for both of you, with family on Satellite One."

Randy asked, "How's Iya doing?"

"Iya's okay. Both of us are staying on as Chief Amaechi's special advisors until the war is over. Needless to say, Iya's committed to finding a peaceful resolution."

Randy spotted Maxine coming. "Here she is."

Maxine lowered herself onto the bench in front of them. "Jarius, Akane, I'm glad you're willing to contribute to the Truth Commission's investigation."

Jarius nodded. "We might be telling you some things you already know, but—"

Maxine cut in. "But different perspectives and additional tidbits of information are always useful in investigations like this. Tell me anything." She clicked on her wristcom's recording app.

Randy, Akane, and Jarius looked at one another, unsure who should speak first.

Randy broke the silence. "Like Jarius mentioned, you've

probably heard some of this from the Chief's addresses. But there were a lot of messed up things that happened in Khanoria."

Since the Chief had assured Guardians they wouldn't face legal repercussions for disclosing information about the CDF's actions, even if it had been obtained unofficially, Randy revealed specific details from the files Conlan had provided. This gave Maxine a granular picture of the atrocities the Chief had mentioned.

Akane shared her experiences as an immigrant in the CDF, detailing the prejudice and hostility she had faced from fellow Guardians. She also told Maxine about similar incidents Simone had experienced. Jarius spoke about his conversations with Coalition rebels regarding their mistreatment under martial law as civilians.

In light of all the evidence of Guardian misconduct that had been presented, Jarius felt the need to say something positive. "Not sure how relevant this might be, Maxine, but I want to say that there are *plenty* of good men and women in the CDF, people who genuinely want to be upstanding Guardians—and who disapprove of the unforgivable behavior of their comrades. Also, before the war broke out, the Ambassador Corps had been actively working to repair the damage to the CDF's reputation."

Maxine said, "Noted. I should mention that this report isn't just about collecting testimonies. The Truth Commission also welcomes suggestions from Guardians on how to improve the CDF. Beyond revising its training curriculum, what changes do you guys think are necessary?"

"A significant overhaul of leadership is crucial," Jarius stated. "We need to elevate a new generation of leaders."

Akane concurred. "Yeah, out with the old, and in with the new. A fresh start is what Simone believed in too."

Maxine pressed on. "Suppose the investigation identifies

government leaders and Guardians responsible for atrocities, like some of the Guardians deployed to Khanoria. What do we do with them? Should they face trial? Is it fair to blame them solely for their sins, or are societal influences and indoctrination the true culprits? Should they simply be let go with severance packages?"

"Honestly, my first instinct would be to fry them," Akane admitted, "but I understand the situation is more complicated."

Randy steepled his fingers. "I guess the answer isn't clear-cut for any of us."

Maxine shut off the recording app. "I appreciate all of you for giving me your time today."

Randy stood. "Well, it was good seeing you guys. Gotta go. I have dinner plans with Stacie later. With retaliation efforts underway, who knows when we'll get some alone time again." He made his way back to his sports cruiser.

The war was going to separate Randy and Stacie. He would join Vanguard Alpha on deployment, while she would ship out with her unit. They were savoring every moment together before the inevitable.

Maxine looked at Jarius and Akane curiously. "Both of you are fond of Randal Scott, aren't you?"

Jarius said, "Yeah, the guy's practically a brother. And you have to admire a man who wears his emotions on his sleeve. I never have to figure out how Randy's feeling about something."

The adoration on Akane's face spoke for her. "He's a fantastic lover, and he was my rock during one of my darkest times—he helped me overcome my trauma. He's not flawless, but he is undeniably one of the finest Guardians I've ever met."

Maxine said, "He certainly seems like a good man." She got up. "Have a great day, you two."

Everyone departed, bracing themselves for what the war with

the Alliance would throw their way.

Epilogue

"The Commonwealth would remain a fractured society for some time, unless some catastrophic event suddenly brought everyone together. Oviereya prayed such a thing would never happen."
—*Republic Under Siege: Threat from Within*

Acknowledgments

I want to express my gratitude to Leilani Dewindt of XandLCreative for her outstanding work as a developmental editor. Leilani worked on *Republic Under Siege: Threat from Within*, and once again, she proved invaluable in refining the story and pinpointing inconsistencies in my characters' behavior.

I'd like to give a shout-out to my paperback cover designer Kristy P. and hardback cover designer Justine S. Florentino for creating such amazing art.

Finally, I want to thank anyone who made the choice to read *Republic Shattered: Sins of Before*. I really appreciate it!

About the Author

Michael J. Brooks holds a BA in Art and an MFA. He is a member of the Independent Book Publishing Professionals Group (IBPPG), and his debut novel, *Exodus Conflict*, was a finalist of the 2013 Next Generation Indie Book Awards, in the sci-fi/fantasy category; earned honorable mention from the 2013 London Book Festival, in the science fiction category; and received five stars from *Readers' Favorite*. He has been featured on The Authors Show and in the Spring 2022 edition of Review Tales Magazine.

Exploration of social issues, unpredictable plot twists, and vivid action and adventure are the crux of his novels. Dedicated to being the best wordsmith possible, his goal is to deliver absolute quality and a fun, well-written story. When not writing, he enjoys reading comic books, watching Netflix, and reading sci-fi and fantasy books.

Website: www.authormbrooks.com
X (formerly Twitter): @AuthorMBrooks
Threads and Instagram: book_author_mjbrooks
TikTok: @book_author_mjbrooks

Contact Michael J. Brooks at authormbrooks@gmail.com.

Other Books in the Wars of the New Humanity Series

Republic Falling: Advent of a New Dawn
(book one)

Republic Under Siege: Threat from Within
(book two)

Wars of the New Humanity: Collection One
(books one and two)

Glossary
(nonalphabetic order)

Earth Era: the era of humanity before intergalactic migration from Earth

Commonwealth: humanity's star nation consisting of four planets —Eden and satellites One, Two, and Three

Eden: humanity's utopian motherworld inhabited by three-fifths of the human population

Satellite One: humanity's dystopian secondary world inhabited by two-fifths of the human population

Advanced Exascale Global Information-collection System (AEGIS): the AI computer system created during Earth Era to divide humanity between Eden and Satellite One

Satellites Two and Three: vacant worlds belonging to the Commonwealth, used for military training exercises and mineral excavation

Edenite/Eden citizen (synonymous terms): human beings living on Eden, whether born on the planet or during Earth Era

Highborn: a moniker referring specifically to human beings born on Eden

Colonist/colony citizen (synonymous terms): human beings living in the colonies of Satellite One, whether born on the planet or during Earth Era

Immigrant: a colonist who has been granted Eden citizenship either through the lottery system or because they were among the first laborers transported from Satellite One to Eden

Link: a psychic connection between two Edenites through a nanochip; colonists lack these chips

Commonwealth Defense Force (CDF)/Defense Force (synonymous terms): the Commonwealth's military force

Guardian: a soldier in the Commonwealth Defense Force

Cadet: a Guardian in training

Shell: a mechanized, armored combat suit used by Guardians

Sleeve: the suit Guardians wear under the Shell

Commonwealth Government/central government (synonymous terms): the governing body of the entire Commonwealth, which includes the Parliament and Chief Executive's Office

Republic of Unified Colonies (RUC): the republic formed by colonies One, Four, and Six after they declared sovereignty from the Commonwealth

The Three-Week War: the war initiated and won by the Commonwealth Government to reclaim colonies One, Four, and Six after they declared sovereignty from the Commonwealth

The Coalition of Rebel Factions/the Coalition (synonymous terms): a coalition of rebel factions formed by the remnant fighters of the RUC to continue combating the Commonwealth Government

The Quad: the Chief Executive's Manor, Parliament Building, Supreme Judiciary, and Defense Force Academy, on Eden, which are situated in a Quadrangle in the middle of Eden's capital, Cornerstone City

Operation Hammer Fall: the Coalition's operation to invade the Quad, commandeer the Parliament Building and use its broadcast center to cast files exposing government corruption across the net

The Battle of the Quad: the historic battle between the Coalition rebels and CDF Guardians during Operation Hammer Fall

The Interplanetary Union: the intergalactic alliance consisting of the Commonwealth and planets Ghanrax, Dhalgratt, Varsh'Ru, Zirkran, Rumanoah, and Taramassia